The Learning Curve

Melissa Nathan was born and raised in Hertfordshire. A journalist for twelve years, she turned to writing novels full time in 1998 and shortly afterwards *Pride, Prejudice and Jasmin Field* and *Persuading Annie* were published. Melissa discovered she had breast cancer whilst writing her first novel for Random House, *The Nanny*, which hit the *Sunday Times* Top Ten in the spring of 2003. She went on to write another top ten bestseller, *The Waitress*, and finished her fifth novel *The Learning Curve* in February 2006. Sadly she died two months later, aged 37. She is survived by her husband, Andrew, and young son, Sam.

Praise for Melissa Nathan

'You'll find this very moreish' *Daily Mail*

'This is one to gobble up in a single sitting' *Company*

'Hugely enjoyable' *heat*

'A witty novel about love' *B*

'Tremendous fun' Jilly Cooper

'A modern-day Lizzy and Darcy tale you won't be able to put down' *Company*

'A witty spin on the nation's favourite novel . . . with a loveable, contemporary heroine at its heart' *Good Housekeeping*

'Hugely entertaining . . . a memorable read – funny, warm and intelligent' *Woman's Own*

Also by Melissa Nathan

Melissa Nathan
The Learning Curve

arrow books

Published by Arrow Books in 2006

7 9 10 8 6

First published in Great Britain in 2006 by
Arrow Books
Random House, 20 Vauxhall Bridge Road,
London SW1V 2SA

www.randomhouse.co.uk

Addresses for companies within The Random House Group Limited can
be found at: www.randomhouse.co.uk/offices.htm

The Random House Group Limited Reg. No. 954009

A CIP catalogue record for this book
is available from the British Library

ISBN 9780099504269

The Random House Group Limited makes every effort to ensure that the
papers used in its books are made from trees that have been legally sourced
from well-managed and credibly certified forests. Our paper procurement
policy can be found at: www.randomhouse.co.uk/paper.htm

Typeset by SX Composing DTP, Rayleigh, Essex
Printed and bound in Great Britain by
Bookmarque Limited, Croydon, Surrey

To Jeremy

Oh brother, have you more than compensated for rolling
me up in a rug when I was a baby.
Thank you for everything.

In memory of Rebecca Lawson,
1950–2004

Acknowledgements

To all at Tetherdown Primary School, especially Annie Ashraf for allowing me into her classroom, being so generous with her time and energy, being so perceptive, intelligent and kind, and for being nothing like my old primary school teachers.

Also to Deborah Nathan, for giving me invaluable insights into the world of top City finance, even with a bad knee. And Joshua Nathan for his invaluable details into the world of an eleven-year-old boy, with two good knees.

My heartfelt thanks, as ever, go to Alison Jones for all her plans.

And also to my wonderful agent, Maggie Phillips. I still can't get over that she wants to represent me.

And, of course, my enormous thanks go to the fantastic editor, Kate Elton, who is happiness and professionalism on legs. (Really long ones.)

And all at Random House, especially the spectacular Rina Gill, Georgina Hawtrey-Woore, Ron Beard and Rob Waddington.

I am in the unusual position of knowing that this book will, in all probability, be published posthumously. And so please indulge me in a rather unusual set of acknowledgements. First, to my wonderful parents. You have given me a life suffused with love, support and friendship. I have been lucky enough to see eye to eye with you both and look up to you at the same time. You are two of my best friends. Please never feel that I have had a hard life. I have had thirty-seven wonderful years and I'm grateful to you both for giving me that. I am happy and at peace.

To Jeremy. It turned out that our dynamic was to be that of doctor and patient. I never would have chosen it to be that way, but there it was. You were always there for me, from the first phone call I made when I was nineteen, telling you I'd found a lump, right through to – and beyond – the night you stayed in hospital with me, sleeping on an inflatable lilo on the floor when I had my first mastectomy, some seventeen years later. You have been everything a brother could have been and more. Thank you.

My wonderful Andrew. I respect you as much as I love you, and that is saying something. You, of all people I know, will get through this. After all, you've got through nearly twelve years of marriage with me and that's no easy feat. I have been so lucky to know you. You have been my steady rock, my gentle giant, my best friend, my everything. I wish you a happy life, full of love and joy.

And my amazing Sammy. I wanted to know you for longer, my love, but it wasn't to be. Still, at only three years old, you have already left an imprint on my heart that will go with me, wherever it is I'm going. Motherhood made my life worthwhile. And you gave me that. What does a mother wish for her son? I wish you happiness. You have a wonderful daddy and a family who adores you. Go into the world knowing that while you were everything to your mother, you won't have to deal with an annoying woman who can't stop kissing you when you're fifteen. I will be in the sky, kissing you from afar.

1

Nicky Hobbs's bedroom was dark and silent. The smooth planes of her wardrobe doors and matching bedside table revealed nothing of their contents. In the middle of her tidy room, in the middle of her tidy bed, lay Nicky Hobbs, tidily. Her body was almost completely still, apart from her eyelids, which fluttered like butterfly wings, tremulously hinting at the dream-world evolving beneath them. For there, the distant sound of church bells lifted towards her as if on a silken breeze, while she lay heavy with dreams in the empty barn. Suddenly Pierre, the farmhand, was silhouetted in the open door, his pitchfork sharp against the cerise sky. He stared at her and then, slowly, started to approach with a languorous stealth which whispered of oiled hips.

Then he turned into Rob. 'Hello, Nickers!' he said and winked. And she was wide awake.

And alone.

One hand landed, bang! on her alarm clock, and the distant church bells, which she now realised had sounded suspiciously like an alarm clock, gave way to silence. Her other hand lost no time in pulling off her duvet, for Nicky Hobbs was not one to waste time. She knew that getting out of bed in the mornings, like many things in life, was much worse in the premeditation than in the actual fact. Like homework. Or doing your hair in the mornings. Or visiting your sister. (The only exception – and there was usually one exception to any rule – was going on a blind date. In her experience, the anticipation was usually the best bit.) So the only thing was to get on with it, and before you knew it the worst was over.

After a quick shower, she strode across the polished floor to her bedroom wardrobe, opened the door and scrutinised herself in the full-length mirror, with the same mindset one might adopt when marking an essay. An essay that, at first sight, gives a good impression with its neat handwriting, but on closer inspection reveals a cavalier attitude to grammar. At first sight, her young, curvy figure looked good even in a shabby old towel; and her heart-shaped face was winning. But, on closer inspection, she could not avoid the facts: her Cupid's-bow lips were dry, her skin was so pale that she looked like she was in the process of vanishing, and the only quality shining out from her eyes was potential. And then, of course, there was her hair. She stared at the copper coils which radiated from her head like an advert for headache pills. She nodded her head up and down just to see the coils go 'boing'. (For even in moments of despair, Nicky Hobbs could always see the funny side of life, and there was little funnier than her hair going 'boing'.) She allowed herself one large sigh. Oh! To be able to flick sleek locks across her shoulder and feel the weight of them against her back!

She turned and went into the kitchen.

From her kitchen window she could see the sun bleeding through heavy treetops and it almost made her stop in her tracks. Instead, she just smiled, told herself that there were benefits to getting up so early, and flicked on the kettle. While the water boiled she prepared a packed lunch of sandwich and apple, and only then did she allow herself to look at the early-autumn morning view. It was at moments like this that she loved her small but perfectly formed first-floor maisonette. From every room, she had an aerial view of the sky as it changed colour before her eyes. Nature was a marvellous, miraculous thing, she thought in wonder. Then she went back to her bedroom to try and turn her hair straight.

Fifteen minutes and much huffing later, she finished. Not so much improved, she thought, frowning at herself in the downstairs hall mirror, as changed. 'Could Do Better,' she told her reflection with a small but firm nod. As she picked up her briefcase and left, she reminded herself that it wasn't always imperative to get 'Excellent'. Sometimes it was healthy to have something to work towards. Goals were necessary in life. They kept you striving, which kept you learning, and learning was A Good Thing.

The girl from next door overtook her on the path with a quick hello, her long, blonde hair gleaming down her back like polished gold. Nicky slid her hand down the length of her still-damp hair. The bottom had already reverted to curls. She'd always hated that girl.

She slid into her car, dropped her case on the passenger seat, slammed the door shut, took her mobile phone out of her handbag and put it on to hands-free, pulled her make-up bag out of the glove compartment, and placed it in her lap. 'Right,' she murmured as she started the engine with one hand and took out an eyeliner with the other, 'I want a "Very Good".'

Nicky adored her car. It was more than just a vehicle to

her, it was a much-loved room that happened to be on wheels. Specifically, a boudoir. In its boot lay her favourite hats and scarves, and two pairs of long, tight, leather boots that enjoyed more space in here than they ever would if they were squashed inside her wardrobe or allowed to clutter up her hall. The glove compartment was tightly packed with her make-up bag, tissues, nail varnishes and earring collection. The 'boudoir' had grown organically (as all good boudoirs do), first as an outpost for those early mornings when she'd run out of time, and then gradually as the ideal place to finish off her face, hair and accessories while listening to the radio in comfort. Even though the journey was not a long one, London traffic and ever-increasing roadworks meant there was never any doubt that she would have ample time to do all of these things. In fact, technically, she lived near enough to school to walk there, but she always had too much to carry even when there hadn't been any marking the night before – and anyway, she loved being in her boudoir. The only drawback was that sometimes, due to diversions, her eyeliner was uneven because of road bumps.

This morning was no exception. Most of the schools went back today and, true to fashion, there were two new temporary traffic lights and one diversion. After texting her sister and listening to the news, she still had time to apply two shades of eyeliner, one of mascara, one of lippy (twice), and even tried on three different earrings before arriving at school.

She parked in the school car park, and just as she was about to give herself a once-over in the rear-view mirror, she got a text from Ally. She smiled and wondered if Ally might actually be in the staffroom already.

Morning! R U up yet?

She texted back that she was already in the car park and got another text immediately.

Swot. Put the kettle on.

She tutted.

A quick glance in the rear-view mirror, a final flick of mascara, and she was ready. (It was always worth giving the final version a once-over before handing it in, as she often told her pupils.) She allowed herself the faintest glimmer of a smile when she saw Rob's car in the nearest space to the school building. She tidied her boudoir, picked up her briefcase, and climbed out, shutting the door behind her. And then, silence.

She smiled at the long, wide, gently curved path leading up to the school. Beneath her elegant, yet comfortable high heels, the softened tarmac yielded pleasingly, as if helping her on her way. On the right-hand side of the path stood the younger children's classes, bordered with conifers, which, if there had been rain the night before, smelt like heaven. On the left of the path stretched the playing fields, and on the ground, in faded rainbow colours, ran the numbers 1 to 10 beside corresponding numbers of brightly coloured insects, followed by the alphabet beside corresponding animals. It doubled as the reception year's playground. She couldn't remember who had dubbed the path 'the learning curve' – probably Ally or Pete – but it was perfect. At the end of it, you came to the school itself; an imposing, red-brick building, with tall, rounded windows and a large, welcoming front door. Nicky always slowed her pace as it came into view. The building seemed to pulse with potential at her across the empty playground. She walked slowly across the main playground, so as to put off the moment when detail would take over emotion. As she did so, she realised this was A Moment. Nicky Hobbs liked Moments.

For here she was, a young teacher for Year 6 (the ten- and eleven-year-olds), only just turned thirty, on the career path of her choice, on her way to a fresh new academic year with a class who were by all accounts fantastically enthusiastic learners. She loved her job and knew she was good at it. She still had the energy of youth combined with an increasingly confident air of expertise. She had good friends, good health and owned her own home. Not only that, but she'd lost three pounds in the summer and could fit into her favourite skirt. Life was good. She allowed herself a childish grin – the kind of grin her pupils never saw till Christmas. She Had It All.

Whoops.

Crash bang wallop. The Moment was over. Her teeth unconsciously sought out her lower lip and gave it a small but satisfying chew. OK, maybe not everything, she told herself, but there were many worse off than her. She pushed the sudden image of her sister out of her mind.

Opening the school door, she came face to face with Rob Pattison, teacher to Year 5. They grinned at each other.

'Nix!' he exclaimed.

'Prattison!' she exclaimed.

Term had begun.

'Anyone else in?' she asked as they walked past the empty, glass-fronted administration office towards the staffroom. The school was absolutely silent, as it always was before the children started arriving, and Nicky always found the silence uncomfortably eery. All it took was one child to race in and the place would come to life. Before then, everything felt wrong somehow, as if she was trespassing in a forbidden dream. But usually, within minutes of the first arrival, the noise levels slowly rose; children's spontaneous laughter echoed out from behind closed classroom doors, as did their lusty singing from the music room, their exhilarated shrieks and shouts from the PE fields and their wild running from the corridors wallpapered with *WALK, DON'T RUN!* notices. All these noises combined to make the unique noise of school, probably because adults had forgotten how to make them years ago.

Nicky looked straight ahead as she and Rob proceeded down the corridor together, only turning her head to glance into any open doorways. She did not turn her eyes towards him once, even though she knew he was looking at her every time he spoke. She'd long since stopped questioning her need to play these games with him after all these years. It was simply girlish pride and she was allowed her little foibles.

''Course no one's in,' said Rob, as they passed the photocopier outside the bursar's office. 'Lazy slackers.' He was smiling down at her.

'Not even Amanda?' Her eyes finally rose to his and she gave him a knowing smile. She saw his lips twitch.

'Not even Amanda,' he said. No more.

She opened the staffroom door and tried to ignore the plummet in her stomach this always caused. 'I must get some posters,' she murmured to herself.

The staffroom at Heatheringdown Primary School, London N10, was a TV makeover producer's wet dream. Government funding never quite stretched to the staffroom because, technically, it was still standing. It was small and square, yet could never be called cosy because the ceiling was so high it could have comfortably housed a mezzanine level. Around the edges of the room squatted old, low chairs which made anyone who sat in them look as if their diaphragm had been sucked out through their back. In the centre of the room lay a multicoloured carpet that was so faded not one colour was discernable; on one wall was propped a kitchenette, which looked as if it was taking a tea break on its way to the junkyard; on another wall stood a bank of small, padlocked lockers. The room was basically a skip with a roof.

Nicky glanced up at the clock. 7.30 a.m. She had half an hour to pop up to her classroom and reacquaint herself with her interactive whiteboard before the Head's first morning meeting of the year. She didn't want to miss a moment of that meeting. Exciting things were afoot: right at the end of last year, the Deputy Head, Miss Fotheringham, who had also been the Reception class teacher for the four- and five-year-olds, had suddenly announced her retirement. She had spent an amazing thirty years in the same job, and almost twenty-five of them in the same skirt. After she'd made her shock announcement, there had only been one more full day of the year left, so Miss James told her staff that she would sort out a replacement as soon as they were back at work next year. But they were to forget this and enjoy their holidays, as there was nothing anyone could do about it now. This was uniformly accepted as typical of her 'team-spirit' attitude. It meant that six teachers were able to enjoy their holiday with an extra spring in their step at the thought of possible promotion next year, without having to deal with competition or interviews during the summer.

So not only would there be a new Reception class teacher to welcome to Heatheringdown this term, but there would be a bit of politics to add a touch of excitement to the proceedings. Nicky wondered if the teacher might be male. They could do with some more men in the staffroom.

By the time she had returned there after playing with her interactive whiteboard, the entire staff of Heatheringdown Primary had arrived. Which meant seven teachers and five assistants were fighting over the kettle, folding themselves into chairs, and, with their knees now somewhere near their eyes, describing their holidays and making the same jokes about how glad they were to be back at school. And one new – female – Reception teacher was pretending it was fun.

Nicky looked round the room. Her older sister, Claire, had once told her that ninety per cent of marriages started as office romances. Whenever she thought of this statistic, Nicky wondered where the other ten per cent met their match. Wherever it was, she would have to start going there soon. Out of the seven full-time teachers here, only three were men. One was Ned and the other two were Pete and Rob.

Pete was great, of course, but he was not what you could call boyfriend material. His frame was slight, bordering on petite, at little over five foot six, and in some trousers it looked as if he had no bottom at all. Ally and Nicky often wondered if it hurt him to sit down. His features seemed to have been painted on with the thinnest of paintbrushes. Delicate eyelashes framed soft blue eyes, the finest of lips curved around small, even teeth. Were he a woman, every man he ever met would have wanted to protect him. As a man he was invisible. He was Rob's best mate, right-hand man and all-round good laugh.

Rob, though, was something else altogether. Everyone knew that Rob Pattison, teacher of Year 5, the nine- and ten-year-olds, was the best-looking guy in the whole school. It was one of those things that just went without saying. It mostly went without saying because the other thing that went without saying was that Rob Pattison knew he was the best-looking guy in the school. In fairness to him, it would have been hard for him not to know. Apart from the way women reacted to him, there were always mirrors. Rob was tall, dark, broad and handsome.

To anyone who did not know Rob and Nicky's history, which meant everyone except Ally and Pete, it appeared that Nicky was the only woman in the school who had been given a Rob Pattison vaccine. ('One short sharp prick and then it was all over' had been a favourite staffroom joke during their first year at the school.) And she was also the only attractive woman who escaped the Rob Radar; that is, he refused to treat her as a potential notch on his bedpost, but rather as a close and respected friend and confidante.

To anyone who did know their history, such as Ally and Pete, it sometimes appeared that Nicky and Rob were simply taking a sabbatical from a relationship that had begun – and ended all too precipitously – seven years ago, and they would one day slip back into it as comfortably as if they were slipping on an old sock.

'You'd better be careful,' Ally warned Nicky once, after an entire lunch-break of raucous flirting. 'People will talk.'

'Oh don't be ridiculous!' laughed Nicky lightly. 'It's just friendly banter. He's like a brother.'

'If I looked at my brother like that,' muttered Ally, eyeing her gravely, 'my parents would call social services.'

The plain, and sometimes uncomfortable, truth was that Nicky and Rob did have a colourful history – and not an ancient Greek sort of history; more a post-Blair-to-present-day sort of history – which gave their friendship that special glow. Unfortunately, the other plain fact was that it had been Rob who had ended it.

And the problem with that was (as Nicky often reminded Ally) that when you weren't the one to finish a relationship, the general assumption made by everyone was always that, given the choice, you would still be in it. But plain facts don't always tell the whole story. Yes, technically, Rob had been the one to finish their six-month-long affair, just two weeks after Nicky's twenty-third birthday, all those years ago. Yes, at the time she had thought her life might as well end. Yes, at the time she had thought she would never find love again and might as well give up her dreams of ever getting married and having a family.

But that was a long, long time ago. Seven years! A lifetime! And she was a very different person now. In fact, as a happy thirty-year-old career woman, she now sometimes wondered gratefully if she had subconsciously, all those years ago, pushed him into finishing what she knew, deep down, was fundamentally a terminally flawed relationship.

After all, at only twenty-three, there she'd been, telling the college Romeo whom she adored (and who had fallen so dramatically in love with her that he'd chased her for a whole year and then stayed faithful for the longest period of his entire life) that if he couldn't promise to marry her this side of twenty-five and provide her with the babies she so desperately yearned for, there was frankly no future for them. How could she have known that instead of dropping

11

to his knees and proposing, he would spend a week ignoring her calls and then chuck her? Fickle, fickle boy! After all those wonderfully worded declarations of adoration! After such exquisite nights and mornings of love-making! After swapping favourite books (with his grave assurances not to break the spine) and pencilling secret notes in the margins! What girl could possibly have predicted such an outcome?

Yet here again, the facts do not reveal the whole story, because he ended their relationship so beautifully that she almost believed that his heart was breaking more than hers. Almost. He broke down and wept. He told her that she deserved more. He confessed that he wasn't the man for her because he never, ever wanted to marry or have children. His own parents' doomed relationship had put paid to that. He told her that it was because he loved her so much that he couldn't let her waste the best years of her life with a man who ultimately could not give her what she wanted. He told her that he had loved her more than any other woman in his life. (And he'd had a gap year, so was talking from experience.) He told her he would never forget her. And he made her promise that they must always remain friends. It was a chucking that left her shell-shocked and traumatised, but not ashamed. She lost no respect in its recounting.

Even more amazingly, they did manage to remain friends. So successfully, in fact, that when four years later, both of them fully trained teachers with some experience behind them, Rob heard about two jobs coming available at the same school, he gave Nicky all the details, they both applied, and were thrilled to start work together at the same time. And so, three years ago, they joined Heatheringdown as bosom buddies, and soon her friendship with Ally and his with Pete formed a tight-knit foursome.

Over the years since their relationship had ended, Nicky couldn't help noticing that while Rob had had many flings and one-night stands, he had never started another relationship. She herself had made a couple of attempts, but they didn't last long. During these, Rob had always maintained a keen interest in their outcome, but he never seemed too alarmed. However, it was always during these relationships that his gentle teasing began. He would drop into conversation how his mind was slowly changing over the issue of children; did she catch that programme last night about adoption? Wasn't that little girl cute – she almost made him want to be a dad! He wondered what kind of children she'd have – adorable ones with ringlets and dimples, etc. etc.

In fact, due to unhelpful comments like these and the easy, good-natured fun of their post-relationship friendship, if Nicky was really deeply honest with herself – and it usually took the imbibing of a certain amount of wine for that to happen – she could not answer one simple question. A simple, yet worrying question: If Rob asked her out again, would she say 'No' or 'Yes'?

On the side of 'No' there were many solid, stout arguments. Seven years on she had far more reservations about him as partner material than she had had in her inexperienced early twenties. Back then his relentless sexual conquests made him appear lusty and passionate, now they just made him seem cynical and jaded. She also found his choice of lifestyle deeply unattractive. He had chosen almost a decade of empty one-night stands instead of a purposeful, loving life with a woman he'd loved (if indeed he'd been telling the truth) and who had loved him. From the string of affairs he'd gone on to enjoy after her, and still energetically pursued, it was abundantly clear that their priorities in life were directly opposed to each other. She wondered now, looking back at the 23-year-old Rob, how he had even managed to stay faithful to her for six long months – if, in fact, he had.

But it wasn't only that. She'd noticed over the years that what masqueraded as laddish behaviour was actually more akin to a cruel streak. He broke hearts with as little regret as other people broke eggs. He could tease someone till they cried. And he could freeze anyone out with a single look. He was perceptive, sharp-witted and clever, but sometimes he used these attractive qualities as weapons. Just because he hadn't done it to Nicky (recently) didn't make it less forgivable, just easier to defend.

Then there were his looks. She genuinely didn't find him as devastatingly handsome as she used to. Yes, he was still good-looking, but somehow his looks had moved away from what had first drawn her to him. She had fallen for the skinny lope of a little-boy-lost and the uneven shoulders of his self-conscious, Jimmy Dean stance. Now that he had broadened out and held himself squarely towards the world he'd lost that boyish uncertainty that used to reduce her to tingling mush with a single glance.

So while the facts were that he had been the chucker and she the chuckee, the truth was that she genuinely sometimes thought that she had made a lucky escape. In fact, it was terrifying to contemplate what might have happened had they settled down together so young.

In her most lucid moments, she felt indebted to him for

making such a mature and prescient decision about their lives at a time when she'd been blinded by the promise of a happy-ever-after cloud-cuckoo-land ending. And thanks to the sharp focus of hindsight, after spending half a decade watching the post-happy-ever-after ending of friends – and of course, her sister, who had married young and started sprogging almost immediately – she knew that many were now unhappy with their lot. Yes, she may sometimes envy them their beautiful children, but she could never say that she envied them their lives. So thanks to his decision, here she was, a happy, fulfilled thirty-year-old who hadn't wasted the best years of her life on the wrong man, who had a career that fulfilled her and promised her a future of satisfaction, and who had all the excitement of love and marriage still to come, instead of firmly behind her.

What, then, could be the arguments for her saying 'Yes' to him? She had two theories: One was that it just so happened that with all her other relationships, pre- and post-Rob, she had always been the one to end things. But because Rob had got in there first with her, she'd been robbed of ever *really* knowing what would have happened if he hadn't. Would she have been the one to finish it, albeit three years later, or would they have four beautiful children, a golden retriever and two guinea pigs by now? She was stuck in the perennially inconclusive limbo of the chuckee, living for evermore with an emotional scar that would never be allowed to fully heal because someone else had done the stitches with half an eye on the exit.

And so, when she and Ally had sometimes shared more wine than was wise on a school night, she had been known to explain her wickedly wild revenge plan of manipulating

Rob to ask her out again, just to prove that she could say a final 'No' and was therefore Completely Over Him.

Ally always vehemently disagreed with this crackpot theory.

'No!' she would shout, shaking her head firmly and, depending on how much wine had been drunk, thumping her fist on the table. 'You'd be proving *exactly* the opposite if you did that!'

'How come?'

'Because if you spend your life trying to get him interested just so you can reject him then you're proving that you're *not* over him, aren't you?'

'I'm not spending my life doing it!' Nicky would shriek.

'Seven years!' Ally would explode.

'I just want to *know*!' Nicky would explode back.

'But that's the whole point! If you were completely over him, you wouldn't *need* to, would you? You wouldn't care!'

'Yes I would!' Nicky would shout. 'I'm just like that.'

'Like what? A glutton for punishment?'

'No! An organised person. I need everything neat and orderly. I need to close the book. I need to shut the drawer. I need nothing unanswered. I need closure.'

'You need help,' was Ally's usual response. 'Don't get me wrong, I love Rob, but he is not The One. You'd have children with him and then wonder why they look like every other child in North London. He's probably sired fifty children already. He just doesn't know about it.'

'Bleagh,' was Nicky's only response to that. 'What a lucky escape.'

'Exactly,' Ally would usually conclude. 'Where's the corkscrew?'

Nicky's other theory as to why she might say 'Yes' (and

this was one she never admitted to anyone, not even Ally) was far more worrying, and tended to strike late at night when she was on her own. This theory was that all her stout, solid answers explaining why she'd say 'No' were mere subterfuge. She protested too much. She was a one-man woman and the man for her was Rob. And the only real reason she was happy being friends with him was because friendship was all he was offering. Should he ever ask her out, she'd drop like a fly; his easiest conquest yet. Whenever these terrifying thoughts occurred, spiralling her into doubt and confusion, she would force herself to imagine Ally's response and slowly talk herself back to sanity.

Thank goodness for Ally. Ally kept Nicky sane – and that was saying something. Ally had the soul of an angel, the wit of a US sitcom writer and the patience of a saint. She was, after Nicky, the favourite teacher in the school. All the kids loved her. Unfortunately, all her wonderful qualities were packaged in a body a bull terrier would be proud of. Ally had shoulders Pete would die for. To say that her body was barrel-shaped would be to slight a barrel. It was only on closer inspection that one noticed the warmth in her eyes and the dimple in her smiling cheek, or heard her contagious laugh.

When Nicky had returned to the staffroom, the others were in the usual corner by the lockers. Rob was leaning against them, looking everything like the school stud. Pete and Ally were studying the new Reception teacher, Martha.

'I'd say seven out of ten,' commented Pete.

'Hmm,' replied Rob. 'More a four.'

'Yeah, well,' tutted Pete, 'not all of us can afford your standards.'

17

Ally frowned and gave them both a look. 'Do you have any idea how offensive you're being?' she asked. 'Reducing a woman to a number, based on your narrow little Western aesthetic ideal?'

'Of course!' replied Pete, without taking his eyes off the girl. 'How else am I supposed to feel superior?'

Ally looked at him and shrugged. 'Your Xbox score?'

He looked at her. 'Hey. Don't knock my second-favourite hobby.'

They continued to watch Martha for a while. This was Martha's first full-time job. She was a bit nervous, very smiley and very young. She drank her instant coffee and listened to everyone's jokes with a smiling sadness, as if all the fun in her life had ended. Meanwhile, everyone showed her the full extent of their dullness by being genuinely excited to have her there.

'You'll get used to us all soon,' Ned, Year 3's teacher, kept telling her, like a proud elder owl.

'Oh yes,' said Gwen, Year 2's teacher, nodding firmly. 'And all our silly little quirks. I suppose it's a bit like your first day at school.'

They all laughed uproariously at this because, they explained, it *was* her first day at school, and then, when Gwen realised what she'd said, they all laughed again.

Nicky tried looking at them through Martha's eyes and realised that the staff, as a whole, were very depressing. When had she stopped noticing this? She decided it was probably as long as a year ago, and felt suddenly despondent. Then she remembered *ER* was on tonight and cheered up. She caught Rob's eye and they shared a small, private grin. As she flicked her eyes away, she caught Amanda's eye, on the other side of the staffroom. She chose to smile widely at her. It was a mistake because Amanda saw this as a green light and came to join them.

As she crossed the staffroom to approach the gang, Nicky tried to look away from Amanda's glossy black mane but couldn't. Long, straight, thick hair the colour of ebony framed Amanda's face. As if that wasn't enough, she was tall and willowy with a year-round tan and legs up to her armpits. All the men pretended they didn't fancy Amanda because that would make them look obvious. But they did. And all the women pretended not to hate her because that would make them look pathetic. But they did.

For some reason unknown to anyone, Rob, while thoroughly enjoying everything about Amanda's charms and their happy effect on him, always stopped just short of doing anything about it. He would play the Rob game with her, flirting, teasing, working her up into a crescendo of expectation and then, nothing. Maybe it was because he was getting older. Maybe it was because he was saving that conquest for a special day. Maybe it was because she had the sense of humour of a stick. Or because she rarely opened her mouth without saying something unpleasant about someone. Or because the gang ripped the piss out of her so mercilessly that the peer pressure was too much, even for him. Amanda had tried gamely to penetrate the gang, but had always failed. Possibly because most of the gang knew that she was only after one thing.

'Hello, everyone,' said Amanda, looking at Rob.

'Hello,' said Rob, smiling.

'What do we think of the new addition?'

'Nice,' said Pete. 'I like her eyes.'

'Nice arse.' Rob nodded. 'Something to sink your teeth into.'

Amanda turned, purportedly to watch Martha, exhibiting the long line of her hips and thighs in her new jeans. Then she yawned, which involved stretching up very slowly and exposing her flat, smooth, soft stomach. Both men looked at her long, taut, tanned flesh and then back up to her face, all thoughts of Martha's eyes and arse gone.

At five to eight, the Headmistress entered, and the room found its focus. It was impossible not to respond to Miss James's warmth. She managed to be effusively batty yet highly efficient and over the years had made this state school hugely popular with middle-class parents. Miss James was almost single-handedly responsible for transforming this humble postcode into a lottery winner's number.

Her personal uniform of choice at school was long skirts, high-heeled boots and big necklaces with exotic-looking stones, which clinked against her bejewelled glasses chain. She carried an old satchel under her arms that was bursting with bits of paper and folders, and she had thick wavy shoulder-length hair that bounced round her friendly face. She had been Head for twenty years and was quite possibly mad.

'Good morning, Team!' she boomed, beaming from ear to ear in the doorway.

'Good morning, Miss James,' boomed back her staff.

'Now!' she began, pigeon-stepping over all the bags and coffee mugs on the floor to her spot by the kitchenette, 'Are we all happy, happy, happy to be back?' Her staff responded by laughing. 'Excellent, excellent, excellent, excellent, *excellent*.' She smiled, putting down her satchel, taking off her coat and scarf, and resting her glasses on the tip of her nose. She gasped suddenly and whipped her glasses off again.

'Good morning, Martha!' she exclaimed, arms out-stretched towards the girl. 'Have you been made welcome?'

Martha said that she had.

'Good, good, good, good, good, *good*.' She then handed Martha her coat. 'Here's your first task as Heatheringdown Reception Teacher. Hanging up my coat! There's a dear!'

There was an explosion of laughter. Miss James rested her glasses back on her nose and pulled an A4 notebook out of her satchel. On it were scrawled notes so illegible they could have been a picture drawn by one of the Reception children. She scrutinised it for a moment before looking up quickly, her big half-moon eyes fixing on their target with precision. Her glasses were taken off again.

'Ned, would you?' she said, picking up the whiteboard pen and holding it out for him. 'Your handwriting's so neat.'

Ned leapt up from his chair, almost causing an avalanche of tea and custard creams. He made his way, almost balletically, across his seated, folded colleagues, grabbed the pen from his esteemed leader, and proceeded to take her dictation of today's timetable in perfect, rounded lettering. Nicky wondered if his beautiful lower-case alphabet would secure him the post of Deputy. She spotted Roberta and Gwen, Year 1 and 2 teachers respectively, eyeing each other. Roberta and Gwen were in a lifelong competition to be the biggest victim. Roberta was a large, lumpy woman with a face like a deflated balloon and a double chin that was enjoying a far more active life than her first one. All she had to do was blink and her double chin almost started a conga along her neck. Her husband had left her twenty years ago and she was still smarting. Her son moved out on his eighteenth birthday. Gwen had cropped orange hair, red lipstick, multicoloured dangly earrings and a middle child with behavioural problems. Roberta's eyebrows rose significantly and Gwen harrumphed in response. Nicky looked back to Ned.

Ned taught Year 3 because he was good at it, and because if he taught anyone older they'd bully him. Every day, his wife sent him off to school with a packed lunch, and every lunch-time he phoned her to thank her and discuss his sandwich fillings. Nicky was extremely fond of him, but had made a pact with Ally that if she ever grew to be like him she would do the decent thing and shoot her.

Miss James finished her list of today's items and looked at everyone. 'Right. One hour to make friends with our new, nervous little bubbies and then we shall all assemble together . . . for assembly.' This was met with good-natured laughter. 'Good luck, Team!'

Nicky rummaged around her briefcase for her hair-band and glasses case. She pulled her hair into a tight ponytail and put on her snappy, black-framed glasses. She had started wearing her hair up for assembly as a simple way to control it whenever it was most wayward, but it had soon become a habit. She liked feeling tidy and formal. Even on the first morning of a new year, when every teacher had a vital one hour to meet and greet their new children before the first assembly, she assumed the ponytail-and-glasses position. It gave the children the correct impression of her. These were children who had only ever seen her in assembly, sometimes on lunch or break duty, but never in the classroom. They thought she was strict and poker-faced all the time. This way when she was fun and kind they got a nice surprise. In fact, the truth was that during the first term she found it an effort not to call each one 'sweetheart' and 'my love', sometimes even 'darling', which seemed to trip off her tongue as soon as she looked at a child. But if a teacher did that too early, children could smell weakness and even the nicest child could not help abusing that. No, children had to smell authority when they saw a teacher. And then, slowly, during the term, the teacher should allow them small sniffs of someone who was on their side, as if they'd just caught the whiff of freshly cut grass on a summer breeze. Nicky knew what she was doing and it started with scraping her hair up in a ponytail and putting on her glasses.

Year 6's classroom was at the end of the top corridor of the school. The view was right over the playground. Nicky, or Miss Hobbs, now stood at the door, holding it open for her new class to file in past her. Thirty nervy ten- and eleven-year-olds did so, overcome by the newness of everything.

'Sit anywhere for now,' she said. 'We'll sort out the seating later. We have much more important things to do first.'

She watched as each child exhibited more about themselves than if she'd installed a two-way mirror in their bedrooms. Every class had its own complex hierarchy, and watching children seat themselves was the easiest way to discover it. Thirty children ran to the five desks of six seats, racing to sit next to their best friends and far away from their enemies. She watched kids overpower weaker classmates with brute force, personality, or just plain cruelty; she watched girls hold hands, secure each other seats and hug themselves with glee as they watched the rest of the class race round them. She saw a crush in a boy's hopeful upturned eyes as he watched an Amazonian ten-year-old girl, and a play at hatred between a sparring boy and girl who had found themselves sitting back-to-back on different tables in the middle of the room. She waited until everyone had sat down before speaking quietly enough for them to have to be silent to hear her properly. And then she gave them all a beatific smile and said the magic words.

'Hello! I'm Miss Hobbs and I want to know all about you.'

This always generated an excited murmur. They all had blank pieces of paper ready and waiting for them on their tables and she asked them to write Ten Amazing Things About Myself, to be read out to everyone. She observed them as they did this, some squirming with excitement, others slowly sucking their pencils as they pondered, and again, picked up more about them than if she'd interrogated them for hours. Finally, they'd finished and, one by one, they stood up and read out their Ten Amazing Things. Before she knew it, the hour was up, it was time for assembly and her kids adored her. It worked every time. She hadn't been soft and she hadn't shouted; she'd just shown genuine interest in them. By the time the new Year 6 went to assembly, they would have defended their new teacher almost to the death.

Year 5 had not been quite so lucky. Mr Pattison was a tough teacher with his eye on top management, and he sometimes had a tendency to treat his class like lower management rather than children. His habit was to spend his first hour explaining what was required of his new team in their new job. Silence was big on the agenda, synchronised standing whenever he entered the classroom came in a close second ('who knew what synchronised meant?'), hard work of course was third, and good timekeeping was

24

fourth. Tenth was no fussing and the ones in-between were lost for evermore in a fog of boredom. Basically, he expected a lot, and by the time assembly came, his kids were in no doubt of this. Ned's kids, at the tender age of seven or eight, knew in just one hour that they were made of tougher stuff than he. He blushed, stammered and laughed inappropriately from nerves at the situation he was in. If it wasn't for the fact that most of them were also blushing, stammering and laughing inappropriately from nerves at the situation they were in, he'd be doomed. But Martha, new girl herself, was having the toughest first hour of all the teachers. Her kids were the only ones who had spent the last year in the bosom of their families, and whose worst nightmare was that school, unlike wizards and monsters, did actually exist. They were even more horrified by their new reality than she was. As soon as one stopped crying, another one started. There were two accidents, one case of vomiting, and little Josephine O'Marney got her feet caught in her chair and thought she was stuck there for ever. She cried till she had an accident and vomited simultaneously. It was a baptism of fire but, by assembly, Martha felt confident in her new job. In the staffroom she was the new girl. In the classroom, she was the Bionic Woman.

An hour later, as the entire school made its way to assembly, Nicky felt a sharp jab on her shoulder. At first she thought it was Rob. But it was Miss James, prodding her with a blunt pencil. 'Pop in and see me after school, would you, Nicola dear?' she whispered. 'Four o'clock sharp.'

Miss James walked abruptly away, and Nicky glanced back. Rob was watching her, while keeping a practised eye on his silent kids, and he raised his eyebrows questioningly at

25

her. She entered the main hall and saw a sea of eager little faces stretching back to the gym apparatus against the far wall. She crossed her arms at the sudden drop in temperature and felt a little squiggle of excitement, like a gold star being drawn in her belly.

Oscar sat cross-legged and watched Miss Hobbs, his new teacher, walk round the assembly hall and towards the back, arms crossed, heels click-clicking, stern eyes observing everyone from behind her glasses. He sat up, so his back no longer leant against the climbing apparatus. She sat down on the chair at the end of his row, picked up her hymn book, crossed one leg over the other, and scrutinised her new Year 6.

He liked his new position of sitting at the back of the school. He was sitting next to his best friend Matthew. Matthew was funny and nice. Daisy was in the row in front and he poked her in the back, managing to whisk his hand away before she hit him. Matthew snorted. Miss Hobbs looked at them, just too late. He saw her look over the top of her glasses to focus on them.

'Year 6,' she said, her voice harder than it had been in class, 'less talk, please.' It was weird being called Year 6.

Daisy didn't mind Oscar poking her in the back. She was having too much fun with her best friend Sophie. They were watching Miss James, sitting at the front of the room facing everyone. She'd got her glasses chain caught in her necklace. Daisy and Sophie giggled but stopped when Miss Hobbs looked up from her book. They had always been far more scared of Miss Hobbs than Miss James, although they liked her much more after spending the morning with her.

The piano music stopped and Miss James walked up to

the central podium at the front of the hall, glasses in her hand, necklace firmly attached, causing her to bend her neck to one side. She reached the podium, looked at her pupils as if they were all fluffy kittens and gave a big smile.

'Hello, everyone,' she said in a warm voice. 'I'm having a little problem with my glasses! What a start to the new year!'

Everyone laughed. Oscar looked over to Miss Hobbs, who blinked to acknowledge the joke.

'Hymn number 32,' announced Miss James.

There was a rustle as 210 children stood up, and the first few firm chords from the piano were followed by a lusty, if not entirely tuneful, rendition of 'In My Heart'.

Daisy's shoes were new. She stared at them intently all the way through the hymn and when everyone sat down, she wondered if God would punish her for loving the angle of her shiny new buckle more than singing a song about Him. Probably, she thought. She would probably die young as punishment. Mummy and Daddy would cry at her funeral and fall in love again. Oscar would regret ever poking her in the back. The boy from the bus stop would come to the funeral and stand at the back because he didn't even know her name. She rubbed her nose, looked up, and saw Miss James beaming and nodding at everyone. Everyone stood up. Assembly was over. That was a shame, thought Daisy. She liked assemblies.

As Daisy walked-not-ran up the stairs to their new classroom, Oscar overtook her and gave her pigtails a friendly tug.

'I'm not coming to yours tonight,' he said. 'Dad's picking me up from school.'

'Good,' she said. 'More chocolate for me.'

She walked past him, satisfied that his expression had altered ever so slightly.

After a pause she heard him shout after her, 'You're not having chocolate.'

She pretended not to hear.

As soon as they were in the classroom, Year 6 spotted a subtle difference in their new teacher. She seemed a little firmer, a tad stricter, a bit more like a teacher than this morning.

Nicky glanced up at them quickly and then, as if pulling out a gun in a Western, flipped open the register. Without any warning, she instructed them to stand up and read out their own names *in the correct order*. There was an almost audible gasp. No clues. No help. All on their own. Nicky knew this sounded much more difficult than it was. Children always knew who came right before them in the register and this trick had never failed her yet. More importantly, it helped her remember their names immediately and always made her new class feel just a bit wrong-footed and self-conscious enough to take her seriously. Worked every time.

When they had finished, she allowed them a small smile.

'You see,' she said, almost seductively, 'you are Year 6 now, so you can do your own register.'

As she took off her glasses (they were only for mild short sight and she hardly needed them), she knew they were eyeing each other across their new desks. Without looking up, she called out the name of one of the boys sitting on the back table, and held out thirty pieces of paper in his direction.

'Will you hand these out, one for everyone, please?'

She looked up as he approached her through the desks and gave him a soft, slight smile. 'You didn't think you were going to get away with hiding at the back, did you?' she said teasingly.

He smiled sheepishly at her. As he held the paper, she refused to let go and waited for him to look up at her.

'Pardon?' she asked, gently.

'No.'

She raised her eyebrows, any hint of a smile on her lips gone.

'No, Miss Hobbs,' he said.

She gave him a genuine smile and let go of the pieces of paper.

'Thank you, Marcus.'

She kept her class busy right up until the bell went for lunch, and only gave them some light relief after it, when she allowed them into the library to choose the books they would read (in silence) every morning before register.

At precisely 3.15, five minutes before the final bell, she turned off the whiteboard, sat on the edge of her desk facing her class, and asked them how they were feeling after their first day as Year 6. One boy said he was excited. She asked what about. He told her he was excited because he was now the tallest boy in the whole school. She laughed with the class and suggested putting up a height chart, so they could all see if they grew this year. One girl said she had been a bit nervous this morning. She asked her what she had been nervous of and the girl had said, a bit quietly, of her. She laughed again and told her she would let them in on the best-kept secret in the school.

'Only Year 6 ever know that if they are good,' she reduced her voice to a whisper, 'I'm a complete softie.' The class laughed. She put her finger over her lips. 'So now it's *your* secret.' She made her eyes big. 'No telling Year 5.'

A wave of excitement swept round the room.

'You promise?' she asked.

'We promise,' they chorused, laughing.

'We promise, *what*?' she asked, cupping her ear with her hand.

'We promise, Miss Hobbs.'

'Excellent!' she cried. 'You're fast learners. I think we're all going to get on very well.'

The bell went, loud and rasping, and the class waited for her reaction. She smiled. 'Have a lovely evening, all of you. You've done well today.'

And they filed out.

She picked up her case and sat for a moment before standing up. Her head was aching, her throat was tired and her cheekbones and eyebrows throbbed from the effort of keeping her face keen and interested all day. She pulled her hair-band off and felt coils of hair spring out in all directions. She didn't care, the relief at her temples was so great. She turned at a noise in her doorway.

'Good day at the office, dear?' asked Rob, head cocked.

'Knackering,' she said, wondering whether to tell him about Miss James's request.

'It's all right for some,' he said, ambling into her room as she packed up her things. 'Some of us have still got work to do before we go home.'

'Oh yes?'

'Miss James wants to see me now,' he said.

'Oh! Interesting!' exclaimed Nicky.

'Mm. Well, I don't know what it's about yet.'

'No, what's interesting is that she's asked me to see her too.'

Nicky noticed that his face showed blank surprise before polite interest.

'Ah,' he said simply. 'The plot thickens.'

They wandered down to the staffroom together in silence. Then they wished each other luck and Rob left for his meeting with Miss James. Nicky had thirty minutes to wait before her meeting, and in that time she did some preparation for tomorrow's lessons, walking past the after-club room on her way to the photocopier. On her way back up the stairs, she glanced in to see if any of her new children were in there.

She only spotted two. The boy who had been fidgeting in assembly and the girl he'd sat with his back to all day. Oscar and Daisy, she said to herself, practising their names. They were playing chess. She watched them for a moment before the boy, Oscar, spotted her. She smiled at him through the door, but he had already looked back down at the chess set.

2

Oscar frowned at the chessboard. If he wasn't very much mistaken, Daisy had won. If he moved the rook, she would take his pawn and checkmate him. He glanced up at the clock over the classroom door and suddenly saw, standing outside, a mad woman, her hair wild, staring right at him. He looked down quickly, before realising who it was. After a moment, he looked up at the clock again. Miss Hobbs had gone. Only half an hour to go before his dad picked him up. He started swinging his legs. If he kept stalling, Daisy wouldn't get to play her next move and it would be a draw. Could he hang on for that long? He put his chin in his hand and looked up at Daisy. She was looking out of the window.

'My dad's coming in half an hour,' he said.

She turned to look at him. 'So's my mum.'

'Yeah, but your mum doesn't drive a red sports car.'

Daisy shrugged.

'I get to sit in the front,' he continued.

She shrugged again.

'Your mum only has an old Renault.'

Daisy's lips pursed like one of the Tweenies. 'Play your next move now, or I've won.'

'That's not fair! Cheat.'

Oscar's mobile phone rang Greenday's 'American Idiot' then beeped. He flicked it open.

'It's my dad!' he exclaimed, and read the text, his head so low his chin touched his chest, his feet hitting the table legs.

'Play your next move now or I've won!' repeated Daisy, firmly.

Oscar suddenly jumped up and walloped the chessboard which made her, and all the pieces, jerk up in the air.

'I don't care about your stupid chess game!' he cried, and ran out of the room.

Miss Gregory looked up from her marking.

'Daisy, what just happened?' she asked.

Tears pricked Daisy's eyes. 'He ruined our chess game,' she said, 'because I was winning.'

Nicky sat down in front of the Headmistress's desk, while Miss James frowned at some notes in front of her. Eventually Miss James looked up from her notes and took her glasses off her nose. She twinkled across her messy desk at Nicky and leant her elbows on the Vesuvius of papers between them.

'How was your first day?' she asked, her voice honey-thick.

'Great, thanks,' said Nicky, nodding and smiling. 'It's good to be back.'

'Ah, that's what I like to hear,' said Miss James enthusiastically. 'You do have wonderful optimism. It's a fantastic quality. I was telling my mother about you last night – you know I tell my mother everything.' She winked. 'And my mother said there is no substitute for optimism when it comes to teaching Year 6.'

'Thank you.' Nicky smiled. Everyone knew that Miss James lived with her mother, a fantastic eighty-year-old who used to be Headmistress at one of the country's top private schools. How many bosses would confide in you so unguardedly about how much they rated you?

'So, my dear,' continued Miss James, 'I have decided. That's just what Heatheringdown needs in a new Deputy Head. Optimism.'

Nicky swallowed.

Miss James gave her a slow smile. 'I'm not interested in making you jump through hoops, though goodness knows the governors want me to. I don't have anything to prove to anyone, so the sooner this is sorted the better. So. We're going to get round the boring legal technicalities by saying it's a temporary staffing position – which, who knows?' She shrugged her shoulders right up to her ears. 'It might be! So get comfortable in the role and we'll make a decision at a later date. It also gives me a chance to see you in the job.' Miss James flashed her a quick wink. Nicky stared blankly back at her and Miss James suddenly went serious. '*I* know you're up to the job,' she told her simply. 'The question is do *you* know you're up to the job?'

Before Nicky processed this question, she smiled and nodded vigorously. This was no time for thinking.

'It would mean a lot more work,' continued Miss James, increasingly grave. 'As you know, Miss Fotheringham was busy all the time.'

Nicky nodded again.

'But because you are our much respected Year 6 teacher, not a reception teacher, I know that you can't possibly have the same amount of time as Miss Fotheringham did. And that is why I have instigated a brave new world order!' Miss James sat back from her desk. 'You and young Mr Pattison are to be my *Joint* Deputy Heads.'

'Oh!' Nicky felt instantly hard done by, then ashamed, and then excited. She gave what she hoped was a confident, optimistic smile. 'I'm absolutely delighted,' she said. 'I can assure you that you won't regret your decision.'

Miss James leant across her mound of papers.

'I know I won't, my dear. I have every faith. Now!' She held up her finger. 'This is all hush-hush until I announce it to the rest of the staff in a few days' time, after the glorious Janet has finished all the relevant paperwork. So! No gossiping!'

Nicky nodded. 'No gossiping,' she repeated.

'Good girl,' said Miss James. She stood up, straightened her long skirt, and held out her hand to shake Nicky's. 'Congratulations, my dear. You deserve it.'

Nicky raced into the staffroom. Rob was still there. They both screamed and fell into a full-body hug, before Nicky drew away quickly, suddenly embarrassed by such close physical contact. She hadn't hugged Rob for seven years. Goodness only knew how much bigger her stomach was now.

'Congratulations, Nix,' said Rob quietly. 'You've done so well!'

She looked up at him. 'Well, so have you,' she returned, leaning back slightly.

'Thanks,' he said, 'but you know what I mean.'

'No. What?' She wasn't sure if she'd heard him correctly.

'Well, it's different for blokes,' he said, with an offhand shrug.

She stared at him for a moment and moved away from him. 'What does that mean?'

'Nothing! It's just . . . well, it's more expected for men to be career-driven than for women, so it's easier for us to do well. That's all.'

'Easier or more fitting?' she asked dryly. 'So what exactly are you saying?' She couldn't help the hardness in her voice, despite her widening smile. 'That I must be a battleaxe to be this successful?'

'What?' cried Rob. 'Where d'you get that from? Blimey! Defensive or what?'

She forced a smile. 'I'm not defensive,' she explained. 'It's just that me being a woman seems to be something you're more conscious of than me, that's all.'

'Of course it is!' he laughed. 'I'm a bloke.'

'So tell me,' she pressed on, 'would you feel able to pay the same sort of compliment to a black colleague who'd done as well as you, just because they were black?'

'Jesus Christ!' breathed Rob. 'That's the last time I try to pay you a compliment!'

'Why do you need to pay me compliments?' she asked. 'I don't need them any more than you do. Or do you think I do because I'm a little girlie?'

'Right,' said Rob suddenly. 'Shut up with all this feminist shit and listen to me. All I was trying to say,' he explained, 'is that we all know that it's still much harder for women to do as well as men. And you've beaten a lot of men to get this far. So you've done fantastically.'

She took a moment to let this sink in and then grinned stupidly. 'Thanks,' she said. 'Yeah, maybe you're right. Sorry about that.' She allowed herself to bask in the moment. 'I have done really well, haven't I?'

'Too right. You should be proud of yourself.'

She smiled and nodded. 'I am. Thanks.'

They started to pack away their things in a mutually contented silence.

'You know,' he said suddenly, 'sometimes I can't believe you're the same person you were when we went out with each other.'

Nicky's whole body temperature shot up. 'How do you mean?' she managed, her eyes still on her packing.

'Well, back then you were fixated on becoming a mum, weren't you? Nothing else mattered. I was convinced that by now you'd have three kids, with another on the way.'

Nicky tried to laugh, but only managed a rather lame honking noise.

'I remember,' he said. 'I've never told you this, have I? I couldn't believe you didn't try to talk me out of finishing with you. I was so convinced you'd just change your mind about kids that I didn't even have a back-up plan.'

Nicky gasped.

'I know!' he chuckled. 'Arrogant or what? But I just couldn't believe you could be that determined about your future so young.'

'You mean . . . you didn't really want to finish with me?' she almost whispered.

He shook his head, with a friendly grin on his face.

'Nope,' he said. 'Not for one second. Came out of your place in complete shock. And I'd tried every trick in the book – crying, declaring undying love, blah blah blah. But you were absolutely determined. Like a . . . like a rock. It was amazing. I'd never seen anything like it before. It was as if . . .' he mused for a moment, '*nothing* was going to stop you getting your dream.' His voice went serious. 'You're a really strong woman, Nicky.'

Nicky went weak.

'I think I'm over it now though,' he said in mock seriousness, his hand on heart. 'And the pity shags I got for it were blinding.'

She let out another laugh. This one sounded more like a dog in a mixer. 'Aaah!' she sighed eventually. 'Sweet!'

'Yeah, well,' he said, 'I think it all turned out for the best in the end, didn't it!'

'I think so!'

'But now look at you!' he said, in warm wonder. 'You've harnessed all that amazing strength and determination and turned it right round in completely the opposite direction. You couldn't have had a more different life from the one you'd planned then.'

Nicky's stomach went into free-fall. If Rob had just shoved her out of a moving plane he couldn't have created a more jolting physical reaction.

'You're an inspiration,' he was now saying. 'You know what you want and you don't let anything – or anyone – get in the way.'

She was completely unable to reply. Partly because she didn't even know what the cliché response was to such a statement let alone the genuine one, partly because the Nicky he was describing was nothing like her and she'd always assumed he knew her better than anyone, partly because she was still in shock from discovering he had never really intended to finish with her all those years ago and their whole history might have been different had she reacted differently, and partly because, physically, it still felt like she was free-falling out of a moving aeroplane.

'By the way.' He broke the lengthy silence with a soft, light tone. 'Do you mind if I ask you a question?'

She shook her head. It was all she could manage. In the light of all she'd just been told she was amazed it didn't just loll to one side.

'It's a bit sensitive.'

She touched the table next to her for balance.

'Well, you see . . .' he went on, 'what I sometimes find myself wondering, late at night, is . . .' he paused, and it was only when Nicky came over a bit dizzy that she remembered to breathe, 'when did you change your mind about having kids?'

Her lower jaw now proceeded to follow her stomach. She stared in utter amazement up at Rob, and his open, honest look of enquiry was so unforced she had to remind herself he hadn't just asked her the time. After a while she turned her thoughts to the social aspect of conversation and began to construct an answer. After a longer while, she plumped for, 'Well, um . . . you see, actually, I don't see it as such an "either/or" thing.'

He frowned gently. 'What do you mean?'

'Career or motherhood,' she explained. 'I don't see them as mutually exclusive.'

He nodded thoughtfully for a bit. 'You mean,' he said slowly, 'you still want kids?'

'Of course!'

'Oh!' He shook his head in wonder. 'I see!'

'Well, what did you think?'

He shrugged. 'Well, I just assumed you'd changed your

mind about it all. You know, come to your senses!' He laughed abruptly. 'Because you hadn't had any.'

There was a long pause.

'It doesn't really work like that,' she said shortly.

'What doesn't?'

'Life.'

There was a long pause.

'Oh, right,' he said, 'I see. No. I suppose it doesn't.'

He nodded slowly while Nicky tried to sort out her thoughts, only to conclude that she was so confused she could barely remember her name.

'Mind you,' Rob started again, his tone friendly and light, 'it's worked out best in the end, hasn't it?'

'What has?' she asked.

'Well,' he said, 'you probably wouldn't have just come out of an interview with Miss James about the Deputy post if there was a hubby at home wanting his dinner and three screaming kids needing help with their homework.'

The back of her eyes and nose suddenly went all prickly. 'Oh, I'm sure Miss James would have managed to see me at a different time,' she said, with forced sweetness. 'I didn't get the impression that if I couldn't make four o'clock I wouldn't be up to the job.'

He laughed loudly. 'You're absolutely right. Touché! And anyway, when you start a family late there's more money in the pot, so you'll be able to do nurseries or nannies.'

Nicky was so shocked that she exploded into laughter. Then, just when she'd acclimatised herself to this fact, it turned into crying. Not endearing, feminine, coy little sniffles, but big, fat, racking sobs that convulsed her body.

She turned away from him.

'What? What? What?' he asked.

She shook her head.

'What the hell did I say?' came Rob's baffled voice from behind her.

'Nothing,' she sniffed. 'Nothing. It's just been a long day.'

'Hey, hey!' he murmured. 'I thought that was a good thing.'

She nodded. 'Yes,' she managed. 'It's brilliant.'

'Please, Nicky! Shit! Forgive me! The last thing I want to do is upset you.'

'You haven't upset me,' she sniffed. 'I'm just tired and emotional.'

'Husshh,' he said, putting a hand on her shoulder. She shoved him away and fished for a tissue in her pocket. Why did tears make people treat you like a five-year-old when usually they meant something grown-up was going on inside?

'Just ignore me,' he continued. 'Forget everything I said.'

'OK,' she said. 'Done.'

'And remember, your career's got a shelf-life on it, but you can have kids whenever. After all, there's no state retirement from kids, is there?'

She turned to him. 'Will you shut up about kids!' she cried. 'Anyone would think you're obsessed with them.'

'Ah, yes,' he allowed, somewhat sheepishly. 'You spotted that. Well . . . you know . . . a bloke gets to a certain age and looks at life very differently.'

There was a long pause.

'Really?' she asked weakly.

'Yeah,' he said seriously. 'Really.'

'Wow,' she said. 'You mean, like, you don't think children would make perfect, moving tables for your pint?'

He laughed.

'Right,' she said, suddenly desperate to get away. 'I'm going home. By the way, I know we're not meant to dicuss it with everyone, but what shall we tell the others?'

'Ally and Pete? Dunno.' He paused. 'That we're better than them?'

She hit him on the arm. He hit her back. Then she roughly wiped her eyeliner off her cheeks. 'Right,' she said. 'I have to get home and prepare for tomorrow.'

'Attagirl,' said Rob, and pretend-punched her on the shoulder.

She punched him back. 'Piss off, Prattison,' she said, a bit snuffily.

It was amazing how effective the cold water in the Ladies could be. If Nicky ever needed ice, she should remember to come here. After a thorough face wash, she was as good as new, except with no feeling in her fingertips. Ten minutes later she walked across the playground to the car park, repeating Miss James's words, forcing herself not to give Rob's words a moment's thought. How would the other teachers take the news? Ned? He'd been here for ten years. Gwen and Roberta both had children to support. Ah well, she thought, trying to push any guilt out of her mind and to focus only on the good. They obviously weren't as good as her at their job. She knew she was good. She wondered what would happen if Miss James retired. Could she actually become Head one day? Was it possible to be a sexy, eligible headmistress? Would it, in fact, make her *more* sexy and eligible? Would the offers come pouring in and before she knew it she'd be a headmistress *and* a mother of three? Hah! That would show Rob and his 'change your mind' garbage.

As she walked out of the school an echo rang out across the playground, interrupting her thoughts, and she looked behind her to the main gate to see if a passing teenager was vandalising the entrance. She was surprised to see a young boy – possibly one of the school's pupils – standing on the pavement, head down, hitting the gate with a cricket bat. She watched as he regularly, if rather forlornly, smacked each iron rail of the gate.

As she approached the gates, she recognised the boy she'd seen in the after-school club. One of her new pupils. Oscar. She called out his name and his head shot up at her voice, his scowl relaxing slightly. He clearly had need of the cold water in the Ladies.

'Don't hit the school gate, please, Oscar,' she said, approaching him. 'Is that your cricket bat?'

He looked at it and thought about lying. He nodded.

'Well, I think you know it's far better suited to playing cricket than vandalising the school gates.'

His head hung low. An apology just reached her over the wind.

'It's ever so late,' she said, opening the gate and standing next to him. 'What are you doing still out here?'

'Au pair's late. Probably lost.' He let out a long sigh. 'She's new.' He took out his mobile phone, and Nicky was surprised to see it had a camera facility. 'I'll call her,' he said.

She listened as he managed to have an entire conversation using only one grunted syllable. He clicked shut the phone. 'Two minutes,' he said.

'Right,' she said, hugging her coat to her and sitting on the ground, her back leaning against the gate. 'Sit.'

Oscar sat.

'Three things,' she said. 'One: Don't bring your phone into school again please. You know that can cause problems. If you need to make a call you can always use the school office. Two: Especially a phone with a camera facility because it won't just get lost, broken or stolen, it will get stolen and you will get mugged. Three: Tell me where your parents are.'

'My dad's working late. Again.'

'And your mum?' she asked.

'I don't have a mum.'

There was a pause.

'I'm sorry about that,' she said, her voice softening.

Oscar shrugged.

'Neither do I,' she said.

He looked up at her. 'But you're a grown-up,' he said.

She shrugged. 'I still don't have a mum.'

A car swung into the space in front of them and the driver hooted.

'That's her,' he said. 'I better go.'

'What are you going to do with that cricket bat in future?'

He managed a placatory smile, eyes down. 'Play cricket.'

She cupped her ear, an already familiar sign to him. He gave a half-smile. 'I'm sorry, Miss Hobbs.'

She smiled at him. 'I should think so too. See you tomorrow.'

He gave a nod. 'Bye.'

'Pardon?' She inclined her head towards him.

'Bye, Miss Hobbs.'

'Bye, Oscar. Have a good evening.'

Oscar gave a grunt, stood up slowly and lolloped to the car. Neither he nor the au pair acknowledged each other's presence as the car swerved out from the kerb. Nicky stood up, wiped the back of her coat, and wondered why some people bothered to have children.

She walked to her car gently chewing the inside of her lip.

Oscar stole a cautious glance at the au pair's hands on the wheel. Her knuckles were white, which was stupid, seeing as she was only driving at five miles an hour. He could skateboard faster. He'd stopped bothering to take any notice of their faces any more, except to register – he didn't know what; prettiness, friendliness, motherliness? This one's face was all hard lines. He hated her.

As they drove through the high street Oscar stared out of the window at the children walking beside their mothers as they passed shops; at the babies in buggies being pushed by their mothers, and at the laughing teenagers flirting in their baggy trousers, holding cigarettes or bags of chips. He imagined their mothers at home, waiting for them, baking bread.

He couldn't wait to be older. Sometimes he could almost feel it, as if it was days away, and then, like a mirage, it would fade, and feel like it would never come.

'What time deed your faather say 'eed be 'om?' asked the au pair.

Oscar shrugged.

'Ozkarr?'

He grunted.

'What time deed –'

'He didn't,' Oscar cut her off. 'Something important came up.'

His au pair whistled through her teeth. Oscar clenched his fists under his satchel.

The road took them past the terraced houses of Muswell Hill where there were buses and lots of people, through two woods on either side, and then suddenly rose up towards Highgate. Here there was more greenery, fewer people and buses, large detached homes and a village pond. He watched the posh boys spill out of the local private school in gangs of four and five. His dad had asked him if he wanted to go there. It would have meant exams later this year, but his dad was happy to pay for private tuition if he felt he needed it. Oscar had said no. He wanted to be like the cool teenagers he saw on the street corners in their baggy trousers, not like these saddos.

The car now crawled down a steep hill and, without indication, turned into the spacious side road where he lived. Oscar's dad often said that the houses in this road were so far apart you didn't have to ever see your neighbour, which was amazing for London living. But Oscar knew the neighbours were there because in the summer he heard them splashing in their pool. The au pair stopped the car, held her breath, put the car into Park, got out, pressed the button at the side of their gate and ran back into the car. While the gate slowly opened, she manoeuvred the car down the drive and tried to negotiate it into the garage. What was the problem? thought Oscar. Just park anywhere, the garage was big enough for two cars. As soon as she stopped the car, before she had exhaled, he leapt out and raced through the connecting door from the garage into the hall. He ran through the vast, square hallway, leaving mud marks on the marble floor and scattering satchel, coat and shoes on and around the cream chaise longue. He went straight to the kitchen, opened the walk-in fridge and took out some Diet Coke before his au pair had even come in.

'Whot are you goin' too doo now?' she asked, holding his coat in her arms.

He shrugged. 'Homework,' and went for the stairs.

'Aye weel be mekking pastahr at seven,' she called after him.

'I *hate* pasta!' he bellowed. 'I'll make my own dinner.'

'Yoo know your faather will be upset eef yoo are not een bed by nine,' she called out.

Oscar let out a roar of anger as he raced three at a time up the curved staircase, past the full-length window. He slammed his bedroom door shut behind him. Then he flung himself on to his bed, located the remote control under a pillow in one movement and turned on the TV.

He ate dinner upstairs. Toast with peanut butter and a packet of crisps. Luckily he didn't hear from the au pair again. When he made his toast he could hear her in the utility room talking on her mobile in a harsh, bitty language. It sounded like she was trying to cough up phlegm. She was probably ironing, and thankfully she didn't come out. After dinner, he spent a couple of hours on his Xbox and then did his homework cross-legged on his bed in front of the telly. Then he shook off his clothes, leaving them next to his bed alongside the plate of toast crumbs and empty crisp packet, put on his pyjamas and picked up his well-thumbed copy of *The Lord of the Rings*.

He didn't look at his alarm clock as he turned off his AC Milan bedside lamp, but he knew that he'd got away with later than nine o'clock. Stupid au pair didn't even check. When he couldn't sleep, he turned on his torch and continued to read under his bedclothes. He didn't remember falling asleep.

And he didn't hear the garage door sliding shut hours later.

Mark Samuels slipped off his shoes, threw his briefcase and jacket on the chaise longue, and took the curved stairs three at a time. He tiptoed across the hall and opened his son's bedroom door. He waited. No movement. He coughed. He opened the bedroom door wider, letting in light.

He walked across the room, sat gently on the edge of Oscar's bed and looked at his sleeping son. He leant over and gave him a kiss on his cheek, taking in the smell of sleeping boy, then pulled the duvet up to cover his shoulders.

He watched how Oscar's breathing made the duvet rise and fall steadily. When Oscar made a small grunt and turned over, he smiled. It was always worth waiting. Eventually, he got up, put Oscar's book and torch on the bedside table, picked up the plate, crisp packet and clothes, and took them downstairs. Ten minutes later, he was in bed, setting his alarm clock for the morning.

3

Four hours later, at half past five in the morning, a besuited Mark Samuels was back in Oscar's bedroom. He felt lots of emotions watching his son sleep, but the most visceral one was envy. Holding his tie against his chest so that it wouldn't drop on to Oscar's face, he leant over and softly ran his hand through the boy's growing curls – his mother's curls, nothing like Mark's own hair – then moved the duvet up to cover his shoulders again. Then he kissed his cheek, wondered how his son could look so much like a baby in his sleep while his body filled up so much of the bed, and traced the delicious curve where the back of his head joined his neck. Then he left the pitch-black house.

The roads and tube were always empty this early and he made it into the office in a record twenty-five minutes. He glanced at the clock as he paced into the office. 6 a.m. Half an hour before the rest of the team would start coming in. In a matter of weeks they would be doing all-nighters. It was always like this during a Due Diligence – the massive, secretive project of checking a firm's entire accounts and reporting back to their client before their client bought the firm. And, as one of the newest partners at the City's second biggest firm of accountants – and in fact the partner who had brought in this huge amount of work – Mark Samuels was for the first time in his fifteen-year career, answerable only to himself and the client. And the other hundred partners, of course. His days of drawing pretty graphics or ticking tidy sums might be over, but the stresses of meeting deadlines and keeping the client sweet were now all his. It never got easier, it just got different.

His office had yet to be moved to the partners' rooms, so it – and he – were still attached to his department. So far, it was working well. He walked through the empty office, carrying a coffee that he hoped would see him through to 11 a.m. in one hand and flicking on light switches as he went with the other. He passed the desk of his personal assistant, Caroline, and opened his office door. He kept it open and pulled up the blinds to the window between him and his department so that he could get a good view of his team throughout the morning, until they got their cabs to the firm on the other side of London. The room they were assigned to there was stuffy and badly lit. He opened his window, sat back in his chair and sipped his coffee. He managed to get a full twenty minutes of work done before his team came in.

Matt was the first.

'Yo, boss!' he called out loudly.

Mark smiled a bitter smile. It was so nice to be respected. He would have got up to chat, but that would have meant moving his bones.

'See the football last night?' called out Matt, stuffing half a croissant in his mouth as he shrugged out of his jacket.

'Nope,' said Mark. I was here till midnight, you arse, he thought.

Matt shook his head. 'Referee should be fucking shot.'

Danny entered and Matt made a sort of war-like noise.

'Two-one, two-one!' chanted Danny, arms in the air, legs akimbo.

'That was never a penalty!' cried Matt.

'The better team won, my man. The better team won.'

Anna-Marie came in and the room went quiet for a moment. 'Morning,' she said, smiling. Matt and Danny said hello. She'd announced her pregnancy last week and as far as they were concerned any energy directed her way was dead energy. Matt chucked some paper clips past her, at Danny, and she gave a little jump.

'Oy!' shouted Danny, laughing. 'You're a bad loser, man.'

'Oh, the football, right?' asked Anna-Marie.

Danny raised his arms in the air. 'Two-one!' he sang again.

'Well done.' She grinned. She turned to Matt. 'Bad luck.' Matt gave a quick jerk of his head upwards in response.

Oscar was more mature than these two gibbons, thought Mark. And they were senior managers. By seven o'clock that evening, he thought he might still make it home in time to see Oscar. By eight, he knew that wasn't going to happen. At nine o'clock, he called one of his team over.

'Right,' he said. 'I think I've found a hole in the books.'

'What?' cried Matt. 'You're kidding me. Fuck.'

'Someone will have to go to Birmingham tomorrow to check this out. No one above Assistant Manager. I've got an 8 a.m. meeting with the board, so I'll be in mid-morning.'

'Right, boss,' sighed Matt.

As he walked through the still-buzzing office, he heard Danny telling his wife that he wouldn't be home till midnight and Matt telling Anna-Marie that a car would come and collect her from her house at 6.30 a.m. and take her to Birmingham for a 9 a.m. conference.

Oscar woke early on Friday morning and insisted the au pair drop him at Daisy's flat on the way to school. He stood outside Daisy's front door, his entire bodyweight leaning on the doorbell as the car made its halting exit. Eventually, the door opened and Daisy's mum stood in the narrow hallway she shared with two other flats, looking down at him with an unimpressed expression.

'You know what?' she shouted. Oscar's finger jumped off the doorbell. She lowered her voice. 'The doorbell works.'

'Sorry, Lilith,' he said, running past her up the stairs to her flat. 'Forgot I was pressing it.'

'Daisy's in the kitchen,' she said, following him up, although she knew he wasn't there to see Daisy, he was there to be part of a family breakfast. Most ten-year-old boys didn't want to know girls and Oscar only just scraped into the exception bracket. Lilith knew that he and Daisy barely made eye contact in school, but out of school they leant on each other almost as much as Mark leant on Lilith. She would have been insulted on behalf of her daughter by this double standard if it wasn't for the fact that Daisy felt just as hypocritical about him.

They were in the kitchen in no time, the flat being what an estate agent would call bijou and what Lilith called 'big enough to swing a cat in if you wanted to kill it'.

Daisy looked up from her cocoa pops and *heat* magazine. 'Hi.'

'Hi.'

'Have you got a packed lunch?' asked Lilith.

'No,' said Oscar.

She sighed and handed him a lunchbox. 'How did I guess?'

Oscar froze, staring at the lunchbox. Lilith froze too, staring at Oscar.

'What?' she asked. 'Is there a problem?'

'It's pink,' mumbled Oscar.

Her eyebrows rose into her fringe. 'I think,' she said, 'you mean "Thank you, Lilith".'

'Thank you, Lilith,' he mumbled unconvincingly.

Lilith sighed, took it back and started repacking his lunch in a blue box while issuing orders to Daisy. 'Coat and shoes on! Satchel, lunchbox and homework. Lights off! Wait for me on the pavement!' She shut the front door behind them all, handing Oscar a lunchbox.

'That's my lunchbox!' screeched Daisy.

'I know!' Lilith screeched back, handing Daisy the pink one. 'Why don't you write and tell all those Third World children who are dying of starvation?'

Daisy raised her eyes to heaven. 'God,' she muttered. 'Bo-*ring*.'

Lilith hugged the living breath out of her daughter. Then she did the same to Oscar.

'Ooh, you're both so *scrummy*,' she said. She stood up. 'Be good. And if you can't be good, I really don't want to know. Have fun,' she called after them as they trotted off. 'Don't cross the roads without looking. Don't eat your lunches until lunchtime. Have fun.' Then she saw the 147 appear at the bottom of the hill and ran like fury the other way to the bus stop.

*

The next day was the first Saturday since the new school year had begun. Across the country new pencil cases had been lost, pencil leads dulled and shoes scuffed. Throughout the so-called 'nappy valley' of north-west London, parents like Lilith were lying in bed, enjoying the luxury of not having to scream themselves hoarse just to get out of their homes before 7.30 a.m., while trying to zone out of downstairs's television. No wonder she needed to shout to be heard, Lilith thought idly. Daisy was turning deaf from the TV.

Further outside nappy valley, in slightly less sought-after postcodes, the teachers of nappy valley's children were out cold. The unfortunates who were both teachers and parents of young children were comatose, but as ever there were exceptions to the rule and Nicky was one of them. For a start, she was a teacher who lived in the same postcode as her school and most of its pupils. When her mother had died, eighteen years ago now, she had left both her daughters a tidy sum of money. This was put into a high-interest savings account by their father – one of the most thoughtful things he ever did for them – and by the time Nicky was looking for her first property, she had enough to secure herself a new-build in what was to become one of the most sought-after areas in north London. Not only that, but a week of teaching had given her more energy, instead of less. By the end of the summer holidays she always felt slightly sluggish and it was good to feel bouncy again. She woke relatively early, walked to the shops and brought back fresh coffee, warm brioches and two weekend papers. Ally arrived at ten, as usual, and as it was a mild morning, they breakfasted on Nicky's balcony while Nicky wondered how to tell Ally all her news.

'I can't believe we're here again,' said Ally.

'What do you mean?'

'Back at another school year. When I was a kid, summer holidays lasted for ever. This one lasted two weeks, tops.'

'I know.'

'Before we know it, we'll look round and wham! We'll be dead.'

Nicky looked at her friend. 'Well, I'm glad you came over,' she said. 'I was worried I might spiral down for a while there, but you've brought your magic into my life again and up I go.'

Ally promised not to discuss death until she'd finished her brioche. To keep her mind off it, Nicky told her her news: she was to be Joint Deputy with Rob. Ally stopped stuffing brioche into her mouth and stared at her. Just as she was about to say something through it, Nicky went on. Rob had confided to her that he'd never intended to finish their relationship. He'd just assumed Nicky would cave in and pretend she didn't want children to keep going out with him. Ally's jawline flabbed. Since they had split up and no children had appeared, Rob had made the assumption that Nicky had changed her mind about having babies. Ally's eyes doubled in size. After Nicky had told him she hadn't changed her mind about babies, Rob had finally confided that he was now seriously contemplating becoming a father.

There was a pause. Ally started to say something, but a bit of brioche went the wrong way and she coughed so violently that most of it came up again.

'Dramatic, huh?' concluded Nicky.

'Can't you let a girl just enjoy her food?' breathed Ally, her eyes watering.

'Sorry,' said Nicky. 'I just had to get it all out. I was dying to tell you yesterday, but Miss James swore us to secrecy and someone might have overheard.'

Ally stared at her again. 'So let me get this straight,' she said.

'Mm.'

'You're now Joint Deputy and Rob basically wants to go out with you again?'

Nicky's stomach flip-flopped. She started giggling. She couldn't stop.

'Well,' said Ally. 'There you go.

'What?' snorted Nicky.

'Now you know.'

'Know what?'

'How you'd react if he asked you out again.'

'How?'

Ally gave her a warm smile. 'Like a fourteen-year-old convent girl.'

Oscar woke at six, got out of bed, padded through the hall and nudged his dad. Mark, eyes closed, went, 'Ugh.'

'Da-ad,' said Oscar. 'Can I go on the computer?'

'What time is it?' managed Mark.

'Six.'

The pause that followed told Oscar that his father was not best pleased. Then, after a while, it told him that his father was asleep.

'Da-ad. Can I go on the computer?'

Mark surfaced slowly from his dream. He wanted to say no. He wanted to say that they had a deal not to go on the computer until at least eight o'clock, as Oscar well knew. He wanted to suggest reading a book until then. He wanted to suggest they go and play a board game together until then. He wanted to sleep.

'Yes,' he said.

Two hours later, Oscar was back.

'Da-ad.'

'Ughmn.'

'Can I watch TV?'

'Mm.'

Four hours later the best TV was over. Oscar flicked through the Sky channels again, then went into his playroom and looked at his toys. He plodded upstairs, his pyjama bottoms trailing, got into his own cold bed, and started reading his book.

At one, he went into his dad's room. He sat on the bed. Nothing. He got up and sat down again, harder. Still nothing. He bounced on it. Nothing. He started whining. Mark opened one eye.

'What's that revolting noise?' he growled.

'I'm bo-ored.'

Mark turned over so he was lying on his back. He opened his arm and Oscar lay down next to him.

'On a scale of one to ten,' started Mark, 'how bored are you?'

'Ten.'

'Don't hold back now,' said Mark.

'Ten.'

'Be completely honest.'

'Ten.'

'I can take it.'

'TEN!'

'Goodness me! Ten!' said Mark. 'We'll have to do

something about that.'

Five minutes later, Oscar jabbed him in the ribs and Mark woke with a start. He jabbed Oscar back. Then he started tickling him. Oscar leapt away and shouted 'TEN!' in his ear.

Mark hefted his body up a bit and leant against the headboard, the skin round his eyes aching.

'Right,' he said. 'I've got about an hour's work to do, then I'm all yours. What shall we do today?'

'Go to the park and play football.'

'Excellent. I was worried you'd say watch more TV. Bagsie in goal. Just . . . give me ten more minutes in bed –'

The pillow landed on his head.

'Good shot!' he muffled from under the pillow. 'You're getting better at that.'

His duvet was pulled off him, leaving the rest of him naked to the elements.

Working at the dining-room table wasn't ideal, but Mark wanted to be in the same room as Oscar. Oscar wanted Mark to be in the same room as him too, but he also wanted to watch his James Bond video at top volume. After half an hour, Mark looked up from his work and watched his boy staring contentedly at the television. Eventually, he picked up the phone. Lilith answered.

'Hi, it's me,' he said.

There was the slightest pause. 'Hmm?' she said.

He sighed. 'I've got this stupid deadline –'

'How long?' Her tone was dull.

'One hour. Max.'

'Which means two. And don't call me Max.'

'Fantastic. What time can you pick him up?'

Lilith exploded into laughter at the other end of the phone. 'You can drop him off here within the next ten minutes or we'll have gone to Brent Cross.'

'Oh God,' moaned Mark, 'he hates Brent Cross.'

Lilith sighed. 'So does Daisy. But I've got to go. It's the only time I get all week.'

'OK,' said Mark, 'how about Daisy comes here to play with Oscar and I work upstairs?'

'Perfect. Thought you'd never ask. I'll bring her round in ten.'

Mark rang off and found Oscar looking at him from across the living room.

'Are we going to the park?' asked Oscar, his voice brittle. Mark's heart clenched.

'If I can get my work finished, sweetheart, yes,' he told him. 'But I'm going to have to work upstairs in my office. Daisy's going to come and play.' He looked at his boy. 'Give your daddy a hug.'

Oscar turned his head and stared out of the window. When he looked back, his dad was already halfway out of the room.

Daisy always won Monopoly and Oscar always won Risk. So they played Frustration and after just twenty minutes it had thoroughly lived up to its name. Oscar won two out of the three games.

'Yes! Hooray!' he cried, jumping up and punching the air with his hand. 'That means we get to play football in the garden *and* you're in goal.'

'OK,' conceded Daisy. 'But don't kick it *at* me.'

Fifty-six goals later, he and Daisy sat in the treehouse, Oscar holding the ball in his hands, Daisy holding her thumb which had been throbbing since goal 23 deflected off it before going in.

'What do you think of Miss Hobbs?' she asked.

Oscar thought about it. 'She's all right,' he said slowly.

'Mm,' agreed Daisy.

'I mean, she's nice, but . . .' He thought about it. 'A bit scary.'

'Mm.'

'She hasn't got a mum.'

Daisy looked at him. 'How do you know?'

'She told me. She asked where mine was so I told her I didn't have one, and she told me neither did she.'

Daisy gasped. 'She *confided* in you. She must like you.'

Oscar shrugged.

'*And* you've got something *in common*.' Her tone was hushed.

When they heard Mark climbing the ladder, they screamed excitedly that no adults were allowed in.

'What's all this then?' asked Mark, from halfway up.

'I scored fifty-six goals!' Oscar cried out.

'Oh!' laughed Mark. 'I bet Daisy's had a wonderful afternoon!'

They joined in the laughter. He reached the tree house and beamed at them. 'Who wants to come inside, drink hot chocolate and watch a video?' asked Mark. 'Daisy, your mum's here and she's going to stay all evening. She's brought *Johnny English*.'

Oscar and Daisy were down in minutes.

Oscar and Mark shared a giant pizza with extra tuna and

pineapple which no one else wanted, Daisy had mushroom pizza and Lilith had salad. They sat on boy and girl sofas, Mark's arm round Oscar, Lilith's round Daisy. Within moments, both parents were asleep. Daisy went to the playroom to find a puzzle, but Oscar didn't move.

Meanwhile, Nicky was trying to piece together what the hell she was doing with her life.

Here she was, an attractive, if rather fuzzy-headed woman entering what could be the most exciting decade of her life. And how had she spent her Saturday? An idyllic morning, followed by an entire afternoon of marking essays, all of which had been written in the style of J.K. Rowling, and some preparation work for next week plus more work she'd been given by Miss James. The latter had sounded like a quick nothing when Miss James had asked her to 'run it off', but she'd wanted to do it properly. It had taken her three hours and had for the first time made her wonder if she would be up to the job of Deputy. And how was her day ending? With the blind date from hell. She wondered what Rob was up to tonight.

She looked at Whatever-His-Name-Was across the restaurant table. She must stop trusting her sister's enthusiasm for her husband's colleagues. What made Claire think that just because Nicky was single she was desperate? Why didn't people understand that the chances were single people were *more* discerning, not less, than couples? Take her sister, for example. Nicky was absolutely convinced that one of the main reasons her big sister had married so young was not because she flukily happened to meet the man of her dreams so early, but because she was not fussy. Never had been. It was just her nature. You only had to look at her clothes to see that. Nicky felt sure that if someone else had proposed to Claire first, Claire would now be married to him. It just so happened that Derek got there first. And Derek was not what Nicky would call a catch. If he'd been a fish, no fisherman would be boasting about him in the pub afterwards, put it that way. Derek had no social graces, no sense of humour and no hair. Mind you, the man did have sperm that could fly. Claire had once said she only had to look at him to get pregnant. Which was lucky, thought Nicky.

'But the penalty,' Whatever-His-Name-Was said, 'was outrageous.'

'Really,' remarked Nicky.

Encouraged, Whatever-His-Name-Was continued. 'We should go to a match sometime. I've got great tickets. I bet you'd like it if you tried. You've got to be open to new experiences.'

'You're absolutely right,' said Nicky. 'And then I'll take you to one of my knitting fayres. I can tell you'd be a great knitter.'

He snorted. 'Fuck off.'

The worst bit of a blind date was knowing that you had to get through all the social niceties that delayed getting your make-up off, undoing your tight jeans (by yourself) and climbing into bed. So Nicky didn't bother with niceties any more. She stood up, put out her hand for a confident handshake, and said her usual line.

'It's been nice. But I don't think it's going to work.'

And then she put a twenty-pound note on the table and walked out, leaving him staring at the money. Only half an

62

hour later, she snuggled down in her bed and closed her eyes. And, to her surprise, saw Oscar getting into the car with his au pair. She turned over and snuggled down again.

If she'd known that Oscar was, at that moment, held fast against a warm heart, being carried upstairs, she might have fallen asleep more quickly than she did.

4

The phone woke Nicky early on Sunday morning. She picked it up and put it to her ear; two fruitless activities because she couldn't yet speak. She tried to make a grunting noise and was rewarded with some phlegm lodging in her throat.

'Auntie Nicky?' asked Sarah-Jane into the silence.

Nicky's mouth said, 'Hello, darling,' but no sound came out. There was a considerable pause.

'Aunty Nicky?'

Nicky gave a cough and her voice woke with a start. 'Yes, sweetheart,' she bellowed.

'Gosh, are you all right?' asked Sarah-Jane. 'You sound awful.'

Nicky smiled. Her eldest niece was taking after her mother more and more each day.

'That's nothing,' Nicky said, feeling her hair. 'You should see me. I look like a badger's bottom. And not in a good way.'

Sarah-Jane snorted with laughter. 'Mummy says can you bring your swimming costume today?' she asked eventually.

'Why? Are we having a bathing beauties competition?'

'No. We're going swimming.'

'Phew. For a minute there I'd thought I'd have to wax my legs.'

Sarah-Jane had hysterics. Nicky did enjoy making her ten-year-old niece laugh. All you had to do was be honest.

'What's the time?' she asked.

'Nine o'clock.'

It was Nicky's turn to pause. 'Are you trying to tell me,' she asked slowly and clearly, 'that you woke me at nine o'clock on a *Sunday*?'

'Yes.' Increasingly hysterical laughter.

'Say bye bye.'

'Badger's bottom,' came the giggled response.

'That's good enough for me,' mumbled Nicky, and rang off.

She pressed the off button on her phone and dropped it to the floor. She tried to leave it there, but it was no good. She hung out of her bed to put it back in its holder, her body half in, half out of the bed, her hair skimming the floor. She found to her surprise that this was a spectacularly comfortable position, stretching her back out like a cat. She lay there for a while, eyes shut, smile on her face, before extracting the other half of her body out of bed. She scrunched her neat, pink feet into the beaded, embroidered slippers which lay, ever ready, under the bed, and flip-flopped to the kitchen.

Radio on, kettle on, toaster on. Sunday was on.

After she'd finished a thorough clean of her house, she drove to her sister Claire's house to the *Desert Island Discs* theme tune, wondering idly why none of the radio guests had ever asked for a five-star hotel as their luxury item. This guest – the latest lad-lit novelist to have written a startlingly honest book about contemporary masculine alienation – had just asked for a football, so he could practise 'keepie-uppie'.

'Twat,' muttered Nicky as she parked outside her sister's house.

Nicky often asked the girls to come and visit her at her flat, and when they did, they loved it there, but Claire always found it so much easier for Nicky to come to her place. On the few occasions when Nicky had insisted, Claire had either turned up late or phoned at the last minute to explain why one of the girls was refusing to get into the car. Eventually Nicky just accepted that this was the way it was. She was the free-and-single Mohammed, Claire the mother-of-three mountain.

She opened the wrought-iron gate and walked down the path to her sister's front garden, waving at niece number two, Isabel, at the window. Niece number three, Abigail, answered the door.

'You came!' she jumped on the spot.

'No I didn't!' cried Nicky, mirroring her tone. 'I left him in the restaurant.'

Abigail laughed without knowing why.

Isabel leapt out of the front room into the hall, Sarah-Jane appeared at the top of the stairs and their mother, Nicky's older sister by six years, appeared at the kitchen doorway, tea-towel in hand.

'Please don't teach them new words,' she said with a weary smile.

'And a hello to you too!'

Nicky turned back to her nieces. 'Right!' she cried. 'I want kisses from everyone.'

The girls rushed forward and Nicky kissed her nieces in turn, hung up her coat, took off her shoes and then approached her sister. They went into the kitchen.

'You don't mind taking them swimming, do you?' asked Claire. 'They loved it so much last time.'

'Nope.'

'Can we go to the cinema afterwards?' asked Sarah-Jane.

Claire made the unique sound of an unimpressed mother, a cross between 'Um' and 'Up'. A sort of 'Uhgpt' the *hgpt* silent.

'Please,' added Sarah-Jane quickly. 'If you've got time.'

'Hmm, we'll see,' said Nicky. 'But what film would a ten-year-old, an eight-year-old and a six-year-old all want to watch?'

They were happy to tell her and she found that her Sunday was mapped out.

Eight hours later, Oscar was having dinner with his dad, and he was not going to eat the Brussels sprouts.

'They look like bogeys,' he told his dad.

'Crikey.' Mark grimaced. 'I don't want to see your bogeys.'

Oscar laughed and then scowled. He did not want to find his dad funny tonight. He was angry, and determined to stay angry. Being the last one to be picked up from a friend's birthday party was one thing, but when he'd specifically asked his dad to be on time because his friend was a dork was *well* annoying. His dad had never been on time. But half an hour late! He'd had to sit with the family while his schoolmate had opened all his presents. His schoolmate's mum had made ridiculous clucking noises of worry for him which had made him want to hit her. And then, when it got to half an hour, she'd actually come over to give him a cuddle. He'd thought he was being buried alive. Then finally his dad had arrived.

'God,' he'd heard Mark say to the mum in the hall, 'I'm *so* sorry.'

'No, don't worry! We've been having fun.'

'I just had to get something finished –'

'Yes of course you did. I don't know how you manage.'

Why did they always say that? fumed Oscar. What did he have to *manage*? Most of the kids in his school only had one parent, so why was his dad the only one who was crap at it? Was he a more difficult child to manage than all the other kids at school? He was definitely not more difficult to manage than Stan Smith who could spit from the sandpit to the back of the swings and kept showing you his willy in the playground. He bet no one ever told Stan Smith's mum that they didn't know how she coped. So his dad just must be the most crap parent ever.

So he stopped laughing at the bogey joke and instead tutted, huffed and pushed his plate away.

'Oscar!' cried Mark.

'I hate Brussels sprouts.'

'OK. No need to be so rude. I did cook them for you.'

Oscar sort of snarled, his upper lip curling up. 'Am I supposed to be grateful?'

Mark sighed. He didn't know the answer to that.

'I hate them too,' he said quietly. 'But they're good for you and I want you to be strong and healthy.' He sighed. 'Because I love you.'

Oscar pulled the skin off the corner of his thumbnail and kicked the table leg with his foot while Mark took his plate away.

After the girls were tucked up in bed, Claire and Nicky sat down in the kitchen with a candle flickering in the middle of the table, a celebratory bottle of wine for Nicky's promotion and a Janis Ian CD of lilting desperation on in the background, which was doing an excellent job of bringing them both crashing down into depression just in time for Monday morning.

'We should go away,' suggested Claire suddenly. 'Have a week's holiday somewhere together.'

Nicky raised her eyebrows. They'd never gone on holiday together. She was surprised – by the offer and by how touched she felt. Mind you, it would be hell.

'Mm.' She nodded eagerly. 'Where d'you have in mind?'

'Who bloody cares?' snorted Claire. 'Let Derek see what it's like to do everything – *everything* – breakfast, laundry, ironing, cleaning, lunches, bath-time, night shift,' she counted them off on her fingers, 'completely on his own.'

'Excuse me,' said Nicky. She started counting on her fingers. 'Swimming, lunch, cinema. All by yours truly. I believe you've just had seven hours to yourself today.'

Claire's face expanded as she prepared for more finger-counting. 'I did the vacuuming, washing, ironing, prepared one ballet bag, one Brownie bag, three lunchboxes and two tea boxes, and arranged two play-dates. I'd hardly sat down when you got back.'

Nicky frowned. 'Shouldn't you be having this conversation with Derek instead of me?'

Claire grimaced. 'Thanks for your sense of sisterhood.'

'Exactly!' retorted Nicky. 'I'm your sister, not your partner.'

They downed their celebratory wine in antagonistic silence for a while before Claire spoke. 'Sorry. I must sound so ungrateful. To you, I mean.'

Nicky bristled. 'I beg your pardon?'

'Well, I just, you know.' She shrugged. 'Here I am, with a husband and three healthy children – three healthy *daughters* – and yet I'm complaining.'

Nicky spoke slowly and clearly. 'I would not want to be married to Derek.'

'Well, of course not!' exploded Claire. 'Because he's not bloody here most of the time! And when he is he's playing bloody golf! Of all the hobbies to take up! He has to pick the one that takes up a whole day. I said to him yesterday, "Are you just unhappy here?". And you know what he said?'

Nicky shook her head.

'He said, "No, darling, but you do get so *angry* nowadays."' Claire stared at Nicky. Nicky stared back. Claire let out a splurt of annoyance. Nicky blinked.

'"*Angry*!"' repeated Claire angrily. Nicky nodded. '"*ANGRY*!"' she repeated again. 'I nearly knifed him in the bloody face!' she cried.

Nicky looked down to hide her smile.

'Ooh, how was your date last night?' asked Claire suddenly. 'I can't believe I haven't asked.'

'Two.'

'Out of five or ten?'

'Twenty.'

Claire's jaw dropped. 'Derek thought he was great.'

'Really?' asked Nicky. 'You mean Derek whom you want to knife in the face?'

Claire grimaced 'Hmm,' she conceded. 'Sorry about that.' She leant across to the bottle. 'More wine?'

Later that night, Mark Samuels looked up from his notes at the living-room ceiling. He could actually decipher the lyrics of Oscar's music, it was so loud. He looked at his watch. Ten o'clock. He put his notes on the coffee table, placed his glass of wine next to it, and paced up the stairs. The music was off by the time he opened Oscar's door. How did his son always hear him? He stood outside Oscar's door for a moment. Oscar was on his computer, back hunched, fingers nimble.

'What?' he grunted.

'Osc,' said Mark, 'it's time for bed. School in the morning.'

'I know.' Oscar stared at the screen. He spoke in a monotone. 'I'd have been in bed earlier if I'd come home from the party earlier.'

Mark wanted very much to walk out and slam the door behind him, but instead he came in and sat on the bed behind Oscar.

'Osc, I'm sorry. But, mate, you have to cut me some slack sometimes.'

'Why?' shouted Oscar.

Mark never ceased to be amazed at how quickly Oscar's tears came.

'Just because I was half an hour late picking you up,' he pleaded, as Oscar shoved his hand away from his shoulder, 'it doesn't mean I don't love you. It doesn't mean I forgot you. It means I was half an hour late.'

'Why aren't any of the other parents half an hour late?'

Oscar swivelled round on his chair to face his father. 'What were you doing that was so special?'

'Working. I was working, Oscar. So that we have enough money to pay the mortgage and go on holiday this year.'

'Fine.' Oscar shut down his computer, got into bed, and turned his bedside lamp off. After a moment, Mark said 'Goodnight' and shut the door. He stood outside waiting. He couldn't hear anything.

When he got back downstairs, he quickly downed his wine then poured himself a gin and tonic, going easy on the tonic. Maybe it would have been better if he'd been in the car crash and not Helen. She would have probably thrived on her own. It was a thought he'd had so often that he'd begun to wonder if Oscar ever thought it too. Did Oscar wish his mother had lived instead of his father? He stood up quickly. He thought of phoning Lilith – the perfect mother – for some emotional support, but decided not to. Instead he picked up his notes and got back to work.

By 10.30 that night Nicky was in bed. She didn't like telling Ally everything that went on between her and Claire. It felt terribly disloyal to her sister. But, on the other hand, she was fairly confident that Claire told Derek everything about her. Why else would he continually feel the need to find her blind dates? So sod it. She told Ally everything.

'How dare she pity you?' squealed Ally loyally down the phone. 'You're ten times prettier than her, you've got a fantastic career and she's married to Derek the Dweeb.'

'I know!' squealed Nicky.

'How *dare* she!'

'I know! Bitch.'

'*Bitch*!' agreed Ally.

'Oy,' warned Nicky. 'That's my sister you're talking about.'

'Sorry.'

Nicky sighed an enormous sigh into the phone. 'How the hell am I supposed to act with Rob tomorrow?'

'Like normal.'

'What's normal?'

'You know . . . like you both fancy each other like mad but are too terrified to do anything about it.'

Nicky snorted down the phone. 'But he *has* done something about it, hasn't he?'

'Really? What? He told you exactly how he felt?'

'No, but he said all those things. All those hinty things.'

There was a pause from Ally's end of the phone. 'Hmm,' she eventually said.

'What?' said Nicky.

'Just . . . I don't know,' said Ally. 'The timing's fishy.'

'The timing?' asked Nicky. 'Seven-year itch or something?'

'No! God, you're such a romantic.'

'So what do you mean?'

'Promise you won't tell me off.'

'Just say it.'

'Well,' started Ally. 'OK. Here goes. You both get a promotion and are, in effect, now suddenly rivals instead of just friendly colleagues. And suddenly – *immediately* – he gets you thinking about him seriously again, even about the real possibility of becoming a mother instead of a headmistress. Just when you've turned into a possible threat to his career ambitions.'

'Blimey,' whispered Nicky, impressed. 'With a twisted mind like that you could be a politician. Why are you wasting your time working with children?'

'Well, OK, then,' said Ally. 'Why did he say it exactly *then*? *Just* after you'd both got the promotion? Tell me honestly, did it take your mind off your promotion?'

Nicky thought for a moment. 'Yes,' she answered quietly. 'I suppose so.'

'You see? I bet it didn't take his mind off his promotion.'

Nicky stared up at her ceiling. It needed a touch of paint. 'But maybe it just made him see me differently? Attractive in a different way? A more serious way?'

There was another pause. 'Hmm.'

'What does that mean?' asked Nicky. 'You think he was just faking it all?'

'Well, he's male, isn't he?'

'Last time I looked,' agreed Nicky. 'Mind you, that was a long time ago.'

'Well, there you are then. He's a bloke: so it's fair game. All's fair in love, war and career.'

'Pete's not like that,' thought Nicky aloud. 'He hasn't got an ambitious bone in his body.'

'Pete's not a real bloke,' dismissed Ally. 'He's a pixie.'

'But I really don't think Rob and I see the joint promotion as competition. We see it as something we're doing together. He really congratulated me, Ally. You should have seen him.'

'Well, of course he did! He's not going to twirl his moustache and challenge you to pistols at dawn, is he?'

Nicky laughed. 'I s'pose not.' She sighed. 'Well, *I* don't see it as competition. I see it as sharing a job with a good mate.'

'Yeah, well, that's because you're nice.'

'Mmhmm,' said Nicky slowly.

'Look, I'm not saying he's evil, Nick,' conceded Ally, 'I'm just saying he's a bloke. They see their careers differently from most women. They have to. Especially from most women who've gone into teaching. Let's face it, we didn't go into teaching because we wanted a high-ranking, high-paying career. We went into teaching because we wanted to teach. Someone like Rob will have had his eye on management for years.'

'What do you mean, "someone like Rob"?'

'Someone really competitive.'

'You think he's competitive?' asked Nicky, surprised.

'Of course!' cried Ally. 'Look how he treats women! He sees them all except you (and me for obvious reasons)' – she added dully – 'as personal achievements.'

'He never went for Amanda –'

'If he'd gone for Amanda, he'd have lost the gang,' cut in Ally. 'He's competitive, but he's not a moron. Look, all I'm saying is that now he's Joint Deputy Head, I bet he starts focussing his innate competitive spirit on his career instead of his bedpost notches. Just watch.'

'Or,' suggested Nicky, 'maybe the reason he never went for Amanda is because he's matured. He's finally ready to settle down. And his sudden, unexpected promotion made him realise he could actually afford to, too.'

There was a long, long pause.

'Yeah, well,' sighed Ally. 'I'm thrilled that I've managed to take your rose-tinted glasses off and you're over your crush on him.'

'I have not got a crush! It's just that that might explain

why he suddenly turned all serious and romantic.'

'Yep. Maybe. Whatever.'

'Oh I don't know. It's all too confusing.'

'You know what I think?' asked Ally.

'Go on.'

'If you were meant to be together, you'd be together.'

There was a long pause. Nicky felt strangely relieved. 'I know,' she said. 'You're right.'

'You have got to concentrate on your new job,' said Ally. 'This is incredibly important.'

'Yeah. You're right. Thanks.'

'Just try and forget everything Rob said and focus on your work. You'll only get one chance at it, Nicky, and you'll kick yourself if you muck it up. If you're meant to end up with Rob, you'll end up with Rob. Concentrate on your job.'

'Yeah. You're right. Thanks, Ally. You're such a good mate.'

'It's all right,' yawned Ally. 'I just know how much it matters to you. Maybe more than you even realise.'

Nicky glanced over at her clock. 'Blimey. It's nearly eleven. I need to get to sleep.'

'Beauty sleep?'

'No,' assured Nicky. 'Brain sleep.'

'Good girl. See you tomorrow, focussed on the job in hand.'

'Yeah,' said Nicky firmly. 'You're right. Thanks, Al.'

Then she finished her phone call, turned off her bedside lamp, lay down and dreamt of babies.

5

Nicky and Rob sat next to each other, opposite Miss James's desk at their first meeting as Joint Deputy Heads, waiting for their esteemed Headmistress to finish off some paperwork. To the echo of children cheering from the neighbouring field, they both stared straight at her while she scribbled elaborate, curly notes she wouldn't be able to decipher later.

There were two desks in Miss James's office: one covered with all her papers, where she sat, the other covered by whatever latest puzzle she was finishing. She was a puzzle fanatic. Everyone who came in – absolutely everyone, whether secretary, child, parent, governor, caretaker or teacher – had to put a piece in the puzzle before they were permitted to leave her office. 'It's a community puzzle!' she would declare to them all. This year's puzzle was Europe and it was a complete bugger. Children had been known to miss a whole numeracy class trying to find Portugal. Teachers knew it was useless to complain to Miss James though, because they would be told the benefits of puzzle-solving, even though everyone knew that the only benefit of puzzle-solving was finishing the puzzle.

This morning, a Year 4 pupil was sitting frowning at it, his face drawn and pale. Suddenly he let out a gasp, leapt up and fitted a piece in.

'Off you go, Ralph,' said Miss James affectionately. 'Just tell Miss Jennings you were doing the puzzle.'

Nicky's intestines were jitterbugging with excitement at the thought of having her first meeting as Deputy Head. Out of reverence for her new job she had worn a rather more severe skirt and higher heels than normal. The ensemble made her feel more serious and more respectable, although ironically (not that it mattered of course) she couldn't help noticing Rob continually glancing down at her legs. He'd stopped doing it as soon as they were in the meeting though. She wondered now, while Miss James continued to draw hieroglyphics, how he was able to compartmentalise so easily. She also wondered how he was managing to keep so calm. She could barely sit still. She kept recrossing her legs and pulling at her new-length skirt. It was all she could do to stop herself from standing up and launching into a lusty rendition of 'Climb Every Mountain'. Eventually Rob turned slowly to her and gave her a pointed look. She managed to control herself enough not to offer to sharpen Miss James's pencils. Again.

Suddenly, apparently in the middle of writing a sentence – or sketching an elephant, it was difficult to tell – Miss James leapt up and made it to her door in three long strides, looking like a Quentin Blake pencil drawing, hair swaying, glasses swinging, skirt swishing.

'ELIZABETH-LOUISE!' she yelled down the corridor.

Rob and Nicky exchanged smiles. Miss James could distinguish a child's footsteps from a hundred paces. There was a pause as Elizabeth-Louise made her way back to her headmistress.

'What,' began Miss James, pronouncing the 'h' in the word, 'do we say about these hallowed corridors, my dear?'

'Walk, don't run.'

'WALK, DON'T RUN! Exactly! And what were you doing down the corridor?'

'Running.'

'RUNNING! Exactly. So what will you do in future?'

'Walk.'

'WALK! Exactly. *So* glad we had this little chat. On you go.'

Miss James returned to her desk, putting her glasses back on her nose. She looked up at her Deputies, pulled off her glasses forcefully and nearly broke her neck.

'Now, now, now, now, *now*,' she said, slowly rearranging her neck. 'How are my two generals?'

Nicky smiled and before she could answer she heard Rob say, 'Fine.' He looked at her and she nodded and they all grinned at each other.

'Good,' said Miss James. 'Good, good, good, good, good, *good*.' She clapped her hands loudly. 'Right! What's your *vision* for Heatheringdown?' She stared, unblinking, at one and then the other and then back again.

There was a fraction of a pause. Nicky's brain started to whirr. Then it sort of phut-phutted to a stop. *Vision?* Oh God. She wasn't going to be up to this job. She had no idea what the correct answer to that was.

Miss James stared at her. Without thinking, Nicky looked at Rob for inspiration and inwardly cursed herself. Miss James followed her gaze.

'Um,' said Rob, 'progressive?'

Miss James blinked at him slowly then gave a small nod.

79

Then she turned to Nicky and raised her eyebrows in a question.

'I suppose,' said Nicky slowly, 'I see it as a multi-ethnic, multi-focussed . . .' her voice trailed off. Multi-focussed? She realised she'd stopped talking and then she realised that she felt self-conscious in front of Rob – much more than she did in front of Miss James.

Oh God, she was going to be demoted ten minutes into her job. And all in front of Rob.

'GOOD!' exclaimed Miss James, scribbling what looked like an ancient Greek temple padlocked to a fish. 'I'm *in love* with that. If it was a cat, I'd adopt it! Multi-ethnic, multi-focussed. Good *girl*.' She stopped scribbling and looked up at Rob. 'What was yours again?'

'Progressive,' said Rob forcefully.

'Hmm.' Miss James frowned. 'In what way?'

'Well, take ICT for a start –'

'Ah! Yes!' sighed Miss James dreamily. 'ICT! So many initials nowadays, don't you find? "Information Communication Technology" I mean, what on God's good earth does that mean? In my day we had blackboards and were done with it. You knew where you were with a black—'

'We've really broadened it,' cut in Rob, not a moment too soon. 'It's not just about computers in the classroom any more, we've got digital cameras, webcams and even "roamers" for the Year 1s –'

'I know,' said Miss James, frowning suspiciously. 'And I don't like it one bit. Robots for five-year-olds. Whatever next? Digital desks?'

'But the roamers help them learn –'

'And anyway,' said Miss James, proving with great

aplomb that when it came to interrupting she could give as good as she got and then some, 'isn't that all just keeping up with the times?'

Good gracious, thought Nicky. Rob wasn't as good at this as she was! She kept her head down and looked straight ahead. The thought was incredible. Did this mean that she was going to be the next Head? If so, would she employ Rob as her Deputy? Or would that be a conflict of interests? Gosh, poor Rob.

Rob coughed and shuffled in his seat. 'Yes –'

'Don't get me *wrong*' – Miss James halted him, like a policeman halting traffic, with the palm of her hand almost in his face – 'I *adore* the idea – think it's genius – it's *exactly* what I've always wanted Heatheringdown to be. It's just that I do wonder if we'll ever really get there.' She turned her eyes upward, always a bad sign. 'To be truly progressive,' she mused, 'we need to be truly amorphous. Fluid. Nebulous. Ever-changing. Like a cloud being whipped up by a tempestuous, autumnal sky. And yet at the same time we need to maintain a rigid ethos that parents – and *future* parents especially – can easily identify with.' Her face darkened, not unlike a cloud being whipped up by a tempestuous, autumnal sky. 'Oh, it's all so complicated.'

'That's it!' cried Rob, excited. 'That's it!' He started laughing.

'Is it?' asked Miss James, thrilled.

'Of course *you would* be the one to summarise it so accurately,' he continued.

'Would I?' she asked, delighted.

'And what we need to do is to work out how those two vital elements – progress *and* tradition – can stand side by side, simultaneously bringing the school forward into the twenty-first century while maintaining its twentieth-century morals and values.'

Rob and Miss James looked at each other with something approaching love in their eyes. Love for Miss James, naturally. After all, it was her office. Nicky sat very still, watching them. She wondered if it would be appropriate to clap. Or vote. Anything really, as long as she wasn't sitting there doing nothing. She decided to nod.

'If I may be so bold,' concluded Rob humbly, 'may I congratulate you, Miss James?'

Miss James bowed her head a little. 'You may,' she conceded, almost shyly.

Then, suddenly, she slammed her palm down on her pile of papers and actually stood up for emphasis. '*Won*derful!' She sat down again and beamed at them both. They stared back at her. 'I can see I've got one hell of a team working on my side,' she said enthusiastically. 'Have a custard cream.'

She thrust the biscuit tin under their noses and they dutifully took one each. Nicky felt a bit of a fraud taking one as she hadn't said anything worth saying yet, but a custard cream was a custard cream. She noticed Rob didn't eat his and decided against peeling one layer of biscuit off the cream during such an auspicious meeting. She ate hers in two bites, a personal record.

Miss James suddenly pointed at Rob. 'I want *you* to work out how to turn "Progressive yet Traditional" into a real, working vision of Heatheringdown. That is your job, O esteemed Deputy.' She turned to Nicky again. 'Now, Nicola, Ni*co*la, Nicol*a*, my other esteemed Deputy. We all know that we have to do boring old SATS, blah blah blah,' she leant in and fixed Nicky with her gaze and a pointed finger, '*but,* O worthy Deputy, your mission – should you choose to accept it – is to find out how every single individual teacher in this "progressive yet traditional"' – a wink and a nod at Rob – 'school carries out their own personal assessments throughout the year with an aim towards formulating an up-to-date structure for them all to follow.'

Nicky stared at her, unable to speak for a moment. 'Gosh,' she eventually managed.

'Rumour has it,' confided Miss James, 'that Ned's method of finding the average level of his pupils is to close his eyes and point.'

'Gosh –'

'Not really on,' continued Miss James. 'Especially if he keeps pointing to the ones who are so thick they don't duck in time.'

'Gosh,' said Nicky again.

'So as of today, that is your job, my dear.'

Nicky wondered how on earth the two tasks could possibly be seen as equal in workload. Rob had to find another amorphous, nebulous, fluid, mostly meaningless sentence to add to Miss James's original one, while she now had to observe and encroach on every teacher's private methods, collate them and come up with a completely original method of summation. She wondered if now would be a good time to broach the subject of workload.

'Thank you,' she said quietly.

'Meanwhile,' continued Miss James, 'I will get Janet, my wonderful secretary, my right-hand arm, my limbs, my Janet, to give you all the help or notes you will need. JANET!'

Janet, Miss James's secretary, opened the door to Miss James's office and stood in the doorway, not putting a toe over the threshold.

'Mm?'

'These *won*derful, *won*derful people are now working on the vision and assessment of Heatheringdown.'

'Mm.'

'Your job is to help them in any way they ask you to.'

Janet gave them both a look. 'I'm going home in five minutes and I'm late in tomorrow because my youngest has broken his thumb.'

'Fine.' Nicky and Rob smiled and nodded in unison.

Janet looked back at Miss Heatheringdown. 'Anything else?'

'No, no, no, no, no, no. Thank you, Janet!'

Janet shut the door behind her. Miss James smacked the papers on her desk vigorously and beamed at them. 'We have serious work to do here. So many pupils depend on us. Isn't it thrilling?'

Nicky and Rob nodded.

'And I have every faith in you two,' she said. 'Together, we're going to turn Heatheringdown into *The* top school. Now, you two. One piece in my Europe puzzle each, and your time is yours.'

Nicky leapt up, crossed the office to the other table, and started scouring the unfinished map. The corners had already been done and England was one-third there. As she started looking at the unfinished pieces scattered around the edges, Rob alighted on a piece, stuck it in the middle of Bulgaria and gave her a quick smile. He turned to Miss James.

'Bye then, Miss James.' She looked up at him from her note-making, as though she'd forgotten he was in the room. To her embarrassment, Nicky took a full ten minutes to find her piece. After fitting it in place, she gave a little cough which Miss James didn't hear, and then crept out, hoping she'd been forgotten.

She found Rob in the staffroom. He grinned at her.

'Multi-focussed?' he asked.

'Give me your custard cream,' replied Nicky, in no mood to be teased. 'Now.'

'It's in my pocket,' he said, holding his arms up. 'Come and get it.

She paused for a fraction of a second, then remembered to act normally and came and got it.

'Don't mess with me when it comes to custard creams,' she told him, her hand still in his trousers. 'Or I'll tell Miss James you didn't eat yours.'

'Hello!' greeted Pete, at the sight of Nicky with her hand down Rob's trouser pocket. 'Is Rob pretending he's lost his testicles again? I can't believe you women fall for that.'

Nicky took out the custard cream and showed it to him.

Pete's eyebrows rose. 'He leaves biscuits in there!' he whispered in awe. 'Genius!'

'What's that?' asked Ally, who had just joined them.

Pete turned to her. 'Putting custard creams next to my testicles.'

'What, for ballast?' asked Ally.

Pete burst into laughter.

'I think Garibaldi are probably more your biscuit,' she told Pete.

'Come here and say that,' said Pete.

'No, you come here and say it.'

'No, you come here and say it.'

'No, you come here and say it.'

Rob watched Nicky as she carefully peeled off the top layer of biscuit with her teeth. 'Actually,' he said, 'they weren't near my testicles.'

'I know.'

'My penis was in the way.'

She looked at him over the biscuit and put the rest of it in her mouth in one go.

'Ouch,' he said, smiling.

The rest of the staff was told about Rob and Nicky's promotion the next morning. A bit of a shock, as Miss James hadn't warned either of them she would do this. She announced that some of their new remit now included 'responsibility for the professional development' of their colleagues, so Rob and Nicky would now have to listen to whatever their ten assigned teachers needed to discuss. They were as stunned as the others about this and it could have been a tricky moment if Amanda hadn't said, 'Ooh, does that mean we can bitch to them *officially*?' and everyone laughed. Amanda was one of Rob's teachers, so Nicky was in no doubt that she would be one of Amanda's future favourite topics up for discussion.

But generally, the announcement went as well as could be expected. Roberta and Gwen eyed each other over their coffee with triumphant bitterness, their friendship jump-started. Ned, who had as much bitterness in his make-up as a hungry puppy lying on its back with its tail thumping the ground, was delighted for both Rob and Nicky. He told his wife at lunch-time during their daily phone call and it had been a small interruption from his discussion of his Marmite and cheese sandwiches; 'an intriguing combination and a not unpleasant surprise'. He'd even put his hand over the mouthpiece and told Nicky across the staffroom that his wife, Theresa, wished her congratulations. Nicky was grateful and tried not to pity him.

Martha, the new Reception teacher, was too new in her post to even think of herself in terms of promotion, so she found it easy to be delighted for both Rob and Nicky.

Nicky found Martha an intriguing addition to the staffroom. It had turned out that Martha's private life gave her a unique position among the teachers. She was neither married nor single, which meant that no one understood her. It took them a while to work out exactly what this meant and, even then, they didn't get it. Technically, she had a boyfriend, whom she liked very much, but he was not The One. Her explanation had been met with a short silence before Rob congratulated her in effusive terms, 'Good for you, girl, go for it!' followed by Amanda in agreement. 'Yeah! You go for it!'

Then Martha left the room and they set to discussing her emotional status with more energy than they would ever do once they'd got to know her.

'That is *such* a shame,' started Roberta in an exaggerated whisper. 'Poor girl.'

'What is?' asked Rob.

'Well, she's obviously waiting for her boyfriend to pop the question,' stated Roberta. 'And she's made up the whole "He's not The One" lie to hide her disappointment.

Didn't you see how hard it was for her to come out with it?'

'Rubbish!' exclaimed all the singles in unison.

'And he probably never will,' agreed Gwen with Roberta, ignoring the singles. 'And she'll throw away her twenties for him.' She clicked her fingers. 'And that'll be that. She'll wake up and find it's too late to have a family.'

Nicky noticed Rob suddenly stare at her with determined concern. She gave him a fixed grin, but when it started to wobble she looked away.

'In which case,' continued Roberta, nodding, 'she should get rid of him and get herself back on the market.' She lowered her voice. 'Perhaps I should introduce her to someone.'

'Excuse me!' shrilled Amanda. 'Maybe she is actually enjoying herself! And maybe, just maybe, she actually doesn't *want* children. Not every woman does, you know. And good luck to her.' She looked over at Rob.

'Or maybe she genuinely doesn't believe in marriage,' added Nicky. 'And good luck to her with that too.'

Amanda eyed Rob quickly, before nodding and saying, 'That's right, girlfriend!' She laughed. 'We're career girls, aren't we?' she said, elbowing her.

Nicky decided now was not the time to enter into a debate about why women had to choose career over family whereas men didn't, nor the use of the word 'girl' for adult females, when the word 'boy' was only ever used for boys, let alone the fact that if Amanda ever elbowed her again she could expect to be punched in the face.

'Excuse me!' cried Roberta. 'I've got an ex-husband and a son – does that mean I'm *not* a career girl?'

There was an ugly pause.

'Does that mean,' clarified Gwen, encouraged by Roberta, 'that mothers of three can't be promoted?'

Silence seeped round the room. Nicky changed her mind and decided that maybe now *was* the perfect time to open a healthy debate about all the above, but just as she was wondering how to get started, Rob gave a little ahem.

'Now, now, everyone,' he said. 'I don't think Nicky got promoted because she's carefree and single,' he said with a gently rebuking smile. 'I think we all know that it's because of the qualities she brings to her job.'

'Yes,' rushed Gwen. 'Of course. We all know that.'

'Good.' Rob smiled.

Nicky stared from Gwen to Rob and back again before saying softly, 'And while we're on the subject, I think we all also know that Rob wasn't promoted because he's carefree and single either.'

'Well of course not,' said Gwen. 'We all know that.'

Nicky picked up her bag and walked out of the staffroom.

At break-time, she caught five minutes with Ally.

'You were a bit sharp back there with Rob,' said Ally. 'He was only trying to defend your position.'

'Why does he need to defend me?' replied Nicky. 'We're equals. Why does my promotion need justifying and his doesn't?'

Ally shook her head at her friend. 'Have you looked at his arse recently?'

Nicky moaned and hung her head on her hands. 'You told me not to,' she wailed.

'I didn't say anything about *looking*,' said Ally. 'I just said don't stop concentrating on your job at the same time.'

*

Nicky's main responsibility of summarising every single teacher's method of assessment for a future school template proceeded to swamp her 'management time' and spilt into her 'planning and preparation time' as, over the next seven weeks, she had to sit in on everyone's class. Most marking was now nearly all done by the children themselves – she had long since learnt that the best way for kids to feel a sense of ownership over their work was to let them swap books with their neighbour and mark each other's work. This had released precious weekend time which, up until now, she had spent on the Internet preparing wonderful classes, or back at school finishing displays so that the children could see their handiwork almost as soon as they'd finished it. She had never resented any free time being spent on her children. The way she saw it, the more you put into work the more the children got out of it. She only had five hours a day with them. She didn't want to waste a moment.

But now, suddenly, she didn't have any moments to waste. Her work list – every day started with a list of jobs to achieve – was now too long for her to even contemplate.

She knew she had pulled the short straw, seeing as Rob's remit had seen him interview some of the kids in their lunch hour and then give a talk to Miss James and herself, with the help of an overhead projector. It had been an impassioned forty minutes – almost as impassioned as his original speech had been in Miss James's office. Miss James loved every word of it. He'd been given two custard creams and a Bourbon.

It was after that meeting that Miss James had told them that they were now, of course, in charge of Parents' Evening.

Yet again, Rob and she were to divide the responsibilities, which seemed fairly easy. The two main areas of responsibility were to oversee either timetables or book-marking. For Parents' Evening – in fact two evenings – each teacher was responsible for their own timetable (so that each parent knew exactly when to turn up and how long they would have with their teacher) and they also had to ensure that every single piece of marking was up to date (so that parents could look through their child's work, should they so desire). Rob chose timetables before Nicky had a chance to put the key in the ignition of her brain, and by the time she'd looked at the gear-stick, she realised she was overseeing teachers' book-marking. It turned out that whereas teachers were only too glad to have someone chivvy them along – with the added thrill of some advice and top flirting – with their bit of time-tabling, they did not care to be reminded to do anything as sensitive as their marking. Especially by someone who got her kids to do hers most of the time anyway.

It wasn't long before Nicky's extra workload started to affect her private life. Exhausted by a relentless week full of resentful teachers, she now needed to be in bed on a Saturday night sometimes as early as nine o'clock. Then she would use all of Sunday morning – starting as early as 8 a.m. – to finish off preparing for the week ahead, when she used to do all her cleaning, before a much-needed Sunday-afternoon rest, preferably spent horizontally watching an old John Wayne film with the sound down (she found them more interesting that way). She had to do most of her cleaning on weekday mornings now instead of Sundays, which was just possible if she woke a quarter of an hour earlier, and then she squeezed in the vacuuming during

John Wayne, which, intriguingly, didn't seem to spoil her enjoyment of the film. She ironed in the evenings if she wasn't too tired, and soon stopped buying clothes that needed ironing.

When the clocks went back and the days shrank, it made a bigger impact on her than it had ever done before. Maybe she was getting old, maybe she had more work to do than ever before. Either way, she now found that she was tired most of the time. She started saying yes to Claire's offer of Sunday lunch because it was the only way she'd get to eat – there was certainly no time to cook for herself on a Sunday – and no to looking after Claire's girls the rest of the day. She simply didn't have the time or energy.

It did occur to her that maybe she wasn't cut out for this level of work and that there was a reason more men made it to management level, namely that they had wives at home cooking their food, cleaning their homes, preparing their sandwiches and generally saying 'Aah' at the right moments.

On top of everything else, she had a host of new responsibilities now she was Management. Rob and she both had to sort out assemblies – a relentless task; daily timetables for the entire school – a hellish task; and the school council – a complete nightmare, as well as organising all the teaching assistants and dinner ladies' rotas.

But first there was Parents' Evening to organise.

And it was Parents' Evening which next drew Oscar to Nicky's attention. As the term progressed, she was growing fonder and fonder of her pupils. This year's Class 6 were just as enthusiastic and as much fun as she'd expected. Usually by this stage of the year, there were a couple of children who stood out from the others. Sometimes it was nothing more than Nicky feeling a special affection for them or, conversely, an awareness that it would take time and work for that to happen. But with Oscar it was something else. She felt a new sort of affinity with him; as if she could see right through the disguise of childhood to his essence: she could see all of him at once; the baby, the boy, the man.

Oscar seemed to possess in his eye the look of an adult. His face could express or hide everything, depending on his mood, and his mood was as changeable as the English weather. When he laughed his eyes watered, as if they might overflow. And the skin around them was so stretched it was almost translucent, allowing the finest of blue veins to peep through. His emotions seemed stretched too, taut as a tightrope which he might topple off at any moment.

A sign of the times was that most classes nowadays had at least one set of twins, sometimes a set of triplets, due to the unpredictability of late mothers' ovulation or IVF treatment. There were also more than two languages spoken in the classroom. Also, by Year 6, almost half the class only saw their dads at weekends. Often, a teacher was able to tell the rest of the staff, within weeks of the new school year, which kids' parents they believed would be divorced by Year 6. Some of the less scrupulous ones had been known to place bets on it. Usually the teacher was right. Sometimes the divorce happened speedily; sometimes it would be a long-drawn-out separation, during which younger siblings arrived. Some kids were fine with their parents' divorce, others missed Dad, others felt responsible for the break-up. Nicky had been known to spend her lunch hour – when she needed to catch up on her other duties or do vital shopping – consoling a tearful child.

But it was rare to find a child living with Dad instead of Mum. And it was rare to find a child who wasn't able to talk about it. And it didn't take her long to find Oscar a rare child.

She discovered his background and figured out that maybe this was why she'd felt drawn to him. They'd both suffered the loss of a mother when they were too young. When Nicky was twelve, her mother had gone into hospital for the last time, and from that night onwards, when her big sister Claire came into her bed for a cuddle, she'd got a surrogate mother. The reality of her mother's death hadn't actually been too much of a shock. The truth was she'd been slowly vanishing from them all since long before then. It began years earlier when she couldn't get up in the mornings, then she was too weak or ill to help with home-work or to be there for bath-time. Eventually she was just a shadow on the sofa and then she simply wasn't there any more. It was a natural, gradual fading of all the details, until eventually, like the Cheshire cat, all that was memorable of her was her smile.

Their father had always been a shadowy figure, but after his wife died he became spectral. Three years later, on Claire's twenty-first birthday, when Nicky was fifteen, he moved away to the coast. They only found out that he'd moved in with another woman when she answered the phone the first time they called. It turned out they'd been together for two years. The sisters had not felt any great loss.

The evening after Nicky discovered that Oscar's mother had died in a car crash when he was still in Reception, she tried to take her mind back to when her own mother had died. She lay in her bath, eyes on the tap at her feet, and took herself back to her twelve-year-old self. How had she felt when the slow realisation had dawned that her mother really was never again going to open her arms for a gentle cuddle from the sofa? She realised that there had never been a sudden moment of realisation. It had just been a slow acclimatisation to never feeling cosy or safe again. Or young. Maybe they amounted to the same thing. The part of her life with a mummy was her childhood and that was now over. Maybe it would have actually been more painful if their father had sat them down and discussed it with them. But he never had, so as she grew up and discovered the rarity of having no mummy – through meeting friends who had one – she just hugged her isolated, distinct memories of her mother to her – summer holidays together, swimming in her mother's arms when her mother could still swim, her mother's soft sun-creamed skin smelling of sugar, her mother teaching her the alphabet with Smarties, planting seeds together in the garden, hiding under the duvet together and giggling, queueing in the local bank. She wished there were more memories, but there weren't. Maybe it was easier that way.

She wondered if Oscar felt like that? Did he have key memories? Or did he have no memories at all? Sometimes he looked as if nothing had ever troubled him. Whenever he thought no one was watching him, he would swing an imaginary cricket bat, his loose limbs elegantly swooping through the air, or win an imaginary goal. Or make his friend Matthew laugh. Or pinch Daisy.

There was nothing out of the ordinary about him, and yet somehow, at the same time, nothing ordinary about him. She wondered whether his father could see what she saw.

And whether she would get a chance to meet him at Parents' Evening and let him know.

She added some hot water to the bath and lay back again. Oh dear, Parents' Evening, she thought. There were many things about a parents' evening Nicky liked and many things she disliked. The thing she liked most was telling a tense mother, who was wracked with guilt that she had to work full-time, that her child was doing well. She disliked talking to an interpreter, or trying to tell two parents who could only speak Romanian that their child might have special needs. And she hated telling yet another single father that no, she didn't think it was appropriate for them to discuss his child over dinner, while pretending she hadn't noticed he'd just asked her out. But the thing that irked her most was a parent who simply didn't respond to the school's invitation. And to her increasing frustration, Oscar's dad was one of those. With only a fortnight to go before the two evenings, he was the only one who had still to return the signed form. She hadn't asked Oscar for the form every day because she didn't want to upset him, and yet every time she did ask him, he either gave a non-committal answer or promised he would give it to his father that night. Each time she believed she'd finally got through to him, only to find him more frustratingly elusive the next day. She thought about phoning his house, or emailing his father. But she didn't want to cause a problem out of nothing. In all honesty, Oscar's work was consistent and good. If his father didn't see the need to come, perhaps she shouldn't push it.

Then, only ten days before Parents' Evening, on Hallowe'en, after an afternoon spent making pumpkin candles and costumes for trick-or-treating, Nicky was delighted when Oscar proffered the information that he was going trick-or-treating with his dad and Daisy's mum that night. Nicky felt encouraged. Any dad who went trick-or-treating with his son was the kind of dad who would not miss his son's Parents' Evening. She told Oscar she was delighted and asked him to promise to make his dad sign the Parents' Evening form before he went to bed. Oscar promised. Nicky wished she had a camera to capture the light in his eyes – brighter than any pumpkin candle – whenever he talked about doing things with his father. Possibly to show the man.

That night she decided to finish off her Deputy work at home. She needed to stop off on the way and buy lots of sweets for the night's entertainment before she could settle in and make a start on her work. Some of her ex-pupils came specially to her place on Hallowe'en and she put a lit-up pumpkin face outside her door, poured all her sweets into a bowl and waited in for them. Rob had invited her to his Hallowe'en party, as usual, and she had said no, as usual. Hallowe'en was for children, not for adults trying to pretend they were children. Anyway, she didn't particularly want to see Amanda dressed up as a witch. Although the thought of seeing Pete dressed as a goblin had been hard to resist.

By six o'clock that evening she was ensconced on the floor, her work spread out neatly on the coffee table in her lounge, the silent television as company in the background, all the warm lamps on, the little gas fire blazing, the night outside dark and cold. When her phone went, she picked it up without noticing. She only just remembered to say hello. It was Rob.

'Are you sure you don't want to come tonight?'

Nicky smiled. 'Yes, thanks. I don't want to miss my kids.'

'Don't do it!' he cried. 'It'll only make you realise how old you are.'

'Gee, thanks.'

'Oh, come to the party. It'll be fun.'

She sighed. 'No, thanks. I might miss a fantastic fairy.'

'I've got my Batman outfit on,' coaxed Rob.

She let out a laugh. It was tempting.

'Hey, don't knock it,' he said. 'This Batman has extremely firm thighs.' He was grinning.

She laughed. 'I *want* to see my kids!'

'Oh, don't be ridiculous.' She could hear him mixing drinks in his kitchen.

'Anyway,' she looked at all her notes, 'haven't you got stuff to do for Miss James?'

'Yes,' he said firmly. 'But I decided it can wait.'

There was a pause as her notes went out of focus. How come he was able to host a party when she barely had time to answer her door? Maybe he was more cut out for this than she was.

'You do realise,' he broke the silence, 'that you're leaving me no choice but to spend my evening with Amanda. And she's coming as a wicked witch.'

'I know,' said Nicky, 'she told me today. I managed not to smile.'

'Good,' said Rob, 'because if you had, she'd have turned you into a toad. Actually, I have a confession to make. I have a bit of a thing about witches.'

Nicky hesitated. What was he trying to say? She considered changing her mind and going to the party, but the thought of leaving her home was just too much. It had turned into winter overnight – it was far too cold outside. Anyway, what would she wear?

God, Rob was right. She must be getting old.

'Pete wants to speak to you,' said Rob. 'I've got to go to the Bat-oven.'

Pete came to the phone. He needed to make arrangements with Nicky about staying over that night. He and Ally always walked to Nicky's place after Rob's parties, because that way they were much closer to school for the next morning. It meant they could drink without having to worry about driving home afterwards, and then walk to work the next morning without having to get up as early as Rob. Also, it was fun.

'He's not so much Batman,' said Pete, 'as Twatman. You've got to come.'

'Is Ally there yet?'

'No. I thought she'd be there with you. Where is she?'

'No idea.'

'You sure you're all right about us staying over at your place afterwards?'

'Of course!' said Nicky. 'It's tradition.'

'Thanks,' said Pete. 'I'd stay here, but goblins can't stay in Batman's cave. It brings them out in spots. And there's nothing worse than a spotty goblin.'

Nicky's doorbell went. She made her goodbyes and ran down the stairs where she picked up the bowl of sweets on the hall table and opened her front door into the cold night air.

Three hours later, most of the trick-or-treating had stopped. Nicky was now sitting on the floor watching telly and eating the last few bloody fang chews. Her tongue felt raw from eating so many pear drops. Rob had been right about staying in. (Was he always right? She began to wonder. It was a trait she'd only noticed since their promotion and it was beginning to irk her.) This year, for the first time, seeing her ex-pupils as lanky teenagers, all teeth and hips, like puppies with large paws, had brought home to her how fast life zoomed ahead. It was as if they were all playing giant snakes and ladders and her kids had got a lucky run of dice sending them up ladder after ladder. Meanwhile here she was, getting one or two on the dice or landing on a snake. For the first Hallowe'en she could remember, by nine o'clock she was feeling so low she was contemplating an early night. She wouldn't need to stay up for Pete and Ally, they had a key. When the doorbell went, too late for trick-or-treaters and too early for Pete and Ally, she wasn't sure whether to open it or not.

Slowly, she got up off the floor and plodded downstairs with her practically empty bowl of sweets. Two children – wrapped up so much that they were unidentifiable – stared at her, a weary mum standing behind them. The mum gave an apologetic smile, but the kids stared at her in silence, eyes wide, and then instead of saying 'Trick or treat', exploded into squeals of excitement.

'Miss Hobbs! Miss Hobbs!'

She asked them all into her warm hallway, where she slowly worked out that she was looking at Oscar and Daisy.

Daisy was jumping up and down and screaming at her mother, 'It's Miss Hobbs! It's Miss Hobbs!' Oscar was smiling so wide it made him look like a different boy. After a night of seeing so many of her ex-kids, she found it all too easy to see into the future. She imagined Oscar all tall and gangly and awkwardly beautiful, aged fourteen and full of life. It made her feel happy and sad at the same time.

The woman with them seemed to add some more effort to her smile.

'Hi,' said Nicky, shaking her hand. 'I'm Nicky Hobbs.'

'Lilith Parker,' introduced Lilith. 'Daisy's mum.'

'Oh! Hello, Daisy's mum!' cried Nicky. 'Pleased to meet you!' She stopped herself from saying how young she looked – Lilith must have had Daisy in her early twenties – and instead remarked on how similar mother and daughter's eyes were.

'People are always saying that.' Lilith nodded with a grin. Daisy leant against her and Lilith stroked her daughter's hair. It was always the ease with which parents and children touched each other that made Nicky envious. She handed Daisy and Oscar the bowl. They looked inside it. They saw five Murray Mints and one bon-bon.

'Um,' said Nicky, 'I'm afraid I've eaten all the fangs.' She turned to Lilith. 'My jaw's killing me.'

Before thinking, Lilith said, 'I bet that's what you tell all your kids.'

There was a fraction of a pause before Nicky let out a raucous, most unteacherly, laugh and then admitted, 'You wouldn't say that if you saw the other teachers I spend every day with.'

Lilith smiled. 'Oh, come on, I've met Mr Pattison. He used to make Parents' Evening almost enjoyable.'

Nicky laughed again, but it wasn't quite as raucous this time.

'I'm sorry we're so late,' said Lilith, 'we've kept going in the hope of Oscar's daddy turning up. We're a bit out of our usual stomping ground. In fact, I think we've done a five-mile radius. We're a bit exhausted.'

'I'm not,' said Oscar stubbornly. 'I'm fine.'

Nicky went all serious for a moment before asking suddenly, 'Who would like some real hot chocolate and some toast?' The children turned to Lilith, their faces suddenly urgent with pleading.

'Can we? Please, Mum,' whined Daisy.

'Please,' begged Oscar. 'Then maybe Dad will still get to come.'

Lilith sighed and looked at Nicky. 'That would be brilliant,' she said. 'Thanks. We haven't had dinner. We've been going since six. The kids just wanted to keep going. Well, Oscar did.'

Nicky turned to them and forced a grin. 'That's perfect. If Oscar's dad had come earlier, I'd never have seen you all.'

They followed her upstairs and into the kitchen.

So, thought Nicky, Oscar's father had failed to turn up for the promised trick-or-treating. While her visitors abandoned their coats, scarves and hats and she hustled them into the kitchen, she asked as merrily as she could, addressing the room in general, where Oscar's dad was. Oscar didn't seem to hear her, but Lilith did.

'Work, of course,' she muttered. 'Where else?'

As the milk heated and the bread toasted, Nicky got Daisy and Oscar to put the jam, butter and plates on the table while she spooned flakes of drinking chocolate and sugar into brightly coloured mugs. Then the children sat up at the small breakfast bar and got overexcited. Nicky and Lilith leant against the worktops, by the hob.

'I hope you don't mind me asking,' began Nicky quietly,

while the children laughed and joked with each other, 'but, do you know if Oscar's dad is coming to Parents' Evening? He's the only parent in the whole class who hasn't replied.'

Lilith rolled her eyes. 'Typical. I'll have a word. But I wouldn't hold your breath. Last year, I had to go for him.' She tutted. 'The only thing Mark does – and he does it religiously – is go to the school's AGM. It's a typical accountant thing – thinks he can help somehow by listening to the treasurer's report. He misses Sports Day, the Nativity Play, Parents' Evening – everything because of work – but come rain or shine, he's there at the lousy AGM. Men!' she let out a stab of laughter. 'Haven't got a bloody clue.' When Nicky didn't respond, she added, 'It's OK. We're . . . friends. He's all right really.'

Nicky gave a quick smile. 'It's just a real shame that he can't come.'

Lilith looked at her. 'Is there a problem?' she asked quietly.

Nicky made a face. 'No, but,' she lowered her voice, 'in my experience, if a parent doesn't come – repeatedly – there is usually a reason . . . possibly a reason we might need to know about.'

Lilith gave her a forced smile. 'I can assure you, the only thing going on is work. Mark's just been made a partner at one of the biggest firms in the City. Earns a complete fortune, but in return he has to sell life and soul to the firm. Before Helen died – Oscar's mum,' she lowered her voice even more, 'it was their one major bone of contention. That Mark loved his job more than his family. But he always said he was doing it for her and Oscar. So although it may not look like he cares, he does and he thinks he's doing the right thing.'

Nicky nodded and was about to ask how Oscar had got on with his mum when Oscar's mobile phone beeped. He jumped up, shouting, 'Daddy! Daddy! He's coming!' and flicked open his phone. Then silence.

'Here we go,' whispered Lilith, so only Nicky heard it. She handed Oscar his hot chocolate and toast. 'What is it, sweetheart?'

Oscar's head stayed down as he read the text. 'It's an all-nighter,' he read in a monotone. 'Dad says can I stay at yours tonight.'

Nicky saw Daisy raise her eyes to heaven and shake her head, like a long-suffering wife.

'Of course!' exclaimed Lilith. 'We can all sing along to Busted in the car on the way back!'

Oscar stared at his drink.

An hour later, Nicky slunk off to bed. When the doorbell went, she leapt out and ran to the top of the stairs. She could see the shadows of Ally and Pete's feet outside her front door. She could see from there that they were a bit drunk and wouldn't be able to find their key, let alone put it in the lock. She ran down the stairs and opened the door. Ally was wearing a wizard's cloak and hat. Pete was in full goblin costume, big spiky ears, even bigger spiky hat, fake nose, red cheeks, green tunic and tights. It cheered Nicky up no end.

'Amanda didn't come as a witch!' shouted Ally, taking off her hat.

'SHUSH!' yelled Pete. 'PEOPLE LIVE HERE! *NICKY* LIVES HERE!' He pointed at Nicky. 'SEE?'

Nicky beckoned them both in.

'She came as a witch's cat,' spat Ally in the hall.

They went up to the kitchen, where Nicky made a pot of coffee and Ally and Pete slumped against the counter. Pete's hat boinged almost as well as Nicky's morning hair.

'She looked like a complete and utter slut,' said Ally. 'It was porno-bloody-graphic. Everyone was there, by the way. I think you were the only one who wasn't.'

Pete sighed. 'I'll never look at a cat the same way again. It's most concerning.'

Ally swiped his arm and he tried swiping her back, but missed and almost fell over, which caused silent hysterics in both of them. After a while they stopped.

'She wore skin-tight black leather boots up to here,' listed Ally, touching her mid thigh, 'fishnet tights, a corset and not much else. But more than that . . .'

Pete and Ally exchanged excited looks.

'Yeah?' asked Nicky.

'*Something* happened,' declared Ally importantly.

Pete gave a sad little belch. They took their mugs of coffee into the lounge.

'What do you mean "something happened"? Weren't you there?' asked Nicky.

'We were in the garden most of the evening playing cricket –'

'*What?*' demanded Nicky. 'It's freezing out there!'

'*French* cricket,' explained Pete.

'Oh, right,' said Nicky.

'But when we came in afterwards,' continued Ally, '*something* had definitely happened.' Ally seemed to have suddenly sobered up. She looked at Pete.

'You'll have to find out for me,' she told him. 'Interrogate Rob for us.'

'Knob off,' he said. 'He's my mate.' He turned to Nicky. 'You do it. He'll squeal for you.'

'Do you think he got off with Amanda?' asked Nicky, her voice even.

Pete looked perplexed. 'I don't think so,' he said. Then he turned to Ally. 'I thought he'd go for Martha.'

'Martha!' cried Ally. 'Why?'

Pete shrugged. 'Easy shag. Low maintenance. No commitment 'cos she doesn't want to finish with her boyfriend.'

'Ah, sweet,' said Ally. 'It's enough to make you believe in fairy tales, isn't it?' She turned to Nicky. 'Is the spare room made up?' she asked.

'Of course!' said Nicky, thanking her lucky stars she hadn't gone to the party. If only no one else had, it would have been better still. 'No hanky-panky though. It's not that kind of establishment.'

Pete turned to Ally. 'Did you hear that, Alison? You keep your hands away from me, you randy bint.'

Ally sighed. 'I'll see what I can do, but I can't promise anything. Goblins with fingers for legs really make me hot.'

Nicky went back to bed smiling, the sound of laughter coming from her spare room. She wondered idly as she fell asleep why she always held back from Rob's Hallowe'en parties. Was it a subconscious ploy to play hard to get, to make her different from all the other girls? Or was it because she really didn't want anything to happen between them and knew that, in that context, it would?

No, when it came down to it, she didn't think it was anything as deep as that. Parties were overrated in her opinion. To be honest, she never really wanted to go to the obligatory work New Year's Eve one either, but she somehow always ended up there. It was easier to ignore Hallowe'en. And anyway, if she had gone out tonight, she'd have missed Oscar. She thought of Oscar, opened her eyes and, stretching out her arm, turned on the radio quietly for company in the dark.

6

The next morning was Friday and Nicky walked into the staffroom with a determined step. She had left Ally and Pete still getting ready in her flat and had forgotten about them as soon as she entered her boudoir. Her first waking thought had been about Oscar and now that she was alone again, those thoughts returned. She decided to confront him about Parents' Evening once and for all. And if he couldn't give her a straight answer, she was going to try and contact his father.

But that was forgotten as soon as she walked into the staffroom. There was definitely something strange going on. She couldn't put her finger on it but she felt a raw, almost fresh, atmosphere, as if the air had been spring-cleaned. Conversation was lucid and sharp; time seemed less relevant. It was almost heady. Had she stepped into Shangri-La? Then she remembered: Rob's party. Amanda the witch's cat.

Everyone was in the staffroom, except for Rob and Amanda. Her abdomen clenched. For a moment, she thought the two of them might come in together, but almost as soon as this thought flitted through her brain, Rob came in, and he was very much on his own. He walked in with a smiling, laid-back swagger.

'Hi, all!' he greeted the room and received the heartiest response Nicky had witnessed since her time there. Instead of heading for the kettle and making coffee for himself and Nicky – a routine he had followed religiously for years – he headed straight for his locker. Two children were in the staffroom this morning talking to teachers, so she waited until they'd gone before she approached him, grinning. 'So?' she began quietly. 'Was last night a success?'

'I don't know,' he replied to the room in general. 'You'll have to ask the others.'

They all responded immediately with a selection of enthusiastic, positive noises. It reminded Nicky of when Miss Fotheringham had announced her retirement. Gossip – real, relevant, live gossip – made everyone feel young again. Something had actually *happened* last night. She was going to need to keep her wits about her to find out. She needed to be subtle. That's what was needed. Rob would need sensitive handling. He was not one to give things away lightly.

She heard what sounded like a stampede of wild buffalo storming past on their way to assembly, recorders tooting in preparation for Year 4's rendition of 'Morning Has Broken'. She would need to go and oversee them with their form teacher in ten minutes.

'OK,' she said to Rob, 'what happened?' She had to concentrate to keep up the inane grin. 'What did I miss?'

'Nothing,' said Gwen with forced nonchalance.

'Nothing!' laughed Roberta. She turned to Nicky. 'Only Gwen as a pumpkin doing "I Will Survive". The others had hysterics. Nicky's pupils expanded like ink in blotting paper. She turned to Gwen. 'Were you drunk?' she asked in disbelief.

'No!' retorted Gwen. 'I was enjoying myself. You don't have to get drunk to enjoy yourself.'

'Plastered,' said Roberta. There was more laughter.

Gwen threw a book across the staffroom that landed squarely on Roberta's shoulder. A library book, no less. To Nicky's astonishment, Gwen had hysterics. Jesus, she thought. It had clearly been a momentous party.

'Did you all go?' she asked. They nodded.

'Fantastic excuse not to be at home for trick or treats,' said Roberta with feeling. 'Kids nowadays are a disgrace –'

She was about to continue when Amanda walked in.

There was an immediate and complete hush as if a sudden snowfall had descended. Amanda paused in the doorway and they all stared openly at her. She put her hand out to the doorframe and swallowed hard. Nicky was agog. For the first time in memory, Amanda did not look good. In fact, she looked distinctly rough. The long, slim legs seemed horribly frail and the all-over tan was unattractively sallow. Why did she never have a camera on her when she wanted one? wondered Nicky idly.

The others didn't seem quite so surprised by Amanda's appearance. Eventually, Ned took half a step forward, gave a small introductory cough, and said, too loudly, 'Hello there!'

The others copied him and Ned started nodding and smiling like a dog in the car window, excited that his leadership qualities had shone through.

Amanda made a sort of grunting sound in response, and, head down, stalked to her locker, where, if Nicky wasn't very much mistaken, she started to try and climb in.

'Blinking Ay-*eeda*,' breathed Roberta at Amanda's

hunched back. 'You look like you've been coughed up by a footballer.' There were a few guilty titters.

Amanda froze. She inhaled deeply, and slowly wheeled round from her locker. She swayed gently and put her hand out to steady herself.

'I,' she announced slowly, wincing, 'have got a hangover. I don't expect any of you to understand because your idea of a good time is coming second at Trivial Pursuit.'

A few gentle tuts were interrupted by Rob breaking into unconvincing laughter and leaping forward to take Amanda by the arm. He was all effusiveness. 'You were fantastic last night! We're only jealous!' He turned to Gwen. 'Gwen! A glass of water please.'

'Of course!' said Gwen and rushed to the tap.

Another cough from Ned. 'How . . . er, how much do you remember?' he asked Amanda.

Amanda's mouth opened and shut a few times. Then Rob laughed and said, 'What's to remember? Girl gets drunk, girl says things she doesn't mean, girl goes home with head in bag.' He laughed again.

The staffroom was silent.

'Did anyone make a video?' asked Nicky quietly.

Rob had loud hysterics. '*Funny!*' he said. 'Ah dear, funny!' He let the laughter ease off before concluding with, 'Ah, well.' He gave an exaggerated shrug. 'I guess it's back to boring old work for us all.'

As everyone took his cue and resumed their morning routines, Nicky tried to catch his eye, but he was having none of it. Even when Ally and Pete arrived, he kept his distance. She had no choice but to go and oversee assembly.

For the first time in living history, the foursome didn't get together all day. Rob either wasn't in the staffroom at the right time or, when he was, there was work to be done.

During lunch he spent over half an hour discussing the benefits of tweed over wool with Ned. Until Nicky and Rob's promotion, the foursome had always eaten together – either in the canteen or the staffroom. Today Pete and Ally were in the canteen, but Nicky had too much work to do. She ate her sandwich while working at her laptop. Rob also had work to do and was in the staffroom, but he was making conspicuous conversation with Ned who was throwing caution to the wind and was talking while eating.

Eventually Nicky fished out her mobile from her bag, turned it on (she usually turned it off as soon as she was at work), and texted Rob from where she sat.

I'll find out what happened – on Bonfire Night – by hook or by crook.

She watched him break off from Ned's opinions, extract his mobile from his jeans pocket and read her text. He glanced across the room at her and gave her a look that expressed something she couldn't quite put her finger on, but made her feel both more distanced from him and closer to him at the same time. She comforted herself with the thought that this Saturday's annual trip to the local firework display would probably be their most interesting to date.

This would be the gang's fifth trip to the firework display together, an evening which involved joining thousands of people on the slopes of Alexandra Palace, watching fireworks and bitching about every single member of staff at school. One year, just to be sure they didn't forget anyone, Ally had written a list. This, Nicky wouldn't miss for anything. Usually there were a few days' gap between the

112

Hallowe'en party and the fireworks display, but Alexandra Palace had chosen the weekend before 5 November instead of the one afterwards, so there were only two days between the two. Nicky was glad of it. She wasn't going to let Rob get away with secrets, especially since Pete had also gone silent over last night – his brotherly loyalty was proving stronger than his gang loyalty.

Before that, though, there was a whole afternoon to get through, and of course there was still no response from Oscar's dad concerning Parents' Evening.

'Did you mention Parents' Evening to your father last night?' she asked Oscar first thing after lunch.

'No.'

'Why not?' She tried to keep the impatience out of her voice. 'Do you not want him to come?'

'No!' Oscar seemed annoyed. 'I was at Daisy's.'

She frowned. 'Do you mean you haven't actually spoken to your father since that text?'

Oscar shrugged defensively. 'I often don't speak to him.'

Nicky stared at him for a while.

'He leaves me a chocolate on my pillow,' Oscar rushed. 'To show he's been there. He does that when he comes in after I've fallen asleep.'

She just kept on staring at him. 'That must be a lot of chocolate,' she murmured eventually.

'Yeah.' He nodded, smiling. 'It's great.'

At the end of the day, Nicky asked Ned and Gwen whether Oscar's father had ever come to Parents' Evening. She was staggered to discover that he had only been once and that was when Oscar was still in Reception. Helen, Oscar's late mother, had come that time, too. Later that year she'd died in a horrific, tragic car accident that had been so epic it had made it into the national news. After that, all contact with Oscar's father had been made via the written word or over the phone. Nicky was stunned. She wanted to hug Oscar to her chest and never let go.

But, she thought, as she drove home, this was the boy's last year in junior school – it was his Year 6, for goodness' sake. Surely his father would want to come? Should she phone him? She'd ask the gang at the fireworks display. After she'd found out what happened last night. She chewed her lip all the way home. A tiny lump was forming on the inside of her lower lip that was beginning to feel quite satisfying to chew. Salty.

Early Saturday evening, Nicky began her preparations for the gang's sixth fireworks display outing by running herself a big, hot bath. She was going to make a special effort tonight. She'd realised that Ally genuinely didn't know what had happened at the party and was beginning to tire of Nicky's desire to know. In fact, she'd even gone so far as to say that Rob wasn't worth so much mental energy. Pete was either similarly disinterested or had been sworn to secrecy. So Nicky had tried to work it out for herself. She scrutinised Rob and Amanda all day Friday for signs of intimacy, but all she could detect was an added consciousness of each other which she found a bit alarming. Not so much because she believed there was something going on between them, but just because up until now she'd thought of herself as occupying pole position in the race for Women In Rob Pattison's Life. Now she wasn't so sure. She was going to have to interrogate Rob. But she was also going to have to keep her pride. And where men were concerned there was really only one way to do that.

After her bath she poured herself into her tightest jeans, which she knew did good things for her thighs and the delicious little upside-down triangle of space above them, spectacular things for the soft arc of her hips and extraordinarily flattering things for her bottom. They were like a denim corset. She chose a skin-tight, black V-neck sweater, which gave her a lovely cleavage without being brazen, and her figure-hugging cream furry jacket which stopped just short of the exact spot where her back curved into her bottom. This she completed with her sexy, high-heeled black leather boots, brought in especially from the boudoir in her car boot for the occasion, which added an all-important three inches to her height and made her ankles and calves look like a slalom. She added her toffee-coloured woolly cap, which instantly warmed her dark eyes and hid the most unmanageable of her hair. Then she picked up her keys and looked at her reflection in the hall mirror, chewed her lip a bit and replaced her keys. She pulled her make-up bag out of her handbag (also brought in from the boudoir especially), applied another line of soft khaki kohl to her eyelids, which enhanced their almond shape, and, for a final touch of glamour, brushed her lips with a new deep, red lipstick. She may not be a natural like Amanda, but there was no denying she scrubbed up well. Mind you, she thought, eyeing her jeans, it was a shame she couldn't breathe. She gave her reflection a slow, satisfied smile and when she heard Rob's car horn from outside, did her best to run to the car.

Everyone knew it was easier to walk to Ally Pally than to drive, but Rob always insisted on driving. He would park as near as possible, which involved much huffing, puffing and swearing, making Nicky feel as if they were already married, and much self-congratulatory cheering when he found a space a mile away. He always gave his fireworks-display parking space marks out of ten. This year was an eight and set him up for a good evening ahead.

Half an hour later, they found Pete and Ally at their usual meeting place by one of the park gates, and together, the gang were swept along by a vast throng of people towards the heat of the enormous bonfire. Nicky was absolutely freezing and tense from the effort of trying to keep warm. As the wind sliced into her neck she started to long for the shapeless fleece hanging in her wardrobe. Rob put his arm around her and rubbed her till she was warm, keeping his hand firmly gripped on her shoulder. She looked up at him. He looked down at her. They smiled. People swarmed past them towards the bonfire.

'All right, gorgeous?' He grinned, giving her shoulder a tight squeeze.

'What happened last night?' She grinned back.

He released her and pointed at her like she'd been a naughty child. She thought he was going to respond, but instead he paused and then said, 'I'll get the baked potatoes; Ally, get the mulled wine; Pete, get us a place; Nicky get the sparklers. And, Nicky, don't forget to get one lit this time.'

'Don't ignore me, Robert Pattison,' she said with a stamp of her foot, pointing straight back at him. 'What the fiery buttocks happened at the party?'

He smiled affectionately and said, 'D'you know, you look like a little girl when you do that.'

She let out an explosive noise. '"*Like a little girl!*"' she cried. 'These jeans are like having a rib removed! "Like a little girl" my *arse*.'

Rob eyed her jeans approvingly. 'You're right,' he said with a grin, 'your arse is all woman.' And to her astonishment, he gave her bottom an encouraging little pat that nearly toppled her over. 'But the rest is all little girl.'

'Don't you dare patronise me, Prattison!' she cried. 'I get dangerously immature when I'm patronised. And you don't want me being immature when there are sparklers around. Not in those trousers.' Rob visibly balked and she used her moment wisely. 'Just tell me what the Hilaire Belloc happened last night,' she ordered. 'And why Amanda looked like a rotting corpse afterwards.'

'Oh, just forget it, Nicky!' cried Pete. 'It's old news.'

'What's wrong with these trousers?' Rob looked down at them.

'See you on the hill,' said Pete, 'I'll call you all when I find a place.' He and Ally went about their delegated duties. Rob and Nicky walked together to the potato and sparkler queues.

'*Tell me!*' she whined.

Rob stopped walking. He stared at her. She stared back, raised her eyebrows and stuck out her chin. He spoke quietly and she had to lean forward to hear him against the background din.

'I'll only tell you if you promise to tell me one thing.'

She started squealing, jumping up and down and clapping her hands. 'OK! I promise,' she said.

'Right.' His voice was suddenly serious. 'If you tell me – *honestly* – why you're so desperate to know, then I'll tell you what happened last night.' He crossed his arms and waited.

She frowned at him. 'Because it's good gossip, dur-brain,' she explained. 'And good mates tell each other good gossip.'

To her amazement, Rob turned his back on her and walked towards the food stall, leaving her staring after him. O-K, she thought slowly. Wrong answer.

'I . . .' she started shouting at his back.

He turned round and waited. She paused.

'Yes?' he asked.

'I want extra cheese on my potato,' she told him.

He nodded, turned away, and continued walking. She stood for a while before turning in the opposite direction to make her way to the sparklers.

Buying the sparklers was a unique experience that Nicky absolutely loved.

They were sold from a stand near the top of a flight of narrow, uneven, concrete stairs that only allowed for one single file of people going up and one coming down. Once you made it to the top of the stairs you turned a sharp right and headed for the back of the queue, from where you could look out over the stunning view of London, punctuated by miniature, distant rockets soaring into the night sky like dancing jewels. Once at the front of the queue, a round, rosy man took your money and handed you your unlit sparklers. Then you moved quickly to an ever-changing huddle of people who were all lighting each other's sparklers.

As she approached the steps, she began a thought process that she repeated every year. Initially, the sight of them made her think of a Dickens novel, which led inevitably to the thought that it would be nice to put on *A Christmas Carol* at school this year as part of the traditional Nativity Play. This thought would be followed, immediately, by the thought that Miss James would never allow it, and finally Nicky's conclusion that one day she must become the Headmistress of her own school or she would never truly be fulfilled. This year, as the stairs appeared, she had already finished her annual thought process and moved on to a new sweet epilogue: The realisation that thanks to her recent promotion, she was finally moving nearer to her dream.

Unsurprisingly, the stairs ahead were horribly squashed as people were trying to make a last-minute dash towards them to buy their sparklers before the show began. Nicky couldn't rush in her jeans, so she took her time, merrily allowing people to overtake her before she reached them. She approached the bottom of them and joined the queue at exactly the same time as a man approaching from the other direction. It was obvious that one of them would have to give way before they reached the first stair. She glanced up to check the man's body language for clues as to whether he was going to let her go first or nip in in front of her. He looked down at her at exactly the same moment, and about three hundred rockets roared up inside her body.

Thick fair hair flopped over his forehead and two wide-set, blue-green eyes shone down at her. He smiled.

'After you,' he said, in a voice that was so low she could have sworn the ground vibrated beneath them.

He allowed her on to the steps in front of him, one denim-clad leg stepping back to make room for her.

Now was the moment to say something startlingly fantastic.

'Thanks,' she said.

Bollocks.

She tried to climb the stairs in front of him in a feminine, impressive way, hinting at all the different, fascinating aspects of her complex personality. It wasn't easy in jeans that cut off her circulation. To her horror, she almost tripped, stretching out her hands to the floor, and the humiliation of this was only just lessened by the man's rush to help her. He stepped up to her level beside her, and with one hand on her forearm, the other gently on the small of her back, murmured with concern, 'Are you all right?'

His voice, like an electric current, seemed to follow a direct path to all her best bits. She stood up straight and turned to him. He took a step down, so she was now one step higher than him, almost at his chin level. They smiled at each other, the smiles lingering for vital seconds longer than was strictly necessary. She felt warm for the first time all evening.

'Thanks,' she said.

'No problem.'

'I-I'm usually quite good with stairs,' she said. 'We've got them at work and everything.'

He laughed, seemingly as surprised as he was amused. She knew she only had seconds left to study him. His teeth were great. Fantastic jawline. Lips that –

'Get a move on or we'll miss the bloody show!' came a gruff voice from below.

She turned 180 degrees away from him in one and rushed up the rest of the stairs as fast as her jeans allowed her. Should she turn back and give a conspiratorial smile at the foolish world they shared? No, she'd probably fall over.

She reached the top of the stairs and, without a glance behind, turned and joined the queue. She looked to her right at the view below. She could feel Him (he had a capital

H already. 'Him'! The masculinity of the word made her spine tingle) join the queue behind her, but couldn't think of anything to say. For the first year that she'd ever queued for sparklers, she was infuriated by how fast and efficiently the snake of people moved forwards. Before she had worked out the precise farewell sentence to say to Him, with the correct amount of eloquent smileage, that would stay with Him for ever, she was at the front, fiddling with woolly gloves and coins.

She joined the huddled circle next to the queue of people lighting their sparklers off each other. And there, facing a straggle of strangers, whose faces were lit by a central golden glow, she suddenly felt A Moment of pure joy. Life was all potential. Life was thrilling. And here she was, right smack bang in the middle of it. (Was he looking? She arched her back a little.)

When he joined the huddle, she couldn't bring herself to look at him. It would feel too much of an admission. Instead, she watched the end of his sparkler, which went directly for hers, touched it and stayed there. She forced herself to look up at him and was rewarded by him gently increasing the pressure of his sparkler against hers while raising his eyebrows suggestively and giving her a shy yet cheeky grin.

Hello, World, she thought, as a hot flush spread round her body.

She grinned and then they both looked down at their sparklers fusing together.

Then nothing happened and they stood there like two tossers.

Finally the sparklers fused. They shared a laugh in the

121

sudden golden glow. Then they moved away from the others and approached the stairs together.

'Thank you for fusing my sparkler,' he said, his voice all low.

'My pleasure.'

Just as he was about to say something, his mobile went. She looked down and continued walking, but not before she heard a child's voice exclaim '*Dad!*' at the other end.

The Moment was over. She went down the stairs slowly, feeling ridiculously let-down. By halfway down, she was already lecturing herself. How on earth did she manage to get so excited so quickly? If it took her that little time to go up, then she deserved to come down with a thud. Stupid thing.

At the bottom of the stairs, she got a text from Pete. She didn't understand a word of it, so she phoned him back immediately. He began to give her directions to the spot on the hill he'd found in the crowd, and, concentrating hard to follow them correctly, she stretched her arm out and made an abrupt swivel. She found herself standing an arm's length away from the amazing bloke called Dad and pointing straight at him, almost touching his chest. He stopped dead in his tracks and stared at her. She stared back. Then they both stared at each other. She slowly put her arm down. His mouth tilted into an awkward smile, wobbled a bit, and then he tried again. His eyebrows rose fractionally. It was rather a sad farewell, she thought, as she watched him slowly turn round and go.

'. . . and you can't miss it,' finished Pete in her ear. There was a pause. 'Nicky? Hello? Are you still there?'

Nicky blinked. 'Where?' she asked, watching the bloke being slowly swallowed up by the crowd.

There was another pause.

'You weren't listening, were you?'

'Um. No, not really.'

'Where did you hear up to?'

'Er . . .' she cast her mind back. ' "Hello?" '

She heard Pete mutter something about giving him strength before repeating himself. Half an hour later, she was still looking for them all, glancing around her for the mystery man. If they met again, here amidst five thousand other people, it would be fate, she told herself. A sign. But as she glanced more and more hectically through the crowds, she admitted to herself that the chances of seeing someone she actually knew in this enormous crowd were a million to one.

'*Nicky!*'

She found herself staring into the face of an appalled Amanda.

'I didn't know you were coming here tonight,' accused Amanda.

'I didn't know you were,' defended Nicky.

'You didn't ask.'

'Neither did you.'

'Who are you here with?' asked Amanda.

Nicky had always been able to think quickly on her feet; it came from years of having to answer the most unpredictable questions from ten-year-olds.

'Rob, Pete and Ally,' she told her. She was too pre-occupied to be inventive right now.

Amanda's face went rigid with martyrdom. 'Oh. I see.'

'Do you want to join us?'

'God, no,' Amanda's face set itself into a smile. 'I get enough of teachers all day. I'm here with friends.'

Nicky nodded slowly. 'I'll be sure to give them all your regards.'

Amanda gave her a confiding smile. 'Yes, you *do* that,' she said.

When Nicky finally found Rob, he handed her a cold baked potato, Ally handed her a cold mulled wine, and she handed them all dead sparklers.

'You'll never guess who I've just seen,' she told them.

'Amanda?' said Rob, without taking his eyes off the display.

'How the hell did you guess that?'

'I didn't. She texted me.'

Nicky stared at Rob. 'Right,' she said. 'If you don't tell me what happened last night, I'll tell Miss James you think she's a mad old cow.'

He fixed her with an intense glare. 'I promise,' he said, 'nothing happened.'

'Hmm,' she said. 'So why did Amanda pretend she hated you just now?'

'Because she probably does,' he said simply. 'Especially after last night.'

Five thousand people suddenly gasped and said '*Ooooh!*' as rockets exploded above them. They both looked up.

'So something *did* happen,' said Nicky, looking back at him. He looked at her.

Five thousand people cried out '*Aaaaahhhhh!*' as pretty pink bows cascaded down from the sky.

They both looked up.

'We're going to miss the whole bloody thing if you don't keep quiet,' said Rob. 'It's over in ten minutes.'

'If you promise to tell me when it's over, I'll shut up.'

'Deal.'

'Promise?'

'Yep.'

'Prom—'

Five thousand people laughed in surprised delight at the skies above.

They both looked up.

'I'll tell you, *all right?*' hissed Rob. 'Now shut up.'

Nicky smiled and watched the display just in time to see the finale begin.

They got up and started to queue for the West exit.

Forty yards away, Lilith and Mark were hurrying Oscar and Daisy out of the display. Mark had thought that his mind would be firmly on the Due Diligence tonight, but he had been pleasantly surprised. Lilith had given him the ultimatum of never helping out for another weekend if he didn't come, so he'd legged it straight from the office. He hadn't seen what the fuss was about, but now he got it. Seeing his boy's face light up with joy at the fireworks had been something else. And then there was that amazing girl with the hair and the body and the slightly shy, slightly knowing smile, who had reminded him that maybe, just maybe, there was more to life than work.

He kept his head down, while Oscar pulled at his hand. As he walked on, head down, eyes firmly on the feet of the people in front of him, he conjured up the image of that woman again.

'Oh look! It's Miss Hobbs! Miss Hobbs!' exclaimed Oscar, pointing to his right and nearly dragging Mark off his feet. 'Daddy! It's Miss Hobbs. And Mr Pattison!'

Without thinking, Mark spun round the opposite way, keeping his head firmly down. He did not need to see teachers tonight.

'Hey,' called out Lilith. 'Why don't you meet her? She wants to meet you. Wants to know why you're not coming to Parents' Evening. And Mr Pattison's there too. He's a complete hunk.'

The children started begging him to take them to her, but he was not in the mood. He kept going in the opposite direction, towards the East exit.

Ally and Pete both lived in the opposite direction to Rob and Nicky and took the bus home. Once Rob and Nicky were on their own again, she got to work.

'Tell me,' she whined, trying to run to keep up with Rob, as he neared the West exit.

'Wait till we're in the car,' he said.

She was about to whine a bit more, when she was sure she suddenly heard someone call her name. She turned to look.

She stared for a while. Nothing. Just the usual crowd of families, all fighting their way to the exits. She frowned and then felt herself being pulled along by the arm, by Rob.

'Tell me,' she whined again.

'I'll tell you when we get to the car.'

They got to the car. Just as she was about to whine again, he said, 'I'll tell you when we get to your place.' They got in the car.

'You'd better,' she concluded hotly. He returned her fixed glare, then started the car and pulled out.

*

By the time Oscar and Daisy were being driven away from the fireworks, they had worked themselves up into a state of distraction over missing Miss Hobbs.

'I love Miss Hobbs!' sobbed Daisy.

'Good!' said Lilith. 'Perhaps you'll be able to stay over a few nights a week.'

'So do I!' cried Oscar.

'You *love* your teacher?' asked Mark, glancing into the rear-view mirror.

The boy nodded. 'Yes. And I love her kitchen.'

Mark pressed his foot on the accelerator and stared at Oscar in the mirror. 'What? When the hell did you see her kitchen?'

Lilith turned round to give Oscar a reassuring smile when Mark suddenly slammed his foot on the brakes and swore angrily. Lilith's neck jerked forward and she closed her eyes in pain.

Rob and Nicky gasped. They'd come within inches of a sporty red number. They were so close they could see the startled expression of the driver. Which was how Nicky found herself staring into the eyes of the amazing guy again. And he was staring straight back at her. His lips were now fixed in a grim, if not hostile, expression. Those wide-set eyes were now highlighted by the fiercely angry set of his eyebrows. (Funny, she hadn't noticed those before.) The sandy fringe had flopped forward over his forehead.

The children went quiet in the back. Lilith made a strangled sound. And Mark found himself staring into the startled eyes of the fantastic girl and her arse of a boyfriend who had just tried to kill them all. And she was staring straight back at him. He hadn't noticed how saucer-like her eyes were before. He was considering smiling at her, when her pillock of a boyfriend reversed the car back into the space it had just come out of and someone hooted him from behind. He drove on.

'Flash wanker,' muttered Rob. 'That car costs five times our annual fucking wage. More money than sense.'

'Hmm,' managed Nicky.

As the amazing guy drove on, she got a chance to glance at his car's passenger seat and, sure enough, she could just make out the shadow of a woman. She looked in the back and spotted the forms of two children. She looked away fast. Were all the good men taken? Was she sitting next to the only attractive, single man in London?

'Is everyone all right?' asked Mark, his hands gripping the wheel firmly.

'Yes,' replied the children.

'Osc?' he said.

'Yes.'

'Daisy?'

'Yes.'

'Good,' he said. 'No harm done then.'

'Lilith?' said Lilith quietly. 'Oh! Thanks for asking. I think I may have broken my neck,' she replied to herself. 'Apart from that, we're all fine.'

'Jesus Christ,' murmured Rob, watching the car disappear in his mirror. 'How much money do you have to earn to buy a car like that? A hundred? A hundred and fifty?'

'Wanker,' shot Nicky. 'Two-timing bastard.'

'Yeah,' added Rob, 'probably a murderer too.'

'Wanker.'

'Tosser.'

'Twat.'

'Miss Hobbs's whole house is upstairs,' continued Oscar. 'I like that.'

Mark was forced to focus on the issue at hand.

'How the hell do you know that?' he demanded.

'We were there on Hallowe'en,' said Oscar.

'You were there on Hallowe'en?' repeated Mark incredulously.

'I think my neck's broken,' breathed Lilith.

'Would you like to explain how the hell that happened?' Mark turned to Lilith.

'Well,' she said, 'it happened when you braked so suddenly.'

'You went to their teacher on Hallowe'en,' said Mark, 'and didn't tell me?'

'No, of course not,' said Lilith crossly. 'We happened to trick or treat her.'

'And she invited you in?' asked Mark.

'I was very grateful, as it happens,' said Lilith. 'We hadn't had dinner and had been going for about three hours in the freezing cold, because Oscar was still waiting for you to turn up. She took pity on us and made us hot chocolate. We were there when you texted him to let him know you weren't going to make it or come home that night.'

Mark tutted. 'God, how sad is that?' he said. 'She must have no friends.'

Lilith raised her eyebrows. How was it possible for men to always extract the least important piece of information?

'It wasn't sad!' cried Oscar. 'It was nice. And you weren't there, so you don't know.'

'Good,' muttered Mark. 'She sounds like a complete weirdo to me.'

Lilith was going to tell him that she wasn't, but instead she just said, 'Ow.'

Rob parked dramatically outside Nicky's house. They sat in silence for a while, Nicky's breathing coming fast as if her body had too much breath in it.

'Well,' she said, sharply, 'thanks for the lift. It's good to confront your mortality every now and then.'

After a pause, Rob turned to her. He spoke slowly. 'If you invite me in for coffee, I'll tell you what happened last night.'

'Jesus Christ,' she muttered. 'You know how to spin a yarn, don't you?' She opened her car door. 'Come on, then.'

Ten minutes later, they were in her kitchen and the kettle was on. It felt good to have a man in her kitchen, especially while she was wearing these jeans. She pictured the man at the display, his eyes when he'd looked at her, and then his neat, 2.4 family in his car.

'Tell me now,' she said impatiently, 'or you're not getting your coffee.'

He sighed and eventually started to talk. 'Amanda said some silly things about us. She was very drunk. And some people happened to overhear,' he said.

She stared at him. '*Us?*'

'Us.'

She went on staring. 'You-and-me us?'

'I believe that's what "us" means, yes.'

She was frozen to the spot. Rob took the hint and told her.

'She's guessed that you and I have a history,' he said slowly. Then he shrugged. 'That's it. I promise.'

Nicky stared at him. And kept staring at him.

'And?' she said. She didn't know what made her say it. Maybe it was the fireworks. Maybe it was nearly having an accident. Maybe it was Rob's temper. Maybe it was the way that guy had looked at her. Maybe it was his kids in the back of his car.

'*And?*' she repeated.

Rob sighed. Then he looked up at her, right into her eyes, with an expression she hadn't seen for a long, long time.

Mark parked his car outside Lilith and Daisy's flat.

'How's your neck now?' he asked Lilith.

'Oh, fine,' she muttered. 'It's amazing what a reckless car drive can do for a broken neck.'

'Can you move your extremities?'

Lilith looked at her hand. 'I don't know.' She slapped him sharply on the cheek. 'Yes,' she said.

'Good.' Mark smiled, rubbing his cheek.

The children laughed and started play-slapping each other.

'Ah, look,' said Mark fondly, turning round to watch them in the back. 'You're such a good example to the littl'uns.'

Lilith turned round to Daisy. 'Shall we get out of the madman's car now, sweetie?'

'Yes,' said Daisy. 'Can I hit him too?'

'No, darling. That's just for Mummy.'

She smiled at Mark. 'Thank you for a great night,' she said. 'I'll call you when I can feel my feet again.'

He watched from the car as Lilith opened her front door and waved goodbye. 'Right,' he said to Oscar. 'Where to, sonny? The Casino Royale? Soho?'

He heard gentle snoring and turned to see Oscar slumped in his seat, out cold.

Nicky stared at Rob across her tiny kitchen, the sound of the clock suddenly magnified.

'Rob,' she said.

'OK,' he replied. He paused and then spoke. 'She says she thinks there's more than history between us.'

'Oh for goodness' sa—' started Nicky.

'She thinks there's . . . chemistry too.'

Nicky raised an eyebrow in amazement.

'You mean . . .' she said slowly, 'Amanda made a pun?'

Rob smiled.

'I see,' she said thoughtfully.

'I think . . .' began Rob, his voice barely louder than a whisper, 'that if we're both honest with ourselves . . . she's more perceptive than we thought.'

Nicky's spine tingled. And then melted. And then a far more key part of her body got in on the act and tingled, then melted. Sex! she thought. She was going to get sex tonight. The thought was so overpowering that she almost forgot Rob was there.

'Don't you?' he asked, the bass of his voice causing her body to start a soft, rhythmic throbbing. Just in time, she remembered he was there. Feminine intuition told her that he was staring hard at her. She knew because her jeans were trembling. And it took a lot to make these jeans tremble. Her head started an internal conversation – for even at times like this, Nicky Hobbs's brain had been known to take over when it was not wanted. 'Hmm,' it said. 'This is an unexpected and intriguing position to be in. I must consider it carefully before I –' But her tingling, melting, trembling and rhythmically throbbing body was remembering the guy from the fireworks display, just before she and Rob met in the middle of her kitchen and kissed for the first time in seven years.

7

Five minutes later, Rob finally pulled himself away and stared at Nicky in disbelief, his pupils slowly shrinking.

'You don't mean it,' he moaned softly in her ear.

'I do,' she whispered, her voice now joining in the merry throng and trembling as much as the rest of her body.

'OK,' he murmured. 'In a minute.' He took her by the hips and pulled her gently towards him. It was all she could do not to liquefy at his feet. If he hadn't been holding her by the hips she'd be a puddle on the floor by now. She'd forgotten how good Rob was.

He started kissing her down the neck so gently that the rest of her body got jealous. And then, for some reason unknown to man, she pictured Miss James, smiling at them both from above. She jolted her head back, knocking Rob with her chin.

'Ow!' he said.

'Come on, Rob,' she said. 'I said "no".'

'OK,' he replied, his voice slightly muffled because his lips were busy circling her neck.

Oh what the hell, she thought, and allowed herself two more minutes.

'Right,' she breathed, her voice high. 'Out.'

He slid his hands round and down her bottom, but she pushed him away. Not the bottom, she thought. The bottom had always been her make-or-break point with Rob. She wondered if he remembered.

'Oh, come on –' he started, keeping his hands exactly where they were and slowly pitter-pattering its curve with his fingers. Hello, Satan, she thought. Take a seat. I'll be with you in a minute.

'No! Out,' she heard herself say, pushing him away firmly. To be honest, if someone had come in now and asked her why, she would not have been able to give one convincing argument. She knew she and Rob were good together. She knew it would be excellent exercise, and she hadn't had a chance to get to the gym in ages. She also knew it would ruin her career and, due to the dysfunctional society she lived in, it would be one-nil to Rob. And she did not want Rob to be one up on her. Ooh. Bad phrasing . . .

Rob was staring at her, his focus slowly coming back.

'Don't you think you're a bit old for games like this?' His voice was gravel.

'I'm not playing games, Rob,' she said, flushing. 'If I was playing games, I'd take you into my bedroom now.'

He pulled her in again. 'Let's play Twister,' he whispered hoarsely into her ear.

Her body told her brain to go and do some homework. Rarely had a man spoken more persuasively and with more sense. Her head told her this was not just a man, it was Rob.

She turned her face gently to his ear and cupped it softly in her hand, placing the other one on his buttock. 'OUT,' she said firmly, pushing him, via his bottom, out of the kitchen.

And to his utter amazement, five minutes later, Rob Pattison, *The* Rob Pattison, found himself on the wrong side of her front door, with nowhere for his body to go but home.

He walked as straight and tall as he could to his car, opened the door and got inside. Then he sat for a while, staring straight ahead. When he saw Nicky's hall light go out, he swore loudly and hit the steering wheel hard, before going home.

As she heard his car start, Nicky stood motionless in the dark hall, her heart hammering. Dare she even think it? Yes . . . It had been everything she'd ever dreamt it would be! And more.

'Rob,' she whispered in the silence, knowing that the one tiny syllable, such an inconsequential word, meant something momentous to her now. 'Rob.'

Oh boy, was this A Moment! She savoured it, standing there triumphantly – though a little bent in the middle – in the dark. This was *The* Moment. The moment she realised her life was about to begin again.

First thing Sunday morning, she woke early. She almost jumped out of bed. She was on a real high. She was on top of the world. She could barely wait to tell Ally her news. It wasn't often that suddenly everything made sense. She got to the bakery earlier than she'd ever been before and decided to treat them both to chocolate croissants this morning. After all, life was for living. It was only when she was running across the hall to answer Ally's ring on the doorbell that it occurred to her that she shouldn't tell Ally what had happened. Ally might not understand; worse, Ally might not support her, and Nicky knew she couldn't cope with that.

Not after all these years. In fairness, it was a complex situation. It was far more complicated than it appeared. And everything was different now. It would probably be better to speak to Rob first. As she walked down the stairs, she realised that keeping a secret from Ally would make her feel disloyal yet mature at the same time. She was growing up; she didn't need to offload everything as soon as it had happened. Maybe the rest of her life was already beginning.

As soon as Ally left, she phoned Claire and told her everything. Together they decided that she shouldn't phone Rob today, but should wait to talk to him first thing Monday. Phones were useless for this kind of epic discussion. It didn't take a genius to work out that he wouldn't be phoning her. Nicky slept the sleep of the innocent all Sunday night. She dreamt she was doing a vast puzzle, each piece as big as a suitcase. The last piece was hidden in her bed and she found it! The final puzzle picture was a Barbie birthday cake – the kind she'd always longed for as a child and had never got.

On Monday morning she woke before her alarm. She had to speak to Rob before anyone else was in. Forty minutes later, she parked the boudoir in the empty school car park and sat staring through her windscreen as the wipers squeaked regularly in the rain. Rob's car wasn't there. She felt the first sensation of tension since their kiss. She wondered if Pete would know what had happened? If so, would he tell Ally? For the first time, she considered how much she had to lose should all this go pear-shaped. She had to talk to Rob fast.

She was the first member of staff in. She walked down the eerily silent corridors, aware that her body was ever-so-slightly shaking. Why? Was she thrilled? Or nervous? What the hell was she nervous about? It was Rob! When she opened the staffroom door, she sat down, took out a pen and paper and tried to work out how she felt. After a moment, she put down the pen and let out a big sigh. What was the point of having feelings if you didn't understand them? Was there any other creature in the animal kingdom that had this inability to work itself out? she pondered, as she stood up and stomped to the kettle. She pictured a gazelle coming face to face with a lion, wetting itself with terror and thinking, 'Hmm? What is that overwhelming sensation? Fear? *Joie de vivre?*'

At the sound of the door opening behind her, Nicky whizzed round, her eyes bright, her smile wide. At the sight of Amanda, her mouth went dry.

'Hi!' she said, her lips sticking to her gums.

Amanda's eyes shrank. 'What are you doing in so early?' she asked.

'Oh, you know,' said Nicky, swallowing hard. 'Things to do. People to see.'

Amanda crossed her arms and stared at her.

Nicky's lips came away from her gums and she managed a smile. 'You?'

Amanda gave her a sickly smile. 'Oh, you know,' she mirrored. 'Things to do. People to see.'

Nicky fought the urge to punch her in the face. Just then the staffroom door opened again and Rob walked in. He took one look at them both and made a noise that was part laugh, part retch.

'*Hi!*' he exclaimed, eyebrows high. '*Hi!*'

'Hi!' responded Amanda, her voice light like acid rain.

Nicky smiled. 'Kettle's just boiled. Coffee?'

'Er, no thanks,' said Rob.

She turned her back to him, nausea clutching at her stomach. Instead of making herself a coffee, she joined them in the chairs in the far corner. How come this was going so badly?

'So,' she began, folding herself into a chair, her knees now higher than her face. 'What did you think of Saturday's display, Amanda?'

There was a moment's pause.

'Pitiful,' replied Amanda crisply, staring at Rob. 'A bit like this one. Would you two like to be alone?'

'No!' cried Rob and Nicky in unison. Shit, thought Nicky. She'd meant yes. She'd been in denial for so long she'd forgotten how to come out of it.

'Actually, would you mind?' she said quickly, before giving herself a chance to self-censure. 'Only, Rob and I do need to talk, actually.'

'No we don't!' laughed Rob. 'There's nothing private we need to talk about. Is there?'

Nicky's allegiances switched and she wanted very much to punch Rob in the face. At least Amanda was honest. Amanda got up, making some muttered comment about 'boring lovebirds'. Rob started persuading her not to go and then the staffroom door opened, bringing in Ned and Gwen, and all was lost.

Nicky thought that maybe she'd have time to talk to Rob on their way to the morning meeting with Miss James, until he jumped up, told her he had some preparation to do before it and would see her in there. She would have followed him out, but at that moment Ally came in.

'Hello, all,' greeted Ally, as Rob walked out.

'Oh, hello,' said Amanda. 'Welcome to The Bad School-room Farce. Nicky wants to talk to Rob. Rob's pretending he doesn't know what she's talking about and any minute now a vicar's going to walk in without any trousers on.'

Ally's eyes went round. 'Excellent. I've always had a thing about dog collars and no trousers.'

The door opened and Pete walked in.

'Typical,' said Ally. 'I fucking hate Mondays.'

Everyone turned away from Pete.

'*What?*' he demanded.

Nicky decided to go early to Miss James and try to get her puzzle piece finished before the meeting. Maybe last night's dream was portentous and she'd be able to do it more quickly now. Then she could follow Rob out afterwards.

When she arrived at Miss James's office, she found Miss James scribbling what looked like an upside-down long-division sum and, to her astonishment, Rob standing at the puzzle table. She stopped in her tracks, shock and hurt making her stomach lurch. He'd actually lied so as not to have to talk to her. He didn't even look up as she came in. She joined him at the puzzle table and before she'd had a chance to look at him, let alone speak, he made a little whoop of satisfaction, popped a puzzle piece in place, and almost leapt to his chair opposite Miss James's desk, all without giving her so much as a glance. Now who was playing games? she thought angrily. She stared at the puzzle, trying desperately to find a piece before Miss James spoke. Everything went out of focus and she found it hard to catch her breath.

'Now!' exclaimed Miss James, perching her glasses on her nose. 'Now, now, now, now, now, *now*.'

Nicky sat down next to Rob. There was a long silence as

Miss James tried to look for some notes. Nicky tilted her head towards Rob and he tilted his away. Nicky could hear his breathing. Miss James started humming happily.

'Miss James?' started Nicky, unable to sit in silence for any longer.

Miss James's head shot up. 'Yes, m'dear?'

'Can I ask you a question about Parents' Evening?'

'My dear!' cried Miss James, 'you can ask me a question about anything in the world! My ears are yours! Ask away!'

Nicky smiled. 'Thank you. It's about one of the parents.'

She told Miss James about her concerns for Oscar and her inability to get a response from his father. At the end, Miss James shook her head sadly.

'Always so . . . tragic when the father doesn't get involved.'

'Especially when there isn't a mother,' agreed Nicky.

'I don't understand men,' added Rob quietly. Nicky and Miss James looked at him. 'I mean,' he mused aloud, 'how can you not want to be involved in your child's life?'

Nicky stared at him. He smiled at Miss James. His profile was perfect.

'. . . so I think a letter to him, just kindly prompting him to come, would be appropriate,' concluded Miss James, before turning to the more pressing matter of how many biscuits and chairs there would be for both evenings.

By 4 p.m., Nicky was desperate. She could barely breathe. Rob had managed to keep one step ahead of her all day. In the end, she had to resort to texting Ally for help. It wasn't ideal having Ally – or Pete – there while she spoke to Rob, but if that was the only way it was going to happen, so be it. She couldn't spend another day like today.

She came running up to the staffroom to find Ally and Pete performing some kind of song-and-dance routine while Rob was having hysterics watching. The room went quiet when she entered. Everyone else had gone home.

'Rob!' she cried out, unable to dissemble. 'At long bloody last!'

He looked at her for a moment, then at the other two, whose guilty faces gave everything away, and then turned back to Nicky.

'Nicky!' he responded. 'Finally!'

'Listen, we've got to talk. About Saturday night –' she gushed.

'Shit, Nicky, you don't need to explain anything to me! It's me, remember! Rob!'

'Yes, I do,' she said.

Ally and Pete started making loud exit noises, but both Rob and Nicky ignored them. Nicky realised that they both knew exactly what had happened.

'The kiss,' Nicky started, 'was a complete blinder . . . um . . .'

'I know, I know! I mean, it's . . . not . . . it's . . . look. It's work and everything. It's really complicated. Crap timing. I got home and realised I was really grateful we didn't take it any further. It would have been impossible.'

There was a long pause. Nicky flicker-flacked through what felt like hundreds of possible answers.

'Thank goodness,' she said eventually. 'That's exactly what I wanted to say. It's really, *really* bad timing.'

Rob nodded. 'Yeah. Really, *really* bad timing.'

Pete broke the awkward silence by asking Rob for a lift home. Rob gave Nicky a big smile and the boys left together, leaving Ally and Nicky standing alone in the staffroom. Nicky looked at Ally.

'I was going to tell you, Al,' she said, 'but I thought it would be better to talk to him first. You know, get it all sorted out. But he's been avoiding me all day.'

'Tosser,' said Ally mildly.

'I take it he didn't mind talking about it to others.'

'Apparently not. Pete had told me everything by break.'

'Sorry you had to hear it from him.'

'Hey, don't be daft!' said Ally. 'This wasn't about you and me. I knew you'd tell me in your own time.' She nodded her head to where Rob had been standing. 'Was that all . . . OK?'

Nicky seemed to wake up out of a daydream. 'Unbelievable!' she said, suddenly excited. 'Ally! I can't tell you how wonderful I feel now I know I'm over him. I've been trying to talk to him all day to tell him finally, conclusively, that we are just good friends. It's like a weight's been lifted off my shoulders. After seven years!'

'You're kidding?' Ally started laughing.

Nicky joined in. 'No!' she said. 'Apart from my body almost beating him to the finishing line, I felt absolutely nothing when I kissed him. I mean, emotionally. Nothing! Physically . . .' She mimed her body melting, and Ally laughed. 'Un-be-lievable. But at the same time . . . it felt like I was . . . I don't know . . . lying. And if I'd taken it any further, it would have felt like I was leading him on. And,' she shrugged, 'I just didn't want to.'

Ally screamed. 'You can get on with the rest of your life!' she cried.

'I know!'

'You got closure!'

'I know!' laughed Nicky.

Ally came and hugged her. They drew apart and Ally frowned when she saw Nicky's eyes were full. 'But?' she asked.

'I don't know,' she said, honestly. 'I didn't expect him to give in so easily.'

It was Friday evening and Daisy's nan, Pat, was in a rush. She slid the bread under the grill and called Oscar and Daisy for their tea. There was a moment's lull in the squabbling. In the half-hour before Lilith was due home from work Pat had to pack Oscar's overnight bag, iron a blouse, change for her line dancing, make tea and clear up from tea. She called them again, turned the bread over, added some sliced cheese to it, and slid it back under the grill.

Oscar appeared silently by her side, giving her the fright of her life.

'I want to go home,' he informed her evenly.

She looked at him. 'Don't you want some cheese on toast?'

'No,' replied Oscar. 'I want to go home.'

She handed him some cutlery. 'Lay the table, please.'

'I want to go home,' he repeated.

'Yes, I heard you. Well, Daddy isn't home yet and your au pair's away, so I'm afraid you can't.' She handed him two table mats.

Daisy came in and plonked herself down at the table. Pat gave a warning cough and Daisy tutted, got up, pulled glasses out of a cupboard, and helped lay up huffily. Oscar had insisted they play sports games on her computer all afternoon and she was thoroughly sick of him.

'I want to go home,' he told the room in general.

'And I want to have a fag and a sit-down,' said Pat, shrugging. 'Life stinks. Once you work that out, it all gets a lot easier.'

Oscar stared at her. 'I want to go ho—'

'Yes, well,' interrupted Pat, 'I'm beginning to agree with you, but there's not a lot we can do about it, is there?'

'Yes there is,' said Oscar. 'You could take me home.'

'On what? My shoulders?'

Oscar frowned. 'No. In your car.'

'Sunshine,' said Pat, 'I don't drive. And even if I did, your daddy isn't home yet and your au pair's away. So it's not going to happen. So, I recommend you sit down, eat your cheese on toast and when Lilith gets home, tell her. All right?'

Oscar gave it a moment's thought. 'All right,' he mumbled.

Pat smelt burning, swore, and took out the cheese on toast. She put it on two plates and placed the plates in front of the children.

Daisy scowled at her tea. 'When's Mummy home?' she asked.

Pat sighed. 'My pleasure,' she muttered, wiping her hands on her apron.

'Thank you,' mumbled Daisy, leaving a polite pause. 'When's Mummy home?'

'Mum-*my*,' mocked Oscar.

'Mum,' corrected Daisy before kicking Oscar hard under the table and then swinging her legs up before he could kick her back.

Pat glanced up at the kitchen clock and then swore again. 'Ten minutes. When you've finished, Daisy, you wash; Oscar, you dry.' She'd have to wear a different blouse, there was no way she'd have time to iron the more flattering one. 'Right. I'm going to get changed now,' she said, taking off her apron. 'I want no arguing and no messing up the kitchen –'

When they heard the front door open and Lilith call out a greeting, the children leapt up.

'SIT DOWN!' shouted Pat. They sat down.

Lilith appeared in the kitchen doorway, coat still on. 'Hello, boys and girls!' she greeted them. 'How are we all?'

'I'm going to be late,' said Pat, squeezing past her and into her bedroom.

'Nan burnt the tea,' said Daisy accusingly. 'And Oscar wants to go home. And I want him to go home too. I've had to play cricket all afternoon.'

'I want to go home,' Oscar informed Lilith, his voice increasingly shaky.

Lilith looked at them both for a moment. 'Right,' she considered. 'Daisy, there are some children in the world who would kill for burnt tea. Oscar, I will phone your dad.'

'Good,' Oscar told Daisy, as Lilith went into the lounge. Daisy ignored him and stared at her burnt toast with hot, stinging eyes. Suddenly she flew up off her chair, knocking it on to the floor and followed Lilith into the lounge.

'I don't care about other children in the world!' she shouted at her mother.

Lilith stared in surprise at her daughter. Daisy was standing in the doorway, her fists clenched, her breathing heavy, her eyes defiant. Lilith knew she should probably be cross but the strongest emotion she felt at the moment was one of pure sympathy. It was a lousy answer to always give the kid, but she'd got stuck in a groove, like a bad record. She knew exactly where her girl's temper came from and understood only too well how wretched Daisy was feeling. She also knew that Daisy probably wanted to hit something very hard right now, and if she couldn't, it would feel like a waste of a filthy black mood. She must buy her a punch-bag for Christmas.

'I don't,' heaved Daisy, 'care about other children in the world! Bethany Jones has a trampoline in her garden! We don't even have our own garden! Oscar's got a whole playroom full of toys and a television and computer in his bedroom but he comes here and plays *his* stupid games on our shitty old –'

'That's enough, young lady –'

'THEN STOP TELLING ME TO COMPARE MYSELF TO OTHER CHILDREN!' yelled Daisy, her crying turning into convulsive sobs. Her legs started running on the spot as if they had a mind of their own and her body needed to expel something, but her arms remained fiercely by her side, probably to stop her from breaking something. Lilith hid her mouth with her hand as her daughter tried to exorcise her demons. By the time Daisy had ground to a slow stop, after executing some fine knee jerks, Lilith had composed herself. Finally Daisy stood still in the doorway, her breathing becoming even and her fists relaxing. Lilith paused before speaking.

'Thank you, Daisy,' she said. 'If I'd wanted to see *Riverdance*, I'd have paid for a coach tour.'

With a roar, Daisy stamped out of the room, slamming her bedroom door behind her. Lilith, feeling a great sense of motherly pride and empathy, knew her daughter would be feeling much better after that display, and so turned to the matter in hand. Taking off her coat and placing the keys on the coffee table, she dialled Mark's number.

'Mark Samuels,' announced Mark brusquely into the phone.

'Your son wants to go home. My daughter wants him to go home even more, which means I want him to go home even more than that. Come and pick him up NOW or you will officially lose your free childcare facility.'

There was a moment's pause. She could almost hear Mark swivelling his chair away from his colleagues.

'I *can't*,' he hissed into the phone.

'Yes you can,' she hissed back.

'How?'

'You can stand up and walk out of that fucking office where you spend more time than your home and be with your son. I mean, last time I looked, you were his father.'

'Lilith,' hissed Mark, 'I do not have time for this. Nor do I have any choice about it. I –'

'No, *I* do not have time for this,' she cut in fiercely. 'And he is *your* child, not mine. And don't you dare talk to me about *choice*. Your life is full of choices, because you are a man in a man's world, and you are rich in a rich man's world, so don't talk to me about choice. Believe it or not, you are not the only single parent in the world with a fucking job.'

Mark tried to interrupt, but she was on a roll.

'Now correct me if I'm wrong,' she continued, 'but I don't remember us ever getting married, so I don't need to take this self-obsessed, sexist, abandoning *shit* from you. Come

148

and get your son NOW and make three people happy instead of just you for a change. Or I am putting him out on the street so that my daughter can have the fraction of our tiny little flat that she calls home to herself again.'

'I'm not *happy* with this –' exploded Mark into the phone, but she'd hung up.

She slammed the phone down and whizzed round. She saw a pale-faced Oscar standing by the door.

She smiled grimly. 'Daddy's coming home soon, sweetheart.'

Oscar turned and walked away.

8

A warm, fidgety body snuggled into bed next to Mark. Mark smiled and turned lazily away, flat on his back, so his son didn't get a premature lesson in how the adult male's body worked. He forced himself to stop visualising curvy women with long, corkscrew hair and snug, tight jeans, and when done, stretched out his hand to touch his boy on the arm. The years of cuddling up together in bed were long gone, but sometimes, if Mark played it right, Oscar didn't move away. This morning, Oscar turned his head towards his dad and they lay there with their eyes shut for a while. Eventually Mark risked it and opened his eyes. Oscar was staring at him, his eyes almost questioning.

He smiled at his son.

'Hello, Osc,' he croaked.

'Hi.'

'We've got the whole day to ourselves. What do you want to do?'

'Go swimming!' said Oscar.

Mark visualised curvy women with long, corkscrew hair and snug, tight swimming costumes. He swivelled his hips away from Oscar. 'You're on,' he said. 'Give me five – no, ten – minutes and I'll catch you up downstairs.'

Oscar cheered.

True to his word, ten minutes later Mark shuffled downstairs for breakfast. While Oscar ate toast and stared vacuously at vividly coloured, violent TV cartoons, Mark picked up the post from the front-door mat. Whenever he did this he got a snapshot of Oscar the toddler running to the post and thrusting it, crumpled and torn, into Helen's hands with the proud words, ''Ost, Mama.'

He wandered back into the kitchen, filled the espresso machine and stood at the counter. He didn't think twice before opening the brown envelope with the typed address on it – all his letters were bills of some kind. But he stopped when he realised what he was reading:

Dear Mr Samuels,

I do hope you don't mind me contacting you in this unorthodox manner, but I am increasingly concerned that Oscar is the only child in my class who has, at present, no one representing him at Parents' Evening.

As you know, Oscar is now in Year 6, and next year he will be commencing secondary education. Both myself and Heatheringdown's headmistress, Miss James, feel that it would be appropriate for you to attend this Parents' Evening, so that you feel fully involved in your son's education at this crucial time.

The evening begins at 6.30 p.m. and ends at 8 p.m. and we feel that this timing should allow for all parents to attend, however tight their business or work schedules might be.

I do look forward to seeing you there.

Kind regards,
Miss N Hobbs

Mark stared at the letter, incredulous. He was being *told* to come to Parents' Evening.

Right, he thought. Oh boy, was he going to be there. And he was going to give this interfering bitch the biggest rocket up her fanny she'd ever had in her life. What did she know about bringing up a child? He hadn't slept a full night in six months because he was working so hard to give his son the life he deserved. He bet this old cow hadn't worked a *proper* full day in her long, dull life.

He was still fuming when they got to the pool an hour later.

After he and Oscar had held hands and jumped into the deep end, screaming 'Geronimo!' as tradition insisted, Mark decided to use this opportunity to find out more about Miss Hobbs. When they came up from their jump, they trod water opposite each other, letting the cool water splash over their shoulders. Mark decided now was as good a time as any. It was even worth ruining the perfect moment.

'Osc,' he started, 'tell me about your famous Miss Hobbs.'

He prepared himself for a sudden change in the mood, a sulk maybe, or just a tight-lipped monosyllabic grunt. But to his amazement, Oscar's face lit up.

'She's great, Dad,' said Oscar. 'I love her. She hasn't got a mum either.'

'*What?*' said Mark. 'How on earth do you know that?'

'She told me.'

'She told you she hasn't got a mother? Just you or the rest of the class? When?'

'The first day, she came and sat down next to me on the pavement outside school. It was cool.'

'You mean . . . the first day of term?'

'Mm.'

'After school?'

'Mm.'

'How come?'

Oscar shrugged. 'I said. She came and sat with me. On the pavement. It was cool.'

'So . . . let me get this straight. She followed you out and started telling you intimate stuff about her private life?'

Oscar nodded. ''Spose.' He dived off backwards into the pool.

Jesus Christ, thought Mark. This was serious. How insane was this woman? And why was she seeking out his son?

'You *have* got a mother, Osc,' he started, swimming after his boy. 'She's just . . .'

' . . . in heaven, I know,' said Oscar, through the water. He let himself float away from his dad. Mark followed.

'Has she been nagging you about Parents' Evening, Osc?'

Oscar kept his eyes down. He mumbled a yes, and Mark persisted.

'Has she been . . . annoying you?'

He shrugged. 'A bit.'

'How often does she mention it? Every day?'

Oscar laughed. 'At least.'

'Right,' said Mark, decided. 'I'll be there at Parents' Evening.' Oscar's face shone back at him. 'And I'll find out all about your Miss Hobbs. Don't you worry, young man!'

'Yippee!' yelled Oscar, and splashed his dad to celebrate.

Mark's face was grim as he watched his son swim away from him. Now he had to work out how to leave work early enough to make it to the school before the 8 p.m. deadline.

Meanwhile, a few yards away in the ladies' changing room, Nicky drew back the plastic curtain, looked down at her eldest niece and did a double take.

'Cherub,' she said in shock, 'you'll get us arrested.'

Claire had phoned her an hour previously, in a state of desperation. She needed to buy Abigail some new school shoes before Monday, because some bully had nicked hers. (Nicky knew how much Abigail hated her shoes, but kept mum.) Claire had managed to fob Isabel off on Derek, which made a change, but Sarah-Jane was refusing to join either and was insisting she spend the morning with Aunty Nix.

Secretly, Nicky was rather relieved. She'd been getting depressed at how much her work was eating into her spare time, and she desperately needed to get out of her place. And a spot of exercise would do her the world of good, clear her brain. Especially at that posh pool near her sister's place, where the changing rooms didn't make you want to rush round with a mop before taking off your clothes.

'OK,' she had told her sister, 'I'll take her swimming, on one condition.'

'Anything,' Claire promised.

'Afterwards, over a big bottle of wine, you listen to my sordid little love-life problem and help me sort my head out.'

Claire cheered so loudly down the phone Nicky had to move it away from her ear.

So now, here she was, staring at her niece, feeling suddenly old.

'When the hell did you grow up?' she asked.

Sarah-Jane laughed. 'Shut *up*.'

'No, really,' said Nicky. 'Last time I looked, you were in nappies.'

They walked through to their lockers.

'You do realise that if you go out like that, I'm going to have to follow you round as your chaperone?' said Nicky.

Sarah-Jane snorted.

'I'm telling you,' said Nicky, 'I'll be beating them off with a stick.' She looked around the changing room muttering, 'Now, where can I find a stick?'

Sarah-Jane bent down to pick up her towel.

'Whoa!' cried out Nicky. 'Since when did they make bikini bottoms out of string?'

Sarah-Jane laughed again, blushing furiously.

'Sarah-Jane, chuck, I'm seriously concerned. You'll have old men following you round the pool.'

Sarah-Jane stopped smiling. 'Really? That's horrid.'

She held her niece by the shoulders and walked her over to a full-length mirror. They looked at each other in the mirror and smiled. Sarah-Jane was only half a head shorter than her.

'You are a beautiful girl,' Nicky told her niece. Sarah-Jane beamed. 'But, sweetheart, you're dressed like a woman. You're only ten years old.'

'And a half.'

'And a half. Sweetheart,' she said softly, 'you look like a sixteen-year-old.'

Sarah-Jane's mouth opened and her eyes sparkled. Nicky spoke softly.

'A sixteen-year-old hussy.'

The sparkle in her eyes moistened.

'And you've got the rest of your life to look like a sixteen-year-old hussy.' She winked and Sarah-Jane smiled. 'Do you have a different swimming costume on you?' she asked gently.

Sarah-Jane nodded. She had the school one her mother had packed. She went and changed into it. When she pulled back the curtain, Nicky wolf-whistled.

'Shall we get some jewellery beads afterwards? We can make a bracelet,' she said. Sarah-Jane nodded enthusiastically.

By the time they reached the edge of the enormous pool, it was almost full.

'Remember,' warned Nicky, 'I'm a bit short-sighted. I can't see further than that column over there. Don't go too far.'

And Sarah-Jane dived off, splashing Nicky in the face. Nicky edged to the nearest steps down into the pool and started a slow, even breaststroke along its edge.

She didn't hear Oscar at first because her ears were too full of water. But after a moment, she realised that the wildly gesticulating boy in front of her was him. She squealed back at him and gave his cheek a little pinch. She somehow felt it wouldn't be appropriate for her to get too close – not while wearing a bikini. She trod water, keeping everything under-water except her face.

'I'm here with my dad!' cried Oscar.

'Oh, really?' replied Nicky. 'Fantastic! Perhaps I could say a quick hello!'

Oscar's face brightened. 'I'll go and get him. He's coming to Parents' Evening!'

'That's wonderful! I'll wait here.'

Oscar dived off and swam away at great speed. As she waited, Nicky did wonder if this was the best way to finally meet Oscar's father, seeing as she was basically wearing brightly coloured underwear. She scrunched up her eyes to see where Oscar was, but he'd gone out of her visual range. She leant on the edge of the pool, and scanned the slightly blurred faces over at the deep end. She wondered which of the men was Oscar's father.

At first, Mark didn't understand what Oscar was saying.

'Miss Hobbs is here!' yelled Oscar through the water. 'Miss Hobbs is here! I've just seen her! She wants to meet you! Miss Hobbs! She's here! She wants to meet you!'

When the words finally started making sense to Mark, he almost wet the pool. This was not the place to feel superior enough to give a teacher a rocket. For a start, he was wearing his swimming trunks. God only knew what she'd be wearing. A Victorian bathing costume, hopefully, under a dress. Secondly, he needed to prepare himself before coming face to face with any teacher, let alone Oscar's. He'd never liked teachers, had always been petrified of them, and age had not done anything to improve his fear. Just the smell of class-rooms made him want to puke. Thirdly, he knew it was going to be ugly when he met her and he didn't want Oscar to see him scrape the floor with someone the boy liked. Or worse, he didn't want Oscar see him dissolve in front of some old harridan.

Oscar stopped splashing and looked at his dad.

'Dad?'

Mark just shook his head. 'There's a time and a place, Osc. And this is neither. I'm sure she'll understand.'

Oscar didn't even bother to argue. He just turned his back, muttered 'I knew it', and swam away. Mark also turned his back and tried to swim into the densest patch of people. The last thing he wanted was for the old bat to spot him and come and find him.

By the time Nicky could finally distinguish Oscar swimming into her range of vision and saw that he was by himself, she was not remotely surprised. What had she expected? His father carrying him proudly on his shoulders, beaming with love, and laughing at his good fortune in meeting the woman who spent every day with his son?

'Sorry,' said Oscar. 'Um, I couldn't find him.'

They both knew he was lying. Nicky even wondered if he'd made up the fact that his dad was here at all. He was probably here with Daisy and Lilith again.

She gave him her best smile.

'Not to worry,' she said, her voice upbeat. 'Probably not the best place to meet him anyway.'

'Yeah, that's what he said.' Oscar nodded eagerly.

She and Oscar made a sad little parting and she went back to swimming her even widths amidst the chaotic Saturday-morning crowd. After a while, she decided it was time to get out and started to look for Sarah-Jane.

'Why don't you go on the wave tunnel?' Mark asked Oscar. 'I'll catch you when you come out the bottom.'

'All right,' said Oscar glumly. 'You don't need to catch me though.'

'Yes I do! It'll be fun!'

'Dad.'

'Yes?'

'I'm ten.'

'Oh. Right. OK.'

'And then we can go home,' said Oscar. 'I can play on my PlayStation.'

'Fine.'

Oscar swam to the far end of the pool and Mark watched him till he was no longer discernable. He thumped the water with his fist. How come something always spoilt what little time they did have together? He swam to the edge and heaved himself out. As he walked slowly to his towel he cast a glance over at the pool. He stopped in his tracks at the sight of a woman standing near one of the plastic tables and chairs, wearing a tight, multi-coloured bikini. He looked at her hair – the water had made it darker and straighter, but yes, it was curly. Corkscrew curly. And she was really *wearing* that bikini. It was packed with soft pale curves. He watched as she rung out her hair on the floor and a young girl, possibly the same age as Oscar, ran towards her from the pool and, resting her arm on the woman's hip – one of the most deliciously soft pale curves of all – started towel-drying herself off. He stared as she suddenly flung her head back, spraying water all around her. Then he turned away fast. As he did so, the sharp movement caught her attention. Nicky glanced over, away, and then quickly back again. She stared, towel in hand, at the man turning and walking away. She watched him as he disappeared, his broad shoulders slightly hunched and gleaming with water. The sandy-coloured hair was now wet and dark, but she knew it was the same. She took in all the finer details as quickly as possible. Long, taut legs, topped with clinging trunks which emphasised a bottom tight enough to eat in one; naturally wide, strong upper arms that alluded to healthy exercise rather than time spent pumping iron. She couldn't take her eyes off him until, gradually, his form lost its sharp edges and slowly grew fuzzy. She was now squinting at him. Then, to her horror, he suddenly turned halfway back towards her, as if he'd just realised he'd forgotten something. She whizzed back round, instinctively sucking in her stomach. Shit. He'd nearly seen her ogling. Heart beating a little faster, she clasped Sarah-Jane firmly by the shoulders and led her into the changing rooms, cursing the fact that you couldn't go swimming in heels, make-up and clothes.

9

'Right!' exclaimed Claire, her eyes bright. 'I want to hear everything. And I mean everything.'

'Oh dear,' muttered Nicky. 'I may have given you the wrong impression.'

'Oh?'

'Yes, that there's actually something to tell.'

'Just tell me. I can't bear the suspense.'

Nicky sighed. 'Well, actually, believe it or not, there's been another development since this morning.'

Claire squealed. 'Oh my God!' she said. 'This is almost as exciting as when I started using Ocado! Tell me everything!'

'I saw him again,' said Nicky dramatically. 'Today. At the pool.' She paused for dramatic effect. 'In his trunks.'

Claire paused. 'Who?'

'*Him!*'

Claire's eyes widened. 'Who?' she demanded. 'Who?'

Nicky sighed deeply.

'*WHO?*' repeated Claire.

'The bloke I saw the same evening I kissed Rob,' Nicky told her melancholically.

As Claire's jaw almost dropped into her wine, Nicky's head dropped into her hands.

'Do you mean to tell me,' asked Claire quietly, 'that you're spending your mental energy on someone you've only *seen* instead of on someone you could actually . . . you know . . . play Fill My Sandwich with?'

'Mummy?' came Sarah-Jane's voice from the doorway. Nicky and Claire spun round. Three little faces stared at them. 'Whose sandwich is being filled?' asked Sarah-Jane.

'I want to choose my filling!' cried Abigail.

'GO TO BED!' shouted Claire. 'NOW! Mummy's having *me* time. She's off duty. Daddy will read you a bedtime story.'

'Daddy's asleep on Isabel's bed,' said Sarah-Jane, crossing her arms. 'And anyway, he's hopeless at reading stories. Absolutely hopeless.'

'What am I going to do?' moaned Nicky to Claire. 'I'm going to marry the wrong man, have children with him and then abandon my family for the right one and ruin everyone's life.'

'GO TO BED!' shouted Claire at the girls.

'We miss all the fun,' mumbled Sarah-Jane, as she stomped back upstairs, pushing her younger sisters ahead of her.

'I want peanut butter and banana in mine,' said Isabel.

'Bleagh,' said Abigail. 'That's disgusting. I want cream cheese and jam.'

Claire looked up at Nicky. 'I can't even be crude in my own house.'

Nicky stared at her. '"Play Fill My Sandwich with"?' she repeated, slowly.

Claire started laughing. 'The walls have ears in this house. I was trying to say it without saying it.'

Nicky snorted. 'What with? Mother-of-three rhyming slang?'

'Don't change the subject,' said Claire. 'What the hell is going on with you and Rob?'

'Well, that's just the problem,' said Nicky. 'I was absolutely convinced that it was over.'

'Why?'

'Because we had this amazing kiss –'

'Oh yeah, that sounds over –'

'– and I genuinely didn't want to take it any further. I was completely and utterly unmoved. Emotionally, I mean; physically, I was a wreck. But then the next day, when I was bracing myself to confront him and tell him that I was only interested in him as a friend, blah blah blah, the bastard beat me to it.'

'Bastard!'

'And I felt . . . strangely disappointed.'

Claire held Nicky's hand across the table.

'Nix,' she said softly, 'how do you feel about him?'

Nicky moaned. 'I get motion sickness just thinking about him. The thing is, we finally kissed as adults, not as hormonal teenagers, and there were absolutely no fireworks. Fact. So. It's over.'

Claire let out an almost hysterical burst of laughter. 'Fireworks?' she cried. 'What the hell have fireworks got to do with anything? That *is* adult kissing! Real love isn't about fireworks. It's about safety, security, trust, respect and sharing a mortgage.'

Nicky looked at her sister. 'Oh well, that's really won me over,' she muttered, pouring herself more wine.

'I'm sorry,' Claire firmly told her sister, 'but it's a no-brainer.'

'Good,' muttered Nicky. 'That should help.'

'This is what you have to do,' Claire said. 'Listen to me. You have to stop fantasising about strangers who have wives and children of their own, however "floppy" their hair is and "wide-set" their "blue-green" eyes are. You have to follow all your gut instincts and go for Rob, have two – possibly three – children with him, and live Happily Ever After.' Claire finished her glass of wine. 'You're simply too fussy, Nix, that's why you're still single.'

Nicky stared.

'Look at this kitchen,' demanded Claire suddenly.

Nicky frowned. 'Eh?'

'Look at it.'

Nicky looked round the kitchen.

Claire spoke without taking her eyes off Nicky. 'Couple of dodgy doors coming off the hinges, sink's too small, no dishwasher. But! It's still a kitchen – *my* kitchen – and it's a hell of a sight better than no kitchen at all. Where would I be with no kitchen?'

'In a restaurant?' tried Nicky.

'And it's exactly the same with men,' concluded Claire. 'You may think you're holding out for the Smegging dishwasher, but the fact is you just haven't got one.'

'I have got a kitchen,' said Nicky. 'And a dishwasher. And it's a Smeg.'

'I'm talking metaphorically, Nick.'

Nicky decided now was not the time to tell her sister she

164

was talking out of her metaphorical arse. Claire was still talking.

'The point is,' she continued, 'you're holding out for a fantasy figure, when a perfectly decent, serviceable man – who happens to be particularly pleasing on the eye – is staring you in the face, and if you don't snap him up quickly, someone else will and that will be that. And you'll be alone, while someone else happily compromises with the man who was meant to be yours.'

'You mean,' said Nicky gravely, 'someone else will be having their sandwich filled by him?'

Claire nodded firmly. 'And their tiles grouted.'

'Ooh.'

'And their patio laid.'

'Nice.'

'And their borders hoed.'

'Phew.'

'And their light bulbs changed, after only two sodding months of nagging. By the way,' said Claire, 'while we're on the subject, if you don't ask the girls to be your bridesmaids, I'll never talk to you again.'

Nicky stared at her sister. Next time she'd tell Ally instead, sod the consequences.

'What are you looking at me like that for?' demanded Claire.

Nicky kept on staring.

'*What?*'

'Nothing,' said Nicky quietly.

The morning of Parents' Evening arrived all too soon, and Mark stumbled past his team's empty desks, his briefcase slung across his shoulder, one grande coffee cup in each hand. Feeling bleary-eyed and bitter, he stared crossly up at the clock. Its two stubby black hands told him it was 6.30 a.m. God, he hated that clock. It ruled his life and the lives of all who sat beneath it like an industrial-age foreman. He had seen it in more positions than he had ever seen any clock in his own home. How many times had he seen it for twenty-four hours in a row? he wondered. Countless.

But not tonight. Tonight he was leaving at seven sharp. Less than thirteen hours from now. And his team could lump it. Send the stress down the line and fuck off to the pub, as one of his colleagues always said when they drank together.

Mark heard a noise from the floor and, dropping his briefcase where he stood, knelt down beside the sleeping forms of Danny and Matt.

'Morning,' said Mark. 'Thought you'd like coffee.'

Danny rolled over and yawned. Matt groaned. 'Thanks, boss,' said Danny. 'What time is it?'

'Only 6.30. Plenty of time.'

When the door opened behind them, they turned round. Anna-Marie gave them all a polite smile.

'Morning, boys! Croissants for all!'

Nearly twelve hours later, Mark stared through the wide-open door of his corner office at his team. They were working silently and furiously. It felt like they'd all only just got properly stuck in. He could swear the office clock went at double speed. He lifted his eyes to it. It was now approaching six o'clock and he still hadn't told them he'd be leaving early tonight. He looked over at Anna-Marie. Her brow was furrowed over some paperwork he knew she was desperately trying to finish before passing it on to him to check, so that they could bike it over to the client before tomorrow. How could he possibly walk past her and out of the office as early as 7 p.m.? Perhaps he could crawl? He winced. Jesus, this was ridiculous. He was a partner now. At only thirty-three years old. A future guru, if he didn't have a heart attack before his fortieth. What was the point of being at the top if you couldn't leave early once a year with a clear conscience? He pictured Oscar's frightened little face being shadowed by the galleon-shape of some battle-axe's bust.

The client would just have to wait.

There was only one thing for it. It wasn't fair, he knew, but there was no other way round it. He picked up his mobile and speed-dialled.

Ten past six and Nicky was just popping her head round all the teachers' doors to check that they were ready and didn't need anything.

'Yes thanks,' Amanda told her tightly. 'I've done this before. But I'll call if I need you to hold my hand.'

There were times when Nicky hated being Deputy Head. However, she had found it really interesting to see how differently each teacher ran their own private Parents' Evening. The entire teaching staff spent the two evenings that constituted Parents' Evening sitting in their classrooms while being visited by parents at specifically arranged ten-minute slots. Nicky had always assumed that there was only one way to carry this out – the way she did it: the teacher would sit on one of the pupil's chairs and provide two more pupils' chairs for the parents and they would all sit together at the same height, around a pupil's desk. That way every-one felt on the same level and could chat as freely and openly as possible. But to her amazement, she discovered that one or two teachers stayed seated almost regally behind their higher desk and offered the parents two pupils' tiny chairs to sit on in front of them. Some perched on the edge of their desk, towering over the parents even more, while creating the illusion of trying to appear informal, and others sat in front of it, but still on their own higher chair. Others sat on top of a child's desk, and only a few like Nicky sat themselves down on the children's chairs. The question that occurred to her was whether or not these teachers were aware of how such seemingly subtle seating arrangements might make some parents feel? If they were aware of it, then they were playing nasty power games and were probably masking deep insecurity. If this was so, then the last job they should be doing was teaching vulnerable children for a whole year. If they weren't aware of it, then they were social idiots and, probably, the last job they should be doing was teaching.

Then there was the time-keeping aspect of the evening. With only ten minutes for each set of parents it was a night of rigorous clock-watching for every single teacher, but Nicky just assumed that they would be sensitive to the fact that those precious ten minutes felt very different to the parents than to them, and the most insensitive thing they could do would be to highlight this impersonal aspect of the evening. So, again, she was concerned to see that some teachers actually brought in large clocks from home and placed them on their desk with their backs to the parents. A few even set an alarm to go off every ten minutes. Others still took off their watches and laid them on top of their notes, leaving no one in any doubt of their priorities for the evening. Such tiny details, but so revealing.

When she popped her head round Pete's door, she found him sitting on one of his pupil's chairs, reading a book and biting his nails. He spotted her, pulled a funny face and waved his arms around. He looked about ten years old.

When she popped her head round Ally's door, they shared a grimace. Ally was slumping cross-legged on a child's desk.

'Is that how you sit?' asked Nicky.

''Course not,' said Ally, looking up brightly. 'As soon as they come in I spring up and do a little tap-dance before the slide show.'

'Sorry,' said Nicky. 'It's just fascinating to see how differently everyone does it.'

Ally nodded as she moved to sit on one of the pupil's chairs. 'Has Amanda turned on her spotlights and mirrors yet?'

'Practically,' said Nicky. 'Talk about war paint. Blimey.'

'Yeah. She's the kind of woman who gives make-up a bad name.'

After Nicky left Ally, she popped her head round Rob's door before nipping back into her own room. She stared. He was sitting behind his own desk, two tiny pupils' chairs placed in front it. On his desk sat the largest alarm clock she'd seen yet, its back to the parents' chairs, ticking so loudly she could barely hear herself judge him. He was leaning back in his chair, hands behind his head, humming.

'Hiya,' she called out. He started.

'Hi.' He grinned. 'All set?'

'I think so.'

'Looking forward to seeing the lesser spotted Mr Samuels?'

'Not really.'

'Attagirl.'

'Hello, hello, hello, hello, hello, hello, hello!' came a voice from behind her.

She turned to Miss James.

'I'm taking orders,' Miss James announced, pen and pad in hand. 'Tea or coffee, custard creams, Bourbons or digestives?'

'Yes please,' said Nicky.

Lilith heard her phone buzz just as she was shutting her front door behind her. She cursed loudly and dropped her bag to the floor. She was already late for Daisy's Parents' Evening, which meant another set of parents – or mothers, who was she kidding? – would slip in in front of her and she'd end up paying more babysitting money.

She delved into her bag, furiously grabbing its contents and dropping them out one by one, until everything but the phone was littered around her. By the time she found her phone, it had stopped ringing, as it always had, but she snapped it open anyway. As she stuffed everything back into her bag and hurried to the bus stop, she read the message. It was a text from Mark.

Call me. It's urgent.

How utterly predictable, she thought. Damn, she should have bet him good money he wasn't going to make tonight. It would have covered tonight's babysitter. Well, she was damned if she was going to call him. And she was not going to be a go-between between another teacher and him again. She hadn't minded so much with Mr Pattison, but Miss Hobbs was not her type. No. He could whistle for it. She reached the bus stop, pulled down a seat and sat on it. She hunched in the cold and tapped her foot as she waited for the bus.

'Sugar?' Miss James asked Nicky.

'She's sweet enough already,' answered Rob.

'No sugar, thanks.' Nicky smiled, feeling the first twinges of a headache coming on.

'Now,' said Miss James, clutching her order pad to her chest, 'I will probably get your teas and bickies to you by about seven, as I'm starting with Year 1. Are you both all right with that?'

'Of course!' chanted Nicky and Rob.

'I knew you would be,' said Miss James. 'I know I can always rely on you two. Well done, well done, well done, well done. Now, I've asked everyone how their timetables and marking are and they've all promised me that they are in excellent order. The key question to ask you two is . . . can I trust them all to be telling the truth?' She turned to them, and they both nodded, Rob more energetically than Nicky. There was no way Nicky would admit that she couldn't answer for Amanda who had refused to reveal her term's marking. Even Gwen had been more obliging than her. Ned had practically shown her every page. Again, she'd been amazed at how different his teaching methods were from hers. Every single page had so many comments on it, it was a wonder Ned had time to go to the toilet. No wonder his wife made him his sandwiches every day. They became aware of two people standing behind them and found themselves facing a couple who had arrived early for their ten minutes with Mr Pattison. Rob leapt to his feet and thrust his hand forward for a hearty shake. The parents approached him and Nicky and Miss James bid a hasty farewell.

Lilith looked at her watch again. The bus was now twenty minutes late. Oh sod it, she thought. The only way to get the bus to come was to phone Mark. And she might as well hear his excuse. Giving him a good old bollocking might alleviate the strain in her neck. She dialled his number and was surprised not to have to wait for him to pick up. He answered with his name immediately in a loud, efficient bellow.

'It's me,' she told him through pursed lips.

'OH *HI!*' he yelled into her ear. 'How *are* you? Long time no speak!'

'What?'

'I'm *fine* thanks,' he continued to bellow. 'How are you?'

Lilith frowned and moved the phone away from her ear to stare at the number she'd dialled, to check it was correct. Yes, it was. She put the phone back to her ear.

'Are you drunk, Mark?' she asked.

There was silence.

'Mark?'

'Oh. My. God,' she heard him say in a hushed whisper.

'*What?*' she asked.

'You're . . . *joking?*' he was still using the hushed whisper.

She stood up and started pacing.

'Mark,' she clipped, 'if I was joking you'd be laughing. What the fuck's going –'

'I-I-I . . . I just, I can't believe it,' Mark talked over her.

Lilith paused. She could hear him making mmhm noises down the phone at her silence.

'No,' she sighed eventually. 'Neither can I.'

'I only saw her last week.'

'Goodbye, Mark.'

'Of *course*,' she heard. 'I'll come immediately.'

'So I've heard,' she said tartly, and hung up.

Nicky looked up from her notes at the next parents who had just come in and pulled her face into a smile. She felt a familiar taut throb pulse from her temples down the side of her cheekbones and along the back of her jaw. She was getting one of her heads.

'Hello!' she greeted them softly. 'I'm Miss –'

'What's all this about uniforms?' said the woman, sitting down next to Nicky in a chair the size of her hand. Nicky raised her eyebrows, which hurt. Why were parents always obsessed with what their children wore? And who spread these false rumours anyway?

She gave them a small but kind smile.

'Ever since I've been teaching here,' she began softly, 'there has been a consistent rumour that we are about to introduce school uniforms. Let me put your minds at rest.' She looked at them both. 'We are not about to introduce school uniforms.'

'Good,' tutted the woman, 'because we'd take Anemone out of here in the blink of an eye. We didn't spend £7,000 on stamp duty to have to start buying school uniform.'

Nicky nodded sympathetically, and a thudding pain shot through the base of her skull.

She looked down at Anemone's notes on her lap. She slowly looked up again and fixed them with a grin, which hurt her gums.

'Your Anemone is a very . . .'

She fought for a positive word to describe their daughter. Tall?

She licked her lips.

'. . . she's a very . . . *forceful* character –'

They beamed.

'. . . whose presence,' she continued, 'is *always* felt in the classroom.'

They exchanged smiles.

'And although this is a *wonderful* trait,' continued Nicky, 'in many, *many* ways, I do feel that . . . just *sometimes* . . . through no fault of her own . . . this can come across to others as . . . possibly a bit *too* forceful.'

'HAH!' said Anemone's mother, forcefully. 'No such thing in my book.'

'Ri-ight,' said Nicky. She looked back down at her notes.

'How's her maths?' asked Anemone's father.

Nicky smiled at him. 'Sometimes,' she gave a little laugh, 'it's more creative than her English.'

They smiled proudly again.

Nicky relaxed her jaw and felt some of the pain ease.

Mark stood at his desk, briefcase in hand, staring angrily at Caroline, his PA.

'Tell him I've gone,' he said for the first time in his life.

Caroline looked at her watch. 'At seven in the evening? A week before deadline?'

Mark sighed. 'All right, all right. Tell my cab I'm coming. Put the bastard on.'

Caroline nipped back to her desk and put the client through on the phone before calling down to Ray, the firm's favourite cabbie, who was parked outside.

Mark waited for the phone to connect him.

'Peter!' he cried. 'What can I do for you?'

'Reuters have been on to us. There's been a whisper. We're going to have to bring the deadline forward.'

Mark slumped in his chair. Not tonight. Any night but tonight. 'How early?'

'Tomorrow.'

'Shit.'

'Noon at the latest.'

Mark put down the phone and thought for a moment. He walked into the general office.

'Listen up, listen up.' Four sallow faces looked up, while the juniors knew it was more than their careers' worth to stop working. 'It's going to be an all-nighter for everyone,' announced Mark. 'Deadline's shifted forward to 10 a.m. tomorrow morning. Reuters know.' The room was thick with cursing. Mark went on. 'I want everything on my desk by midnight. If it's not there, Matt, I'll want to know why.'

'When will you be back?' asked Matt.

Mark glanced at his watch. 'As soon as I've bollocked my kid's schoolteacher. Within a couple of hours.'

As he walked through the office, he heard Matt passing the shit down behind him.

10

Nicky raised her head slowly at the next parent hovering in the doorway and instead saw Miss James standing stock-still, staring intently at a cup of tea in her hand, the tip of her tongue peeping out of her mouth in concentration. Then she approached rather unsteadily, crouched down slowly and placed the tea carefully on the pupil's desk where Nicky was sitting. Then she put up a finger as if to halt applause and, with great aplomb, pulled out two crumbly pieces of broken Bourbon biscuit from her cardigan pocket, and popped them on to the saucer.

'I know you said custard creams, my love,' said Miss James, 'but we've run out. Between you and me, I think someone in the *environs* has stolen a whole packet. And between you and me, it's Amanda. No one's more surprised than me. I mean, where does she put them, with legs like that? If ever there was proof that life is unfair . . . anyway,' she perched on the desk, 'I saw them in her drawer when she took out a coaster for her cup and saucer. I don't know which surprised me more, her stealing an entire packet of custard creams or thinking that her desk needs a coaster for a cup. On reflection, I think it's the custard creams. Anyway, no matter. How are you doing, dear girl? Has the lovely Mr Samuels turned up yet?'

Nicky managed a shake of her head. She was gasping for tea. Not just because she was gasping for tea, but because she now had something to take her headache pills with. She took out three, sipped her hot tea and scalded her tongue, but the relief of knowing that pain relief was on its way more than made up for it. Miss James was about to continue talking when a mother appeared at the doorway. She leapt up off the desk, spilling Nicky's tea, and bounded out, patting the mother on the arm as she passed, as if the mother was about to take Grade 1 piano exam. Which might have explained why the mother then entered the room looking exactly as if she was about to take Grade 1 piano exam.

Mark shut his eyes and cursed inwardly. Ray glanced at him in the rear-view mirror.

'Sorry, Mr Samuels,' he said. 'There's been a pile-up in Islington and the tailback's right through to the City. It might actually be faster by tube.'

Mark couldn't believe his ears.

'Five people died, apparently,' continued Ray. 'Shocking business. Drunk driver. They should bring back capital punishment. That would stop the buggers.'

'How long do you think it's going to take?' asked Mark.

Ray sighed long and loud. 'Forty minutes? Possibly half an hour.'

Mark sat back. 'That's fine,' he said and fell asleep.

Nicky forced herself up from her seat. Every hair on her head felt screwed in. She knew the painkillers had started to work because her limbs were now leaden, but the headache was unchanged, which meant she'd taken them too late. She was now only waiting for Mr Samuels and had miraculously managed to get ahead of her timetable by five valuable minutes. She was going to use every single one of them with her face under cold running water, or, if possible, uncorking her head and replacing it on a looser fitting.

As she left her classroom with measured steps, she glanced over into Rob's classroom. He was holding forth in front of two parents who looked like overawed children in their ridiculous-sized chairs. She frowned, but it hurt, so she stopped.

She pulled off her glasses. Nearly there, she thought, tiptoeing down the corridor.

Mark swore loudly in the back of the cab. Since when was the main entrance of a school closed to the public? How else were you supposed to get in?

'Absolutely typical,' he muttered to Ray. 'They insist you come to school and then make it as difficult as possible to succeed. Just like bloody exams.'

Ray chuckled.

'What's the time?' asked Mark.

'Ten to.'

'Right. We don't have time for this shit,' said Mark. 'Ignore the sign and drop me off outside the front door. If anyone bollocks you just tell them Miss Hobbs told you to do it.'

The car stopped, he leapt out, slammed the door shut and raced up the stairs to the front door of the school.

*

178

Nicky leant against the sink and looked at her reflection in the Ladies' cloakroom mirror. Two perfectly matched red patches under her eyes were all she had to show for such pain. She pulled the hair-band out of her hair. Respite was instant. Then she twisted the cold tap, slowly bent down over the sink, and cupped nearly freezing water on to her aching features.

It was official. Mark was lost. He had now passed the display board three times and knew without any shadow of a doubt that this was the Chinese Year of the Dog. He undid his tie as he ran, scanning each room for a sign on the door saying 6 and an old dragon sitting inside waiting to breathe fire on him.

Nicky watched her hand twist the cold tap until the water slowly stopped dripping. Her face was so cold she almost couldn't feel it. She hoped it would last all evening. She patted her cheeks softly with the paper hand-towel and stared at herself in the mirror, sighed long and low, and closed her eyes. Pain tunnelled into her skull from them. Surely someone was tightening her eyeballs in their sockets? She thought of everything she had to get through before the sweet oblivion of sleep.

Then she left the loos, closed the door behind her, and came face to face with the man from the fireworks display with floppy fair hair and wide-set blue-green eyes.

Mark stopped dead in his tracks. The girl from the fireworks display was standing right in front of him, and she looked even more amazing than before. Her skin was almost translucent, her eyes were bright and two perfect apples of pink highlighted her cheeks. Of course! She was a parent. The little girl with her at the swimming pool must be in Oscar's class.

'Hello!' he beamed.

'Hello,' Nicky breathed, putting great effort into a smile.

She didn't seem too pleased to see him, he thought. Maybe she didn't recognise him. Or maybe her husband was down the other end of a corridor.

'We met at the fireworks display –' he started.

'Oh yes!' she said, smiling a bit more. 'Of course. I remember.'

'I thought I was lost for a minute there,' he said. 'Thought I'd never leave this place alive.'

'Ooh, stuck in school! Horrid thought,' she said.

'Well, I wouldn't mind now,' he allowed.

Nicky's girlie bits went all girlie.

He held out his hand.

'I'm Mark. Pleased to meet you.'

She shook his hand.

'I'm Nicky.'

'Hi, Nicky.'

'Hi, Mark.'

They smiled.

'Well, well,' he said, slowly letting go of her hand. 'This is a pleasant surprise.'

'Thank you.' She smiled. 'Likewise.' They moved away from the wall and began to walk down the corridor together.

'So, did you enjoy the fireworks display?' he asked.

'Ooh yes,' she said. 'My favourite yet.'

180

He gave her an unmistakable look. 'Me too. Me too.'

To stop herself from giggling like a schoolgirl, she forced herself to remember that he had a family. 'Are you here for the Parents' Evening?' she asked.

The question had an immediate and dramatic effect. The smile went, the flirting stopped, and he sucked in his breath. 'Jesus, yes,' he said, suddenly grave. 'I'd managed to forget that. I had a three-line whip.'

'Oh,' she said. 'I see.' So. Not getting on with the wife.

'Yes,' he sighed. 'My boy's having problems with this nightmare teacher.'

'Oh!' Nicky was shocked. There had been a couple of complaints about Amanda's strict approach, but she had never heard her described as a nightmare before. If there were any complaints, she needed to know about them.

'I'm sorry to hear that,' she told him. 'Do you mind me asking what's wrong?'

By now they were approaching her classroom. She wondered briefly where he was going, but he seemed content to follow her lead.

'Oh,' he went on easily, 'nothing I can't handle. But the old bat's clearly using my boy as a substitute for her own lack of children. Desperate old spinster, you know the thing.'

'Oh,' murmured Nicky, fascinated. That didn't sound like Amanda. Maybe it was Gwen he was talking about.

They reached her door and both walked in, hovering inside the door.

'Tragic, really, when you think about it,' confided Mark. 'To be surrounded by children when you don't have your own. I suppose I should pity her instead of being angry. But I'll be giving her short shrift tonight.'

'Crikey,' said Nicky, shutting the door behind him before this got too personal. 'Sounds serious.'

'Well, yes it is. She actually –' he interrupted himself with a laugh – 'you won't believe this – but, she actually sent me a prissy, school-ma'am letter insisting – not asking – *insisting* that I come tonight.' He let out another laugh. 'Like I'm one of her pupils. I've had to leave the office specially. We're working through the night and I've left my whole team there. Unheard of. I'm a partner. It's absolutely unheard of.'

Nicky blinked.

'And that's not the half of it,' he continued. 'She invited my son round to her place on Hallowe'en without my permission – how inappropriate is that? I could probably get her suspended for that alone – she probably bought the sweets specially – God! It doesn't bear thinking about. And she cornered him outside school hours to tell him all about her own private life. He's only ten years old! God knows what she's doing to him emotionally.'

He looked at Nicky for reassurance. She was staring at him, wide-eyed. Reassured, he continued.

'You see, Oscar – that's my boy – hasn't got a clue. He's too young to pick up on these things. So he thinks she's the bee's knees. You know, loves him like the mother he doesn't have. Doesn't stop going on about her. You see, he's vulnerable; hasn't got a mum – I'm widowed – and of course she plays on that, doesn't she? Uses it to her advantage. Even tried to imply they were in the same boat because she hasn't got a mother either. Can you believe that? Here is a grown woman telling a ten-year-old boy that they can both be motherless together. If you ask me, the woman needs help.'

He looked at Nicky again.

182

'I wonder if you know her?' he asked suddenly. 'Miss Hobbs?'

Nicky felt the floor tilt slightly.

'Mr . . . Samuels?' she heard herself say. 'Isn't it?'

He gave her a surprised beam. 'Yes! Mark Samuels! How did you know?'

'Oscar's father?'

'Yes! That's right! Oscar Samuels! Do you know him? Cute kid, six freckles on his nose.'

Nicky put out her hand. Mark looked at it and then frowned at her.

'Perhaps we should begin again,' she said quietly.

He shook his head in bewilderment.

'I am Miss Hobbs,' she said faintly. 'Nicky Hobbs. Oscar's form teacher.'

Mark opened his mouth to speak, but it soon became clear to both of them that this was an empty gesture. A gargling noise came from the back of his throat, and then it stopped.

Nicky waited.

'I didn't –' he began. 'I –'

She raised an eyebrow.

'You're much –' he began again. 'Um –'

She raised her eyebrow higher.

'I –' he resumed.

'Well,' she said softly, 'it gives me a warm glow to be pitied by such an eloquent man.'

She scraped her hair back into a ponytail and whipped on her glasses.

'Oh,' he said in some alarm, stepping back slightly. 'Oh.'

'Mr Samuels,' she spoke quietly but firmly, 'no one forced you to come here tonight, but I am not remotely surprised,

183

from what I have already gleaned about you, that this enormous sacrifice you've made – for the first time since your son's been at the school – has been made under such duress.'

Mark started to open his mouth, but he was nothing if not a fast learner, so he shut it again fast.

'My "prissy, school-ma'am" letter,' continued Nicky, 'was written after considerable thought and concern, and, of course, with the consent of Heatheringdown's much-respected Headmistress. It was intended to be a kind, if last-ditch, attempt to create some glimmer of interest in your son's educational and emotional life.'

'How –' Mark's vocal chords gave a spasm.

'A son', she continued, 'who lives with a constant, daily awareness of the loss of not one loving, full-time parent, but two.'

Mark's voice gave a brief cameo appearance.

'As for your concerns about me, let me assure you,' she went on, 'I have not confided one detail of my private life to Oscar that is in any way unsuitable. It just so happened that I too lost my mother when I was a child, and had an emotionally absent father. Unlike Oscar, I was lucky enough to have an older sister who became my surrogate mother, but I know, to this day, as an adult, which parental loss pained and confused me most. An absent dead parent you can grieve, an absent living parent you never get over.'

Mark made a small guttural noise.

'When I happened to chance upon Oscar,' she continued, 'he was the last pupil to be picked up on the first day of a new school year. We have more than two hundred children at our school, Mr Samuels, and that includes some who live in care, some from traumatically broken homes, and some whose parents still live in war-torn parts of the world. Oscar was The Last Child to be picked up and taken home. Unsurprisingly, he was crying. He was also vandalising the school gates, while waiting for an au pair whom he hated and didn't even know the name of. I mentioned, briefly and in passing, my late mother, to allow him what I already felt (after knowing him for less than a day) might be a rare moment of adult empathy.'

Mark let out a low grunt.

'Now, to your next accusation. I did not "invite him round" on Hallowe'en. As it happened, earlier that day in school he told me that you were going trick-or-treating with him that night. Allow me to tell you just how excited your son was at the thought of spending one evening with you. He could barely concentrate in class. However, it just so happened that he, along with Daisy and her mother, rang on my doorbell at nine o'clock – hours after everyone else had stopped – because he was so determined for you to join them that he couldn't accept that you weren't going to. They were all exhausted and hungry after a long night out in the cold. I don't know how you'll feel to know about this, but I'm going to tell you anyway. Daisy showed absolutely no surprise when she found out that you weren't coming after all. She is ten years old. I asked them all in and so I happened to be there to pick up the pieces when you *texted* him to let him know that, yet again, you were going to let him down.'

Mark blew air out of his nose.

'You have a wonderful son, Mr Samuels. And you are right. I don't have any children of my own. But let me assure you, I would much rather not have any than bring one into a world I had no intention of sharing with them. I am very fond of your son, but I do not need your cast-offs, thank you very much.'

'CAST-OFFS? How *dare* y—'

'Well, what would you call it, Mr Samuels?' she shot, leaving Mark livid that when he had finally found his voice she hadn't let him finish using it. 'Leaving him chocolates on his pillow instead of being there for him? Abandoning him with another parent for days and nights on end –'

'I have to earn a fucking salary!' exploded Mark finally, glad to have found something he could say.

'Oh of course!' she exploded back. 'The all-important salary. That male substitute for love.'

'*What?*'

'Do you have any idea how many single mothers I've seen tonight? And not one of them needed a letter to force them to come.'

'WELL,' shouted Mark, determined to finish one full sentence, 'they've probably got some poor bastard working his balls off to pay them shitloads of alimony –'

'Oh, poppycock!' shot Nicky so ferociously that they both almost got whiplash. 'They hold down two jobs and still manage to put food on the table – literally – *and* be there for bedtime. The difference is, Mr Samuels, they know what being a parent means. Look it up in the dictionary some-time. It doesn't mention anything about a salary.'

'How *dare* you –'

'Oh I dare, Mr Samuels. I dare. The only tragedy is that, clearly, no one ever has before.'

They stared at each other.

'Oh and by the way,' she said primly, opening the

classroom door to indicate that their interview had concluded. 'We don't allow swearing in this school.'

With that, she turned her back on him and walked to her desk where she began to collect all her notes together.

Five minutes later, Nicky walked towards her car trying not to think about the fact that there was every chance she had just ruined her career. At this moment she just didn't care. All she wanted was bed.

Just then a taxi roared past her across the playground.

'Absolutely typical,' she muttered, as she saw who was in the back of it.

Mark looked away sharply from Miss Hobbs as the taxi sped out of school. The expression of contempt on her face was unmistakable even in the dark. When the taxi drew up outside his office he opened the door before it had stopped. Then he stood on the steps of his office staring up at the front door. He walked up the steps and came to a final stop at the top. After a full five minutes, he buzzed the door and pushed it open, muttering 'Poppycock' to himself and trying to find it ridiculous.

11

The sun peeked out at Mark from the edge of a neighbouring high-rise, promising a fine, bright winter's day. He
scrunched up his eyes, glanced at the clock and took out his
mobile.

'Wakey, wakey!' he sang into the phone, his voice raw
from lack of sleep.

'Wha— *Dad?*' came Oscar's morning voice.

'Hi, gorgeous boy. Sleep well?'

There was a beat.

'What's up?' asked Oscar.

'Nothing!' replied Mark. 'Just wanted to speak to you
before you went to school.'

He heard Oscar roll over and pictured him lying on
Lilith's sofa. He'd offered to buy a put-you-up for her flat –
which in effect would be for Oscar – but she'd always
adamantly refused it on the grounds that she didn't need
charity. But now that Oscar was growing so tall, surely she'd
have to agree that they needed to do something about the
sleeping arrangements. Maybe he should suggest bunk beds?

'Did you sleep well last night?' he asked.

'Mm.'

'What's on for today?'

'School.'

'I met Miss Hobbs last night.'

Oscar's voice was suddenly alert. 'Did you? What did you think? How am I doing?'

Mark smiled into the phone. 'You're doing fine, sweetheart. It's me she's got problems with.'

'What do you mean?'

Mark heard Caroline's phone ring and knew he had seconds left.

'I'll see you tonight,' he told his son. 'If you're asleep, I'll wake you and we'll have a midnight feast.'

Caroline popped her head round his door and he nodded at her.

'Bye, Osc. I love you.'

He pressed number 4 on his phone.

'Peter!' he said.

'So! So, so, so, so, so, so. What nuggets of information do you both have to tell me?'

Due to the longer post-Parents' Evening meeting, Rob and Nicky were to miss assembly today. Ned would be taking Miss James's place.

'Anything?' asked Miss James, staring from one to the other.

Nicky stopped breathing. Had Mr Samuels already complained? Was Miss James giving her a chance to confess all, before she had to extract last night's appalling behaviour from her? Her headache was, of course, still there, but less dramatic than yesterday, leaving just a thudding heaviness. Four-hourly painkillers and lots of water would see her through today. She knew it was on its way out because the sound of two hundred children rushing past Miss James's office on their way to assembly didn't physically hurt her cranium.

Miss James smiled at her two generals and then suddenly, without any warning, hurled herself towards the door.

'TOBIAS MATTHEWS!' they heard her yelling down the corridor. There was a pause. 'Don't think I didn't see you laughing all the way through yesterday's assembly, young man,' she said. 'Not really appropriate when we're talking about the benign graciousness of Our Lord Jesus Christ, is it?' There was another pause, as Tobias Matthews doubtlessly said a quiet no under the hubbub around him. 'None of that behaviour this morning, young man,' said Miss James, with only half a smile in her voice.

Then, just as suddenly as she'd leapt out of her seat, she returned to it, grinning from ear to ear. 'Now!' she said, rubbing her hands together. 'Where were we before that charming little interlude? Ah yes! Yes, yes, yes, yes, yes, yes, yes! Did we all have a *lovely* time meeting our lovely parents?'

Maybe, thought Nicky, just maybe, Mr Samuels hadn't had time to complain yet. Too busy at work, probably. She might even have an opportunity to right the wrong before it was too late. Hmm. When would be a good time to confess to bollocking a parent who had come to his first Parents' Evening in six years? Before, during or after puzzle time?

To the tinny sound of two hundred pupils singing an unrecognisable hymn, Nicky wished with a childish longing that she could watch Ned stumble over his lines instead of having to stumble over her own. This made her question for the umpteenth time that morning whether she was up to this job. When a sudden explosion of laughter came from the assembly hall, she had to forcibly stop herself from running out to see what had happened.

Even Miss James looked startled. 'Ooh!' she said. 'It all sounds very exciting in there, doesn't it?'

'I'm sure Ned's doing a wonderful job,' agreed Rob. Nicky nodded with them both, trying hard not to picture something more like the truth, such as his trousers having fallen down.

'Now!' began Miss James. 'Have you both managed to squeeze in a little tête-à-tête with your allotted teachers yet?'

They nodded.

How did she do it? thought Nicky with grim awe. How did Miss James always manage to make the jobs she gave them sound so inconsequential? 'Squeezing' in a 'little' chat with their allotted teachers had meant them coming in an hour and a half early, and everyone else coming in at least an hour early, which invariably meant great festering mounds of resentment from those teachers who had been doing Parents' Evenings since before Nicky and Rob had been out of school themselves. Even Ally had resented it and had turned up late.

And of course, as usual, there was nothing much to relay, except the usual frustration at the volume of SATS preparation and a perennial, unfounded paranoia that the school was about to instigate a uniform.

And a parent who was bollocked to within an inch of his life. She waited for Rob to finish his patter while pondering what career she'd have a stab at next. Pottery teacher? Traffic warden? Lollipop lady? She'd be a good lollipop lady. If she played her cards right, she might even get an OBE.

'Nicky? Where are you, my dear? You look miles away!' Miss James was smiling graciously at her. She wondered what the woman would look like angry. It came as somewhat of a shock to realise that she'd prefer it.

'And what of the notorious Mr Samuels?' asked Miss James. 'Did he make an appearance after your charming letter?'

Nicky decided this was as good a time as any to start a discussion on what had happened the night before.

'Ye-es –' she started.

'And?' asked Miss James, agog. 'And, and, and, and, *and*?'

'Nothing much to tell, really,' she said, her voice hollow. 'But at least he turned up.'

'Well done, my love!' sang Miss James. 'Consider yourself congratulated!' She thrust the biscuit tin under her nose and Nicky took a digestive without any sense of the usual pleasure.

She sat in silence for the rest of the meeting.

By noon Mark had opened the bubbly and the office was a mess. After his second glass, he poured himself a cup of water and walked shakily back into his office, shutting the door behind him. Champagne didn't usually have this effect on him, but then he wasn't getting any younger. He sat behind his desk and laid his head gently on it. He'd just stay here until bedtime.

'Mark?' Caroline was standing in the doorway to his office.

'Hm?' he gazed across the room at his personal assistant.

She stared pointedly back at him.

'Yes?' he croaked.

'Mark,' she whispered, 'you look absolutely dreadful.'

'I don't feel that great, actually,' he whispered. Caroline was seriously alarmed. In Mark Samuels speak that meant he needed hospitalisation.

'Right,' she said firmly. 'I'm calling you a taxi.'

He didn't have the energy to nod, let alone thank her.

Nicky couldn't shake off the feeling that something very bad was going to come out of her argument with Mr Samuels. She wanted to talk to Ally. She needed advice from a teacher who was also a friend. She needed someone else's take on whether she should confess to Miss James before the inevitable complaint came through. Or should she just act dumb when it did and say that he was overreacting?

But there was something even more disconcerting about the row than its possible negative repercussions. Mr Samuels's harsh accusation that she was overcompensating for not having her own children had set her off on a chain of depressing internal questioning. Was she going to end up being like that? After all, what was she actually doing to meet men? How often did she go out? Never. How many new people was she meeting? None. She spent all of her spare time working. And for what? For a job that she might have just thrown away.

And so she continued in ever-decreasing circles.

As soon as the gang reconvened at lunch, she asked Ally to come over for dinner that evening. Unfortunately, Ally was busy all week.

'I've got a college friend staying,' she said sadly. 'Otherwise I'd have loved to. Sorry.'

'What's up?' asked Pete.

'I need help,' admitted Nicky. 'From a friend who's also a teacher,' she said.

'Damn,' Pete replied. 'I've got football tonight.'

There was an uncomfortable pause.

'I'll come,' said Rob.

'Mm,' she said, 'I'm not sure that's . . . I'm probably not up to it tonight. I'm going to go straight to bed. I've still got my headache.'

'All right,' he said. 'I'll come tomorrow.'

'It's a three-dayer. A migraine.'

'Right. Friday it is.'

She gave him a weak smile. He gave her a friendly one back. 'After all,' he said, 'we're still mates, aren't we?'

Nicky nodded and realised the feeling she was experiencing was gratitude. Yes, they were mates. And maybe what she needed was a bloke's take on it all.

Three days after Oscar's Parents' Evening, Mark had still not been back at work, but at least he felt well enough to phone Lilith.

'You *what*?' she cried into the phone. 'You mean . . . you *went*? To Parents' Evening?'

'Yes,' murmured Mark from the sofa. 'And I haven't been able to walk since.'

'You went?' she repeated. 'You *went*? You didn't send some lackey from your office? *You? Went?* How did you know where to go?'

He let out an exasperated sigh. 'And,' he repeated, 'I haven't been able to walk since.'

'Hold on a minute. How come you've got time to phone me from work?'

'I'm not at work. I'm ill. That's what I've been trying to –'

'Jumping Jehovah!' she cried, which was her latest favourite saying from Daisy. 'This is *Mark Samuels* I'm talking to, isn't it?'

'I had to come home the morning after and I haven't been in since.'

There was a lengthy pause.

'I can't pick up Oscar today,' she said, her voice suddenly flat. 'I'm doing a double shift, to help pay for this week's baby-sitter. Mum's picking Daisy up on her bike. Next question?'

'I wasn't going to ask that – Jesus, you make me sound like I'm always asking favours.'

'You are.'

There was a long pause.

'Right,' said Mark. 'Well then, here's the last one. Please come over for dinner tomorrow night.'

'That's the favour?'

'Well, not exactly . . .'

'Oh no! Mark! It hasn't come to that, has it?'

'Come to what?'

'Mercy sex?'

'Please. Please,' he begged her. 'Shut. Up. The truth is I would very much like to pick your brains.'

'Thank God for that,' said Lilith, intrigued. 'You are so not my type.'

'Halle-fucking-lujah,' he breathed.

'It just so happens that Mum's not line dancing tomorrow night, so I can manage it.'

'Thanks, Lil.'

'Don't ever call me that again. It makes me sound like a washerwoman.' And she hung up.

It was Friday evening and Nicky was sitting in her lounge, waiting for Rob to arrive.

'Grateful,' she said aloud to the room. 'I'm grateful. This is really good of him. He doesn't have to come in his own time to help me out when I need it. He's a good mate. After everything, he's still a good mate. Yes, we've kissed in the past, but that's over. Yes, he's good-looking, but I'm totally over him. Yes, he was my first love, but . . .' She stopped. This wasn't working. She heard the kettle boil in the kitchen and went to put the pasta on.

Mark switched off the phone and lay back on the sofa. Lilith was getting bitter in her old age. Maybe he should tell her. After all, they were friends and it was a particularly unattractive trait in a woman. Maybe that was why she hadn't had a boyfriend for years. I mean, he thought, she's actually trying to imply that I only ever phone her if I need help. He proceeded to mentally argue the case with her, beginning with a list of all the times he'd phoned for a chat, or to see how she was. After a few moments, he turned into a foetal position on the sofa and made a low groaning noise.

Rob stood outside Nicky's door waiting to be let in. He had never, in all his life, been in this position before. He genuinely had absolutely no idea where tonight would lead. Would they end up in the kitchen again? If so, would he be thrown out again? Or were they really just going to talk? Wow, he thought, as he waited for her to open the front door. This must be how the other half lives. When Nicky opened the front door, he used his tightly honed skills to appraise the situation within seconds.

Mixed signals. Didn't have a clue.

He followed her up the stairs. She was wearing a faded tracksuit and her hair was in a loose plait down her back. There were dark shadows under her eyes and her lips were pale. Two bowls of pasta lay on the coffee table in the lounge.

He flung some flowers on to the empty two-seater.

'Saw these on the way,' he said. 'Thought you needed cheering up.'

'Oh, thanks! That's so sweet!' She picked up the flowers.

'Sweet,' he thought. '*Sweet*.' Shit.

She smiled up at him, gave him a peck on the cheek, and squeezed past him out of the room. She smelt of rose petals. He watched her bottom as she walked into the kitchen. He reconsidered. She must know how good she looks in that tracksuit, he decided. Those were unnecessarily tight track-suit bottoms.

Oh yes, he thought. The tracksuit was a double bluff.

'I'll just put these in water!' she called out from the kitchen. He stood for a moment and then suddenly followed her, only to be met by her at the kitchen door. They both jumped, him higher because she was pointing a corkscrew at him.

OK. It wasn't going to be the kitchen this time. Maybe she felt more comfortable in the lounge . . .

'Oh!' she said. 'Did you want a cold drink? I thought a nice bottle of wine would be a good idea. I know I need it.'

'Perfect,' he said as they wandered back into the lounge.

Oh yeah, baby, he heard that one loud and clear. Dutch courage for the little lady.

She sat close to him on the two-seater. Bring it on, he thought.

Then she crossed her legs in front of him, hunched over them and let out a long sigh.

Hmm, he thought. Certainly not textbook. And very defensive body language. He couldn't get past those legs if he tried.

'Do you mind doing the honours?' she asked, passing him the corkscrew and fluttering her eyelashes faux-coyly at him, traces of a soft blush creeping up her neck.

'My pleasure.' He smiled.

He heard her sigh and felt her eyes bore into his back as he opened the wine beside her. He tried to imagine what he looked like to her – his hands were large and agile and he opened the wine with no trouble, on just the second attempt. He poured it slowly and carefully into the wine glasses, then turned to her with a practised smile and found her day-dreaming out of the window.

She turned and gave him a faint smile. Their fingers touched. She sighed again, louder this time, and stretched her head back, exposing a smooth, almost luminous neck.

He gulped down the wine.

'Help yourself to whatever you want,' she murmured.

'Thanks,' he murmured back, trying to put the wine glass back on the table without taking his eyes off her.

She looked back up. 'Sorry it's only pasta.'

'Pardon?'

'I'm just so exhausted I didn't have the energy to do anything more fussy. I feel like I'm about seventy. I feel . . . spent. Totally and utterly spent.'

OK, he heard that one loud and clear. Not tonight,

Josephine. He was almost relieved. He was beginning to feel a bit tired himself.

So he was rather surprised when she then slowly shuffled sideways, moved up, and leant towards him, resting her head on his shoulder.

Mark stared at Lilith across the kitchen table in disbelief. He must have misheard her. There was no way she'd have said that. Especially after the meal he'd just made. He asked her, in a calm, steady voice, to repeat herself.

'You heard,' she replied, just as calmly and steadily.

'What the hell do you mean by that?' he asked.

'I mean exactly what I said,' she said. 'It was about bloody time someone told you the truth. It should have been a friend, but it happened to be her.'

'I don't think you could have heard me right. That uptight little bitch accused me of – she . . . she said "poppycock", for Christ's sake.'

'I know, Mark. I heard every single word. And she's right.'

'I thought we were friends,' he whispered.

'No.' She shook her head sadly. 'I haven't been much of a friend to you. I've been helping you disguise your problem instead of helping you get out of it.'

'What problem?'

'If I was a real friend, I'd have said all that years ago.'

'You have!' cried Mark. 'You threatened to put him out on the street the other day.'

'Yeah, but I always got angry on behalf of me or Daisy. But the real one who's been suffering was Oscar. And he has been for years. And I've never actually said it.'

'Oh Jesus,' he muttered. 'Not you too.'

199

'You only have one chance with kids, Mark. And that's it. Then they're gone.'

He shivered suddenly.

'I also think,' Lilith was now speaking in a gentle whisper, 'that you know – deep down – that she's hit the nail on the head. You have fucked up big time. You've completely failed Oscar as a father. And that is massive.'

He shook his head.

'Which is why,' she continued, 'your body is purging out all the shit that you've been in denial about since Helen died. 'Cos you hate to get things wrong, 'cos you're a perfectionist. But you've been doing the wrong thing perfectly.'

Mark closed his eyes and hung his head down.

His mouth formed the word 'Poppycock', but no sound came out.

'There, there,' Rob comforted Nicky, shifting so that he could put his arm round her without giving himself a hernia. 'What's all this, eh?'

She moved away stiffly. 'God, I'm really sorry,' she sniffed. 'I can't stop crying.'

'That's all right by me. Here,' he poured some more wine in her glass. She drank it down.

'I – I . . .' She drank some more wine.

He waited.

'I feel,' she said with some difficulty, 'like I'm waiting for something . . . monumental . . . to happen in my life.'

Rob stared at the two freckles on her upper lip and slowly leant in towards her.

'Something awful,' she continued. 'Something terrible. Something catastrophically bad.'

He leant back.

'And I just felt,' she said, wiping her eyes with the back of her hand, 'that I needed to get it off my chest or I'd end up vomiting it up or something.'

He let out a long sigh and poured himself another wine.

'Shoot,' he said.

Mark and Lilith moved slowly into the living room, so that Mark could lie down. He needed to be horizontal.

'So, let me get this right,' he said slowly, from the day-bed. 'On Hallowe'en, Miss Hobbs made you hot chocolate because you happened to be in her flat when I texted Osc to say I wasn't coming?'

'Yep,' sighed Lilith. 'And toast with jam and butter. And that was when she asked me, quietly and out of the kids' earshot, where you were.'

He grimaced. 'And what did you say?'

Lilith shrugged. 'What was I supposed to say? I told her you were still at work. Again.'

Mark stared at her. 'You didn't think,' he said slowly, 'to tell Oscar's form teacher that I was helping starving kids in Africa –'

'Why the fuck should I lie for you, Mark?' She sat up on the sofa indignantly.

'Yeah, you're right. Sorry.'

'And the fact that you said that shows that you know damn well that being at work is a shitty excuse not to go to your child's Parents' Evening.'

'Yeah,' he murmured, shaking his head. 'Fuck,' he whispered to himself.

There was a pause. Lilith looked at her watch before downing her glass of wine.

'So, go on then,' he said suddenly. 'How did she react?'

'Funnily enough, she wasn't that impressed, as I recall.'

'Yeah, well, you recall right. She was not impressed. She was most *un*impressed. Oh yes,' he said bitterly. 'Miss Hobbs was most unimpressed.'

'As was I.'

'Miss Hobbs, prim Little Miss School-ma'am, was unimpressed.'

'As was I.'

'But she doesn't understand how it works in the city. You don't get anywhere if you're half-hearted about your career. It doesn't –'

'Blah, blah, blah, blah, blah, blah, blah,' cut in Lilith, holding her hands over her ears.

Mark frowned at her.

'Oh don't be –' he started.

'Blah, blah, blah, blah, blah –'

'Oh, grow up –'

He stopped and there was a long, heavy silence before he spoke again.

'Blah,' he whispered, closing his eyes before they filled too much.

Rob stroked Nicky's hair out of her face and kissed her gently on her forehead.

'Of course you're not going to lose your job,' he soothed her.

'But maybe I should,' sniffed Nicky. She moved slightly

away and stared at him. 'Then I could focus on what's staring me in the face.'

He stared into her face.

Then he leant in.

'If –' started Nicky.

He leant out.

'If I ask you a really important question, will you promise to answer me truthfully?'

'God, yes,' he said firmly.

'Rob?'

'Yes,' he said.

'You know you said, when we got our promotion, that you were changing your mind about wanting kids?'

He held his breath. He gave a brief nod.

'Tell me,' she continued, 'do you think it's possible for a woman to have a good career as well as a family?'

'Of course.'

She nodded. 'OK, take it one step further. If you had a baby with a successful career woman – a theoretical successful career woman – who loved her job and was good at it, would you expect her to give up work to be with the baby?'

He blinked at her. Fucking hell. They hadn't discussed babies since . . . well, since . . . Shit, this was big. Keep calm. He'd completely misjudged it last time. Think. *She's changed now. She's a successful career woman. But she still wants kids.* Talk about the million-dollar question. It was tricky, but it wasn't impossible. She probably didn't know the right answer herself. Sweat beaded his forehead. If he got this right, they could be shagging within minutes.

'No-o,' he said finally. 'Of course not. Unless, of course,

y-she wanted to be a full-time mother, which would be absolutely fine with me . . . you know, fantastic.'

'So . . . deep down you would want her to?'

'N-nooo. I didn't say that.'

'So you'd *want* her to work?'

'No-oh. I'd want her to be happy –'

'More than you'd want the baby to be happy?'

'No! I'd want the baby and her to be happy.'

'But you'd see it as her responsibility – not yours – to change her life to keep the baby happy.'

'I think,' answered Rob slowly, 'deep down, that *she'd* probably see it as her responsibility.'

'Well, of course she would,' answered Nicky, 'she's been socialised to think that's her role, whether she's naturally maternal or not.'

'Right, yeah.'

Shit, she'd changed. Think, man, *think*.

'If she *did* want to be with her babies,' she continued, 'and wanted to keep up her career, then what?'

'Um.' Rob had lost concentration. He poured himself more wine.

'Would you like her to work part-time?' suggested Nicky.

'Yes!' he cried. 'Brilliant! Part-time! Perfect! Absolutely perfect. Win-win! Everyone's happy!'

'Which would, of course,' mused Nicky, 'ruin any of her long-term career ambitions, thus preventing her from being any kind of threat to your masculinity.'

'Um . . . right . . . well . . .'

'It's all so confusing, isn't it?'

'Fuck, yes.'

'I mean, what is the right answer?'

'Bugger me.'

'Sometimes I wonder if the last generation didn't get it right. No questions asked: father worked, mother looked after the kids.'

'Yeah,' murmured Rob, relaxing slightly. 'Father got the best armchair, kids in bed before he got home, female teachers left if they got married. I mean – obviously, that's appalling.'

'And of course a whole generation of mothers were depressed, angry and unfulfilled and took it out on the children who'd ruined their lives.'

'Shit. Yes –'

'But on the other hand, at least they knew what lay ahead for them. Everything was so certain in those days.'

'Exactly.'

'Still. It must have been hell. A life of making sacrifices. Inevitable depression. Isolation. Bitterness. Resentment. Watching their self-esteem seep away while their men got on with their lives.'

'Well . . . I wouldn't go that far. It wasn't a piece of cake for the men either. Same job for forty years. Mortgage, wife and kids to support.'

Nicky looked at him. 'Kudos, respect, money, companionship, illicit affairs.'

'But it didn't work out well for all of them. I mean – no . . .'

'No.'

'And life's not a piece of cake for us now.'

'How so?'

'Well,' pondered Rob. 'OK, just for example, just plucking it out of the air. You and I certainly wouldn't be sharing a job.'

'No, you're right,' agreed Nicky. 'I'd be stuck at home ironing your shirts.'

'Exactly.'

'I mean, hypothetically.'

'While I'd be providing for you.'

She gave him a look.

'Hypothetically,' he added.

'I would *hate* to have someone providing for me,' she muttered.

He spoke softly. 'And I've got someone to do my shirts.'

They stared at each other. OK. He was back on track.

'I suppose,' said Nicky thoughtfully, 'we're in the dark together. I mean, men and women.' She smiled. 'On the same learning curve together.'

He nodded, leaning in. 'Sometimes that's nice,' he murmured.

'I hate it,' said Nicky firmly. 'I need to be in control.'

He leant out again. 'But you're completely in control, Nix,' he whispered. 'Even when you don't think you are.'

'Am I?'

'You always have been.' His voice was low.

'I feel totally out of my depth. I don't know what's going to happen next.'

'Well, just wait and see,' he murmured again, leaning in. 'You might get a pleasant surprise.' He moved his arm to turn off the lamp.

'God, no,' she said fiercely. 'I hate surprises.'

Rob went limp. He rested a hand on her knee and looked seriously at her. 'Nix,' he whispered, 'I'm too old for this shit.'

She returned his gaze. 'Oh my God,' she whispered. 'I

was just about to say that. I know exactly what you mean.'

'Do you?'

'Yeah. Sometimes I feel . . .'

'Yes? What?'

'*Old*. Really *old*.'

He stared at her. 'Well, I certainly do tonight,' he said.

She blinked in surprise. 'Why tonight?'

He snorted. 'I love you to bits, but you're doing my head in.'

She frowned hard. 'I'm doing your head in?' she repeated faintly.

'Sweetheart, don't take this the wrong way . . . but you send such mixed messages I don't know whether to jump your bones or run for the hills.'

Nicky's eyes were saucers. He held his breath. This was the moment. Make-or-break time.

'Do help me out here, Rob,' she said softly. 'But what's the *right* way to take that?'

Oh dear. He had a moment to put it all right again.

'No!' he said suddenly, with almost ferocious certainty. 'I would not make a successful career woman give up work.'

Nicky's voice was ice. 'Well, whoop-de-fucking-doo for her.'

'Oh for fuck's sake!' he wailed, a sob escaping.

'You told me we were friends –'

'Oh don't give me that "friends" shit . . .' His voice trailed off. 'You prick-tease me for three years,' he began, 'then finally launch yourself at me in your kitchen.'

'I did not launch –'

'Then, just when you've worked me up to a crescendo, you throw me out of your flat –'

'Right.' She stood up. 'I think –'

'*Then* you get me round for dinner –'

'You offered to help me –'

'Spray on a tracksuit –'

'Wha –?'

'Try to get me drunk –'

'I did not try to –'

'And start a poor little girl "*Oh help me!*" act –'

He stopped and looked at her face. It was a picture. Unfortunately, it was a really angry picture.

'Oh *shit*,' he groaned as he collapsed back on the sofa.

'That's right, Rob,' she said coolly. 'My life is all about you getting your end away.'

'Oh come on, Nix –'

'Rob, answer me this. If the governors found out about us snogging, whose job would be on the line? Whose reputation would be tarnished and whose would be improved? How many governors are female and how many are male?'

'What?' cried Rob. 'Don't try and turn this into something political. That stuff went out with the ark.'

'Bollocks!'

'Haven't you heard of post-feminism?' He was shouting now.

'Oh, is that what they're calling it in *Nuts* this week?' So was she.

'I don't read that crap, Nicky, and you know it.'

'Really? Because you sounded just like a reader's letter back then.'

There was a long pause.

'Right,' said Rob eventually. 'I hear you loud and clear.

Let's just never bring us up ever again.'

'Right,' Nicky took stock. It would probably not be a good idea to slap him. She still had to work with him. 'Yep,' she managed. 'Let's just try and forget any of it ever happened, and act like adults.'

'Right,' said Rob. 'Adults.' There was silence for a moment, before he said quietly, 'So. It's actually quite nice to know where we stand finally.'

'Yes.'

'We're never going to have sex ever again.'

He felt the sudden tension in the air around him and made sure not to glance up at her. Genius. Absolute fucking genius.

'Bye, Rob,' she said quietly.

He got out, trying not to smile that she hadn't answered his last point.

12

During her drive into school on Monday morning, Nicky wondered how on earth she had got herself into this situation. Just last week everything had been completely normal. Now she was waiting for a complaint from the parent of her favourite pupil and she and Rob had finally admitted that their years of flirting were officially over. She could barely concentrate enough to apply her make-up, let alone make right turns.

But she kept finding that there was something more tenuous about her low mood. After much soul-seeking, she worked out that she had lost hope. Every morning since she'd seen Him at the fireworks display, she'd woken up to the sure knowledge that somewhere out there was a man who made her insides go fizz. Every single day was backlit by a golden ray of hope, and now that had vanished. That man didn't exist. She was alone again.

Fortunately, Rob didn't appear in the staffroom that morning. Unfortunately, Ally and Pete did.

'Did Rob manage to help you out on Friday?' asked Ally. They hadn't shared their usual Sunday breakfast due to Ally's college friend staying over.

Nicky glanced at Pete. He had an easy, open expression. She decided Rob hadn't told him his version of Friday night. Yet.

'Yeah, I think so,' she said. She'd tell Ally what had happened later.

She found Rob, as she had suspected, already in Miss James's office. He was sitting at her desk humming. Behind him, at the puzzle table, Ned was sitting staring miserably at a patchy Europe. He looked considerably worse than Rob, who looked fine. Absolutely fine. What had she expected? Had she expected him to be a broken man? Because he wasn't.

She paused in the doorway and he glanced up. There was a fraction of a pause, then he gave her a quick raise of the eyebrows and a small but definite smile. Then he glanced away, just before saying hello. He would obviously have to work up to keeping eye contact and speaking to her at the same time. But at least he was trying.

Right, thought Nicky. He'd done his bit, now it was her turn. She came into the room and started saying something vague about her journey in. Luckily she was interrupted before she had to come to anything approaching a full or meaningful sentence.

'Nativity Plays!' came a wild exclamation from behind them. They turned to see Miss James's entrance. 'Can you *believe* it's that time of year again?' she said, as she paced past them both and sat down behind her desk.

A downhearted sigh came from behind them at the puzzle desk.

Rob launched happily into his ideas for this year and Nicky watched, hardly noticing Ned's increasingly loud sighs from the puzzle table punctuating Rob's soliloquy. As Rob eagerly discussed his pupils' contribution to the Christmas play, she found his seeming indifference to their squabble last night rather attractive.

Which worried her greatly.

But what worried her more was Rob's sudden revolutionary idea that, this year, Year 6 could start a new tradition of putting on an ironic, updated nativity play with their own script, including modern references, as a treat for being the top class of the entire school. After her initial shock, Nicky attempted to include Year 5 in it, but Rob said that would complicate timetable issues and prevent it from being a specific treat for having got to the top of the school. Was this revenge for Friday night? She wanted to kill him. Maybe it would have been simpler just to shag him.

After usual business, which included the resignation of the bursar, a row between two dinner ladies and a new timetable issue, Rob and Nicky were allowed to join Ned at the puzzle table. Half an hour later, the three of them walked down the corridor wordlessly. Nicky needed time before she broached the subject of a Year 6 ironic, newly scripted nativity play with Rob in private, otherwise the only words would be blasphemous ones, which seemed somehow inappropriate.

At lunch-time, she completed a hundred errands, but when she had finished them all, she found herself with a full fifteen minutes to herself. She texted Ally, but Ally was working with one of her pupils. So she decided to pop into the staffroom.

She found Rob and Amanda having a quiet tête-à-tête on the only two-seater, while Ned chatted on the phone to his wife about houmous with cream cheese. She decided to bite the bullet and join Rob and Amanda, and after flicking on the kettle, wandered over. As she arrived by them, neither of them acknowledged her presence, but continued with their animated chat. She was surprised how hard it was to be furious with someone who was ignoring you. She pretended not to notice and sat beside them, already seeking only a greeting from Rob instead of a heartfelt apology. After a while, she picked up the trade paper on the table in front of them and flicked through it. As she did so, it dawned on her that this was what Amanda must have felt like every time the gang had ignored her. She promised herself that she'd be nicer to the girl in future, however much she detested her.

Then Amanda laughed loudly, told Rob that she had to get on with some photocopying, touched him lightly on the thigh, got up and walked away. Rob brazenly watched her bottom leave the room.

'She's always photocopying, that one,' said Nicky, as soon as her bottom had left.

Rob didn't answer.

'Do you think she ever does any actual teaching?' she tried again.

He looked at her as if he'd only just noticed she was sitting there.

'Yes,' he said before getting up and leaving the room.

Nicky sat mute for a moment, motionless apart from her chest which had to work extra hard to breathe, her finger-nails which bore into her palms, and the two fine lines of steam escaping from her ears.

As the day wore on, the more she thought about Rob the more she wanted to race into his classroom and hurl a blackboard rubber at his face in front of all his kids. That was just one of the many tragic losses that had come with the introduction of new technology in the classroom. Interactive whiteboard cloths just didn't cause as much damage to the face as good old-fashioned blackboard rubbers. Maybe she could suggest Rob reintroduce them as part of his Progressive Yet Traditional ethos.

Such thoughts helped her get through the day.

At a quarter to three that afternoon, she still hadn't been called to Miss James's office to face a livid Mr Samuels brandishing a subpoena in her face. She was so relieved by this that at the end of the afternoon, she decided to give her kids a treat and ask them to talk about their weekend. Children always loved to talk about themselves and it gave a fantastic insight into their home lives.

She looked around the room as every single child fought to put their hands up higher than everyone else.

'Matthew,' she said to the boy sitting next to Oscar, causing all the other hands to go down. 'What did you get up to?'

'I went to Hampton Court and it was brilliant and they've got a maze there which I went in with my dad and my sister went with my mum and we won so I got to get a DVD on the way home and I got *Shrek 2* which is really funny have you seen it at Hampton Court I got a family tree map thing of all the kings and queens and I can bring it in there was one king who was younger than me I think he was called Edward . . .'

As Matthew continued his breathless monologue, Nicky fought the urge to interrupt him. It was, she supposed, incorrect to speak as if punctuation didn't exist, but it added so much to the charm of his subject. If only adults talked like this, the staffroom would be a far more endearing place, she thought. When Matthew finally ran out of breath and information, she picked two more children and discovered that last weekend a new baby sister had been born and a new football had been bought, both of which were given exactly the same amount of detail.

Before she knew it, it was time to go home. As the children began to pack up, she wandered round the classroom to the windows where she leant on the window-sill and looked out across the playground. The reds and oranges of the last few leaves on the trees never failed to stun her. Her gaze wandered idly to the left, settling on the road which came to a gentle bend just outside the school entrance. Then her attention was arrested by movement at the gate. Nicky glanced over and involuntarily gasped. There, against the wrought-iron school gates, leant Mr Samuels, staring intently at the school.

This was it. Her career. Over.

She knew it had been too good to last. He must have made his complaint and was now waiting for Oscar to come out of school. Or maybe he was waiting to make the complaint with Oscar. She stared at her accuser, the man who was about to threaten her dreams of headship for ever. God, she thought, his legs were good. He wore faded denims and the same deep blue fleece jumper he'd been wearing when she'd first seen him at the fireworks display. Had he taken a whole day off work just to make this complaint? When had he fixed the appointment? Had Miss James known this morning? Yesterday morning?

Then suddenly he stared straight up at her. She stepped back from the window and turned her attention back to her class. She watched Oscar race out and forced herself away from the window. She didn't need to see the father-and-son reunion.

Mark continued to stare up at the window, even after she'd gone. It was only when thirty children charged towards him from the front door that his attention was drawn elsewhere. A tentative smile came to his lips as he spotted the top of Oscar's head. He watched as Oscar chatted animatedly to his companion – a boy he'd never seen before, but who looked like a good friend – with the intensity of an old man discussing politics over a malt whisky. Mark got a flash of the man inside the boy and felt a lunge of love. He felt an impatience for the future and longing for the past at the same time. Then Oscar spotted him, grinned and raced over. They hugged a loose-limbed boyish hug and then Oscar moved away – too soon, it was always too soon – discarded his schoolbag into his dad's arms, and fell into step beside him down the road. Mark felt a swell of pride.

Nicky sat in the empty classroom. She turned on her phone and checked it. No texts from Ally. She'd phone her tonight. She needed Ally's take on Rob's behaviour today. Was she imagining it, or had he declared a silent war? Then she slowly tidied her briefcase. She closed the door behind her and refused to glance into Rob's room. She descended the stairs and, bracing herself, walked along to Miss James's office.

'Hi, Janet,' she said to Miss James's secretary. 'Is she in?'

Janet looked up at her over her glasses.

'Who? The cat's mother?'

Nicky sighed. 'Miss James.'

'No. Miss James is not in. She has not been in all afternoon. She is at the latest assessment strategies meeting.'

Nicky frowned. 'She's been out all afternoon?'

'Yes. You will note that that is why I specifically used the phrase "all afternoon".'

'She hasn't had *any* meetings – *at all* – this afternoon?'

Janet gave an impatient sigh. 'Not unless they were about the latest strategies meeting and at another school in the borough.'

'Right, thanks,' said Nicky.

'Oh,' muttered Janet, getting back to her work, '*de nada*.'

It was only on her way home that Nicky realised two things: one, that Miss James would be presenting the hours of work she had been delegated to do on the subject of individual teacher's assessments; and two, she wished she'd been invited to attend.

'So,' continued Oscar, beside his dad, 'I played my king and it was checkmate.'

'That's great, Osc –'

'We find out what parts we've got tomorrow!'

'What for?'

'*The Celebrity X-Factor Nativity Play*. Miss Hobbs said she's decided after watching us in drama. I want to be Ali G singing "Away in da Manger".'

'Do you?' Mark laughed. 'Brilliant! I didn't know you liked performing.'

Oscar shrugged. 'It'll be fun. Miss Hobbs is directing.' He turned to his dad and spoke as Ali G. 'Is it 'cos I is de Son of God?' he asked, in a perfect accent, and when his dad laughed, continued until they got home.

When they got home, Mark realised he had no idea what to do now. Did Oscar eat anything before he did his homework? Did he watch television first? What time did he have supper?

'How much homework have you got?' he asked, following his son into the kitchen.

He watched bemused as Oscar opened the fridge, took out a carton of orange juice and raised it to his lips.

'About half an hour,' replied Oscar.

'What are you doing?' cried Mark. 'Use a glass!'

Oscar stopped and looked over at his dad. 'Why?'

'Because it's unhygienic! That carton's for everyone. You might as well go round kissing us all on the lips.'

'Yeagh.'

'Exactly.'

'Whatsername always lets me.'

'Well, I'm not letting you!' Mark opened the cupboard where the tumblers were kept. It was empty. He frowned. 'Where are the tumblers?'

'Dishwasher?' Oscar shrugged. He took one out and slammed the door shut before pouring juice into the glass.

'Hey, hey, hey, big man,' said Mark. 'Are you going to empty the full, clean dishwasher?'

Oscar stared at him and then slowly shook his head.

Mark laughed. 'I'll do it this time. But in future, whoever finds it clean, empties it. OK?'

Oscar sat on the stool at the kitchen island. 'Dad, when do you think you'll be well enough to go back to work again?'

While Oscar was upstairs finishing his homework, Mark prepared spaghetti bolognese. While it was cooking, he phoned Lilith and invited her and Daisy over that Saturday evening. Daisy could stay overnight if she wanted. He would take them both swimming the next morning. And he'd make dinner.

Meanwhile, Nicky was having a busy evening. She spent four hours preparing for next week, two choosing pop songs that could double as hymns for the Nativity Play and then seven lying awake in bed.

13

It was that time of year when everything suddenly takes a turn for the worse. Nights are longer, days are darker, and the sky just gives up hope. Friday morning started damp and grey and the last of the autumn leaves had finally fallen in the playground, leaving a soggy carpet underfoot.

And like the shift in season, there was a seasonal shift in the gang's energy too. Nicky had finally got a chance to tell Ally about the humiliating row with Rob and was, for the first time, grateful for Ally's deep-felt loyalty towards her and prejudice against him. However, it was hard to stay angry with him over the Nativity Play because she soon began to thoroughly enjoy working on it. She had known that her kids were wonderfully enthusiastic, but she'd had no idea that they were also so witty, self-ironic and keen to work as a team. She got a great buzz from telling them that these abilities would, one day, be just as important as academic achievements – if not more so – and seeing their eyes light up with excitement. Usually the Nativity Play was pure 'aaah' factor as the Reception children pretended to be Joseph and Mary and assorted biblical animals. This year it was going to be pure X-factor. She couldn't wait. Yes, it had added more work on to an already heavy workload, but in fairness, Miss James had allowed her the rest of the term off timetabling duties, which were now down to Rob alone.

She and Rob were managing to strike a balance between friendly and indifferent, even, on occasions, helping each other with their joint tasks, but there was definitely something missing now. Sometimes she wondered if their friendship had all been about that something. She still didn't know if Rob had told Pete about their ugly row at her place, or if Pete and Ally had ever discussed it, but she did know that the easy camaraderie between the four of them had gone, and every comment now seemed barbed. Worse still, Amanda was now always with the gang and Rob was suddenly refusing to play the I-Hate-Amanda Game. Her presence changed everything, partly because Nicky and Ally hated her, partly because she just didn't fit in, full stop.

'OK, everyone,' announced Ally one morning. 'I'm having my hair cut this weekend. What shall I get done?'

'Number one,' said Pete, 'with a Mohican on top. Probably pink.'

'Is there any way you can get it to go over your face?' suggested Rob.

'Blue rinse!' added Pete.

Nicky was about to suggest a mullet, when Amanda, with a look of mildly surprised disdain at the boys, said, 'You really are horrid to her, aren't you?' Then she turned to Ally and patted her knee. 'I think you should try layers. It would soften your . . . features.'

At that moment, they were all interrupted by Gwen coming in and moaning to the room in general about wasting twenty minutes of her life trying to find the 'g' of Bulgaria.

221

'I was joking about Ally's hair,' Rob told Amanda with a kind, almost secret, smile.

Nicky stared at him in disbelief. It felt like an era was over.

One day later, on Saturday evening, Lilith and Daisy were led into Mark's kitchen where they stared in astonishment at the beautifully laid-up table.

'I baked the potatoes!' announced Oscar. 'And Daddy roasted a chicken.'

Lilith smiled, while Daisy frowned at her friend. Was she supposed to be impressed? She'd been baking potatoes for tea since she was six. And everyone knew roast chicken was easy.

'Have you heard?' asked Mark, as they sat down and he started to carve. 'You are sharing a table with Ali G.'

'And Anne Robinson,' said Daisy. 'I'm Anne Robinson! "You-are-the-weakest-link-goodbye!" '

Lilith smiled at Mark. 'Daisy only chose Anne Robinson so she could have plastic surgery to look as young as her. And, may I add,' she went on, 'that I'm absolutely thrilled that my wonderful daughter has let me get away with buying a Primark suit instead of having to make a costume this year.'

Mark smiled. 'Tuck in, everyone, before it gets cold.' Then he stopped suddenly.

'Osc,' he said quietly, 'who's going to make your costume?'

'You, of course,' said Oscar, tucking in to his dinner before it got cold.

After dinner, Lilith and Mark cleared up and poured

themselves more wine while the children watched a video. Now that the children were in the other room he gave up the pretence of being on a high. His legs ached.

'I've got something to tell you,' he announced, as soon as the dishwasher was on.

Lilith smiled at him from across the kitchen table. 'I had a feeling something was up,' she said.

Mark sat down at the kitchen table opposite her and took a deep breath.

'Go on, then,' she said.

'As soon as this year's bonuses are announced, I'm resigning.'

Lilith stared. Then she stared some more. Mark began to explain himself. In the week he'd been at home, he'd discovered more about his son than he'd ever known before. At the end of it, he'd asked Oscar if he'd enjoyed seeing his dad this much and Oscar had burst into tears at the thought of next week returning to normal.

That was it, Mark told Lilith. He was decided. He was going to do whatever it took to spend more time with his son. And once he'd decided that, it felt like a massive weight had been lifted off his shoulders. He could finally breathe out. It was amazing.

He was going to sell their five-bedroom detached house and get rid of the au pair, then downsize to a three-bed semi nearer school. Then he was going to put the substantial savings into a high-interest earning account and get an independent financial adviser to spend some more on some shares. This would give them something to live on while he looked for a local job he could fit round Oscar's school hours.

'But –' said Lilith. 'The pay cut! It will be absolutely *vast*. Enormous. Are you sure you've thought this through?'

'Yes.'

'You'll lose a hundred a year.'

'More.'

'How the hell will you manage?'

Mark gave a bitter smile. 'I never had the time to spend the money anyway. Most of it's been in savings since Helen died.' He smiled. 'That's the one thing I have done for Oscar. I've been saving religiously for him since he was born. He's – well, *we're* – sitting on a small fortune.' He shook his head. 'Anyway, what's the point of all that money when we haven't got any quality of life? As you said, you only have one shot at it with kids. I realised that there are men in my office twenty years older than me spending every hour of every day at work while the wives bring up their teenage kids whom they hardly know.' He shrugged. 'I just realised that I don't love my job that much.'

Lilith stretched across the table and held his hands.

'That is absolutely fantastic,' she said.

'I've already started looking for jobs nearer home,' he told her. 'And there's already a couple of good ones I want to go for.'

'Good for you.'

'So . . . would you mind babysitting on Sunday while I fill out some forms?' he begged. 'As one last favour?'

She unclasped his hands. 'Oh no,' she said, leaning back again. 'Daisy and I are doing Wood Green all day Sunday. I have to buy a suit that my daughter likes and that costs less than a tin of cat food.'

'Oh dear,' sighed Mark. 'When will I do these forms?'

Lilith leant across the table and whispered to him: 'You'll have to do it when he's asleep. That's when I'll be busy doing the laundry and ironing. And hundreds of single mums all across the country will be doing their Open University homework. Or degrees. Or applying for jobs. Or –'

'Yeah, all right. I get the point.'

14

The rehearsals for the Nativity Play began in earnest in early December. Children with acting parts had written their lines with the help of Miss Hobbs and now had a deadline by which they had to know them off-by-heart. And while the rest of their class had singing practice, the actors started having real, actual rehearsals.

Nicky congratulated herself on her controversial casting. As well as the obvious performers, there had been a few surprises from some of her less confident children. She had managed to give everyone a part of some description and she was beginning to realise that for some of them – if not all of them – she was literally giving them the experience of their lives so far. And watching them blossom during the month of rehearsals made her feel wonderful. Getting them to learn their lines, however, was making her feel tetchy, to say the least.

Except for Oscar. He had learnt his within a week. Not only that, but he seemed to know everyone else's too, whispering to them ear-splittingly across the classroom when they dried, or jumping up and down on the spot with excited frustration when they got it wrong.

Now, Nicky Hobbs had always known that she loved children. Not in a blanket, indiscriminate way. Children were people, and it wasn't possible to love everyone, unless part of your brain was missing. But she loved the potential of children. Ironically, this was something she had known about herself since her own childhood. She could remember the visceral yearning of wanting to cuddle babies, of needing to give love to a warm bundle of humanity; a tiny scrap of possibly enormous potential, from as early as she could remember. She also knew that she especially grew to care for the children she taught. However unruly they might appear at first, they always seemed to become tame under her care, and anyway, there was rawness to them; a roughness around the edges of their personality, that made being in their company something akin to watching God in the act of creating. A bit like sitting in on a divine rehearsal.

And, during her years as a teacher, she had come to recognise that she especially loved those children she taught who had that vague, special quality; a twinkle in the eye, a hint of depth in the soul, a lust for life. And every so often, there would be one of those who also happened to adore her back. Those children came along rarely – she'd only had one before – and she was lost to them.

She honestly felt it was a privilege to be with children at this special time in their lives, as they tiptoed towards the precipice of adolescence. But, with Oscar, she felt more and more that he had already jumped off. She recognised the signs because she'd seen it in her own mirror when she was growing up. It was what came of losing a parent before one's time. She knew that, eventually, his body would catch up with his spirit, but it seemed unfair that he was saddled with it so early. Sometimes she just wanted to brush the signs away, like a mother wiping a dirty mark off her son's face with a firm but loving touch. Sometimes, when she was away from school, either at home or shopping, or even with Claire, she'd suddenly experience a fleeting burst of happiness that she'd never felt before. She'd try and picture what or who her mind had subliminally thought of. Was it Rob? Was it Mark? Then she'd picture Oscar. And the happiness would return. It was a feeling she'd never experienced before and it made her feel good to be alive.

After a fortnight there was still no news of a complaint from Mr Samuels, and Nicky began to hope that perhaps Oscar's fondness for her had prevented his father from making one. And as each peaceful day went by, she gradually began to allow herself the happy thought that he had merely come to pick up his son the other week.

One night after rehearsals she was walking through the car park and spotted Oscar waiting outside the gates. She watched him for a moment, smiling irrepressibly. This was not the same boy who'd been hitting the school gates on his first day back after the summer holidays. He was practising his moves for the Nativity Play with boundless vitality. He spotted her, waved and ran towards her. They met in the middle of the playground. She bent down to his height and stretched out her hand, touching him lightly on the arm.

'Au pair not here yet?' she asked.

'Nope. 'Sall right though. I can go through my lines.'

She smiled and stood up straight, dropping her hand. 'Do you like her a bit better now?'

Oscar gave an indifferent nod. 'She's all right,' he

allowed. 'Dad's at home much more now. And they're together a lot. She's much nicer when he's around.'

A car hooted from outside the gates and Nicky watched, still as a statue, as Oscar trotted off. Surely not? Mr Samuels surely couldn't have . . .? She shook her head in wonder. So. Daddy's started shagging the au pair. No wonder he hadn't bothered to complain about their little tiff. He's had other things on his mind! Silly her – to think he'd waste any time on something as trivial as his son's teacher, when he had a young au pair girl living in his home. She squinted at the car as Oscar hopped inside. She couldn't make out what the girl looked like, but she thought she caught the careless flick of long, straight hair as the car turned round and sped off.

As she stormed across the playground to her car, she bit the inside of her lip so hard it bled.

It was early December when Mark discovered that his bonus would cover all the house-moving costs including stamp duty, and prevent him from having to touch his savings for the first few months. From then on, he'd started leaving the office by 6 p.m. sharp – at the latest – every night. And he needed to, because his exhaustion wasn't improving. He had started going to bed almost immediately after Oscar and was still having difficulty getting up in the morning. He felt like he was fighting off a virus.

After a rush of inspiration, he'd started paying the au pair extra for her to teach him the basics of housework. It was amazing how rusty you got after years of avoidance. It was also amazing how different he felt about his home now that he was learning how to run it. He felt pride in the smoothness of a newly cleaned duvet cover, satisfaction from dust-free taps, and smugness from a clean oven.

He wasn't going to send his partners a letter of resignation until he'd officially been offered a new job and signed a contract, and only then would he tell Oscar the news. He didn't want to get Oscar's hopes up, only for the boy to then have to wait six months for it to happen. But within weeks of his applications going out, the interviews started flooding in and all the signs were good. He was experiencing the rare delights of being in demand. Over the past decade of moving up the City ladder, competition had been horrendously tough. He was good at his job and had a fine CV, but he'd lost his fair share of promotions and new jobs due to the equally impressive candidates belonging to the right golf, squash or gentlemen's club. But that was all different now. Now, his City training and experience was a rare and prized commodity. From the few rivals he'd happened to see while waiting to be called into an interview, he knew he was now competing with one of two things: mums who hadn't done any sums for the past decade – apart from very basic ones in crayons – and who were demanding two days off a week, or older men who had failed in the City and who emanated a stench of failure. It didn't take him long to work out that all he needed to do in his interviews was convince the inter-viewers that his reasons for such a change of heart and career were genuine. Once he'd done that they were practically eating out of his hand.

At first he started applying to local accountancy firms, but on visiting them, discovered that they made him want to throw himself out of the windows, which invariably looked out over the backs of local restaurants. Luckily the windows didn't open and he began to wonder if that was deliberate. Worse, the offices were peopled by losers. After two of these companies offered him a job with unattractive haste and he refused both with similar haste, he was forced to reconsider where he really wanted to spend every weekday.

And then, one evening when he was catching up on the Sunday papers in bed (it was the only time he got to read them nowadays), he stopped and stared at a job advert. He was so excited that he got out of bed and started writing his application immediately. He hand-delivered it with a thumping heart the next day.

It was three nail-biting weeks before he was called for an interview.

Unlike the other jobs he'd been applying for, this one held its interviews smack bang in the middle of the day, so he decided to make a few estate agent appointments for that afternoon and then, when the day arrived, he did something he'd never done in all his years as an office worker. He called in sick. It was an uneasy revelation to discover how easy it was.

Then he finished his last bits of preparation, showered, dressed, had his third espresso of the day, and set off.

Half an hour later, he found himself in the toughest, weirdest interview he'd ever been in. Never, in his entire life, had he had to answer the kind of questions that were being posed to him. And certainly never in his life had he had to talk about himself so intimately.

Every time he thought he'd answered suitably, his interviewer just peered at him, squinted, and then asked for more. By the end, he was ready for counselling.

'Hmmm,' said his interviewer finally. 'OK, so I know why *us* and I know why *you*. So. Why us and you *now*?'

He frowned.

'What,' continued his interviewer, leaning forward, 'on earth has been the catalyst for such a dramatic change in your life? What life-altering, all-changing, monumental catalyst has led you here to my humble little office this fine winter morning?'

Mark opened his mouth but no patter came. Instead, he heard his voice falter and felt his eyes sting. It was while answering this question that he realised two things. One, he was experiencing a mid-life crisis so profound that it had made him physically ill. And two, it was all that Miss Hobbs's fault.

He forced himself to speak slowly, concentrating hard before every word. At one excruciating moment, his voice cracked, but thankfully he was able to push his emotions back down with a cough and a shrug before starting again. After he finished his answer, he sat staring at the hands in his lap, as if they were someone else's. He felt exhausted yet lighter, as if he might slowly float up to the ceiling.

After a pause, he looked up at his interviewer as if he'd forgotten she was there.

'Excellent.' She beamed. 'Excellent, excellent, excellent, excellent, excellent, *excellent*. Now,' she peered at him over her specs, 'how good are you at puzzles?'

Nicky was halfway through a science experiment when she realised she'd left all the books for her next lesson downstairs in the staffroom. This was most unlike her. The last time she'd done it was about two years ago. She couldn't leave the children on their own and she had no teacher's assistant today. There was no way out, she'd have to ask Rob to look in on her class. It was something other teachers did a lot, but Nicky hated doing it. Not only was it a big favour to ask of another teacher, who had their own class to control, but it was admitting to someone that she had made a mistake. Still, she had no option. She told her class to keep quiet for a moment and ran across the corridor to Rob's classroom. To her surprise, Amanda was in there, leaning over his desk, pointing to something on it, her long hair falling on to his shoulders.

Nicky had seconds to make a decision. Should she lower herself to ask Rob a favour in front of Amanda? Should she enquire who was looking after Amanda's class? Should she be jealous? Professionally concerned? Or should she just take a long holiday somewhere in the sun?

Rob and Amanda looked up at her and she looked straight past Amanda at Rob.

'Mr Pattison,' she said, 'sorry to trouble you, but I've got to go downstairs and get something, can you keep an eye on 6, please?' she asked him.

It was Amanda who replied. 'I'll do it, Miss Hobbs,' she said smilingly, leaving Rob and approaching her. 'I've got an assistant in for an hour and I'm using the opportunity to get something sorted out with Mr Pattison. I'll just nip in now.'

'Thank you, Miss Taylor,' said Nicky.

As they left Rob's room, Amanda gave her a big smile. 'No problem. We've got a timetable nightmare we're trying to sort out. Nice to have a break.'

'Great,' said Nicky. 'Thanks. I won't be long.'

As she raced down the stairs she wondered if they'd started going out with each other yet.

She marched to the staffroom as fast as possible, determined not to give Amanda an excuse to make her feel indebted to her. She wouldn't be surprised if she'd started a stopwatch. In the staffroom she collected the thirty slim textbooks and, gripping them under one arm, shut the door carefully behind her.

If, after Parents' Evening, she had ever predicted when she would see Mr Samuels in the school again, it would not have been now, more than a month after the event. Which was why, as she shut the staffroom door and glanced out into the playground to see what the weather was doing, she couldn't believe her eyes.

It was Him. Standing in the porch like he owned the place. She'd know the cut of those suits anywhere. He was standing with his back to her, one leg bent, one straight, like some period anti-hero, staring straight ahead at the rain. He must have just come out of a meeting with Miss James. There was no other possible explanation. This was it. He had finally made his complaint.

She stared in horror at his back, all thoughts of hurrying back to her class gone. A couple of books slid slowly out of her arms, pad-padding softly on to the floor by her feet, waking her out of her trance.

She started. Damn. She had to get back to her class. Amanda! And yet, strangely, her feet weren't moving. Then, when she thought it couldn't get any worse, Mr Samuels suddenly turned round and looked straight at her.

She swallowed and felt her whole body flush. He would now know that she knew he'd just complained about her.

They stared at each other, both seemingly paralysed. Then, without warning, her feet sprang into action and she whisked herself away, speeding along the corridor. She started to run up the stairs when she heard little whimpering sounds escaping through her chewed lips.

Mark could not believe it. She'd seen him. Typical! Why the hell had he turned back? What dark force had compelled him to take one last look inside? With great effort, he turned round and pushed through the drizzle, across the playground, the searing image of her, in her school-ma'am heels, knee-length skirt and neat little white blouse tucked in at the waist, branding itself into his mind. Hell and damnation. What if she asked Oscar why his father was in school today? This thought made him freeze in the middle of the playground, as if he was playing Grandmother's Footsteps. Should he go back in and ask her not to tell the boy that his father had been in school? No. He couldn't. He might be spotted by Oscar on his way in.

And he couldn't face talking to her. He felt a wave of nervous fatigue at the thought. Anyway, dammit, the woman didn't deserve an explanation. She was so rude! He'd actually been considering approaching her and apologising for his shocking behaviour at Parents' Evening, or at least smiling and giving her a polite nod of greeting, but before he'd had a chance, she'd turned her back on him in a huff and walked away, making it categorically clear that he was being ignored.

He cursed under his breath, carried on down the ridiculously long winding path to his car, got in and shut the door. He rested his elbows on the steering wheel and hung his head in his hands.

After a minute, he pulled out an *A–Z*, checked it, started the ignition, and drove out of Oscar's school, making sure to follow the signs this time.

Within minutes, he pulled up outside a two-up two-down cottage. He peered at it through his windscreen and frowned. Too small. He shouldn't even bother to leave his car. Unfortunately, the sight of a parked, empty Mini, splattered all over with the garishly printed name of his estate agent, announced that his contact was already inside. He sighed and got out of his car. He was directed by way of a lavender-lined cobbled path up to a small white door with a knocker. The winter remnants of jasmine languished over the door and fringed the top of the white-framed bay window. He rang the doorbell and soon heard footsteps approaching. If the door had been opened by Peter Rabbit he wouldn't have been too surprised. Instead, he faced his estate agent, which, frankly, jarred with the whole country cottage feel going on.

'Hell-*oh*,' greeted Steve, the estate agent. 'Come on in, come on in.'

He stood back and Mark squeezed past him into a hall so small he thought of getting into a lift to feel the benefit.

'Isn't it beautiful?' said Steve.

'Well, it's certainly small.'

'*Bijou*,' corrected Steve.

'Ah, *bijou*. Is that what you call it?'

Steve laughed so energetically that Mark thought he might have to go back outside to give him more room.

'Come and see the kitchen,' encouraged Steve. 'I think you might be surprised.'

'Why?' asked Mark. 'Is it made of Lego?'

Steve laughed uproariously again, and then took two steps backwards into a galley kitchen.

Mark stood in the doorway. Then he looked at his watch.

'Right,' he said. 'Well, I think I've seen everything I need to see here –'

'Fully fitted kitchen –' interrupted Steve, opening and shutting cupboard doors.

'Mate,' said Mark, shaking his head, 'my time is precious. So is yours. So here's the thing: Look at me. I'm six foot two. I have a ten-year-old son who looks like he has every chance of growing taller and broader than me within five years. Please do not make any more arrangements for me to see houses designed for hobbits.'

'You don't want to see upstairs? The views are fantastic.'

'They'd have to be,' said Mark forcefully. 'Right. Let's go to the next one.'

Steve shook his head. 'I think you're making a big mistake.'

Mark wondered how rude it would be to tell this man that he cared significantly less about his opinion than he did about upstairs views. He took out a crumpled list from his pocket.

'Demby Place?' He looked at his watch again. 'We'd be early. Is that a problem?'

Steve replied sulkily. 'We could walk. It'll take ten minutes.'

Demby Place backed on to a car mechanics with no doors. Capital Gold blared out so loudly that the mechanics had to yell to be heard. Apart from that it was perfect. Hadley Gardens needed serious work and Onslow Avenue was a sprawling top-floor flat with no lift.

'Right,' said Mark as they stood outside the flat. 'Here's the other thing: I'm a very busy, very tired family man, so no top-floor flats – no flats at all, in fact – no noise pollution and no redecoration requirements.'

Steve sucked in air through his teeth, shaking his head slowly, like a plumber inspecting a new job. 'I really don't know how easy that's going to be, to be honest.'

Mark gave him a look of surprise. He spoke quietly. 'I don't care how easy or difficult your job is. I will not be cajoled into living in a house I don't like, just so you get commission and can buy yourself a new Ford Capri. If you waste any more of my time, I'll make a formal complaint and take my business elsewhere. I don't care if you like me. I just want to buy a house off you. Do you understand?'

Steve blushed and Mark recognised hatred in the firm set of his jaw and determined nod. I'm the client from hell, he thought. At last! About time it was my turn.

They had one more place to see before Mark's plan to pick Oscar up from school as a surprise. It was in a road on the other, less affluent, side of the school, a road that was described as 'Muswell Hill borders' because it wasn't in Muswell Hill.

Mark drove down the street distractedly, taking no notice of it because he knew he didn't want this postcode. You had to think about resale with these things. He'd have told Steve to cancel the appointment, but Steve had already gone back to the office because, for this one property, Mark was actually meeting the homeowner. Typical.

He parked outside the property and drummed his fingers angrily on the steering wheel. As he walked to the door he took note that it was a halls-adjoining 1930s end-of-terrace, probably the least inspiring architecture he'd seen all day. He stood at the front door waiting for the person to answer, and wondered idly what dinner he'd make Oscar that night. He'd see his boy soon. The crap day vanished.

He watched the front door open and set his face into a smile in preparation. But as soon as the door was pulled back, his smile stuck as he found himself looking straight past the owner at an airy, elegantly decorated hall with a staircase to the right that beckoned him up to a light, spacious landing. He would not have been able to describe the person standing at the door ten minutes later, because the harmonised shades of the walls and floor, the spotlessly glowing veneer of the doors and the widening vista of the kitchen/diner beyond were taking up too much of his brain space. It was an instant, primitive thing, like falling in love. Everything else about the property would pale into insignificance compared to that first impression, and in the next few days, he wouldn't be able to stop thinking about it because it would make him feel so good. And that good feeling would overcome any possible warning bells. If the house had had no indoor toilet, he'd have seen this as a great opportunity to get more fresh air.

Luckily, the rest of the house matched the hall. Every room was beautifully proportioned, with high ceilings and freshly painted cornicing, and yet there was a cosiness to them that made him feel snug. Only one or two sets of curtains were not to his taste, and that would be easy enough to change. Apart from that, every box was ticked: the kitchen had been extended backwards into the long garden, with a vast Velux window making it large enough for a good-sized dining table and small sofa; the living room and dining room had been 'knocked through', leaving a long, wide room, big enough for several guests to sit in comfortably, a coffee table to rest dinner on and a vast sofa to sprawl on; and the garden was a good enough size to kick a ball about in. In addition, the garage had been changed into an office, and the box-room above it had been extended into a decent-sized guest room with en suite shower. Oscar's bedroom would be smaller than his room at home, but if he needed a lot of space for homework projects, he could share the office with Mark – another desk would fit in there easily.

By the time the owner had finished the tour, Mark could barely speak for excitement. Thankfully, he'd had years of training as a man, so was able to fully control his emotions. When his mobile buzzed in his pocket he ignored it. He nodded silently as the owner explained why her family was leaving such a beautiful, well-loved house and showed him where the boiler was. He shook her hand firmly and then slowly walked down the path. When he got to his car, his mobile phone buzzed in his pocket again, telling him that a message had been left for him. He took it out to see who the message was from. If it was the office, he wasn't answering.

He didn't recognise the number, but it was local. He barely dared imagine what it was as he selected to listen to the message.

He stood with the key hovering near the car-door lock, listening intently. And then with a smile on his face, he turned round and walked straight back to the front door.

The owner opened the door and smiled openly at him.

'Sorry to trouble you,' he began, 'but I just wondered if I could check one other thing?'

'Of course,' she said. 'Come in.'

This time they both walked straight into the lounge.

'This may sound silly,' said Mark, 'but where do you put your Christmas tree?'

The owner pointed to the front bay window of the living room. He hadn't noticed it was a bay. 'And we also have a tree in the kitchen,' she admitted a bit sheepishly. 'The kids love them so much.'

'Ah!' he murmured, nodding slowly. 'Yes. I see.'

He asked her if it would be convenient to come back in half an hour with his son. It would give him twenty minutes to tell Oscar that, if Oscar approved, Dad was going to be the next bursar at Heatheringdown Primary School, and as of 3 January next year, would walk into school with him every day, be at home during every afternoon, and have no office work during the school holidays. Oh, and he'd found a new home for them to live in so that they could still afford holidays.

An hour later, with Oscar's hysterically giggled blessing, he made an offer to the owner of the halls-adjoining, three-bed semi in Muswell Hill borders, of the asking price.

15

Nicky clapped her hands again and waited for the hubbub to die down. Trinny and Susannah had been whispering all the way through David and Victoria's rendition of 'All I want for Christmas is a Baby Girl'.

'Trinny and Susannah!' she cried eventually, interrupting the Beckhams. 'If you don't stop whispering, I shall make you do one of your own makeovers.'

Rarely had a threat worked so effectively.

Miss James was due to pop in later this afternoon to watch today's rehearsal. During any other rehearsal Nicky would have been delighted, but after seeing Mr Samuels at school yesterday, it just made her feel incredibly anxious. Miss James hadn't mentioned him in this morning's meeting, but then she might feel it inappropriate to bring up a complaint about her in front of Rob. Would she use this opportunity to ask to see her privately, while smiling sweetly at her? Or would she actually try and talk to her during the rehearsal in front of the children? There was no knowing with Miss James.

Nicky got the kids to start their rehearsal again and just as it began, she heard the door behind her swing open and shut. She turned and watched Miss James approach. She was making a grand show of coming in very slowly on tiptoe like a cartoon character, which made her tilt at a precarious angle, necklaces and glasses swinging like a pendulum. When Nicky gave her an uncertain smile, Miss James beamed back so widely that what remaining part of her body wasn't tilting, now hunched. The overall effect was something like a demented tortoise. When she finally reached Nicky, she gave her shoulders a squeeze and huddled up to her in the vast hall, as if for warmth.

When the rehearsal finished, she clapped so loudly that Nicky's head almost burst.

'More! More! More! More! More! *More!*' she cried out.

The children cheered, which finished any work Miss James hadn't finished.

'Are we all having fun?' yelled Miss James.

'Yes!' shrieked ten children.

'Three cheers for Miss Hobbs!' yelled Miss James. Nicky managed a gracious smile.

Miss James turned to Nicky.

'Right. I'm off home, my dear. See you tomorrow morning, bright and early!' She gave her a wink and waved as she tiptoed out, hunched precariously.

Nicky watched her go. Would she talk to her about Mr Samuels then? In front of Rob?

Later that night Oscar stood in front of the bathroom mirror with a look of undisguised derision on his face.

'What do you think?' asked Mark, standing behind him and frowning at his son's reflection.

Oscar managed to screw his face up even more. 'I think I look like a twat.'

Mark grimaced. 'Oscar! Don't use that word. It doesn't become you.'

'Neither does this costume. It makes me look like a twat.'

'Oscar!'

'Ali G wears expensive glasses, not swimming goggles.'

'But they look like swimming goggles.'

'It's not the same thing. I'm going to look like a twat.'

'Right,' clipped Mark. 'That's it. Time for bed. You'll have to work out what to wear yourself. I've got to get up in . . .' He looked at his watch and groaned. 'Five hours. We'll go costume shopping at the weekend.'

'Great,' moaned Oscar.

'Yeah, I can't wait either.'

'I'm not wearing swimming goggles,' shouted Oscar as he went to his room. 'Everyone else is going shopping with their mates, not their dads.'

Mark followed Oscar into his room so fast that Oscar felt sure he was going to get walloped. He backed into his room, almost falling over his feet. He tried to finish this with a look of defiance, but he knew he'd given his fear away.

'If you want to go clothes shopping with your ten-year-old mates, you can, young man,' hissed Mark furiously. 'And you know what?'

Oscar shook his head numbly.

'*Then* you'll look like a twat.'

And he slammed Oscar's bedroom door shut on him.

Ally came round on Sunday and Nicky discovered just how much her friend really detested Amanda. She'd always assumed that the onus of hatred for the girl lay on her shoulders, due to Amanda's obvious intentions towards Rob. But it seemed that Ally had plenty of her own motives for hatred where Amanda was concerned.

'That *body*,' she almost spat. 'It's a stick with breasts. I mean, what's so attractive about that? It'd be like necrophilia. What is *wrong* with men these days?'

Nicky shrugged miserably. 'They seem to like it.'

'Yeah. Because they've got shit for brains.'

'I'm not arguing there, girlfriend,' whispered Nicky.

'And Rob's a piece of shit for including her in all our conversations. Why should we have to spend time with someone we hate, just because he wants to sleep with her?'

'Do you . . .' began Nicky, 'do you seriously think he's going to go for it?'

Ally looked at her. 'Is the Pope Catholic?' she asked rhetorically.

'But she's not even his type,' she said weakly.

Ally gave a bitter laugh. 'Maybe it's time you finally wised up about Rob, Nicky,' she said. 'Amanda's putting that stick-insect body on a plate for him, like something out of *I'm a Celebrity*. He's a bloke who's used to getting his end away as quickly as looking at someone. And his pride's been hurt.'

'I think you're being a bit harsh –'

'No!' cried Ally. 'The sooner you realise Rob's just another bloke the quicker you're gonna get closure.'

'I've got closure!'

'Oh yeah, sorry,' said Ally. 'I forgot.'

Nicky stayed silent.

'And as for Pete,' continued Ally, 'I'm losing all respect for him.'

'Why?'

'Because he gives Amanda the time of day, and –' She stopped suddenly.

There was a long pause. 'And what?' asked Nicky.

'Nothing. Dunno. Nothing.'

'Tell me.'

Ally shrugged uncomfortably. 'Oh, he just always sides with Rob whenever you two have a . . . you know, thing.'

Nicky felt uncomfortable. 'Well,' she mumbled, 'I suppose . . . I'd like to think you always side with me because you're my friend.'

'No,' said Ally firmly.

Nicky couldn't speak.

'I side with you because you're right,' said Ally. 'Pete sides with Rob 'cos he's a bloke and they have bloke rules. And they are pathetic.'

They looked at each other sadly. Ally finished her brioche and swigged it down with the last of her coffee.

'Maybe,' attempted Nicky, 'we just raised our expectations because we got on with them so well. But deep down, they're just men. They can't help themselves.'

'That is not good enough!' cried Ally. 'Don't forgive them just because they're men! How come everyone damns women just because we're women but forgives men just because they're men. I'm sick of it. They're human beings too. With souls. With morals. With empathy.'

'With willies.'

Ally pondered for a moment. 'Hmm,' she murmured eventually. 'I'm not too sure about Pete. Where would he put it for a start?'

Nicky snorted. 'Maybe it's a fold-up one. Like a Swiss army penknife.'

They built on this for a while until they felt better, and when Ally had to leave, they shared an extra big hug.

Exactly one week later, the great day had arrived. Today was the day that Heatheringdown would re-enact the humble birth of Jesus and hear Thierry Henry sing 'Wish I Was at Home for Christmas'.

Miss James still hadn't mentioned the mysterious appearance of Oscar's father and, feeling brave one day, Nicky actually managed to mention that she'd seen him in the school without blushing. Miss James had winked at her and said enigmatically. 'I know, my dear. I know. More of that later.'

And so Nicky forced herself to forget it. And what with rehearsals and the increasingly excited atmosphere at school, she occasionally managed to.

At the end of the school day she wished her pupils good luck, and told them that she was proud of all of them and couldn't wait to see them perform in a few hours. Then she drove back home, prepared a quick dinner, cleared up and took herself into her bedroom to get dressed for her favourite evening of the term.

Ten minutes later, she was still standing in front of her wardrobe, now in bra and knickers, frowning, awaiting inspiration. After a while she padded across her flat to the bathroom, where she ran a scaldingly hot bath with plenty of bubbles. To the soothing accompaniment of a running bath, she returned to her wardrobe. After a while, she padded back across her flat, past the bathroom to the kitchen where she filled the kettle and switched it on. Now with her home full of sounds heralding pleasant sensory experiences, she returned to her wardrobe and awaited inspiration.

Then she went and made herself a mug of hot, sweet tea.

Comforted, she brought it back to the wardrobe, stood in front of it, sipping her tea and awaiting inspiration.

Then she had a bath.

She slipped off her underwear and pointed her toes daintily into the water. Her eyes closed blissfully. She sank in, relishing the nearly painful heat as it spread up her body.

She rested her head back and floated in the bubbles. She smiled. In just two hours, her favourite pupils for years were going to take a massive leap towards the adults they would one day become, and she would be watching from the wings. Tonight they would find confidence and faith in themselves. Tonight she would see their parents glow with pride. Tonight –

She balked. She sat up so quickly that water splashed on to the floor.

'Great futting scum,' she whispered.

Oscar was playing Ali G. Oscar's father would be in the audience. Tonight she would have to face Mark Samuels again.

She washed quickly and got out of the bath, splashing more water on to the floor, picked up her tea and returned to her wardrobe, where she took out a dress that went in and out exactly where dresses were meant to. She took out a pair of shoes that provided something for all; comfort for the wearer; pleasure for the voyeur; a week's mortgage payment for the designer. Then she prayed to the Goddess of Make-Up and began work on her face. The Goddess chose to be kind to her and lo, when it was done she looked fab. And finally, she geared herself up to the task of doing her hair with a determination she'd never felt before. In fact, she was so determined that she knew she'd succeed. Half an hour later, thick, glossy curls accentuated the heart-shape frame of her face and her upper arms ached from the exercise.

An hour later, she was back at school. She walked straight to the corridor behind the stage where the children's changing rooms were, her dress silkily skimming her knees. She scanned the furthest section where her class was meant to be. No one was here yet. She wondered when they would start coming. Several of the Reception children were already here, dressed in biblical garb, their excitement causing all sorts of bodily functions to go awry. Feeling not dissimilar, she turned to go to the Ladies and give her make-up a final check. She had a feeling one or two of her eyelashes weren't giving their all.

She walked down the darkened corridor towards the toilet. It was only after she had finished appraising her reflection that she heard a murmur followed by some giggling. She walked out of the Ladies hoping to tiptoe back unnoticed but found herself staring squarely at the door of the Gents when it was flung wide open and there stood Rob and Amanda, Rob squeezing Amanda's waist. She forced a quick, wide grin and then turned and walked on.

'Aren't you going to say hello?' asked Amanda brightly after her.

Nicky turned back to them quickly enough to catch Rob eyeing her rear view.

'Hello!' she said, just as brightly as Amanda.

'We were just –' started Rob, following her.

'We were just, *you know* . . .' giggled Amanda, following him.

'So, how are you anyway?' asked Rob.

Nicky turned round at them and beamed. 'I'm fine, thanks,' she said.

They all walked together to the changing rooms, Nicky wondering if it was a good or bad sign that she wanted to punch Rob as much as she wanted to punch Amanda.

Back at the changing rooms an entire dwarf-sized nativity tableau had arrived and Nicky's heart expanded at the sight of so many cutie-pies. Mary was edible, especially when she held the baby Jesus by his left foot. One of the donkey's mothers had made his costume to match Eeyore and Joseph's obligatory tea-towel had cricket rules on it. She wanted to scoop them all up in her arms and hug them till their freckles fell off.

Then she almost shrieked with delight when she saw the back of Oscar's head. She called out across the changing room and ran towards him. He turned round, his face radiating so much happiness it almost warmed the entire room. He was dressed like Ali G, complete with tight hat and big gold rings. 'Yo,' he said, and then snorted hysterically.

'Dad's in the audience,' he announced in his normal voice.

'Well of course!' she replied.

'It's the first time he's ever come,' he announced again.

She managed not to repeat herself.

'He wants to see you tonight,' continued Oscar.

Nicky bit her lip. 'Oh,' she managed. 'Does he?'

'Yes. He has to tell you something. About meeting Miss James.'

Nicky's blood chilled. She managed to nod. Then she stood up and looked round to see if the rest of her children were here. As she did so, she spotted Amanda leading Rob out by the hand. He turned his head just before he was out of sight and she looked away quickly. She had more important things to think about. Like the fact that Mr Samuels couldn't wait to tell her about meeting her boss himself.

The sudden sound of loud clapping from Miss James set off a Chinese whisper of shushes, followed by giggling, followed by more shushing. This moment was usually Nicky's favourite bit of the whole event, the anticipation, the thrill, the fun. But tonight she could have happily hit someone. Her nerves were so jangled she was amazed she was still able to function. She was covered in goose-bumps at the same time as sweating. It was times like these you needed a mum. She got up quickly and started fussing with Bruce Forsyth's shiny seventies-style suit.

'Now, everyone,' called out Miss James, 'your family and friends are all seated and ready.'

More hysterics and shushing.

'And I know you're all going to show them the most wonderful Nativity they've ever seen.' She smiled dotingly at all of them. 'Now,' she said, 'where's my trusted right-hand man? Mr Pattison? Mr Pattison?'

Nicky waited for Rob to appear suddenly, hair unkempt, lipstick on his cheek, grin on his lips. But no. He was obviously being shown too good a time. Men, she thought bitterly. If it's not their au pair girl, it's their colleague just before curtain-up. She wondered if Oscar's au pair would be out there in the audience. Oscar hadn't mentioned it so possibly not. Or maybe –

'Miss Hobbs! Will you step into the breach, my friend?'

Nicky looked at Miss James.

'Of course,' she replied. What had she just been asked to do?

'Excellent, excellent!' said Miss James. 'All you have to do is introduce the Nativity and then read out this little list of announcements.' She held out an A4 piece of paper and Nicky made her way through the changing room to take it out of her hand. The list was made up of ten points, including a request for fundraising ideas, a car-park notice and copious thank-yous to everyone who had been involved in tonight's production. Miss James smiled at her.

'I've got a bit of a throat coming,' she whispered with a smile that Nicky was beginning to despise. She stared at the piece of paper and wondered why it was shaking so much. Then she realised it was because her hand was. She hadn't spoken underneath a spotlight since her own nativity plays, about twenty-five years ago. And Mr Samuels, who hated and pitied her, was sitting in the audience, preparing himself to give her a piece of his mind.

Just then Rob appeared.

'Ah!' cried Miss James. Thank the Lord, thought Nicky, her body instantly relaxing. 'Looks like you've missed your chance of stardom,' Miss James told him happily. 'Nicky's going to introduce tonight's show. You'll have to do next year's.'

'I don't mind,' said Nicky faintly.

'I'm sure you don't,' Miss James held her hand in a tight grip. 'But tonight's your chance to shine.' Another smile. 'Come along, my dear. Beginners in five.'

Nicky looked down and watched her feet follow Miss

252

James out to the front of the changing room. She kept her eyes down as she passed Rob and Amanda, but she felt fairly sure she was not missing any great expressions of enthusiastic solidarity. The next thing she knew, she was standing next to Miss James in the wings. Her heart was pumping so fiercely she was worried that the audience would be able to see it through her sheer dress. And as she stood there, the thought struck her that there was every chance tonight would be the first night that a teacher, and not a pupil, had an accident in the wings.

Outside, in the auditorium, Mark could not believe how terrified he was. His hands were sweating so much he could barely hold the camcorder. He showed Lilith, who was sitting next to him.

'Well, what did you expect?' was her unsympathetic response. 'To enjoy this?'

'What if he forgets his lines?' he whispered. 'Or falls over? Jesus Christ. This is torture.'

Lilith stared at him. 'What did you imagine it would be like?'

He shrugged. 'Fun?'

She laughed. 'Fun? You make it sound like a trip to the cinema. Parenthood isn't a leisure activity, it's an extreme sport.'

'I'm beginning to see that,' he said quietly.

Lilith sighed. 'You have so much to learn.'

'I think I'm going to be sick,' mumbled Mark.

The lights went down.

'Well, you'll have to hold it in,' said Lilith harshly. 'Ooh look,' she cried suddenly, as a few wolf whistles sounded from the auditorium. 'It's Nicky!'

Mark forced himself to look up at the stage. Fully expecting to see his only child trip up out of the wings, break his neck and die, he was pleasantly surprised to see Miss Hobbs standing in the centre of the stage, ignoring wolf-whistles.

He stared. It dawned on him that although he'd met her several times now – and one memorable time while she was wearing only a bikini – he had never really had the chance to look at her properly; to study her, to take her all in. This was mostly because it was rude to stare, but also because it was hard to study a woman when she was shouting abuse at you.

He sat back. First he looked at her face. It was too cute to be called beautiful, but there was definitely something arresting about it. A dimple appeared in one cheek whenever she smiled. He traced the ringlets of lustrous, chestnut hair that shone with auburn highlights under the spotlight and came to rest on her chest, rising gently with every breath. Her dress flowed in and out like a river, and, although he was no expert, to his eye the only thing keeping her high heels on were tiny little bows at the front of her dainty ankles.

Once he felt he'd accumulated enough visual data, he decided to turn his attention to what she was saying. He was surprised to find that the voice that had seemed so strong when it had been screaming at him, was now distinctly soft and even quite tremulous. He observed that every few words were punctuated by a little cough and she kept coiling her hair behind her ear, a futile action, as it kept popping out again. When she got annoyed with it he smiled to himself. She was cute. Definitely cute.

After collating all the visual and aural data he came to the conclusion that Miss Hobbs was suffering from stage-fright. And was extremely cute.

His neck stretched forward every time she coughed. Bloody hell, he thought, as he watched her lick her increasingly dry lips, the poor woman was terrified. She came to a faltering end, gave an apologetic smile – there was that dimple again – and then walked extremely cautiously off the stage. He was surprised to hear clapping around him.

He didn't take much in after that, especially as he knew Oscar wasn't on until the second half. The first half was the Reception class re-enacting the Nativity scene. Any other year he'd have found it a grotesque waste of an hour of his life, but this year, it moved him almost unbearably. He found himself occupied with wondering what was happening backstage. Did the teachers stand in the wings? Was Oscar with her right now?

During the interval, he and Lilith queued for some mulled wine and he grimly studied all the other parents over the rim of his paper cup. When he realised some of the teachers were milling around among the parents, he watched them with surprise. He had no idea they'd be so young. He almost choked on his wine when he saw Rob wander past. He recognised him immediately as the tosser who had almost got them killed by his dangerous driving at the fireworks display. This bloke had definitely been driving Nicky home that night. He gave him the once-over. So, this was her type, then. He almost dropped his cup when Rob recognised Lilith and grinned happily.

'Ms Parker!' he greeted her. 'How lovely to see you.'

To Mark's disgust, Lilith seemed just as delighted to see

him. He stared as they openly flirted with each other, growing increasingly disconcerted at the discovery that this young bloke, who couldn't drive and was screwing Miss Hobbs, had been Oscar's teacher for all of last year. He went off and queued for another two plastic cups of wine, contemplating the thought that this bloke had spent every day of last year with his son and had probably worn those ridiculous trendy jeans in the classroom. No wonder Oscar's clothes sense was screwed.

After Rob wandered off, he joined Lilith, tutting loudly and shaking his head.

'What?' demanded Lilith.

He nodded towards Rob. 'Thinks he's God's gift.'

Lilith watched Rob go. 'Well, maybe not God's *gift*, but a voucher, definitely. I wouldn't mind choosing something off that.'

'You're kidding?' said Mark. 'That's good-looking, is it?' He finished his wine and went straight on to hers.

'God, yes,' said Lilith enthusiastically. 'Sex on legs.'

'Looks like a tosser to me,' muttered Mark and looked away from Lilith to avoid her amazed stare at him. By the time the lights went down again, he was feeling much more relaxed.

When he felt a sharp stab in his right rib, he woke with a start. He sat up. Where was Oscar? He scanned the stage for an extortionate pair of shades that looked like naff swimming goggles.

'Where is he?' he hissed to Lilith.

Two parents in front shushed him.

Lilith pointed to the tall boy at the back, standing in a parody of a rapper pose while Busted sang a song about what they went to school for. It hardly seemed an appropriate song, but it was surprisingly good.

Then Oscar swaggered to the centre of the stage and the lights dimmed. Mark stared at the stage breathlessly, waiting for the lights to come back up. When they did he was struck by how tall Oscar was. When he first heard him speak his lines – lines Mark knew off by heart – he let out an audible gasp. Oscar's voice was so clear, so loud and so confident. He thought his heart might burst out of his ribcage. He lifted his camcorder up to his eye so quickly he hit himself in the face. No matter, he flicked it on to record and took in the sight of his son grasping himself by the goolies and singing 'Away in da Manger' to increasingly hysterical laughter from the audience. When the rapturous applause finally came, Mark made noises he'd never heard himself make before. On the tape it sounded like crying, but he swore it was laughter.

When her pupils trooped off-stage into the wings, they all hurled themselves into Miss Hobbs's arms. And she forgot all the PC rules that stated she wasn't allowed to touch them and made up for a year of caution by hugging them all so fiercely she almost winded them. Miss James always turned a blind eye to such goings-on after the Nativity Play. She felt Jesus would understand.

She always insisted that the teachers appeared out front after the performance to gush with all the proud parents. Usually Nicky loved doing this and then she adored dissecting it with the gang the next day. This year she felt there was little to look forward to. It had long been one of her inspired traditions to hand out goody bags to all the children backstage as soon as they had finished changing. It stopped them taking two hours to get out of their costumes and ensured that the teachers got home before midnight. This year she was loath to let go of them, such was her terror of what she was about to face in the auditorium tonight. She busied herself giving each child a hearty hug and telling them exactly what was inside their goody bag before handing it over. Then she set to, finishing clearing up the inevitable detritus left by children so eager to bask in the glow of parental pride that they forgot the costume the parents had taken months to make.

As she did so, she wondered idly if Miss James had even noted Rob's late appearance tonight. Then she wondered if Miss James would ever call her her right-hand woman, as she'd referred to Rob as her right-hand man? And although she'd hated every minute of making the announcements before the performance, she did wonder why Miss James had assumed it should be Rob's job? For the first time she found herself wondering if Rob was getting the better deal as Joint Deputy. Or, if she was honest with herself, was she just feeling bitter, not because Amanda had finally got Rob, but because Amanda's glee at doing so was so clearly directed at her?

She was relieved when the noise lessened around her. She hadn't noticed she was alone until she heard Rob's voice telling her that she was.

'Hi,' she said, not looking up from her tidying.

'What's up? You're missing all the fun out there,' he said, leaning against the coat pegs and looking down at her as she knelt on the floor picking up stray belongings. 'I've come to look for you. I've been asked by three parents where you are,' he went on. 'I told them you were powdering your nose.' He gave her a wink.

'You *what*?' she said, looking up at him for the first time, suddenly angry. 'You didn't feel like telling them I was clearing up, then?'

He gave an uncertain shrug. 'It was only a joke.'

'Really?' she said. 'I'll remember to say that you're just having a quick shag with another teacher next time Miss James asks where you are, shall I? And then say it's just a little joke.'

Rob came nearer. 'Hey, hey, hey,' he soothed. 'What's up?'

She stood up and knocked his hand away. 'Don't "hey, hey, hey" me. Telling my pupils' parents that I'm powdering my nose is a derogatory, unprofessional – and sexist – slur, especially when I had to go on-stage tonight while you were . . . you were –'

'Hey. Now, listen. We didn't do anything . . . we were just –'

She exploded. 'I couldn't care less if you were doing it doggy style on the puzzle of Southern Europe! Just don't tarnish my reputation after I've had to go out there on-stage to protect yours.'

He chuckled. 'Crikey, that was funny! You were really nervous, weren't you?' he said. 'I thought you were going to pass out.'

'Thanks!' she cried.

'Don't worry!' he said. 'I don't think anyone noticed.'

'Just go away,' she said and went out front.

She stood at the door leading to the auditorium, trying to get her bearings. When she heard Rob follow behind her, she stepped into the hall, pulling the door shut behind her, hopefully in his face.

She stood there for a while, still holding on to the door handle, trying to spot Ally or Pete. When the door opened behind her, she walked ahead, not quite knowing where she was going. When a grinning Lilith stepped into her path, she stopped to chat to her and Daisy.

While she was doing so, she grew aware of Rob joining them beside her and she steeled herself to maintain a smile on her face. She tried to concentrate on the conversation but found it almost impossible as Amanda also joined them, hovering behind Rob. Lilith, laughing at one of Rob's jokes, took a tiny step back, possibly even with the intention of stepping nearer to him next time. Amanda stepped quickly into the gap and joined in the laughter.

When Oscar appeared at Nicky's elbow, she was so glad to see him that she practically flung herself on to the floor to his level and cried on his shoulder. To her embarrassment, her eyes filled. She made do with holding him by the shoulders and telling him how proud she was of him. She became aware of someone standing behind him and looked up to see a similarly moist-eyed Mr Samuels. He looked younger than before.

She stood up again, nodded at him, and let go of Oscar. As she did so, she noticed him put his hand on the boy's shoulder. Her hackles rose.

'This is my dad.' Oscar beamed. She smiled at Oscar and then looked back at his father.

She nodded politely. 'Yes, we've met.'

He offered her his hand and she took it. As he shook it, and gushed nonsensically, she noticed that his eyes were bright, his cheeks were flushed, and there was a bruise forming above his left eye.

'It was wonderful!' he rushed. 'Absolutely wonderful. I've never been before. I had no idea. Oscar said you wrote most of it. How did you do it? It was so funny! You must be exhausted. I bet you're glad when the Christmas holidays come round!' He laughed. 'Oscar's loved every minute of it, haven't you, Osc?'

Oscar nodded happily and leant into his dad.

'Well, congratulations, anyway!' finished Mark, releasing her hand.

'Thank you.' She smiled. 'He's been absolutely fantastic. A star performer.'

She spotted Lilith give Daisy a little wink and turned her attention to the girl. 'And you, madam, you sang exquisitely too. Quite one of the strongest links.'

Daisy glowed.

'You spoke very well at the beginning,' Lilith told Nicky in return.

Nicky grimaced. 'Oh don't,' she said, blushing furiously. 'I was awful.'

'Ah yes,' came in Rob loudly. 'Our Miss Hobbs is a real little trooper.'

Amanda gave half a laugh at this in agreement, as though this was a shared opinion or a statement they had discussed previously. Nicky ignored them both. She was beginning to pray that Rob and Amanda would leave before Mr Samuels laid into her. When Miss James appeared she almost turned and fled.

'Aha!' exclaimed Miss James. 'I see you've all met, then.'

Here it comes, thought Nicky. Have a mince pie and a P45.

'What do you think of the news, eh?' asked Miss James, her eyes wide with excitement.

'Actually,' said Mark, 'I haven't told them yet. I was just about to.'

'Oh!' said Miss James. 'Well, I won't spoil the surprise! Don't let me spoil the surprise, will you!' She winked at Nicky and Rob and then cocked her head in Mark's direction. Then she turned back to them. 'You'll want to keep in his good books!' She looked back at Mark. 'Well, go on, then!' She said. 'Tell them! I'm in suspenders!'

Mark looked at Oscar. 'Go on, then!' he said. 'Miss James is in suspenders.'

Oscar laughed and then, embracing his father, said, 'Daddy's the new school bursar. He's starting next term. And we're moving nearer school. And we're going to walk into school together every morning.'

Nicky stared at Oscar. Then she stared at Mr Samuels. In fact, she was so amazed, she was only slightly aware that the deeply sheepish grin he adopted suited him so well.

'That's right.' His arm was firmly round Oscar as the boy hugged him. 'Looks like you'll be seeing a lot more of me in the future, I'm afraid.'

'Wow!' exclaimed Amanda and stretched out her hand to him. 'I'm Amanda. Miss Taylor. I look forward to seeing you at school in the New Year.'

'Fantastic, mate,' said Rob, stretching across Amanda and Nicky to shake him firmly by the hand. 'Absolutely fantastic. And you know what they say? Better late than never. Better late than never, mate.'

Nicky was preparing herself to say something suitably anodyne, but Rob carried on loudly and, feeling thoroughly exhausted, she left them to it.

16

Oscar couldn't get to sleep. He almost did at one point, but then he thought he heard something and he woke up again. He wasn't an idiot; he knew Father Christmas didn't exist, but it had definitely sounded like a roof tile dislodging . . .

There it was again! And then something moved on the landing. It was definitely on the landing. He sat up and called out to his dad, giving him plenty of warning that he was still awake. He didn't know what he was more afraid of, hearing a stranger on the roof or waking to find his dad standing in the middle of his room clutching a full pillow-case. Both images were so mortifying that he had now tossed and turned for two hours. Had he felt like this last Christmas Eve? He had no idea. In fact, he couldn't ever remember feeling this weird mix of excitement and dread before. If this was what growing up felt like, he didn't want to grow up.

He called out again, but there was no reply. He jumped out of bed and hurried to his bedroom door. He opened it slowly, wincing as the bright hall light stung his eyes. There was something so alien about the house at night; like it wasn't his house any more, and his dad, who inhabited this alien space, was now a stranger. He couldn't wait till they moved house. He was going to get to choose where the furniture went and was going to be allowed to redecorate his room. And he was going to have his own bathroom. It was a smaller house, so he'd always know where his dad was, but he was going to have a bed that converted into two beds, so he could have loads of sleepovers.

He peered down the stairs.

'Dad?'

Silence.

'Dad?'

He opened the door fully.

'Da-ad!'

Mark appeared on the landing, wearing baggy pyjama bottoms and an attempt at a frown.

'Hello, young man,' he said. 'This is no time for children to be awake. You do realise that if you see Father Christmas, he has to kill you, don't you?'

'Da-ad,' whined Oscar. 'That's not funny.'

He padded over to Mark and rested his head on his chest. Mark loved Oscar at night-time. He seemed to regress five years. They stood like that for a while.

'Come on now,' Mark whispered eventually, stroking his son's hair and then gently turning him round and leading him back to bed. Oscar got back under the covers and Mark lay on the edge next to him.

'What are you looking forward to most about moving?' he whispered. This was their favourite game. It had helped calm them both while waiting to exchange, and now, in the weeks leading up to completion, they did it just for fun.

And they seemed to be having more fun generally. This had been the best Christmas for years. And it was the first one since Helen's death that had made Mark feel he could give Oscar just as good a Christmas without his mother. Or rather, that this Christmas was not going to be saturated with poignancy. He hoped that this feeling lasted through to tomorrow. Truth was, you never knew how you were going to feel on Christmas Day until it arrived.

But this year he felt confident. Relaxed. Dare he say it, he felt happy. Which had made him realise for the first time that, for as long as he could remember, he had not felt happy. Which meant that he had probably been *un*happy. An odd revelation, when you'd assumed you were.

He, Mark Samuels, was happy again.

And then the guilt had come. How could he be happy when Helen was dead?

Then, to his own great surprise, he found a way to deal with this new emotion. Early December came and he visited Helen's grave. He'd always said he never understood people who did that. The grave was just a deposit box for decaying bones. The spirit of the person was in your heart. In the past, whenever Oscar had wanted to visit, he'd let Lilith or his own mother take him.

Yet this December had seen him visiting her grave with a bunch of wildly extravagant lilies. She'd always loved the lingering aroma of lilies. He'd bought some already blossomed, some still to bloom. Silly, he knew, but it made sense to him.

It had been a beautiful, crisp winter's day, the air a fresh kiss on his skin, the sun a friend. He had felt Helen was with him. And he got a jolt of simultaneous joy and grief. Their marriage had been stormy and complicated, but there had never been any doubt they'd loved each other. Helen was a

265

complex woman and a straight-talker, in fact that had probably been what had first attracted him to her. Yes, they'd rowed a lot, mostly about how much time he spent at work, but she'd been a wonderful mother and a fiercely loyal wife. He used to call her a mother lioness, defending her young against everything. He smiled now at the memory. He'd forgotten that.

At the beginning, after she'd died, he'd been inconsolable and had thrown himself into his work even more than he had previously. At first he'd thought that had helped, but he was amazed when, a year later, he'd had a minor nervous collapse and had had to go to see his GP. There he'd discovered that it was quite common for people who repressed their grieving to simply experience it later. He took a fortnight off work – the most he'd ever taken without a holiday booked – and cried all day every day. By the time Oscar came home every afternoon, he'd be spent. But to his amazement, the break did actually help. He went back to work and felt fully awake for the first time since her death. And over the recent years, thanks to his friendship with Lilith – Helen's best friend – he'd been able to pick up the pieces again.

And now, here he was, actually feeling happy again. It made him feel nostalgic. It wasn't a constant high, it was just little ups throughout the day. Feeling a sense of optimism as he woke in the mornings. Feeling happy at the thought of his first espresso of the day. Feeling great huge waves of love for his son.

He'd sat at Helen's grave, reading and rereading her inscription until it became a jumble of letters instead of a stab of pain.

After that he'd spent as much time as possible with Oscar. And doing so made him realise that Oscar was his tonic. Not alcohol, not work, not oblivion. Oscar. If Oscar was happy, he was happy. If Oscar was learning the skills to help him live in the world from a dad he loved, he was happy. And if Oscar was happy just because he was with his dad, he was dizzy with happiness. And that was OK. It was more than OK, it was good. Life was good. They were lucky. They had each other. They had life.

He looked down at his son's head and felt something that was part emotion, part prayer. Oscar smiled drowsily on the bed beside him.

'I can't wait to have my own bathroom.'

'And?'

'Being able to redecorate it myself.'

'What colour will you want?'

'Green.'

'I thought it was blue.'

'No,' yawned Oscar. 'Green.'

'Green it is, then. And what else?'

'Walking to school.' He yawned again. 'With you,' he whispered.

Mark crept out of the room and when Oscar woke up four hours later, he could make out the shape of a bulging pillowcase at the end of his bed. He was so relieved that he fell asleep for another two hours, making it the latest Christmas morning ever in the Samuels household.

Mark was right, this Christmas was different. It was the first year without Helen that they were making a full Christmas lunch at home, not having it at a friend's house or at Mark's

267

parents' house or at an expensive hotel. Mark had donned a specially bought apron with a picture of Father Christmas on it and a tiara of tinsel in his hair as he dutifully cooked turkey, stuffing, sausages, sprouts, roast potatoes and parsnips. And Oscar was his sous chef.

But there were two other major differences this year. The first was that Oscar received a fraction of the presents he usually got. Mark had prepared a speech explaining the need for some restraint, but there was no need, because the other difference was that Oscar hardly noticed the presents. He was so excited to prepare the meal with Dad, he was so excited at the thought of them watching a video together tonight and going to see a pantomime in town together on Boxing Day, he was so excited at the thought of what next year would bring, that he forgot to play with his brand new shiny toys. Usually, Mark was unable to extract him from them.

As they began peeling the vegetables, Oscar sitting at the kitchen table, with a serious look on his face, holding a peeler in his hand as if it was Excalibur, Mark wondered how he could have got it so wrong for so long. Then he told himself just to enjoy the moment and appreciate that he'd got it right before it was too late. At that thought he got a flash vision of Nicky Hobbs and felt a jolt of nervous excitement.

He decided that now was the perfect time to break the news to Oscar that it wouldn't be a wise idea to go on an expensive summer holiday next year and how did Oscar feel about going camping in Cornwall instead? Oscar's reaction was yet another lesson in his education.

'Camping!' he shrieked ecstatically. 'Just us two?' He ran over and hugged his father, potato peel dropping on the floor. 'This is the best Christmas ever, Dad,' he whispered into Mark's ear.

'I thought you loved your summer holidays abroad,' Mark replied, thickly.

Oscar's voice was muffled. 'Only 'cos I'm with you.'

Mark was speechless, which was a shame because as he watched Oscar return to peeling the spuds, he realised that, were this an American film, it would have been the moment to tell him how much he loved him. Instead he switched on the television to a children's pop programme and they continued their food preparation to a typically crappy combination of memorable Christmas hits and unmemorable recent ones, Oscar filling Mark in on all the details of his favourite bands.

Mark had thought carefully about inviting his parents to their special lunch. Christmas was about families, and Oscar needed all the family he could get. He had lost one set of grandparents when he'd lost his mother. Helen's father had died before she had, and Oscar had never known him. Helen's mother had emigrated to New Zealand after she'd lost her daughter. Oscar received a birthday cheque and a Christmas cheque and that was it. Mark knew why; Oscar was the image of Helen. Photos of Helen as a baby and a child looked like Oscar in drag. It wasn't just his colouring, it was his features; the spaces between his features; the shape of his face; the speed of his smile – it was everything. Sometimes Mark would catch Oscar glancing up and see Helen's face hover across his features. It shook Mark sometimes, so God only knew how it made Helen's mother feel. The tragedy was that instead of this compelling her to see Oscar more, it compelled her to flee from him. She had remarried in New Zealand and had adopted her Kiwi husband's grandchildren as her own.

As for Mark's parents, he had no choice but to invite them. He loved them of course, but he loved them most when he was greeting them and saying goodbye. The bit in the middle was hard.

Virginia and Harvey Samuels had never liked Helen, always believing that their only son had married beneath him. It wasn't anything specific about her they didn't like, except, Mark used to think, that she wasn't of royal blood. Then when she died in a car crash, they were horrified. When Mark began to pay for a string of foreign hired help instead of grabbing an eligible, young wife to begin with all over again (after all, he was still attractive, young and highly eligible himself), they decided the only way to persuade him to remarry was to argue in favour of it whenever they saw him. After a few years of this not working, they moved on to a different method, namely that of expressing disappointment in him whenever they saw him.

Virginia's face suited this method perfectly. It expressed disappointment effortlessly. Her features just fell that way. Her eyebrows had been plucked away decades ago, and every morning she drew them on in a high arch of disdain. Her upper lip curled down as if in a perpetual state of resisting speaking her mind, and all it needed was a glint of bitter contempt from the hard, brown knots of her eyes and the person at whom they were directed would be struck down with guilt. Her husband, Harvey, had Mark's even, open features, but a lifetime of being struck down with guilt had hardened them.

By the time they had turned up (early) and Lilith, Daisy and Pat had joined them (late), the food was ready and Mark and Oscar were dressed in matching sweaters (*'Whatever'* scrawled in orange against a black background) and jeans. After lunch, they played a game of charades that lasted two of the longest hours of Mark's life, and after Lilith, Daisy and Pat had gone home, Oscar went upstairs to play on his new computer game.

Mark sat his parents down over mince pies and port to tell them his career news.

He poured the drinks – a double for him – and put the warmed-up mince pies on the Conran occasional tables in front of them all. His mother perched, motionless, on the edge of the sofa, her back straight, her ankles pinned together, her hands clasped and resting on her knee, her head tilted in readiness for good news, as if she were a piece of live art. His father sat back in the armchair holding his drink, his eyelids drooping. Mark waited until their port needed refilling. Then he began.

'Mum, Dad, I've got some news,' he said.

Virginia audibly gasped and stared at him, willing him to make her a happy woman.

'I'm not engaged,' he rushed, realising his mistake.

She sighed loudly and pursed her lips hard together. Harvey downed his second port.

'So, my news is,' continued Mark, slowing down with every word, 'that I have resigned.'

This announcement was met with a total, 100 per cent silence, made up of 80 per cent shock and 20 per cent port. In it, Mark poured himself another drink.

'I've got a new job at Oscar's school,' he went on, 'so I'll be able to walk there and back with him every day and take school holidays.' He coughed. 'And we're moving house,' he went on. 'It's a smaller place but it's much nearer school. It means –'

'Are you going to be . . . a . . . a *teacher*?' his mother whispered.

'Christ,' shot his father, sitting bolt upright for the first time all day. 'He's having a mental whatyoucallit.'

'No,' said Mark firmly. 'I'm still an accountant. And I'm not having a breakdown.'

'Oh, thank God,' breathed his mother. 'Everyone hates teachers.'

'An accountant in the public sector?' quizzed his father, in a damning tone. 'What sort of accountant is that?'

'It's the type of accountant who wants to spend more time with his son, Dad.'

'Why?' asked Virginia. 'What's the matter with him? Is he in trouble?'

'Son, you are a *partner* in a *City* firm,' reminded his father. 'Do you have *any* idea how –'

'No, I'm not a partner in a City firm any more, Dad. Because I resigned. To spend more time with Oscar.'

His parents stared at him uncomprehendingly.

'So –' started Mark.

'Now listen to me –' began Harvey.

'Ruining. His. Life,' Virginia staccato-ed to her husband. 'He is ruining his life. Apart. From. Breaking. His. Mother's. Heart.'

'Actually –' began Mark.

'I suppose we should be grateful that he's not engaged to

272

that Lilith woman,' continued Virginia, talking only to Harvey now. 'Did you see what her mother was wearing? Plastic earrings. *Plastic* earrings.'

'You see,' said Mark, 'I was very unhappy. And so was Oscar. We weren't seeing anything of each other. I was at work all the time.'

'Of course you were!' snapped his father. 'You're his *father*. I didn't see you properly till you were eleven. I never saw my father at all.'

'Being with the child is the mother's job,' Virginia explained, attempting to speak softly.

'Yes, Mum,' replied Mark slowly. 'But Oscar's mother died, so I am his mother *and* his father.'

Virginia spoke slowly and clearly. 'If you *remarried*,' she said, 'he *would* have a mother. And possibly some siblings. And a family. And then you wouldn't have to sacrifice your *career*.'

'We *are* a family,' replied Mark.

'Oh no you're not,' shot Virginia darkly, 'and you are fooling only yourself if you think you are. A family is a mother, a father and their progeny. Not a father and a son and a string of Eastern European help. Nor is it a mother, daughter and grandmother with plastic earrings.' She turned to her husband. 'What is wrong with this generation?' she asked him. 'Did they learn nothing from us?' She turned back to her son. 'You have a responsibility to the next generation and you are falling short, young man. You are falling short. I only thank God I'll be dead before the next generation are adults.'

Mark sighed. 'Actually, I did learn a lot from you. Even if it was only learning from your mistakes.'

'Mistakes!' exclaimed Virginia. 'What on . . . we didn't make mistakes! We did everything for you. We didn't go out in the evening for the first ten years of your life. We never left you with a stranger once.'

'All right,' said Mark, 'I have just *realised*, then, that I only have one opportunity to be with my son. And I'm not going to miss it.'

'So you're going to sit at home like a bloody woman?' His father was now shouting.

'No,' said Mark. 'I'm going to do a job that fits round my son.'

Virginia's voice sliced through the men's. 'Speaking as a "bloody" woman,' she said tightly, now talking directly to Mark, 'if you are going through some mid-life crisis, dear, why don't you just have an affair with your secretary? It worked for your father.'

There was a pause.

'*What?*' breathed Mark.

'Right,' muttered Harvey, standing up. 'We're going.'

He walked out of the room, taking his car keys out of his pocket.

'Do say goodbye to Oscar for us, darling,' said his mother, standing up.

Mark jumped up and called out to Oscar.

Oscar didn't notice anything strange in the chilled atmosphere as his grandmother touched his cheek with hers and his grandfather patted him on the shoulder. After the kitchen was tidy, Oscar went to the cabinet in the lounge. He carried a heavy box carefully to the coffee table. They sat down on the floor, Mark with his whisky, Oscar with his chocolate orange, and opened the box. It was full of photos

274

of Helen; an exhausted Helen with newborn Oscar; Helen and Oscar smiling the same smile to the camera; Helen, Oscar and Mark on holiday together. (Mark noticed that he was never touching Oscar in any of the photos.) Mark recounted the story behind every photo that Oscar picked out, stories Oscar knew so well himself that if Mark left out any details he filled them in.

Then they watched a video together and went to bed.

17

Once term time was over, the Christmas season stopped being Nicky's favourite one. Christmas always did the same to her. She looked forward to it – because that's what you did with Christmas – and then afterwards she was always inexplicably struck down with a depressed lethargy.

Most of her friends were not originally from London, and so at this time of year, they took the opportunity to vanish to their own homes across the length and breadth of the land, to be clasped to the bosom of their festive families. One year, Nicky accepted Ally's invitation and joined her in Leeds, during which she learnt that the only thing worse than spending Christmas with your own dysfunctional family was spending it with someone else's.

So for the past few years, she had spent the social desert that was the interminable week between Christmas Day and New Year's Eve getting on with work. From 8 a.m. to 3.30 p.m., she found something soothingly positive in such industry. Then as dusk settled, her life became epically tragic. She felt like a Brontë, old before her time, overlooked and unloved, sinking into the quagmire of work to escape the echoing loneliness of her life. Then she'd watch day-time telly and eat chocolate.

Usually, though, at least Christmas Day was enjoyable. She always went to stay with Claire, Derek and the girls on Christmas Eve and came home on Boxing Day. She was able to ignore Claire's mother hen-ness and the tedium of Derek because their daughters' exhilaration always rubbed off on her. But the girls were getting older and this year only the youngest really believed in Father Christmas, and Nicky found nothing sadder than spending Christmas Day with a cynical ten-year-old and a jaded eight-year-old. Not only that, but when the girls had been babies it had been far easier to imagine that one day they'd have cousins to share their youth with. Now that she could see the young woman inside Sarah-Jane bursting to get out, and even Abigail showing early signs of menstrual moodiness, she couldn't escape the painful thought that maybe they'd never have any first cousins. Or if they did, they'd be babysitting them rather than playing with them, and probably at ridiculous rates. The older her nieces got, the more she felt a witness to their family than a part of it.

Maybe that was why this year Nicky's depressed lethargy started early. On Boxing Day morning she made an excuse to get home straight after breakfast. On opening her front door and climbing the stairs to her flat, she found winter sunlight streaming in through the windows, creating an aura of light and air and peace. She breathed a sigh of relief. Perhaps she should spend less time with her sister's family. The truth was they weren't her family, they were her extended family, and there was a difference. Perhaps it was time for her to extend the other way a bit. Yes, too much of their company wasn't good for her.

Then Claire phoned her mid-afternoon on Boxing Day

and she clung to the call like a hung-over alcoholic clings to their first drink of the day.

'How you doing?' asked Claire.

'Oh, all right,' said Nicky. 'You?'

'Knackered. The kids miss you – I'm talking to Aunty Nicky. Go away. I'm talking to Aunty Nicky.'

Nicky could hear Abigail whining in the background.

'What did I just say?' Claire asked her daughter. 'I am talking to Aunty Nicky. Go. Aiy-waiy.'

Nicky walked her phone into the kitchen and looked out of the window over her treetops. She wondered if she would ever tell her own child to go away.

'Well, go and put them upstairs,' continued Claire. 'I am talking to Aunty Nicky. Upstairs. Now. UP!'

Nicky heard Abigail stomp upstairs. One day she was going to buy herself a cat. Not because she wanted a cat, but just to have something to talk to during phone calls with her sister.

'So anyway,' continued Claire. 'Have you got any plans for December 30th? New Year's Eve Eve?'

'Yes, actually,' said Nicky brightly. 'I'm going on an expedition to Everest. There's a few of us going. We're trying to set up the first Internet and knitting café at the top, with loads of new coffee flavours and varieties. We think it's the perfect place for a fucaccino.'

There was a pause.

'I SAID UPSTAIRS!' shouted Claire. 'I am having a conversation with Aunty Nicky!'

'Oh no! I forgot,' said Nicky. 'I'm going to a sixteenth-century fancy-dress ball as a high-class courtesan. Or is that the week I'm learning to sail?'

These were both things she had actually done in the past

and this was the nearest she ever got to confessing that she was hurt when Claire forgot to ask how they'd gone.

'What was that?' asked Claire. 'Can't get a moment to myself in this place.'

'Um, no,' she sighed into the phone. 'No plans for December 30th.'

'Excellent! Derek and I want to have an adult evening. No kids, smart dress, civilised conversation, posh music in the background and real, proper food. Probably M&S. What do you say?'

Nicky felt a hop of hope inside her. 'Sounds great.' She smiled. 'Thanks.'

So, the night before New Year's Eve, feeling fondness for her sister and something approaching friendliness for her fellow man, with all her school work finished, Nicky rang her sister's front doorbell, wearing a posh frock and high heels and clutching a Sauvignon Blanc. And then Claire's front door was opened by a stranger. A man stranger, who was about ten years older than her.

'Hi!' he exclaimed. 'You must be Nicky.' He gave her an appreciative once-over, then stepped back to let her in. He offered her his hand. 'I'm Don. I've heard so much about you.'

As he took Nicky's hand in a weak shake, and wobbled it about a bit, Claire's voice called a greeting from the kitchen and Derek arrived in the hall. He said, 'Aha! I see you two have already met,' and smiled benignly at them, like a godparent at a font. And so began the evening from hell.

First there were pre-dinner nibbles in the living room, during which Claire and Derek popped in and out pouring wine, whilst finishing the cooking and showing off their cosy coupledom by teasing each other and making gratuitous physical contact that put Nicky's teeth on edge.

Nicky felt as if she'd stepped into a timeshare sales pitch for marriage. To the soundtrack of Claire and Derek's advert for wedded bliss, which she found as monotonous and unrealistic as most adverts, Don quizzed Nicky about her job while squeezing in amusing anecdotes to show how much he liked children, pets and his mother. To be honest, there was nothing absolutely detestable about the man, and Nicky wondered if that had been Claire's criteria when she'd said yes to Derek.

After for ever, Nicky and her future husband were led into the smart dining room, where the table had been laid for the second time that year, all red baubles and matching napkins. Don and Nicky were seated opposite each other while Claire and Derek popped in and out of the room, dishing up, checking on the food, opening another bottle, squeezing each other playfully as they passed in the doorway, and causing a fine layer of acid to line Nicky's stomach.

As Derek brought in the hors d'oeuvres, Claire plonked two garlic baguettes in the middle of the table, sat down and suddenly exclaimed, 'Oh! I forgot! Nicky! You'll never guess. Don *loved* that film you liked.'

They all looked at Nicky.

'Really?' she said, turning to him. 'Let's get married!'

There was a pause before Claire did a fantastic impression of a terrified horse trying to laugh. The men followed.

'You see? What did I tell you!' Derek winked to Don. 'Wicked sense of humour. Absolutely amazing. The kids dote on her. Dote on her.'

Nicky grew concerned that Derek might suddenly stretch

over the table and open her mouth to show Don her healthy gums.

Don confided to her over his mozzarella and tomato, 'I love Ken Loach. I love his . . .' he pondered, 'his beautiful bleakness.' He let this hang in the air, as if to give her time to appreciate it fully, before asking her, 'What's your favourite Loach film?'

Nicky gave him a steely glance. 'Um . . . was *American Pie* one of hers?'

Don and Derek laughed like machine-gun fire and it was only politeness that stopped Nicky from sticking baguettes in their open mouths and pushing hard. After half an hour, she excused herself and went into the kitchen where Claire was taking out the roast.

She came and stood next to her sister. Her throat caught. Claire looked up and smiled over the roast. Then she saw Nicky's expression and stopped smiling.

'What,' breathed Nicky, 'are you doing?'

Claire stared at the roast. 'You think it needs more time?' she asked, her eyes still down. 'I don't want it to go tough.'

Nicky's neck muscles went twang. She spotted the bottle she'd brought, yanked open the corkscrew drawer and proceeded to open the wine, her hands trembling with rage.

'Give him a chance,' Claire whispered to her sister's back. 'You never give anyone a chance.'

Nicky swirled round, brandishing the corkscrew at her sister.

'When did I *ever* say to you "If *only* I could meet a man who loves the beautiful bleakness of Ken Loach, my crappy little life would be worth living"? WHEN?'

'I –'

'When?'

Claire wiped Nicky's spit off her cheek and spoke slowly and pointedly.

'I was only trying to *help* –'

'"*HELP*"!' exploded Nicky. ' "*HELP*"!'

'Who needs help?' Don grinned, leaning nonchalantly in the doorway.

'I do,' squeaked Claire.

Nicky turned to him with a wide grin. 'I'm *so* sorry, Dan –'

'Don –'

'Dom –'

'Don.'

'– but I've suddenly remembered I left the . . . kettle on,' and she stormed past him, still holding her bottle, and left the house.

Twelve hours later, now New Year's Eve, neither sister had phoned the other. Nicky certainly wasn't going to phone Claire. She was just relieved that she'd finished all her school work already, because after that evening she was in no fit state to do any. She was unable to sleep, due to the increasingly furious imaginary arguments she kept having with her sister. At five that morning, she found herself pacing around her bedroom in her pyjamas shouting to herself.

This year she couldn't even look forward to the New Year's Eve work party. Usually she would have a laugh there with Ally and Pete, safe in the knowledge that there would be plenty of good-natured flirting with Rob. But not this year. By the end of Christmas term it had become clear to all that Rob would be arriving at the party, and leaving it, with

Amanda. They were now officially an item. In disgust, Ally had announced at the end of term that she was going to stay up in Leeds with her family for an extra week after Christmas, thus missing the party for the first time ever. As she told Nicky later, she did not want to spend New Year's Eve being pitied by that spidery witch.

As the party approached, Nicky felt stranger and stranger about going without Ally, as if she was going there naked. She decided to go very late, in the hope that Pete would already be there.

Gwen's house was a mid-terrace in a pretty, tree-lined street near the school. Most of the houses and trees in the street were adorned with small, white twinkly lights. Gwen's house had real oak floors in the hall, a real coal fire in the front room and real mince pies throughout. The kitchen was large and square and about thirty years out of date. Nicky spotted the mistletoe over every doorway and made a note not to loiter.

She pushed open the kitchen door and smiled a greeting at everyone. After increasingly feverish glances round the room, she realised that there was not a single person there whom she actively liked. It dawned on her that maybe Pete wasn't coming.

Apart from Rob, Amanda, Ally and Pete, the Heathering-down's staffroom had simply transported itself into Gwen's kitchen and donned tinsel and big smiles. It was as familiarly surreal as usual. She found herself next to Ned and his wife by the kitchen back door, with whom she began an energetic debate on the art of making the perfect packed lunch.

By 11.30, she realised that she was the only one using irony. By 11.31 this hit her badly. She was young and healthy and discussing sandwiches with Ned and his wife on New Year's Eve. Maybe Claire was right. Maybe she did need help.

At 11.55, she decided there was only one thing for it. She would have to exit the kitchen to prevent seeing in the New Year discussing Marmite. No amount of alcohol could make that a good thing. But by now, the kitchen was so packed that she realised she'd left it too late. Panic seized her. There was only one option left. She made a noise about being hot, flung open the back door and rushed into the night air, shutting the door firmly behind her. It was pitch black but surprisingly mild. The pencil-shaped London garden seemed to be completely empty. She stepped carefully down it until she hoped she was no longer visible from the kitchen and there she took a long, deep sigh. Then when she felt she was safe, she started laughing.

'Hello!' cried a familiar voice from what looked like a tall, skinny tree.

Nicky nearly jumped out of her skin.

'We're over here!' said Rob, stepping out from behind what turned out to be Amanda.

'Oh! Don't let me interrupt you,' Nicky begged, backing away.

'Don't be silly!' said Rob, following her up the garden. 'It's lovely to see you! You haven't interrupted anything.'

Nicky wanted to scream. Why were couples so patronising? Just because there were two of them and one of her, it was assumed that the pleasure was all hers and the kindness all theirs, when the truth was that they had interrupted the sanctity of her solitude.

Rob and Amanda had now approached, and from the

kitchen light Nicky could make out the delightful sight of Amanda rearranging her smudged make-up and pulling her bra-strap up her bony shoulder.

'Where's Pete?' asked Nicky, getting straight to the point.

'He's not coming.'

'Why not?' She was outraged.

Rob shrugged. 'Said he didn't fancy it this year. So how long have you been here?' he asked.

'In the garden? About two seconds,' replied Nicky.

Rob laughed maniacally.

'Not "here" in the garden, silly,' clarified Amanda, standing in front of Rob so her head nestled into his shoulder. 'Here at the party.'

'Oh! Right!' said Nicky. 'Um,' she lowered her voice. 'About fifty years. I've been talking to Ned.'

Rob snorted very loudly and then snorted again. He tried to stop but this made him snort again. Nicky guessed he was drunk.

'So who else is here?' asked Amanda.

'I don't know,' replied Nicky curtly. 'I was comatosed in seconds.'

She hated Amanda. It was because of her that Ally wasn't here.

'Is that gorgeous new bursar –' began Amanda, when a muted cheer interrupted her from inside. Nicky turned back to the kitchen and watched everyone hug each other.

'Well!' she turned back and forced her face into a fierce grin. This was her worst New Year ever, and that included the one where she went to a Chas & Dave tribute band with Claire and Derek. 'Happy New Year, guys!' she cried.

'Yeeeaaah!' cried Rob, stepping forward and almost

falling into a long, hard hug with her. Nicky wasn't sure what amazed her most, him hugging her, or Amanda literally yanking him back to her side. 'Happy New Year, Nicky!' he said. Then he stepped forward and began again. 'Happy New Year!'

'We were just going, actually,' said Amanda tightly, pulling him back again.

'Yeah,' said Nicky, suddenly tired. 'I think I might too.'

'It's different when you're a couple,' confided Amanda. 'New Year's Eve is for doing other things, if you know what I mean.' She winked.

'Oh, I see.' Nicky turned to Rob. 'Back to the Scrabble then.'

Rob roared with laughter and Nicky allowed herself a sheepish grin first at him and then at Amanda. Amanda's expression was pure hatred. Nicky stopped grinning. Then Amanda's expression changed into one of sympathy and she took Rob forcefully by the hand and led him into the kitchen. Nicky stood motionless in the garden, struck by the utter crapness of her life. Determined to talk herself out of a dive into depression, she took a grip and started compiling a list of all the good things in her life.

I've found a really good lipstick, she started, when Rob suddenly appeared again and to her amazement, pinned her to the wall. His eyes were wide.

'Listen carefully,' he breathed, no sign of a slur. 'We haven't got long. She pees from nought to sixty in one second.'

'Wha—?'

'Just give me a hug,' he said, taking her in a fierce, quick bear-hug. 'Happy New Year, Nicky. I love you to bits.'

The kitchen door opened and Rob suddenly sprang away from her as if his pants had just been set on fire. He beamed maniacally up at the door.

'Hi, darling!' he exploded.

Nicky looked at him sadly, and then, with a guilty expression – even though she knew she had nothing to feel guilty about – she followed his gaze to the door. To her amazement, instead of finding herself looking up at Amanda, she found herself staring at Mark Samuels himself.

'Oh, thank fuck for that!' laughed Rob. 'We thought you were – HI, DARLING!'

'Hi,' said Amanda, peering at him from behind Mark. She stared at Nicky and then back at Rob. She said to him in a voice that could curdle cheese, 'Started already, have you?'

'AHAHAHAHAHA!' said Rob, clapping his hands and rubbing them together. 'SHE'S TALKING ABOUT NEW YEAR'S RESOLUTIONS!'

Nicky frowned at them both.

'RIGHT!' he said. 'WE'RE OFF HOME. YES WE ARE. OH YES SIREE. OFF WE GO. HOMEWARD BOUND.' Rob was now standing a good foot away from Nicky, yet he still looked guilty as sin. As for her, she was standing against the brick wall with her arms crossed, like a teenager who'd just been given a forbidden love-bite. It was all getting too complicated. She wanted to talk about sandwiches again.

Unable to look either Rob or Amanda in the eye, she stole a glance at Mark. He raised his eyebrows slightly at her. Suddenly, from behind him, Amanda let out a sexy laugh and pointed above his head at the mistletoe. Then she landed a smacker on his lips, pulling him towards her. After coming up for air she looked over at Rob.

'Well,' she said to him huskily. 'New Year's Resolution *that*.'

Nicky knew it was rude to stare, but she couldn't help it.

Rob laughed. 'Happy New Year, mate,' he said to Mark.

'Thanks,' said Mark quietly. 'Same to you.' He looked at Nicky. Her insides flamed. 'Excuse me,' he said. He gave them all an uncertain look before disappearing into the kitchen.

'What the hell's he doing here?' whispered Nicky to Rob and Amanda.

Amanda stepped down from the kitchen to stand next to Rob.

'Gwen invited him at the Nativity Play,' she replied. 'He's staff now. Hey! Maybe we should try and fix you up with him, Nicky.'

'AHAHAHAHAHAH!' laughed Rob, pushing Amanda back into the kitchen and following her.

Nicky let them go and stood in the dark for a while. What had all that been about?

She decided to continue her list to cheer herself up, but her mind had gone a complete blank. It was no good. All she could think of was that her local supermarket had started stocking organic chocolate. When she went back in, she found Gwen, her husband and Martha's boyfriend tidying up the kitchen. She made her goodbyes and Gwen came with her to the front door. There they found Mark talking to a totally inebriated Martha. She was leaning against the wall and it was clear that were the wall not there, she would be lying on the floor.

Mark glanced at Nicky and, when she returned the

glance, he looked away with cool disdain.

'I'm afraid you missed the best of the party,' Gwen told Mark apologetically. 'Most people have to get back for the babysitter just after midnight.'

'So I see.' Mark smiled. 'I always try and see in the New Year with Oscar.'

'Aaaaaaaaaah,' sighed Martha, looking up at him dreamily. 'Isn't that *lovely*?' She turned to Gwen. 'Gwen, isn't that *lovely*?'

'Ooh *yes*.' Gwen winked. 'There's nothing lovelier than a devoted dad.'

'I think that is just *lovely*.' Martha turned to Nicky. 'Nicky, don't you think that is just *lovely*?'

'I do,' agreed Nicky. 'And the *really* lovely thing about it is that he only has to do it once a year.'

'Aaaaaaah,' agreed Martha. 'That is just *lovely*.'

'W-ell,' said Mark uneasily, 'I'm . . . I'm not doing it because I'm nice or anything. I mean it's totally selfish on my part. I just want to be with him.'

Martha gasped. 'Oh! Did you hear that? Did you hear that? Oh! That is just *lovely* –'

'You'll have to excuse Martha,' cut in Nicky. 'She teaches Reception; she's used to repeating things.'

'Do you know . . .' said Martha suddenly in a hushed voice, 'I saw Amanda and Rob leave together.'

She gave a very slow, very dramatic wink with both eyes.

'Martha!' exclaimed Gwen. 'You *are* behind the times! They've been going out with each other since last term. Haven't they?' She turned to Nicky. 'Poor Nicky missed her chance there. Unless the rumours are true and it's a rebound thing.' They all stared at her.

'Ahahahahaha!' said Nicky, her brain hurting. She had absolutely no idea what to say. 'Ah well,' she said, 'time for me to go.'

'Oooooh,' Martha put her finger to her lips, 'love triangle, eh? Say no more, say no more.' She smiled. 'Say. No. More.'

Nicky pretended to yawn. 'Thanks ever so much, Gwen. It was a lovely evening.'

'I hardly saw you, my dear,' replied Gwen. 'You were in the garden most of the time, weren't you?' She winked. 'In your cosy little love triangle.'

'No I wasn't!' corrected Nicky. 'I was in the kitchen! I was talking to Ned for hours.'

'Were you?' said Gwen, surprised. 'Where was his lovely wife? Not like Ned to be separated from Theresa. Gosh, Nicky, what effect are you having on all the taken men?'

'You're right, Gwen!' echoed Martha. 'Not like Ned at all. Were you leading him astray, you wicked girl?' She giggled. 'Where was his lovely wife?' She turned to Mark. 'She's *lovely*.'

'She was with him!' said Nicky, wondering if she was shouting. 'She was with him and me! We were all together. Talking about sandwiches. All evening.'

'Sounds thrilling.' Mark smiled.

She turned and stared at him. Then she turned to Gwen.

'Thanks for a lovely evening, Gwen.' She kissed her on the cheek. 'You excelled yourself once again. Happy New Year. See you next term. Bye, Martha.'

And she walked out without looking back.

18

Nicky greeted the brand new year with a big pot of filter coffee and an even bigger slab of organic chocolate. Then she settled down in front of the television for as long as it would take her to stand up again. She was estimating ten hours.

It was half past nine and Claire still hadn't phoned, and she was certainly not going to phone her. She did not need to be patronised today. Not when she had this much television to watch. And not by someone married to Derek. Nope. She would just sit in big fluffy pyjamas all day, eating crap and watching crap. There was something deliciously decadent about being lazy when you only did it once a year.

Her fury at Claire had subsided somewhat, but only because it had been shoved out of the way by her resentment towards Mark Samuels, anger at Rob, hostility towards Amanda and disappointment with Ally and Pete. As she got comfortable on her sofa, it became apparent that the only way to deal with all these negative emotions was to find out how to make snowflakes out of doyleys.

Just as she was learning, in reverse order, the ten best

places to hang them up for maximum effect, her doorbell rang. Reluctantly, she muted the television. It went again. She padded over to the landing and waited. It rang again. She lay on the floor to see if she recognised the shadow of the feet outside her front door.

'It's me,' shouted Claire through the letter box. 'Are you going to let me in or do we have to do this through your front door?'

Nicky considered this for a moment before swivelling on the floor, getting up and stomping downstairs to open the door. The sisters stared at each other. Nicky's first thought was that Claire was beginning to look old. There were dark puffy bags under her eyes.

'Well?' said Claire eventually. 'Are you going to ask me in? What's with the scissors?'

Nicky opened the door wide, standing back to let Claire in. She followed her into the kitchen, where Claire suddenly turned round and began.

'I've had to leave Derek with the children to come here, you know,' she said, accusingly.

Nicky blinked. 'Well, I'll try not to let you all down,' she said quietly.

Claire ignored her, waited a moment, then, seemingly too tired and emotional to argue, suddenly seated herself on a bar stool. Nicky put down the scissors, moved the other stool a bit further away, and flicked the kettle on. She would have to live without discovering the top ten places to put her snowflakes. She saw Claire glance at the clock.

'Well, *you* may have the whole day to watch television in your pyjamas,' began Claire, 'but I haven't. What the hell is going on?'

Nicky balked. 'Correct me if I'm wrong,' she said slowly, 'but I sense, from your tone, that you blame me for what's going on.'

'I most certainly do.'

She nodded slowly. 'Hmm.'

'What does that mean?'

'It means that that's rather intriguing, because I hold you entirely responsible for it.'

Claire's eyes almost sprang out of her face on sticks like a cartoon.

'Did *I* walk out of a dinner party?' she yelled. 'Did *I* insult a perfectly nice friend of yours? Did *I* hurt your feelings after you'd gone to every effort to make a nice evening –'

'*NICE?*' exploded Nicky, and Claire jumped, a little squealy noise escaping from her.

'You . . . patronising –' began Nicky.

'*WHAT*?' Claire screamed back, a little recovered now. '*Patronising?* What the *hell* do you mean by that?'

Nicky paused and tilted her head. 'It means to talk down to someone,' she explained softly.

'How the hell was I patronising?' roared Claire. 'I was trying to help!'

Nicky had trouble controlling her voice. 'Have you any idea how offensive you were the other night?' she asked. 'And how crap you made me feel?'

'Offensive!' exploded Claire. 'I made a delicious dinner and invited someone over I thought you'd like. How the hell is that offensive?'

'Calm down,' ordered Nicky. She realised this might take some time. She made a pot of tea, put it on the worktop and took out two mugs. 'Right,' she began, pouring the tea. 'Tell me – honestly – why you didn't let me know Don was coming.'

'Because I knew you wouldn't come.'

Nicky nodded. 'Exactly! Because you thought *you* knew what was good for me and *I* don't.'

'No, because you're too damn proud.'

'Of course!' roared Nicky. 'It's always *my* fault. It's all *my* fault my life isn't more like yours!'

'What?'

'How would you like it if I put myself on a one-woman mission to find you a job because, you poor thing, you haven't managed to find one by yourself?'

Claire looked at her sister as if she'd finally lost the plot.

'How would you like it,' continued Nicky, 'if every time I saw you, I brought a teaching job application with me and insisted you go for it?'

'Wha—?'

'If I insisted that instead of me visiting you at your house, you would have to come to me at school, because I was *far* too busy building my all-important career, and after all, you didn't have one, so you had loads of spare time to visit me? And then, while you sat there in the corner, watching me teach, I brought in my boss and, with all the subtlety of a bitch on heat, introduced you both and listed your CV in front of you, as if you were unable to talk for yourself?'

Claire was breathing heavily.

'And then,' continued Nicky, her voice rising steadily, 'whenever you tried to tell me to mind my own business, I turned on you and criticised your personality, telling you that it was your fault you didn't have a job.'

Claire was staring at her.

Nicky paused for a while, before asking, more quietly, 'What do you think all that would do to your self-esteem? If I constantly chip-chipped away at you – for *years* – implying that your life was crap because it wasn't like mine, and all you had to do was modify your personality to be more like mine and everything would be OK?'

Claire blinked.

'And,' continued Nicky, 'how do you think you'd end up feeling about me? Your only family in the world who cares whether you're alive or dead, but who relentlessly reminds you your life's crap?'

She sat down. Then suddenly she stood up again.

'And I do not want to meet a man like Derek!' she cried emphatically. 'I barely want to meet *Derek*!'

'All right!' croaked Claire. 'Shut up. Just shut up.'

Nicky stopped and stared at her sister. A tear was sliding down her cheek.

'What's the matter?' she asked, amazed. 'Why are you crying?'

Claire shook her head, unable to speak. Nicky waited for her to say that she had never known such remorse in her life. If only her sister could find forgiveness in her heart –

'I've thrown my life away,' whispered Claire.

Nicky blanched. 'How can you say that?' she murmured. 'You've got three amazing daughters.'

'But what about *me*?' Claire thumped her chest with her fist. The tears were coming in pairs now. 'What about me?' She wiped her nose with the back of her hand. Nicky forced herself not to respond and, after a while, Claire spoke again.

'I genuinely thought I was helping,' she sniffed.

Nicky sighed. 'Yes,' she replied firmly. 'I accept that.'

'Good.'

'But,' continued Nicky, 'that just proves that you genuinely believe I need your help, even though I've never ever asked you for it.'

'You moan about your life –'

'That's completely different from saying "Please fix me up with someone. Anyone. Just as long as he likes the beautiful bleakness of Ken Loach."'

Claire let out a snort of laughter.

'I just think sometimes,' sighed Nicky, 'that your emotions for me are founded on pity.'

'Well,' said Claire, 'you were only a kid when Mum died.'

'I know. I know. And you were fantastic. But I'm not a kid any more. And unlike you, I had a big sister to help me through that time. And no one to look after. So you could say that I had it far easier than you, not harder.'

Claire stared at her. 'I never thought of it that way,' she murmured.

There was silence.

'OK,' sighed Claire. 'I hear what you're saying. I've been . . . annoying.'

'Patronising,' said Nicky.

'Patronising.' Claire nodded.

'And you're really sorry,' said Nicky.

'Jesus Christ,' muttered Claire.

'Well, are you?' asked Nicky. 'For making me feel my life is crap?'

Claire nodded. 'Yes! When you put it like that.'

Nicky raised her eyebrows. 'What? Like it *is*.'

'Well,' said Claire, 'when you put your side of the argument forward. But that's only one side, isn't it?'

'No, it's how I feel. There is only one side to how I feel.'

'Yes, but my feelings are in there too.'

'Go on, then,' said Nicky, crossing her arms. 'This should be good. What's your side?'

'We-ell,' began Claire. 'Has it ever occurred to you that I might be jealous of your career?'

Nicky blinked. 'No,' she said firmly, putting her mug to her lips. 'Not for one second.'

'Well, there you are, then. You don't know everything.'

'What on earth have you got to be jealous of?' asked Nicky.

Claire shut her eyes and spoke with them still shut.

'I . . .' she whispered, 'have to ask Derek for money.'

Nicky stared at her sister. 'What?' she whispered back. 'Don't you have a shared bank account?'

Claire shook her head. 'No. He's set up a monthly direct debit into my housekeeping account. It hasn't gone up in ten years. If I need more, like if the girls need new shoes or I want to treat myself, I have to ask him. But, of course, if he wants to buy himself a new car, he just does it. And he uses his annual bonus on a treat for himself. Says it's his bonus and he deserves it.'

Nicky's eyes were saucers.

'Although he's never said it,' said Claire, 'I know he thinks he's better than me because he's got a job and I haven't.'

'But you have got a job,' insisted Nicky, 'you're bringing up his children. Fantastically. They're going to be future world leaders, those three.'

Claire shrugged. 'Anyone can do that.'

'Anyone except Derek,' shot Nicky. 'He can't even tie their shoelaces without a map.'

297

Claire let out a deep sigh. 'I just always assumed I'd have a career,' she said. 'I completely took it for granted. Instead, I'm slowly watching that life drift off in the other direction. And the further away it gets, the less likely it feels that I'm ever going to have it.'

Nicky's eyes suddenly filled and then overflowed. Why did this keep happening?

'What's the matter?' whispered Claire.

Nicky shook her head and waited for the feeling to pass.

'I just, I just,' she sniffed, 'I know how you feel,' she whispered. 'It's terrifying.' She suddenly got a flash fast-forward of her not pushing Rob out of the kitchen after their kiss and instead taking him into her bed and her life, giving him her key, marrying him a year later, and then popping out three children and baking Barbie cakes with *Woman's Hour* on in the background.

'But it's not too late for you,' said Claire. 'You're still young.'

'Nor you! There's loads of women going back into the workplace at your age. Older.'

Claire shook her head. 'I'm terrified. I haven't had a boss for over a decade.'

'No, you've had Derek! And three tyrants! You're going to find a boss a piece of cake after all that. Bosses are only people in smart clothes.'

After a moment's silence, Claire sipped her tea.

'Nice tea,' she said.

'Thanks.'

They both seemed to suddenly run out of energy at the same time. There was a tacit agreement that the argument was over.

'Tell me something,' said Nicky.

'Hmm?'

'Why do we feel that we can't have both? There are loads of women out there with careers and family. It's tough, but they do it. I work with enough of them. But how come you and I both seem to feel the two are mutually exclusive?'

'I don't know,' pondered Claire. 'Maybe Mum and Dad typecast us.'

It had been so long since they'd discussed their parents that it almost sounded to Nicky as if Claire was making up some fairy tale.

'Did they?' Nicky whispered back. She tried to picture her mother and father as they were when they were together, but only saw shadows against the wall of their old family kitchen.

'Yep.'

'I don't remember.'

'Well, I knew them for longer, I suppose.'

Nicky felt a stab of envy. 'Why . . . how do you mean "typecast"?'

Claire shrugged. 'You played with dollies and I didn't? Something and nothing. They said you'd be a mother and I'd have a career. I always felt they were criticising me.' Claire continued musing while Nicky sat in silence. 'I suppose, I always felt they were opposing lifestyles. You were going to have the babies, I was going to have the career. And then I met Derek and happened to marry young. And then before I knew it I was a mother of three. I had your role while you were the one with the glittering career.'

Eventually Nicky dared to speak. She spoke softly, and it felt a bit as if the voice wasn't coming from her. 'Sometimes, when I'm at your house, watching you with the girls, I feel like you got the kids . . . so I can't have any.'

Claire's face whitened. 'That's very, very weird,' she whispered. 'Because that's how I feel about you. You got the career. So I've got to make do with the kids. Don't get me wrong,' she rushed. 'I love them. But sometimes I feel like I'm living their lives and not mine.'

'And you got the husband,' allowed Nicky.

'Don't mention him,' whispered Claire. 'I've cried enough for one day.'

Claire went home and asked Nicky to pop by later. Nicky suggested they go out for lunch together instead. For the first time since she could remember, Claire accepted and so they didn't chat in her kitchen, being interrupted by the girls, they chatted in a café, being interrupted by waiters. It was Claire's idea to stay on for a coffee. Afterwards, when Nicky dropped Claire back at her house, she was preparing to say something suitably gooey. Instead, Claire said, 'I do love Derek.'

'Of course you do,' said Nicky softly.

'And it's not as bad as I made it sound.'

'Of course it isn't,' she said. 'I know that.'

'Good. Good. Well, thanks for a lovely lunch.' She gave Nicky a wide smile. 'Right. Back to my lovely family.'

Nicky watched Claire open her front door and then she put on some loud, shouty music for the journey home.

19

Mark's alarm clock leapt into action and so did he. He was in and out of the shower in five minutes. Towel tied at his waist, he knocked on Oscar's door, now only a stretch away from his own.

'OK!' shouted Oscar, a laugh escaping.

Ten minutes later, they met downstairs in the kitchen.

'Right,' said Mark, glancing up at the clock, which now swamped the new kitchen wall. 'Cereal or toast?'

'I'm not eating,' said Oscar.

'You have to,' said Mark. 'It's the first morning of your new term. You have to have breakfast.'

Oscar giggled. 'Toast.'

Mark ran to the fridge.

'No!' yelled Oscar. 'Cereal.'

Mark stared, hand on the fridge handle. 'The clock is ticking, Osc.'

'Cereal,' said Oscar firmly.

'Right. You get the cereal. I'll get the milk.'

Mark made himself an instant coffee and then threw it down the sink when he realised he'd forgotten to boil the water.

Oscar finished his cereal and leapt up from the table.

'Er!' said Mark. 'What's that?' He pointed at the cereal bowl.

Oscar tutted. 'Da-ad, it's only –'

'In the dishwasher. Now.'

Oscar ran to the bowl, squeaking with repressed excitement, ran it under the tap and put it in the dishwasher.

Coats on, bags collected, new house alarm set.

They ran out of the front door, Mark slamming it shut behind them. They sped off down the empty road. When they approached the silent school gates, Oscar ran the last few yards, hit them and shouted, 'NOW!'

Mark ran to join him and stopped his stop-watch.

'Not bad,' he said. 'Not bad at all.'

'Go on, tell me!'

'Twenty-eight minutes. A record.'

Oscar cheered.

'Which means,' said Mark, 'we can get up tomorrow as late as 7.15.'

Oscar cheered again.

'But to be on the safe side, perhaps we should make it ten past.'

Mark walked home slowly, savouring the last day of Oscar's Christmas holiday, while Oscar did his Tigger impersonation of running a few steps ahead and then running back to walk with his dad, then running ahead again only to come back again. Excellent exercise.

The next morning, first day of the spring term, adrenaline was pumping fiercely through the Samuels household. The very fabric of the house seemed to pulsate with it and everything looked somehow different today. When Mark knocked on Oscar's bedroom door, Oscar appeared fully dressed. By the time Mark sped downstairs, Oscar had already put the cereal bowl in the dishwasher. By the time they were on their way to the school, they were well on their way to a new personal best. Oscar ran the last ten yards and hit the school gates. It was Mark's turn to cheer.

'Twenty-*two* minutes!' he shouted.

They did a high-five outside the school gates.

'How are you feeling?'

'Fine.'

'You'll be great,' Oscar told his father. 'I know you will.'

'Thanks, Osc,' said Mark. 'You have a good day too.'

Just then Oscar saw his friend Matthew. Mark felt he now knew Matthew quite well after having been at home when he'd come to play with Oscar. Mark had even made them lunch together. Oscar shouted across the road to Matthew and they raced each other across the playground to the school entrance. Mark watched through the gate and when Oscar hit the door first, he kept the cheer to himself.

A child – possibly as old as nine – walked past him and through the gate. He followed.

It was 3 January, the first day of the new term, and the staffroom was empty when Nicky arrived. She made herself a cup of tea and had just concertinaed her diaphragm into a chair when Janet, Miss James's secretary, appeared at the staffroom door. She glanced round the room and then back at Nicky. She raised her eyebrows and pointed to Miss James's office.

'Miss James's office?' Janet gave a quick nod. 'Now?'

Nicky's breath caught. She heaved herself up out of the

chair and followed Janet down the corridor. The photo-copier was set back off it, just outside the bursar's tiny office. Both were opposite Reception and Miss James's office. As she passed the photocopier, Nicky heard office furniture being moved in the bursar's office, giving her the excuse to look at it. The door was ajar. So, she thought, he's already in. Mark Samuels was in the building. And in his own office, not in Miss James's office. Which meant he wasn't waiting for her in there, ready to brandish a P45 in her face.

Janet's usual style was to sit down at her desk and give a curt flick of her head to indicate that Miss James was ready for her, but today, she gently tapped on the open, connecting door to Miss James's office. Miss James started with shock.

'Miss Hobbs is here,' said Janet with a quiet significance that Nicky found most ominous.

Two Year 5s, who had come in early for an assembly meeting, were now standing at her puzzle. Miss James turned to them.

'Don't worry about that now,' she said. 'Off you go.'

Both children stared at her in disbelief before running out fast. Nicky swallowed hard. Now she was frightened.

'Hello, my dear!' cried Miss James. 'Come in, my love. Come in, come in.'

Nicky walked into the office. She heard the door softly click shut behind her. Miss James gave her puzzle one last look, and then stepped slowly to her desk. She smoothed the back of her skirt with her palms, sat down, and gave Nicky one of her long, slow smiles.

'Do sit down, my dear.'

Nicky sat down.

'How are you feeling?' she asked.

'Fine!' Nicky replied throatily. She coughed. 'Looking forward to the new term.'

Miss James nodded. 'Good girl, good girl.'

Nicky's throat closed.

'Well now,' said Miss James. She paused. She cocked her head. She straightened it again. She looked across the desk at Nicky and sucked her lips in, with an air of sad finality. Nicky's ears started whistling.

'I have some news,' announced Miss James with an air of concluding sorrow.

Nicky's blood rushed from her extremities straight for the door.

'I think you may have guessed it, my dear,' said Miss James kindly.

Nicky's head nodded. So this was it. Mark Samuels had said he couldn't work in the same school as her and Miss James had chosen him.

'I am . . .' Miss James gave a sigh, her eyes down, 'leaving.' She looked up at Nicky. 'I am leaving, my dear.'

Nicky stared.

'Retiring,' continued Miss James. 'Yes, I am . . . retiring.'

Nicky's blood came back, agog. Meanwhile, her mind went on a little journey. She had no idea Miss James was of retirement age. She'd always imagined she was in her fifties. Blimey. The woman looked fantastic for her age. Hardly any lines round her eyes at all. Her skin was absolutely amazing. And her figure was still good too. But then she hadn't had any children, had she?

'You're very quiet,' said Miss James.

'Oh, I was just thinking . . .'

'Ah! Were you? Were you, indeed. Good girl. And *what* were you thinking?'

'Um, well, I was actually thinking how good you looked for sixty.'

Miss James roared her approval. She leant forward and whispered, 'Clarins.'

'Wow,' Nicky whispered back.

Miss James snapped back into work mode.

'Now,' she said, 'this, of course, leaves a little opening, does it not?'

Nicky's ears whistled again.

'Have you, my dear, ever considered being a head-mistress?'

Oh, only every time I look at you, thought Nicky.

'We-ell,' she said slowly, 'it's something I definitely aspire to, yes.'

'Good *girl*,' accentuated Miss James. 'Good girl, good girl, good girl, good *girl*.'

Nicky decided now was not the time to question the use of the word 'girl' for a woman of thirty who was the Deputy Headmistress of a school. Did Miss James ever call Rob a 'good boy'? she wondered.

'The reason I ask, my dear, is because I would very much like you . . .' Nicky's ears started to whistle an almost distinct tune, 'to apply . . . for my job.'

'Gosh,' whispered Nicky. 'Gosh.'

Miss James smiled beneficently at her.

'Thank you so much,' breathed Nicky suddenly. 'I'm honoured.'

'You are most, *most* welcome,' said Miss James. 'But,' she almost shouted, 'this is not a decision to be taken lightly. The job would mean, of course, far less contact with the children (unless you wanted to be a teaching head, but I don't recommend it), a nice little pay increase and possibly,' she smiled, 'some more headache pills.'

Nicky laughed heartily.

'There is of course *considerably* more administrative work –'

'Of course.'

'– you would be constantly walking the tightrope between keeping the governors, the bursar, all your staff and your pupils happy.'

'Of course.'

'And, let us not forget, not all good teachers make good heads,' continued Miss James. 'The two are very different jobs. Hardly any crossover at all, in fact.'

Nicky was beginning to wonder why she was here.

'But,' concluded Miss James, 'there are exceptions.'

Nicky smiled.

'Now,' said Miss James, 'it just so happens that I have also asked Mr Pattison to apply.'

'Oh, obviously.'

'He happened to pop into school a couple of weeks ago during the holidays to do some preparation work and I was here doing one thing or another. I decided to use the opportunity to have a word with him about it. So he already knows. And of course, he also knows you will be going for the job too. And you'll be thrilled to know he's as delighted for you as he is for himself!'

Nicky smiled wanly.

'I trust that will not be a problem for you,' said Miss James.

'Oh no, no, of course not,' said Nicky, smiling properly.

'After all, you are both professionals.'

'Absolutely.'

'But I am aware that you're both friends too. Would that I could insist they create two Headship posts!' She laughed heartily and Nicky joined in. 'But alas, they can't.' Miss James stopped laughing abruptly and so did Nicky. 'And so I find myself in the awkward position of having to tell my two best candidates to apply for the same post.'

'Thank you.'

Miss James leant in. 'I made him promise faithfully to me that he wouldn't mention any of this to you until I had had a chance to speak to you properly.' She waggled her finger at Nicky. 'So you must forgive him for keeping a secret from you!'

'Of course.'

'Now, naturally, you know the legal situation. I have no choice but to advertise this vacancy nationally.'

'Of course.'

'And confer with all my wonderful governors.'

'Right.' There was a pause. 'Well,' Nicky laughed, 'I won't get too excited, then.'

Miss James banged her desk. Papers flew. 'Oh! You must get *very* excited,' she ordered. 'Very excited indeed!'

'Right.' Nicky smiled. 'OK.' Miss James stared at her, nodding regularly. 'I am . . . very excited indeed,' offered Nicky.

'Good! *Life* . . . is exciting,' trilled Miss James, practically vibrating with the excitement of it all.

It occurred to Nicky to look for hidden cameras. It would explain a lot. She nodded and gave her boss a respectful smile.

'Now,' continued Miss James. 'Technically, the job isn't going to be available until the end of the summer. And it's only going to be made public knowledge to the rest of the school in the spring. Of course, Janet knows, but she is my right arm; my appendage; my other limb. And of course, our new wonderful bursar is, as they say in the classics, "in the know". But none – no, not one – of your fellow teachers knows. So! You have three months to think long and hard about whether or not you want to go for this. And yes, during those three months, it will become my task to observe you – and Mr Pattison – with an even keener eye than of yore, but it is always kindly, my dear, it is always kindly. And then, of course, should you decide to apply, the very process of doing so will mean more work, facing some rather stressful interviews, and directly competing with at least one of your colleagues. Obviously, others may apply. So I have chosen to give you – and Mr Pattison – a long time to really think this through. Think of what you want from your life. This is a big step. You want it to be one in the right direction.'

Nicky nodded, utterly focussed and completely confused.

Miss James stood up and extended her hand across the mound of papers on her desk. Nicky rose and shook it.

'Good luck,' whispered Miss James, shaking her head in nostalgic wonder. Nicky wondered if perhaps she was waiting for her to kneel and offer the top of her head to be kissed. She gave what she hoped was a professional yet polite, confident yet not cocky, assured yet warm, firm yet friendly handshake. Then she waited for her hand to be released and left the room on only slightly trembling legs.

She didn't cry this time. She wanted this job. She went to the toilets just to look at herself in the mirror. Did she look different? Did it show? Thank God she had never taken things further with Rob. And that they had got over their hiccup like adults. She smiled at her reflection. She was 'gonna whip his ass'. She returned to the staffroom, trying to look as calm as possible. When she was nearly at the door, she was stopped in her tracks by a noise behind her.

'PSSST!'

She froze.

'OY!' An excited whisper from behind her shook the corridor. 'NICKY!'

Slowly she turned round to face Rob, who, from the expression on his face, had just been in to see Miss James and now knew that she knew. He ran down the corridor, ending in a skid at her side. He was grinning widely until he saw her face.

'Hello!' he said. 'Someone died?'

'How appropriate do you think it is to call me that in the corridor?' she asked. 'Especially the corridor outside Miss James's office?'

'Oh, yeah, sorry,' he said. 'Didn't think.'

'Well, Didn't Think was made to think.' She started walking.

'How?' He followed.

'Dead arm.' She opened the door. Amanda looked over and gave her an unmistakable scowl. Then she looked away and ignored them.

Nicky turned away from Rob to join Ally, who immediately turned her back on Pete.

'Morning!' greeted Ally. 'God, you look like shit.'

'Thanks,' said Nicky.

Pete turned to look at her. 'What happened?' he asked.

'Don't tell me you accidentally hugged a child? That's ten years, eight with good behaviour.'

'Nothing happened!' she retorted. 'Can't a person just look like shit occasionally?'

'Of course,' said Ally. 'Pete does all the time. He's an inspiration to us all.'

'Well,' said Pete shortly, 'where you lead, I follow.'

They stared at each other. Nicky wondered if the atmosphere would get even worse with a secret. If that was even possible. Amanda and Rob wandered over. As she watched them, it occurred to her that there was every chance that Rob might actually tell his girlfriend this secret and not his colleagues. Was the gang's heyday, in effect, over?

'Hello, Gang!' exclaimed Amanda.

Yes, thought Nicky. It was.

She decided to eat on her own in the canteen that day. She hated the fact that she had to keep a secret from Ally. She also didn't trust herself not to tell her. She needed a day to stop jigging in her seat before she could trust herself to spend time with her. As she started to eat, a shadow fell on her lunch. She looked up. Rob was sitting in front of her, an expression of intense earnestness on his face.

'I chucked Amanda,' he whispered urgently. 'It's over.'

She blinked. She wasn't quite sure how to react. Obviously, this was good news because Amanda was a sly bitch and deserved a good chucking, but there were other things to consider. Firstly, why was Rob telling her as though it was of huge significance? Secondly, they were, as of this morning, rivals for the same job. Thirdly, and perhaps most importantly, she had just put an enormous amount of shepherd's pie in her mouth.

'I know you've been asked to apply for Miss James's job,' he rushed. 'And I know you know I have too. And I know you know that I've known for a while.'

She slowly circled the pie over her teeth to the other side of her mouth. It was good pie.

'Nicky,' he urged, 'Miss James wouldn't let me tell you. I promise. Nicky, don't do this to me. This is me talking. Rob.'

Her eyebrows flickered with a hint of a frown as she swallowed and then washed down her mouthful with some water.

He sighed. 'Shit, Nicky. I know I've been acting a bit . . . crap recently. You know . . . since . . . you know. Look, I'm sorry. I'm sorry about the Nativity Play. That was mean.'

'I absolutely loved the Nativity Play,' said Nicky. 'Can't believe we never thought of it before. And the kids loved it too. And the parents adored it.'

'That's great! Well, it really was very good. It was quite your night that night.'

'Hmm,' said Nicky, her mind returning to Rob and Amanda's liaison.

'So!' he rushed. 'Can we just put all that behind us?'

Unsure how to react, she decided to delay the need. She put another enormous bite of shepherd's pie in her mouth.

'OK, I'll admit,' continued Rob, 'my stupid macho pride was hurt. And I really . . .' he reduced his voice to a whisper, 'I really wanted you. Badly. So I dealt with the hurt by acting like a twat. Amanda was . . . I don't know. Revenge? Not nice, but I couldn't help it. But that's all over now. Thank God. Just forgive me, please.'

Nicky stared at him. Then she sucked the sweet meaty

juices from her gums, wondering how words like that could still do unmentionable things to her, even when she was eating. She had no idea her insides could multi-task. Wasn't the human body amazing?

'Come on,' he begged, his voice urgent. 'Let's . . . start again? Just . . . you know, us. Being the good-looking half of the gang again?'

She nearly choked. 'Rob!' she shrieked. 'That's a terrible thing to say!'

'Friends?' he grinned.

'Friends,' she agreed, grinning back.

'Oh! Thank God, Nicky. I missed you.'

There was a pause. 'Me too,' said Nicky.

'Right! Now!' he exclaimed. 'One thing: One, promotion does *not* mean you won't have children.

'I know that!' she squealed. 'Crikey, I'm *so* over that.'

'Really?'

'Yes!' she said. 'I can't believe I cried about it. I think it was just the shock of the promotion. But, don't worry, I'm not shocked this time.'

'That's fantastic,' he said, slapping the dinner table with his hand. 'Absolutely fantastic. Brilliant. And more importantly, I'm just glad we're talking again. I couldn't have gone on like that for much longer.' He gave her pie a pensive gaze. 'Is that as good as it looks?'

'Better. And you're not having any.'

'Hmm,' he said, shaking his head. 'Can't resist a cooked breakfast, myself. My appetite's come back now we're talking. I feel like I've been living a lie for the past few months.' He gave her hand a squeeze. 'Don't go away, Nick.'

He got some paper serviettes and a great big cooked breakfast while Nicky sat back watching him, smiling. They were friends again and all was well with the world.

As Rob queued for his food and Nicky savoured the last of the pie, Mark Samuels spent his first lunch-time in his new job wishing he could see more than the long coils of hair down her hourglass back.

20

Miss James always allowed her new members of staff one full day of relative anonymity in their new job before formally introducing them to everyone. So today was the day to introduce the new bursar to her band of merry men.

'Hello!' she exclaimed from the doorway. 'Hello, hello, hello, hello, hello!'

She tiptoed through the assorted paraphernalia towards her spot, followed by a rather sheepish-looking Mark. The room hushed. For want of anywhere else to look, Nicky looked at everyone else as they all looked at Mark.

This was a momentous occasion indeed. A brand new male in the tired old staffroom! And not just any brand new male, but a tall, broad one with an open, handsome face, warm eyes and a gorgeous smile; a man with two legs, both as long as each other, a man who didn't have too much hair sprouting from his ears or nose, nor too little from his head; a man wearing a close-fitting, stylish, expensive suit that fitted him in all the right places. A man, in short, who had no immediately obvious reasons for working in a place where most of the people were under four foot.

As Nicky glanced round the room, she thought she could

almost hear excited ova whooshing down Fallopian tubes.

Mark reached Miss James's side at the front of the room. His mouth hinted at a shy smile. The silence intensified.

'Now,' confided Miss James, 'the more observant among you will have noticed that I am Not Alone this morning.'

Hearty laughter rang out in the staffroom; a laughter that told Mark loud and clear that he didn't have to be mad to work here, but by George, it helped. Miss James put a motherly hand on his arm and squeezed it. He smiled at her. Several of the weaker ova fainted.

'This is Mark Samuels,' announced Miss James proudly. 'Some of you will know him simply as Oscar Samuels' father . . .'

There was utter silence compounded by many blank faces. Had a pin dropped, people would have jumped. Nicky was pleased to see that at least Mark had the decency to look embarrassed.

'. . . and some of you, I believe, met him at Gwen's wonderful New Year Eve's party.'

A couple of people nodded a hello to him.

'But for the rest of you,' continued Miss James, 'you are meeting Heatheringdown's new bursar.'

There was a murmur of surprised approval from most. And from those who had met him before, there was a murmur of unsurprised approval. Miss James suddenly launched into raucous applause. Everyone joined in. As it died down, she continued.

'I am absolutely delighted to welcome Mark to Heatheringdown,' she said. 'He comes fresh from a top City firm of accountants, where he was one of the youngest partners.' There was a gasp of female admiration. 'And he will be bringing all his financial genius, wisdom and experience to us here at Heatheringdown.'

Nicky wasn't sure if Mark's increasing look of panic was from the expectations being laid out before him or the determined devotion in the eyes of most of the female staff.

'His first job,' went on Miss James, 'will be to come up with some fantastic fundraising plans for us. So if anyone has any ideas they want to put to him, you know where his office is. His door will always be open, isn't that right, Mark?'

'Absolutely,' he said firmly.

'Then,' continued Miss James, 'he will be putting that fantastic mathematical brain of his to work on our ever-depressing budget, so that Heatheringdown continues to be the top state school in the area. Now. Do any of my trusty team of top teachers in the borough have any questions?'

After a moment's pause, Amanda put her hand up and her chest out.

'Hi there, Mark.' She smiled.

'Hi.' He smiled back.

'I'm Amanda – Miss Taylor – and I teach Year 4. We met at the Nativity Play. And the party.'

'Yes, I remember.' A hint of a blush highlighted his cheek-bones. 'Hi there, Amanda.'

Smiles all round. Nicky remembered the mistletoe kiss and stared at Amanda in some awe.

'You may find my question slightly impertinent,' Amanda went on, 'but –'

'Ooh!' said Miss James. 'How exciting.'

More laughter. This was a totally mad morning.

'Well,' Amanda said, smiling, 'I should imagine this is the question on everyone's lips . . .'

Nicky wondered if she was about to propose.

'. . . um,' continued Amanda, 'it's just that I'm fascinated . . . what on earth made you leave the bustling City life for our humble, little, albeit excellent, school?'

There was a Mexican wave of nodding.

'Good question!' cried Miss James. 'Go to the top of the class!'

Mark leant against the table behind him and rested one hand on its edge. He slowly ran the other hand through his sunlit-sand hair while his full, though masculine, lips slid into a modest smile, accentuating his firm jawline. Several menopausal symptoms reversed.

'We-ell,' he began. 'It's funny you should ask that question, because I actually have one of you to thank for that.'

Silence.

'You see,' he continued, 'thanks to the observations of your very own Miss Hobbs at Parents' Evening, I went on to make one of the biggest decisions of my life.'

All eyes turned briefly to Nicky. Nicky blinked.

'It was Miss Hobbs's highly perceptive comments about Oscar that made me realise,' he went on, 'that I wanted – and needed – to spend more quality time with my boy. Yes, City firms pay well, but in return they want your life, so you miss the fundamental, important things. Hopefully, with this job, I can put my training and experience to excellent use, as well as see my boy grow up.'

Had there been a scientist in the room this would have been a Eureka moment. The room was experiencing a monumental rise in fertility. One of the teachers opened a window.

Miss James gave a little clap. 'So, Nicky! We have you to thank for our new addition!'

'Well, *I* certainly have her to thank,' answered Mark modestly. 'Whether *you* guys do is something we have yet to find out. I am new to the world of schools, but I promise you all, I'm a fast learner. And as Miss James said, all advice will be most welcome.' He smiled out at his audience.

'Did you have any idea about this, my dear?' Miss James asked across the room to Nicky.

'No,' she said. 'None at all.'

'And now that you do,' twinkled Miss James, 'do you have anything to add to this confession?'

'Yes.' Nicky smiled. 'If he's not any good, I never saw him before in my life.'

There was an explosion of laughter, followed by applause. This was an extraordinary morning in an extraordinary place.

After the applause died down, Amanda sat upright in her chair all pert and polite.

'Well, either way,' she beamed, waiting for all eyes to return to her before continuing, 'thank you, Mark, for answering my question so honestly.'

Another smile flashed from Mark. 'My pleasure,' he said softly.

Nicky glanced at Rob, who was staring intently at a speck of dirt on his trouser leg.

The bell rang for assembly and Nicky gathered her belongings and her wits together. Could this be the same man she had rowed with at Parents' Evening? She stood up and looked over to where Mark was standing. Only the top of his head was visible. A crowd of women had gathered around this marvel of manhood to welcome him into their world and into their hearts; for here was a man who wanted to spend more time with his child and had cheekbones you could slice cheese with. He was more than a man, he was a phenomenon. Just wait till they find out he's a widower, thought Nicky. There won't be a dry seat in the house.

She did not begrudge them their admiration. Had he been a beautiful female he would now be swamped by male teachers. It was only biology. But it did make her feel less inclined to join the throng of extras, when she had, a while ago, daydreamed about being the female lead. She glanced again at his growing circle of admirers. Just a teensy-weensy part of her wished that they had seen him pre-Parents' Evening. And a slightly bigger part of her considered being the one to paint that picture for them.

Nonetheless, he had just given her the best reference she'd ever had – and in public, in front of all her peers and her boss. For that, and that alone, he deserved a big thank you. Just not now.

She sat down again, pulled her hair back into its regulation assembly ponytail and slipped on her glasses. When she stood up again, Ally was by her side and Rob by hers. They caught up with Pete and it almost felt like old times again as they ambled to assembly together.

'Please, Miss Hobbs,' joked Pete. 'Can I touch your hem?'

'No,' said Nicky. 'But you may lick my shoes.'

'What do you think of our new bursar?' Ally asked her, ignoring him. 'Eight out of ten?'

Nicky smiled. 'Oh easily,' she said. 'Nine possibly.'

Ally nodded. 'Yeah. I think you're right.'

Pete tutted. 'That is so offensive.'

'And crap,' muttered Rob. 'He's a complete tosser. Did you notice how he had to get in a mention of his big pay packet?'

'Oh yes!' gasped Ally. 'I noticed that. When he leant back against the desk.'

'Me too!' giggled Nicky. 'Ten out of ten.'

It was lunch-time before Nicky had a chance to speak to Mark properly and to thank him. As soon as she'd eaten, she hot-footed it to his office, giving a fearless knock on his door. The door opened slowly and Amanda appeared in front of her.

'Oh!' cried Amanda. 'It's the perceptive one herself!' She opened the door a fraction wider and welcomed Nicky into Mark's office. As Mark had moved his desk to the other side of the room, Nicky was now facing a wall.

'Oh no, it's OK,' she said, stepping back quickly. 'I can come back another time. It wasn't important –'

'Don't be silly!' cried Amanda, taking her by the arm. 'We were only having a quick chat. Weren't we, Mark?'

Mark was now standing beside Amanda. When he ushered Nicky in, she saw why it had taken him so long to appear. The tiny office was full of packing boxes yet to be emptied. He had clearly had a bigger office in the City.

Amanda propped herself up against the window-ledge, where she casually picked imaginary bits of fluff off her blouse while giving a running commentary of Mark's ideas for his office.

Mark and Nicky stood opposite each other. She noticed that his cheeks were seriously flushed. He had either just lugged a heavy box across the office or given Amanda an energetic seeing-to. She remembered Oscar's au pair. Then

321

she pictured Mark and Amanda spreadeagled on his desk. Then she had visions of Mark going through the female staff like a dog out of a trap.

Gosh, it was hot in here. Meanwhile, Mark's flush was haemorrhaging down his neck. He was turning puce in front of her eyes. Nicky noticed how pungent Amanda's perfume was. She looked out of the tiny window and watched the clouds race by.

'It's not much of a view,' said Amanda, following her gaze, 'but at least it's a bit of light.' Then she stepped across the office and perched on the edge of Mark's desk.

'I thought we could set up a brain-storming meeting for fundraising ideas,' she announced. 'In a pub. One evening. What do you think, Nicky? Good idea?' Nicky opened her mouth to answer. 'Mark?' asked Amanda, turning away from her.

'Yes, great idea,' replied Mark, nodding to Nicky. 'It would be a nice way to get to know everyone properly, too.'

Nicky wondered who would babysit Oscar. 'Or,' she said, 'we could ask the children to come up with some ideas. It's their school. And they're usually really imaginative.'

'Oh yes! Of course!' said Mark. 'Brilliant. Of course.'

Amanda laughed. 'I don't think they allow children in pubs, Nicky,' she said. 'I'll put together a few dates and see if there's any interest in the staffroom. In fact, we could do that now, couldn't we, Nicky?' She hopped off Mark's desk. 'Or did you want . . . a little private tête-à-tête, just the two of you?'

'No, no, it's fine,' said Nicky. 'I'll come with you.'

'Hold on!' laughed Mark. 'Did you want a word, um, Miss Hobbs, Nicky?'

'Um . . .'

'Amanda.' Mark looked over Nicky's head to Amanda. 'If you don't mind . . .'

'Of course not!' sang Amanda gaily. 'I'll get those dates together. Cheerybye.'

Nicky tried to smile. She turned back to Mark. He looked at her with an expectant smile.

'Hello,' he said.

Nicky was almost fazed. The word seemed so personal, somehow.

'Um, I just wanted to say,' she began softly, 'how much I regret my outburst to you at Parents' Evening.'

Mark stopped smiling.

'It was,' she continued, her head down, 'unforgivable and highly unprofessional of me, and, I can assure you, completely out of character.'

There was a pause. She was just wondering how she could turn this into a thank-you for his performance this morning, when he spoke.

'Ri-ight,' he said slowly. 'I see.' There was silence. 'Well, thank you for that. But,' he said quickly, 'I don't regret it at all.'

She gave him a questioning look.

'And,' he spoke quickly, 'it's me who should be apologising.'

'Oh?'

'It wasn't long before I grew absolutely appalled by what I'd said to you that night. Having met you, I now know that I was so utterly and completely wrong.'

She decided now was the moment to say her piece, albeit much more softly than she'd ever practised.

'For the record,' she said, her eyes wide and direct, 'I don't mother my pupils. I teach them.'

'And, for the record,' he joined in, with a smile, 'I have always loved my son. I just hadn't realised the best way to show it.'

There was a knock on the door and Amanda popped her head round it.

'I've got three possible dates, so get your diary out, Mark!' she said.

Nicky smiled at him, able to ignore Amanda now that she was happy again.

'And I wanted to thank you for that brilliant job reference you gave me this morning. That was very generous of you.'

He gave her a serious look. 'All true.'

That night she decided to break with tradition. She was not going to do any homework. She deserved a night off. Not only that, she would give herself a home-spa evening – complete with hot, aromatherapy bath followed by face-pack and *EastEnders*. Possibly a packet of Maltesers. As she walked out of the school and across the playground, she was struck by how warm the air was. Her shoulders dropped.

When she got home, she walked straight to her bedroom, dropped her clothes where she stood and climbed into bed. Within seconds she was asleep, so she didn't hear the answerphone message from Claire an hour later, who, coincidentally, was also breaking with tradition.

21

Nicky didn't hear Claire's message until the following evening. When she did, she played it again, then turned off the radio, sat down in the silence and played it once more. She smiled the sort of smile that only happens when you're on your own; almost invisible to the naked eye but great big clanging bells inside.

She picked up the phone to return the call and then, just for the hell of it, played it again. If she'd had a technical mind, she'd have turned it into her mobile ring-tone.

'Hi there,' came Claire's voice, loud and clear. 'Hope you're OK. Just wanted to . . . well, ask for some help really. Could you call me?'

It turned out that Claire had spotted a part-time job vacancy as a teaching assistant in her local paper. She needed help with writing an application letter and advice on whom to ask for references. Nicky offered to pop over at the weekend to help, but for the first time in living memory, Claire suggested she come to Nicky's flat, 'no children or . . . distractions'.

When Claire arrived on Saturday morning, she brought flowers.

They sat down at the kitchen table and Nicky started quizzing her big sister on why she wanted the job, what qualities she felt she could bring to it and which way up you held a computer. As the two women sat there, Nicky felt as though their roles had been reversed, as if she was a child teaching an adult how to walk. She discovered that when it came to the world of work, interviews and office politics, she knew quite a lot. And Claire knew practically nothing. But Derek knew less than both of them, because he thought his wife was having a body wrap.

'It knocks inches off you,' informed Claire. 'And makes your skin all silky smooth.'

'Won't he notice that you haven't had it done?' asked Nicky.

'Not unless I put an England kit on,' she muttered. 'And even then he'd only be lying back and thinking of England.'

'Maybe I should have a body wrap,' mused Nicky.

'Hah!' exploded her sister.

Nicky bristled. 'Just because I haven't got a man doesn't mean I don't want to feel good about myself.'

Claire stared at her. 'The reason you don't need a body wrap, you moron, is because you have a body that looks like an After picture.'

'Oh. Thanks.'

'I've had two 41-week pregnancies and one 42-week pregnancy,' continued Claire. 'My belly is blancmange. My thighs are jelly. And as for my arse and tits, they're just great big mounds of sponge.' She stared ahead. 'I'm a walking trifle,' she murmured.

Nicky's stomach rumbled.

Over the next few days, Nicky made sure she was on hand

to help with whatever Claire needed. When Claire was sent an application form, Nicky helped her use a computer to fill it in. When Claire was invited for an interview, Nicky asked Miss James if Claire could observe a teacher's assistant for a day. Miss James let her observe for a week. And when Claire won the job, Nicky helped her tell Derek, who would probably have to make do without a casserole on Thursdays from now on. Derek surprised them both by being genuinely delighted for his wife and even offering to make do with takeaway once a week from now on. And Claire surprised Nicky by buying her a voucher for a body wrap as a thank-you present. Nicky decided to save it for a rainy day. Or better still, a really sunny one.

Back at work, now that Amanda was not with Rob all the time any more, the gang had made a comeback. It was difficult to pinpoint how or why, but as with most come-backs, it didn't quite have the same feel to it any more. After she knew that Amanda had been chucked by Rob, Nicky tried never to give her reason to feel jealous. Previously, she had never put much thought into what Amanda might actually be feeling, especially about Rob. But that had changed now. Amanda had an emotional claim to Rob, even if that emotion was anger, and Nicky respected that. Yet Amanda seemed determined to cope well with the break-up and spent far less time being with Rob than she did with Mark. It wasn't difficult to work out how Amanda was planning to deal with heartbreak, if indeed, thought Nicky, hearts made of bark could break. In fact, as the term progressed, Nicky even began to feel a creeping respect for Amanda's stiff upper lip, although it was certainly the only part of her body she had any respect for.

But at least two good things had come out of Amanda and Rob splitting up. One was that the old Rob was back and their friendship was better than ever. It was, dare she thought it, a bit like it had been before the fireworks display, which meant (when she was honest with herself) she was back to a constant background hum of her trying to understand what he really wanted from her, let alone what she wanted from him.

After a while, he started up the flirting with her again, but it had a different feel to it now. It felt somehow far more serious than before. If she ever found herself (late at night in bed on her own) envisaging this as the nearest she'd ever get to motherhood, she would immediately force herself to think of something else. Then she'd go to sleep and dream of babies with Rob's eyes.

Two main concerns were back in her life again; one was that her self-esteem was relative to how much Rob Pattison flirted with her. And the other was that she still felt relieved that she hadn't completely burnt her bridges as far as sharing a future with him was concerned. She sometimes wondered if all she wanted him for was his ripe DNA.

This was getting ridiculous. Was she going to spend the rest of her life going round and round in circles with this man? When would she ever get real closure? Would one of them have to die for that to ever really happen? And if so, how could she commit the perfect murder?

The other good thing about Rob and Amanda splitting up was that Amanda was around less. She spent time with other teachers and wasn't even in the staffroom as much any more. It felt as if a bad spirit had left the building. Unfortunately, there was no avoiding her at the fundraising meeting. Nicky hadn't wanted to go, but she knew that as Deputy she would be expected to. True to her word, Amanda arranged a pub evening to brainstorm ideas and give Mark a chance to get to know everyone better. Or rather, as it turned out, to get to know Martha, Rob, Amanda and Nicky better.

Nicky had begged Ally and Pete to come too, but they were having none of it.

'The perk of not being a high-flyer,' Ally told her, 'is that we don't have to do anything we don't want to.'

'Too right,' said Pete. 'Even if it is arranged by a woman with legs up to her armpits.'

'*Especially* if it's arranged by her,' muttered Ally.

'Yes, sorry, I meant that,' said Pete. 'Hey!' He turned to Ally. 'I've got an idea!'

'What?' asked Ally.

'We could go and see a film instead.'

Ally frowned. 'What? And miss *Corrie*? Have you ever listened to anything I've ever said?'

When Miss James heard of the plan, she was thrilled, not only that there would be 'grand ideas afoot', but that the 'young'uns' were socialising together.

Nicky didn't feel young on the evening of the meeting though. It had been a grim, grey day that had never worked up enough energy to create real light, and by the time evening had resolutely set in, the wind had turned wild, heaving the rain into horizontal, razor-sharp sheets. When Rob phoned Nicky to say he would pick her up on his way to the pub, they both knew that that was the only way she'd have got further than her car door.

Her home was made for evenings like this. She could sink into an armchair and look out over the top of the battered, windswept trees, heat from the flat below percolating up through the floorboards, and feel safe and settled. If she had a log fire and a cat she'd never leave again.

By the time Rob rang on the door, she'd had a hot soak and changed into some warm jeans and a snug sweater. She arranged her woolly cap on her head, gave herself a quick once-over in the hall mirror, rearranged it, and ran to his car. She slammed the door shut against the elements and they drove off in silence. When he eventually started up some small-talk, it felt like he was doing it from a long way away.

The pub was in Highgate, near Mark's old house and so near Amanda's flat that her hair didn't even look wet. She was already there, sitting on a cushioned window-seat next to an old log fire, busily texting someone. Nicky prepared herself for a comment about Rob and her arriving together ('Do you two always come at the same time?'), but instead Amanda lifted her head, gave them half a smile each and then returned to her texting. Rob went straight to the bar and Nicky joined Amanda by the fire. After only five minutes, Amanda finished her text and put her phone away.

'We're a small team tonight,' she said, 'but I don't think that's going to be a problem.'

Rob arrived with both their orders and they all ignored the fact that he knew them without asking. They made polite conversation for the next quarter of an hour, Rob content and at ease with the situation, Amanda aggressively so. For the first five minutes Nicky believed this might be the dawning of a new era. Amanda was obligingly sweet to her, even going so far as to complement her on her hat. She went one further and asked if she could try it on and then, admitting that it didn't work half as well on her, gave it back to Nicky. Nicky reluctantly put it with her coat, watching Amanda smooth down her glossy black hair. When Amanda caught her eye, Nicky looked away. She knew now that her own hair would look as woolly as the hat, but to go to the ladies to tame it would show she cared. It would also take about half an hour. She cursed her vanity for caring. Then she cursed her stupidity for giving her hat to Amanda. Then she cursed Amanda, and felt better. During the second five minutes, she happened to glance at Amanda when she wasn't expecting it and caught real hardness in her eyes before the camouflage smile appeared. They both knew she'd seen it. Into the third five minutes, Amanda was tilting her head at every smile in her direction to compensate, but it was too late. Amanda knew she'd been caught and it was Nicky's turn to start overcompensating. After a while, they were smiling and tilting their heads so much they were both getting one of Nicky's heads.

When Martha arrived she received a rousing welcome. They didn't even mind that she'd brought her boyfriend with her. It turned out that he was seeing a friend nearby, so had been able to give Martha a lift. He kissed her before leaving and passed Mark at the door.

'Hi, Mark!' cried Amanda.

He greeted her back, and gave them all a disarming smile in turn. When he got to Nicky, he gave a miniscule lift of the eyebrows and widening of his smile. Her hand instinctively reached for her hat. Mark put his hand out to Rob who shook it, stood up, and offered him his seat, next to Amanda. Amanda smiled the cool, easy smile of the most popular girl in the class, but Nicky wasn't having any of it. Sitting opposite the woman for the past fifteen minutes had rendered her unable to catch her eye without wanting to scratch it out, so she quickly moved up one, making room for Mark next to her. This way, she was now sitting next to Amanda and wouldn't have to look at her. She didn't care how much Amanda might hate her for doing it, she knew that if she had to look at her for another five minutes, there would be a cat fight. Martha, however, was delighted, as she was now seated on the other side of Mark, with Rob on her other side.

'So!' said Mark, sitting next to Nicky and taking off his leather jacket. 'What have I missed?'

'Oh, absolutely nothing!' laughed Amanda. 'We couldn't have been more bored!'

Rob and Nicky exchanged a look and Amanda's laugh stopped instantly. Nicky finished her drink.

'I tell you what,' suggested Mark. 'I'll get the drinks in, while you guys get your thinking caps on.' He took their orders and left them to it. When he returned, they were discussing Miss James.

'She's sixty if she's a day,' said Martha. 'Ooh thanks,' she took the pint out of Mark's hand and drank half of it in one.

'No way,' said Amanda. 'If she wore jeans she'd look late forties. Those skirts really age her.'

Nicky fought hard not to catch Rob's eye. Amanda turned to Nicky.

'What do you think, Nicky?' she asked in a tone so friendly Nicky realised, properly for the first time, that Amanda hated her guts.

'No idea,' she said. 'I've never really thought about it.'

'Oh, don't be *ridiculous*,' laughed Amanda innocently. 'You're a woman! Of course you've thought about it.'

'I think she's about fifty,' said Mark. 'Rob, what do you think?'

'We-ell,' sighed Rob loudly, 'I wouldn't do her, so that means she's probably over thirty-five.'

Martha made a raucous yeuuch noise and pouted that he was absolutely disgusting. Mind you, she admitted, thirty-five was ancient. As Rob continued in this vein, Amanda openly eyed Mark across the table and gave him an affectedly knowing smile and raise of the eyebrows. Nicky sat back and watched Rob's show, wondering when men would realise that acting like a boarding-school twat didn't do it for bright women. That was, of course, assuming that Rob wanted a bright woman. Maybe now what he wanted was a young girl fresh out of college; a twenty-something whose idea of feminism was to drink pints and belch. Or maybe this was an act for her? Or Amanda? She just couldn't make the boy out. But Martha was easy to work out. Nicky watched her fall, laughing, into Rob's contemporary man-trap of double bluff: pretending that he was only pretending to be an arse.

'All right then,' said Martha, pint glass to her smiling lips, 'so what are your requirements for "doing" a woman, as you so delicately put it?'

'Well,' said Rob, leaning forward to her, 'I like a woman who can take her drink.'

Martha had the kind of full-bodied hysterics that is impossible to do once you hit your late twenties without waking up the next morning and wondering why your neck aches.

'Oh,' said Amanda to Rob blankly, 'does that mean a woman who gets so pissed she has sex with you?'

'I don't need a woman to get pissed to have sex with me,' answered Rob with a laddish leer. 'As you well know.'

Amanda's cheeks went rough with redness and the delicate skin around her eyes tightened, creating the illusion that her eyes were shrinking. Nicky expected to see rays shooting out of them and Rob going splat.

'Right, then!' declared Mark. 'I hereby call tonight's meeting open.'

'I've got nothing to be ashamed of about my sexual past,' Amanda told Rob haughtily, ignoring Mark. 'And you have got no "conquest" to be proud of. Those sexual double standards went out years ago.'

'I couldn't agree more,' replied Rob. 'When it comes to us, I have absolutely nothing to be proud of.'

'So!' Mark clapped his hands. 'Who wants to kick off with the first idea?'

'Oh, now it's my turn to agree, Rob,' shot Amanda. She turned to the others and wiggled her baby finger, whispering, 'Absolutely *nothing* to be proud of.'

'I thought maybe a sponsored something,' said Mark quietly.

Amanda gasped. 'Oh I'm sorry, everyone,' she said. 'Was that below the belt?'

There was a stultifying silence. When it started to clog up pores, Nicky had to speak.

'Wow, Amanda,' she said with an attempt at a conciliatory smile. 'Remind me never to annoy you.'

Amanda let out a shock of laughter. 'Oh, *bless*! Poppet, you couldn't annoy me if you tried.'

Martha put down her pint, only just missing the beer mat. 'Anyway, size doesn't matter, it's what you do with it that counts. If you know what I mean.'

'You're absolutely right, Martha,' said Amanda with feeling. She turned to Rob. 'I think you've just found your perfect woman.'

Everyone's eyes flicked to their drinks.

Rob gave Amanda a sad look. 'Did I hurt you that much?' he asked softly. 'I had no idea. I'm sorry, Mandy.'

Amanda's eyes filled and Nicky turned to Mark. 'I think a sponsored something's a brilliant idea,' she said. 'Like what?'

'Um . . . silence?' he suggested.

After that, the atmosphere was slightly less charged and ten minutes later Amanda even got a round in. And she didn't pour any of it over Rob's head or into his lap, but just left it in the middle of the table.

'You haven't pissed in this, have you?' he asked her as he put it to his lips.

She laughed. 'Oh God, no,' she said. 'I'd have to care about you to do that.'

Rob smiled. 'Touché,' he said, and flashed her a wink over the top of it.

Mollified, she allowed the atmosphere to return to good old-fashioned tension.

Much later, Mark came up with the idea of a fête. By then he was almost the only one still sober, so the idea was greeted with rapturous applause. It was the only proper idea they'd had all evening (apart from Martha's sponsored snogathon and Rob's sponsored wet T-shirt competition), but the evening hadn't been a complete wash-out. Amanda's plan had worked and they had all got to know each other more. More, in fact, than most wanted to.

When Martha's boyfriend appeared behind them, they realised it was time to go home.

'I thought we said I'd phone,' she greeted him, as he stood uncomfortably behind them.

'Yes,' said her boyfriend quietly, 'but when Clive started putting on his pyjamas, I thought it was probably time I left.'

'Well, someone would have given me a lift.'

'Well, I'm here now.'

'So I see.'

She made her goodbyes and walked out. They watched him follow her.

'I give it six months,' said Rob. 'Tops.'

'Six minutes, more like,' said Amanda.

'Nah,' he shook his head, 'she's more used to him than she thinks.'

'Now, you,' she said suddenly. 'Robert. We need to talk. Up to my flat. Now.'

'Ah, sorry, Mand,' said Rob, 'I've got to give Nicky a lift home. Otherwise I'd love to –'

'That's all right!' said Mark lightly. 'I can give Nicky a lift. No problem.'

'There you are!' Amanda declared. 'Thanks, Mark. I really appreciate that. I owe you.'

'Gosh, thanks, Mark,' added Nicky. 'Otherwise, I don't know, I'd have had to hitch, or something.'

She said goodbye to everyone and gave an extra long look at Rob. Despite his pathetic show of laddish flirting most of the evening, her heart went out to him as he stared soulfully up at her. Goodness only knew what sort of bollocking he was in for now.

As she and Mark approached Mark's low-slung, red sports

car, she remembered Rob commenting on how expensive it was and then remembered how Mark had boasted in his introductory speech that his City partnership paid well. She felt a surge of underdog support for Rob.

'It's open.' Mark smiled at her over the shiny roof.

After a while, he spoke again. 'You might have to give me directions. Oscar may have been to your place, but I haven't.'

Nicky directed him. 'Oh yes, I'd forgotten about that,' she said softly. 'That was Hallowe'en, wasn't it?' As soon as the words were out, she remembered the text Oscar had received from his father that night while in her kitchen. She fell silent.

'That's right,' said Mark. 'He was so excited about it.'

'Mm.'

They drove on in a silence punctuated only by Nicky's increasingly monosyllabic directions. She kept remembering Oscar's bitter disappointment of that night.

'I know exactly what you're thinking,' Mark said eventually. His voice was soft.

'Oh yes?'

'You're thinking, "That was the night you let him down again."'

She had to laugh. 'Am I that transparent?'

He smiled. 'No, I just . . . think I know what you think of me.'

She turned to him. 'Oh, do you now?' she said, archly.

'Mmhm,' he replied, just as archly.

'Actually, to be honest,' she confessed, 'I can't make you out at all.'

'Well,' his voice was suddenly serious, 'I'm glad you're trying.'

After a while, he spoke again.

'I tell you what, I'll help you in your efforts to make me out. Of course, I am a bit biased, but I promise to keep just to the facts. That night, Hallowe'en, I slept for two hours on the office sofa with a picture of Osc on my mobile phone next to my face. I set my alarm for when he would wake, and phoned him at Lilith's first thing. As it happened, he refused to speak to me. The next night, after twenty straight hours of work, I came home and fell asleep with him on his bed. I woke at dawn to finish two more hours of work that I still had to do.'

Nicky blinked at him in the dark. 'What would you like me to say?' she kept her tone light, just like when she was telling off her pupils.

He sighed. 'Nothing, I'm just giving you the other side of it. And remember – that was before I realised that I was not being the father Oscar needed. Yes, I was misguided, but I was still trying.'

'It's left here,' she said.

He turned into the drive of her block of flats and parked.

'Look,' she said finally. 'Your relationship with your son is really none of my business.'

He laughed. 'You could have fooled me.' She noticed that his tone was as soft as hers had been.

She frowned. 'I couldn't possibly have known that you'd change your life so dramatically after what I said. And I only told you my thoughts so . . . plainly . . . after you'd insulted me.'

'Accidentally!' he rushed. 'When I said those things I had absolutely no idea you were the famous Miss Hobbs.'

'I'm not famous.'

He laughed. 'You are in my house. Osc thinks the world of you.'

There was a pause. 'Well, it's mutual,' she said quietly. 'I think he's . . . wonderful.'

'Good,' whispered Mark. 'So at least we agree on something.'

They were silent.

'I think . . .' he murmured slowly, his voice suddenly all velvety, 'there's something *else* we agree on as well.'

Nicky's blood flooded, like a tsunami, to all her good bits. Her heart declared an emergency situation and got pumping. Her head tried sending aid, but it was too late. She held her breath.

'I feel,' he said slowly, his voice low and a touch tremulous 'that *you* . . .' – he took a deep breath, as if gathering courage – 'you . . . and . . . you alone . . . deserve that promotion.'

At first, Nicky's ears were confused. They repeated the message to her brain a couple of times, and then, probably through embarrassment, started whistling. What had she expected him to say? What had she hoped he was about to say? She skimmed a hundred thoughts, twice. Then she went off on a few little tangents. When she'd finished each one, she came back to where she'd started from. Finally, she stopped.

She was now completely lost. She decided to wait for help.

'Sorry,' he said. 'That was probably unprofessional of me.'

She decided to wait for more help.

'God,' he said, 'now you're angry with me.'

Ah, she knew how to answer that one.

'No,' she said slowly. 'I'm not angry. I'm just . . .' she let out a long, heartfelt sigh, 'I'm just disappointed.'

Disappointed like needing a big bar of chocolate disappointed.

'Shit, sorry,' Mark said. 'I'm used to City office politics. Maybe you don't do it like that here. All I'm saying is that you have a massive fan. I mean, professionally speaking.' Silence. 'I think the school would benefit hugely from you being the next Head. And I know the kids would absolutely love it.'

Now fully acclimatised to the conversation, she joined in.

'How do you know I'm going to go for it?' she asked squarely, turning in her seat so she was now facing him.

'What?' he exclaimed, turning to face her. 'You're kidding me?'

She shook her head.

'You're thinking of not going for it?' he almost whispered. 'Are you mad?'

Now there was a question she knew the answer to. 'Yes,' she murmured. 'Quite possibly.'

'You *have* to go for that job.' He leant in towards her. His head was nearly as tall as the car roof.

'Why?' she frowned up at him.

He spoke with a compelling urgency. 'Because every cell in your body is made for that job,' he said. She grimaced. He leant in closer still. 'You are a future headmistress. It's what you were made for.'

She turned her face away quickly.

Mark frowned. 'Have I said something wrong?' he asked eventually.

'No,' she said softly. 'That was a very nice thing to say. Thank you.'

'You are brilliant,' he continued, on a roll, 'Rob is an arse;

340

ergo, you should be the next Head.'

She laughed. How could she put this without him thinking she was a hormonal sad case?

'I'm afraid it's not as simple as that. In fact, it's quite complicated.'

'How so?'

'I think . . .' she began, 'it's just . . .' she continued, 'there's just a different set of considerations for women with these things. Especially women of my age.'

He sat back suddenly. 'Are there? Isn't that illegal?'

'It may be for our employers, but the plain fact is that we have to . . . fit in more, shall I say. If we want a family, that is.'

'Oh! I see,' he said. 'Of course. Sorry. I didn't mean to pry.'

'It's OK,' she said. 'It's just . . .' She did not want to use the phrase 'biological clock'. (Funny, she thought, how words describing women's fertility – biological clock, ticking, menopausal – all sounded so pitiful.) Then she remembered she was in the middle of a sentence. 'It's just . . . I don't actually know – for sure – how to get this right.'

'What do you mean?'

'Well,' she sighed, 'I was talking about it to Ro— to a friend recently. We're the first generation of women who've been brought up to believe we should have a career as well as a family.'

'That's good, isn't it?' asked Mark gently. 'I mean, my wife was a wonderful accountant as well as a fantastic mother. And she was happy because she was doing both.'

Nicky stared at him, transfixed. 'Really?'

'Yes,' he said. 'Of course, I'm not saying it was easy. It

wasn't. Oscar arrived much earlier than we'd planned and so Helen – that was my wife – had to really fight to keep her career going. And at times it was very hard. She felt she was being torn in two. Most of the time she felt guilty for not doing either as well as she could. She used to say that a working mother was the definition of guilt.'

There was a pause. 'I think I'd have liked her.' Nicky smiled.

He smiled back. 'I think you would have.'

'Anyway,' she said suddenly, 'that's just it. She – your wife . . .'

'Helen.'

'Helen – had no one to follow. I mean, apart from the odd exception, generally speaking; as a generation, we haven't got any role models to follow.'

Mark frowned. 'How do you mean?'

'Well, whereas our hypothetical daughters will be able to learn how to juggle properly from their mothers, we didn't. In fact, our mothers did the absolute opposite of what we're trying to do; they sacrificed career for family or the other way round. So it's really hard for us.' She shrugged. 'Funny, isn't it?' Her voice dipped. 'We learn so many things at school, but we don't learn how to make ourselves happy. I mean, the nuts and bolts of making ourselves happy . . .'

She turned to see Mark looking grave. Oh God. She'd gone off on a tangent again. The gang would have shouted her down long before now.

'Sorry,' she said. 'Ignore me. I get carried away.'

'No,' he said quietly, 'you're absolutely right. I've actually never realised it, but that's exactly how I feel about Oscar.'

'You? How?'

'Well, exactly what you're saying,' said Mark simply. 'My dad knew precisely what his role was. He didn't have a moment's doubt. He was the provider, full stop. But,' he shrugged, 'it's so different for me.' He let out a heavy sigh. 'To be honest, if Helen hadn't died . . .' he paused, 'and if I hadn't met you, things probably wouldn't have changed much in our household. I can see now that Helen did find it very hard to do everything, which was in effect what I was asking her to do, without realising it. She used to call it extreme motherhood!' He gave a short hollow laugh.

They sat in silence for a while, Nicky desperately trying to find the right thing to say. Finally she plumped for more silence.

'Anyway,' he cleared his throat, 'things did change and I'm here now and I can't ever be that kind of dad again. But . . . anyway, where was I?'

'Um . . . your dad?' asked Nicky.

'Ah yes, role models. You're absolutely right. If I'm honest – I feel like I'm trying to do a job without a job description. And, like you say, I suppose that job is trying to be happy. And of course trying to make my child happy.'

Nicky nodded. 'Yeah. We're all working off-plan,' she said.

He shook his head. 'Scary,' he murmured. 'A whole generation working off-plan. Hoping we're getting it right. Learning on the job.'

They looked at each other and then smiled.

'Look,' he said finally. 'There're lots of things I don't know. But what I do know is who should get that job. But I won't go on about it. Especially if there are other issues for you. Sorry if I spoke out of turn or if it's something you don't feel you should discuss.'

'No,' she said. 'Actually it's . . . really nice . . . to talk about it. I can't talk about it to Rob, obviously. Or any of the other teachers. And . . .'

'Well,' he grinned, 'if you ever want to "brainstorm" it – I'm your man.'

After a moment, she heard herself say, 'I'd invite you up for coffee, but . . .' and then wondered how to end this. She looked at him. He raised his eyebrows. She sighed.

'I'm knackered and caffeine this late gives me the runs.'

Two minutes later, as she heaved herself up the stairs, Mark's laughter echoing in her head, she wished she had a superpower to turn back time. But of course, if she did, it would be a cruel misuse of it, which was probably why that sort of thing didn't happen to her.

As she opened her front door, her mobile phone beeped. It was a text.

Phew, came Rob's text. *I'm still alive. U?*

She frowned as she replied, realising that for all his confusing messages, she'd never had any awkward moments with Rob like she'd just experienced with Mark.

Meanwhile Mark drove home slowly. How on earth had he imagined that a woman like that wouldn't have some bloke in the background? And from the sound of it, some bloke who was pressurising her to settle down fast.

22

Mark and Nicky didn't discuss the promotion for another fortnight, even though it was on her mind all the time. (Well, most of the time.) It wasn't easy to keep the subject to herself. In fact, it wasn't easy to keep anything to herself, and she had certainly never managed it for this long before. She hadn't been able to discuss it with Claire because Claire was now so busy, she had been forbidden to discuss it with Ally, and whenever she touched on the subject with Rob, he would inevitably joke that one day, in a long, long time, they'd laugh together about all this. Possibly over the family Christmas turkey. Obtuse, but she understood it. She stopped talking to him about it.

Which was why, one lunch-time, she found herself knocking on Mark's office door. His office, now cleared and tidy, was very cosy. It even had a plant in it, although it looked rather too suspiciously healthy to be real. There was only one photo facing him on the desk, and Nicky wondered idly whether it was of Oscar, Helen or an au pair. But thoughts like this occurred less and less as their chats continued.

Although Nicky's possible promotion was their main topic

of conversation, it was never their only one. They covered all the important areas of contemporary culture, from whether they preferred showers to baths, aerobics to the gym, reality TV to US sitcoms.

Before long, Nicky felt as relaxed as she was content talking to Mark, and was able to be up-front about most of her concerns about this promotion. Within a month, she had revealed why she'd gone into teaching in the first place and had confessed just how special she thought Oscar was. The one topic she kept well away from was, of course, her biggest block; her concern that with increasing work responsibilities, she might actually be thwarting her dreams of one day having her own family. Only the other day, she'd read an article in the newspaper exclaiming (victoriously?) that men emphatically did not look at successful career women as potential wives. And it was too simplistic to retort that she wouldn't want a man like that for a husband anyway.

Part of the reason she kept away from the subject was because it felt too personal, but the other reason was because it was purely academic, there being no man in her life, and she didn't want to look like a completely sad loon.

Because of her reticence on the subject, whenever the topic came up there were ambiguous pauses and unsatisfactory silences, but she just couldn't bring herself to say the words out loud.

Sometimes she felt disloyal to Rob having such intimate discussions with Mark. But then, she'd tell herself that was ridiculous. She owed Rob nothing. They were friends, nothing more. And anyway, she wasn't doing anything to be ashamed of. Mark was also just a friend, nothing more. It wasn't her fault she was enjoying his friendship so much that she had started to look forward to seeing him in the mornings more than anyone else. Mark was selflessly helping her, with wholehearted support that came from complete belief in her. Not the kind of thing she'd ever got from Rob. And the chats with Mark were getting so enjoyable that they were her first waking thought, giving her a feel-good morning moment before she'd even opened her eyes. She didn't realise it but he was turning into a drug and before long she needed a daily fix of him just to keep her up. Thankfully, due to her difficult decision, and his keenness to support her in making it, she had the perfect excuse to get her daily fix.

But then suddenly it all changed. A few days after the clocks went forward and the longer days pulled everyone out of their winter slump, Miss James had some rather startling news. It was days before the spring fête. During the morning meeting – as soon as the unfortunate caretaker had finished his piece of the puzzle and scarpered fast, probably never to return – she told Rob and Nicky that she planned to announce her retirement during the fête itself. Her mother would be there, as would many of the PTA and governors, and it felt like the appropriate moment. So! She expected all applications no more than one week later.

After the meeting, Rob found a corner of the Mediterranean just off Sicily within minutes, and left the office whistling a jaunty tune. Nicky, however, stood over Miss James's puzzle feeling completely thrown. Not only would she have to finally apply for the post of Headmistress – which felt very different from just being asked to consider it – but she'd have no more excuses to start rambling conversations with Mark. She stared at the occasionally fuzzy map and took twenty minutes to find the northern tip of France.

That lunch-time she popped in to see Mark and when she told him Miss James's deadline he practically congratulated her on winning the job already. He seemed more excited about it than she did.

'At last,' he grinned at her, 'no more shilly-shallying. It's as good as in the bag.'

Why was he feeling so confident? And why wasn't she?

On the delicious spring evening before the fête, as she strode across the playground towards her car, she heard Oscar call out her name. She whizzed round and watched him race his father to reach her. It was close, but Oscar won. He asked her if she was going to the fête tomorrow, and as the three of them ambled to the car park together, she replied that not only would she be there, but she expected both of them to help on her stall. After a picture-book wave goodbye from father and son, she got into her car feeling as if the best-looking boy in the school had just asked to carry her books.

She slept well that night, and woke to blossom on the trees and a girlish skip in her heart. Spring seemed to have had its effect on everything. In the past few weeks, she had experienced global warming. Tectonic plates of relation-ships had shifted and ice-caps melted. She and Mark were close friends.

It was no surprise that Nicky thought of him so instantane-ously after waking that the two practically happened simultaneously. This led instantly to the thought that she was heading for trouble. Trouble like needing-a-mega-size-box-of-chocolates trouble. This led to the next thought that she couldn't be that serious about her career if her first waking thought was of Mark and not of the headship. Which led, naturally, to the next thought that perhaps, then, she shouldn't apply at all. She needed to discuss this with Mark. And then she spotted the deliberate mistake with this theory, realised that she couldn't ever tell him what was really on her mind, and she was, in all probability, doomed.

Coffee. She needed coffee.

Caffeined up, it dawned on her that when Miss James had finally announced her deadline of one week for all applications to be in by, Nicky had had to hide her disappointment to Mark because it would mean no more excuses for their chats. He, on the other hand, had been cock-a-hoop at the news. The only possible conclusion a sane woman could come to was that these chats obviously hadn't meant as much to him as they had to her. Not only that, but why such excitement at the possibility of her promotion? Beginning to feel like Miss Marple, but without the confidence or knitting prowess, she got dressed fast.

At precisely 8 a.m., she arrived at Claire's house. With more bitching, bossing and hierarchical in-fighting than a PTA meeting, Claire's girls poured the contents of thirteen jumbo packets of sweets into a vast bowl. Nicky set up a system of counting in tens and within half an hour, they had counted the entire collection of sweets and only eaten half of them. Then Nicky poured them into an enormous glass jar and twisted on the lid. She made the girls swear and sign a declaration, one by one, that they promised not to tell anyone how many sweets were in the jar. She even made them give her their fingerprints, thanks to a new toy she'd got especially for the occasion. By the end of the process, even Sarah-Jane was excited.

Thanks to the intimidating efficiency of the school's PTA, this was all Nicky needed to do to set up her stall. Of course, she needed to show her face early, but tables, refreshments, rotas and even the marquee had all been organised and set up by mothers of pupils at the school. When the girls filed out of their house and cheered because the sun had appeared, Nicky merely assumed that the PTA had sent a memo requesting it to pull its weight.

The girls had wanted to go to their beloved auntie's school fête because it was always such great fun being at a school that wasn't yours. They wanted to get there early to help, and Claire was only too happy to have a lie-in, so Nicky aimed to get there for nine with her trusty little helpers, three hours before the fête was due to begin.

She drove to the school singing heartily to Busted's latest album, easily making more noise than all her nieces put together. As she did so, she wondered if maybe this was as good as it got. Maybe being an auntie was her destiny. And if so, it wasn't half bad. When she parked in the school car park her singing voice lost its verve due to a spectacular somersault in her stomach. Would she get her fix today? Would he bring a girlfriend? If so, would it be Oscar's au pair? Or some slick City chick with perfect children of her own? As the girls leapt out of her car, collecting all the gubbins needed, she delved into the dressing-up box that was her boot and found her shades. Feeling slightly more confident behind protection, she led the girls out to the playing fields behind the school. Apart from a couple of the most keen PTA members, plus a handful of overexcited children, they were the only ones there.

The smell of freshly cut grass and the girls' excitement

were enough to squash Nicky's nerves and make her feel good to be alive. When one of the mothers offered her some home-ground, organic Kenyan espresso and freshly baked M&S flapjacks (state schools in certain pockets of north London had a unique set of parents), she felt a buzz of contentment.

She and the girls sat on the grass and she began instructing them on how to make the Guess How Many Sweets In The Jar stall the most eye-catching, colourful one at the fête. Each girl was given their task. As the sun rose above the copse behind them, Nicky swirled her hair up on top of her head, using a pencil to keep it up, pulled out an A4 notebook, and drew lines down it, heading each column with neatly worded titles. When the sign was completed, she stuck it to the front of her desk, proudly displayed the jar on the table, and placed the pad and a pen next to it. Then she went to find as many chairs as possible, with the girls in tow.

As they left the marquee and crossed the field towards the school, Nicky sensed movement out of the corner of her eye, near the car park. She sucked in her stomach, held her back straight and looked over. She was surprised to see Rob. They waved at each other.

The school seemed dark after the light outside. The girls ran ahead to the assembly hall, shouting at each other, more excited by the freedom of a strange, empty school corridor than an empty field, and Nicky had a little word with herself. She was thinking too much. Mark was a colleague and friend and here she was turning that into a schoolgirl crush. If she wasn't careful she was going to make a prat of herself. Why was she unable to have a friendship with a man without her mind going into warp speed (let alone warped speed) and turning it into something more? Just focus on work, she told herself firmly, apply for the promotion, and then get back to normal. Mark was the parent of one of her pupils, for goodness' sake, and he was also the school bursar. But perhaps more important than that, he was a man who believed fervently that she had the perfect mind and body to be a junior-school head. Knowing the mind and body of the present junior head, Nicky could only conclude that this was not a man forcing himself to hide his base thoughts about her. Damn.

She reached the assembly hall and called to the girls to stop them playing tag. They took a chair each and formed a neat little procession back to the stall. As she led the way, she continued her little chat to herself. Mark wasn't even that nice. Don't be fooled by this *über*-dad act; this was a man who had spent the first decade of his son's life being an absent parent. She stepped out of the school into the light. Anyway, she continued, more importantly, he wasn't interested in her as anything other than his next boss.

She let out a sudden gasp! If she got the job, she would be his next boss! She'd spotted it! The reason Mark was so supportive of her decision to go for the job! He wanted her to get it instead of Rob! As she stood there, suddenly frozen in the sun, her skirt floating in the warm breeze, she remembered just how much Mark hated Rob. Great billowing arse! Mark would hate Rob becoming Headmaster because it would mean that Rob would be his direct boss. So he *did* have an ulterior motive for persuading her to go for the job after all. Maybe he even thought he could control her in some way. So that was why he was building on their friendship so intensely at this crucial time – to make sure there was real competition for Rob and to make an ally out of her if she won. Oh, why on earth hadn't she thought of that before? It was so blindingly obvious now. What was it, she wondered, that made these men so competitive? And, while she was on the subject, what made them so much better at it than her? She simply had to stop this naïve romantic dwelling on Mark's belief in her and, instead, focus on what *she* wanted out of life. He was just another competitive man after the best deal he could get out of life.

'Hi!' called out Mark, from her left. She almost dropped the chair. God, he looked gorgeous. Gorgeous like good-enough-to-eat gorgeous. He was wearing slim-cut pale linen trousers and a sheer, baggy open-necked white shirt. The sun filtered through it on either side of his V torso. There was no girlfriend, which was also gorgeous. He wore shades, which on anyone else would have looked pretentious, but on him were gorgeous.

She pulled herself together and had another sharp word with herself: he was the parent of one of her pupils. And more importantly, he wasn't interested in her, other than as a means of achieving his own agenda.

She smiled at him. He smiled back. His smile was gorgeous.

'Can we help?' he asked with an even more dazzling smile that turned his jaw to granite.

She took a deep breath and had another little word with herself: he was the pupil of one of her favourite shades. And more importantly, he was an open-necked torso with smile.

Oscar was standing on one side of him, Daisy on the other. They looked like a glossy magazine photo-shoot. While Nicky was thinking of something to say that would make her appear a) attractive, b) witty, c) attractive and a) fully in control of herself and own destiny, Mark approached Abigail who was struggling with a chair that was nearly bigger than she was. He knelt down, so he was her height, and asked her softly if she'd like some help with the chair. The little girl gave a Lady Diana tilt of her head, a wonkily coy smile and Nicky swore she almost fluttered her eyelashes. From behind the safety of her shades, Nicky watched Mark's forearms as he gripped Abigail's chair with one hand and then took Isabel's chair with the other. His forearms were gorgeous, lined with soft blond hairs. Then she turned away to give herself a final, proper talking to: Now look, Nix, she told herself, this is the ulterior man with linen thighs and teeth, granite forearms and nipples.

The swishing in her ears was strangely comforting.

'Osc,' Mark called out, 'what are you waiting for?'

Oscar scrunched his face up into an ugly question.

'There's a young lady needs help,' said Mark, indicating Sarah-Jane with a nod of his head.

Oscar thrust his head and shoulders down as if he'd just been given detention, and took her chair.

'Thanks!' she said breezily. 'I'm Sarah-Jane.'

Oscar grunted.

'I'm Daisy,' Daisy replied for Oscar. 'How old are you? I'm nearly eleven.'

As the children went on ahead, Mark and Nicky followed, and every now and then Nicky shifted her eyes from behind the safety of her shades across to his forearms.

'So, how you doing?' Mark asked her.

'Fine!' she replied. 'Thanks! You?'

Mark was prevented from answering by Rob's approach.

As the children ran into the field ahead of them, Rob gave a broad grin and side-stepped to Nicky's chair.

'Why, Miss Hobbs,' he said, 'what's a pretty little thing like you hefting a great big thing like this?'

'Piss off, Prattison.' Nicky frowned, tightening her grip. 'I'm a woman, I'm not a six-year-old.' There. That would show both of them that she was a woman of her time, chasing her own destiny without either of their help. Then she dropped the chair on his foot.

Rob delicately handed it back to her and gave Mark a conspiratorial grin. 'Good old feminism.' He winked. 'They don't let you carry their chairs but they let you shag 'em.' He ran on to the school, only limping slightly. Nicky stopped still, her mouth an almost perfect 'O'. Mark stopped too.

'I can't believe he just said that,' she said in an almost whisper.

Mark's eyebrows made a brief appearance from behind his shades.

'You know, you're right,' she said, as she started walking again. 'He can be an arse sometimes.'

'I didn't say "sometimes",' muttered Mark.

Nicky was trying to work out how to explain that she hadn't 'let' Rob shag her, in such a way that would not make her appear either a) highly strung or b) totally barking, when she was suddenly squeezed round the waist from behind.

She leapt up, banging her chair on her shin, and found herself staring into the somewhat crazed eyes of Miss James.

'Hello!' cried her boss. 'Hello, hello, hello, hello, hello!'

'Hello!' cried Mark and Nicky.

'How are we all today?' cried Miss James.

'Fine!' cried Mark and Nicky.

'Good, good, good, good, good!' said Miss James. 'Good!'

Feeling anything but good – feeling, in fact, bad – Nicky tried not to swipe Miss James over the head, involuntarily or voluntarily, with her chair. Instead, she walked with Mark and her boss to the field, and contented herself with thinking dark thoughts. How did Rob always manage to turn things around so quickly? What on earth had made him say that? He was not a friend. When would she learn that? Men and women could not be friends. Maybe – she gasped again – maybe he and Mark were in it together? Right. That was it. She'd move to Sicily and learn how to fish.

By ten o'clock, everyone staffing a stall had arrived and the place was jumping. Nicky busied herself helping other people and when there was no more help needed, she began playing games with the girls and various other children, to keep them occupied and, more importantly, to stop herself from thinking about the two scheming men in her life. Spending time with children usually sorted her mind out. And it did this time too. As she kept a game going, she actually managed to forget everything and just enjoy herself. The breeze in her hair, the grass under her sandal-less feet, the sun on her skin, being surrounded by kids' laughter; all of it cast its spell. She was having fun.

Mark stood and watched for a while. Oscar joined him.

'What's up, mate?' Mark asked, nudging his boy.

'Nothing.'

'Why don't you join in? Daisy's there.'

They both looked over at Daisy and Sarah-Jane holding hands and laughing together.

'Leave me alone!' whined Oscar and he stomped off. Mark watched him go and then turned back to watch the game. A circle of children held hands on the grass, all chanting something that made them laugh with excitement. Nicky chased a niece round the circle, and then the niece suddenly slapped one of the children on their back and took their place. That child, in sudden nervous hysterics, now fled from Nicky.

Watching, Mark saw, under Nicky's skirt, a slender curve of leg – alabaster apart from a little bruise on her shin – flash past with every pace. Her hair flowed down her back and her cheeks glowed. But that wasn't what struck him most about her. She wasn't running like a woman, let alone a teacher, she was running like a child, unselfconscious, determined and without a care in the world.

He watched until Oscar returned. Then he put a gentle hand on the back of the boy's neck and guided him towards the game. When Nicky turned to them, let go of the circle, and welcomed them both into the game with a wide-open arm and broad grin that lit up her whole face, Mark realised that his feelings for her had finally overtaken those of his son's.

By noon, the place was filling up and by half past twelve, it was heaving. Nicky's stall was one of the favourites and she hardly had a moment to herself. When Oscar and Daisy came to help, she was so relieved she almost hugged them. She ran to the Ladies and on her way she found the girls queueing to have their faces painted. She ordered them, on pain of the worst tickle in their life, not to tell Oscar and Daisy how many sweets were in the jar. She needn't have worried, they were not going to relinquish such power that easily. When she returned, two tigers and a cat were taunting Oscar and Daisy with their knowledge.

At one o'clock, Nicky took a break from her stall and bought a sandwich for lunch. She watched everyone as they mingled and queued for stalls and wondered how different she would feel if she were Headmistress. She tried to imagine it, but couldn't. Then she spotted Rob in deep conversation with Miss James and felt eaten up with envy. She watched as Rob then walked towards the centre of the marquee with long, confident strides. He jumped up on to the platform, took the microphone and, with the ease of a practised performer, arrested everyone's attention instantly. He introduced Miss James with a speech that was witty enough for the kids to enjoy, respectful enough for the governors to enjoy, and short enough for the parents to enjoy. Nicky watched, her sandwich uneaten. It dawned on her that she was probably watching the future Head. Morning assemblies would be fun if Rob was Head. Were she to get the job, she'd need hypnosis therapy just to walk to the front of the assembly hall without blacking out.

She became vaguely aware of someone coming to stand next to her. She couldn't look. Needles pricked under her arms. Rob started the applause going before leaping off the platform.

'He's good, isn't he?' came Amanda's voice in her ear, so close now that Nicky could almost taste her perfume. She answered with a nod and glanced round the marquee at hundreds of laughing, smiling parents. When she spotted Mark's face, he was staring at her. Paralysed, she stared back. He started pushing his way through the crowd towards her.

As Miss James began her shock announcement to the world, Nicky managed to pull her eyes away from Mark. He reached her side and Rob arrived beside Amanda. The vast crowd gasped in amazement at Miss James's news.

'Well, well, well,' said Amanda, as a slow applause began round the marquee. 'Now there's a turn-up for the books. I thought she was about twenty years younger. Didn't you, Nicky?'

Nicky stared at Miss James as she came off the podium and hugged her mother.

'Oh I see!' sang Amanda. 'Apparently I'm invisible.'

'Who said that?' asked Rob. Amanda dug her elbow into him so fiercely that he swore. A couple of parents turned round and tutted. Rob apologised profusely before giving Amanda a look black enough for Trinny and Susannah to approve of. Nicky was vaguely aware of Amanda offering him a muted apology.

Miss James left her mother and joined them.

'Well!' she breathed. 'I've done it, people. And I want applications in within the week.'

'You'll get mine tomorrow,' said Rob proudly.

'Oh wonderful!' exclaimed Miss James. 'I do like a man who's fast off the mark.'

Rob beamed. He gave a little bow of his head and Miss James clapped. There was a moment's silence. Suddenly scared that Amanda might beat her to it, Nicky spoke up.

'And mine!' she cried.

Miss James cheered and clapped again. Mark joined in.

'Well,' Miss James beamed at them both, 'the gauntlet is well and truly hurled to the floor!'

'So it is!' laughed Rob. 'And may the best man win!' He took Nicky's hand and brought it to his lips, like a gallant knight. Nicky involuntarily curtsied.

'Whoever *she* may be!' added Mark happily.

They all laughed and Nicky felt alive with love and hatred for them all, including herself. If she'd been a computer, her connections would have blown. As it was, she was merely unable to finish her sandwich.

Miss James was whisked away by a governor, and the four of them were left standing in a determined little group. Nicky wanted to be alone.

'Well!' said Rob. 'Well, well, well, well, well.'

'Well, well, well, well, well, indeed!' agreed Amanda.

Rob turned to them all. 'How was the speech?'

They all told him it was good, Nicky satisfying herself with smiling and nodding.

'I love public speaking,' he said. 'That would be my favourite part of the job, I think.'

Amanda gave Nicky a conspiratorial smile. 'Blimey,' she said, 'you'd think the job was his already!'

Confused by Amanda's friendliness, it took a while for Nicky to realise that what she was witnessing was a politician hedging her bets. After all, either of them might be her next boss. She stopped making eye contact with her. Did this mean that she was now going to start pretending to be her friend? Was anyone here genuine?

'I'm going for a drink!' she said suddenly.

'Excellent!' said Mark. 'I'll join you.'

As they walked away, they brushed arms with each other in the throng.

'Congratulations,' he whispered, leaning into her and giving her upper arm a soft squeeze. His hand was warm.

'Well, I haven't got it yet,' she replied. 'I've only said I'm going to apply.'

They reached the queue for drinks.

'Yes, but I have every faith in you,' he said, smiling down at her with, she thought, the look you give your trusty, dying Labrador.

She shut her eyes. 'Thanks.'

'You've applied,' he whispered firmly, 'for a job you more than deserve. It would be a crime if you didn't.' He inched closer. 'You know, I'll tell you something – I've seen so many women let lesser men overtake them because of family commitments. And these woefully inferior bastards end up earning double what the women earn, *and* rip the piss out of them when they leave early to pick up the kids from school. Meanwhile it's all right for them to leave the office early to get plastered in the pub while they've got wives at home sacrificing their careers to bring up a family they never see.' He thought of Lilith. 'Shit,' he said. 'It's so unfair on working mothers.'

Nicky wondered why this speech of solidarity wasn't cheering her up.

'Yes, but I'm not doing it for them,' she said with a gentle smile, 'or for whatever women you may have trampled on in the past. I'm doing it for me.' He was about to say something, but she continued. 'Anyway,' she added thoughtfully, 'you're assuming that bringing up the kids is the short straw.' They shifted forward in the queue. 'Maybe working mums are in on the secret that they're the ones with the perfect life balance and everyone else has got it wrong.'

'Mm,' said Mark. 'But men can get to the top of their field *and* have the perfect family. And get respect for it in both fields, without doing half as much work as the women.'

Nicky nodded. 'Yes, but as I say, I'm not doing it for them, I'm doing this for me.'

'Of course!' said Mark, slightly bemused. 'I'm just saying you're absolutely right; it's all about balance. You taught me that.'

'Yes. Unless you haven't got any children,' she said, composing her voice. 'Without children a woman can focus just as obsessively on her career with all the advantages of a selfish, imbalanced man.'

'Exactly!' he whispered in her ear. 'Thankfully, you don't have to worry about any of that. You are on completely equal footing with Rob. And as such, you deserve that promotion,' he said. 'It's that simple.'

She felt the heat from his body and fought not to lean into it. 'Nothing's that simple,' she said quietly.

An hour later, Ally arrived at the fête. By the time she found Nicky, she'd already eaten half a candyfloss and heard the news.

She greeted her with an urgent, 'I hope you're applying.'

'I am.'

'That's wonderful! Congratulations.'

She took her in a fierce bear-hug, getting candyfloss in her hair. They pulled away and grinned at each other.

'If you get this job, you know what it means, don't you?' asked Ally, taking a mouthful of pink sugar.

'What?'

'It means I can get in late every morning. You have to get this job.'

Nicky laughed, but it came out hollow. Was there no one who would just be happy for her without thinking of the gain they could get out of it?

The fête was a huge success. Hundreds of people came and by mid-afternoon every child's face looked like a cartoon jungle animal who'd eaten too many carrots. After packing up her stall, Nicky dropped the girls at Claire's and drove home. She had a bath and went to bed, but although she was exhausted, it took her hours to get to sleep.

23

The next day was Sunday, so it was only natural that Nicky woke feeling depressed. Lying in bed, staring at her thin, luminous curtains, she pushed her thoughts to the clean, empty teapot in her clean, empty kitchen and it did the trick. She felt the stirrings of just enough optimism to get out of bed. In the kitchen, she leant against the worktop acclimatising to being vertical, while staring at the boiling kettle. As her eyes drifted in and out of focus, she told herself that a watched kettle never boils. She frowned. So how did one overcome this? Was she meant to put it on to boil and then ignore it? Pretend she didn't care, even though she'd been the one to turn it on? Or was she meant to go to extraordinary lengths to double-bluff herself in order to genuinely forget she'd done it? She just hated playing games, even with electric appliances.

Blimey though, it was taking for ever.

Eventually, mug of tea in hand, she crossed the living room to her balcony. She pulled open the sliding door and stepped outside. Cool, fresh air aerated her skin. She'd just made it in time to catch the morning's last dew-filled moments. She sat down on her deckchair and crossed her pyjama-clad legs.

Oh, why were Sundays so suffused with sadness? Even the air felt different. Something was wrong with this world if you spent five days counting down to the weekend, and then half the weekend killing time till *Poirot*.

But apart from it being Sunday, why else was she feeling down? Oh yes! As of yesterday,

Mark Samuels was her staunch ally in her battle to be a childless career woman, thanks to his own hidden agenda of wanting to work for her rather than Rob. And what did she want? She mused on this for a while as she watched the powdery clouds skit by. She knew damn well what she wanted. She wanted the headship, she wanted to work with Mark, she wanted babies and she wanted very much to do base things with Mark.

But not necessarily in that order.

She got up and went inside. After a bath, she deafened the voices in her head by putting on some loud music and filling out the application form for Miss James's job on her laptop while eating a slice of chocolate cake the size of a tent.

It worked! By the afternoon, she was high on caffeine, loud, sassy drum beats and sugar. A quick run, a late tea with Claire and the girls, and by bedtime she had worked herself up into a healthy state of not unhappiness.

On Monday morning, she reread her completed application form before leaving the flat. She found three spelling mistakes. She'd redo it tonight, without any loud music playing, and hand it in on Tuesday. She still had all week.

At school, she and Rob exchanged grins across the staffroom. He approached with two mugs of tea in his hands and, for a touch of nostalgia, Amanda by his side. They had clearly overcome their differences.

'Handed it in yet?' he asked.

'Nope,' replied Nicky. 'You?'

'Eight thirty this morning,' he said. Amanda tutted and shared a look with Nicky.

That night, Nicky took out her laptop, deleted most of her application, and began again. This time with Classic FM on in the background.

First thing Tuesday morning, she reread it before sealing the envelope. She read it again. And again. Yes, there was definitely a weak sentence that made her sound ambivalent towards the job. She must have written it during a distracting advert break on the radio. She'd have to redo it tonight. And no music at all in the background this time.

Half an hour later, she happened to meet Mark in the school car park. She walked past his car just as he was locking it and they smiled at each other. He was wearing a dark pin-stripe suit, a crisp white shirt undone at the top and no tie, his smooth, soft Adam's apple hinting of smooth, soft other things. They fell into step with each other and meandered up the curved path.

'Handed in your application form yet?' he greeted her.

She smiled up at him. 'Don't you mean, hello, how are you?'

'Hello, how are you?' He laughed. 'Handed in your application yet?'

She smiled. 'No, I'm going to do it tonight.'

He sucked in some breath. 'Living dangerously, eh?'

'Oh yes,' she agreed. 'Life on the edge, me.'

Later that evening, she took three hours to rewrite the

whole form, with no music in the background, focussing on making it much more forceful in tone. She decided to try and forget about it and then reread it the next day, so she would be more fresh.

Next morning in the staffroom, Rob was by her side first thing.

'Well?' he asked. 'Handed it in yet?'

'Not yet,' she said, as lightly as she could. 'No point rushing something this important.'

Amanda approached. 'Apparently,' she murmured, turning her back to the staffroom and talking quietly so they had to lean in to hear, 'a surprise internal applicant has joined the race.'

'You're kidding!' gasped Nicky, eyes wide.

Rob sucked in his breath. 'You'd better hurry up,' he told Nicky. 'Don't want to be an unimpressive third.'

'Don't intimidate the girl,' scolded Amanda.

Nicky wasn't intimidated; she was horrified. She scanned the staffroom to see if she could spot anyone watching her from behind an upside-down map. She felt knocked sideways. It had never occurred to her that anyone else would apply from inside the school. The implications of this were most unpleasant. It meant that someone in the room believed they had been overlooked for the post of Deputy and deserved it more than she did. Her first impulse was to seek them out and offer them her job, but on second thoughts she decided she could just go into hiding. She was really beginning to detest all this. She hated all the politics and the rivalry. She hated not knowing who her friends were and who was pretending to be her friend so they could get something out of her possible promotion. She just wanted to teach. Maybe she should just throw in the towel, move to the country and get a kitten.

That night she reread her form and decided it still needed improvement. She did it again, no music on, with a dynamic, forceful and direct tone and a new paragraph which she especially liked.

First thing Thursday morning, she reread it and found a new spelling mistake in her new paragraph. She almost cried. If she'd found one, maybe there were others. She'd have to reread it again tonight. If she couldn't even fill in the form, how on earth would she manage the job?

Maybe a ginger kitten. With white paws.

Then she thought of Mark, and of how stupid she'd look to him if she didn't apply. Especially if her reason was because she couldn't fill in the form. That evening, the last evening before the deadline, she reread her final version. She checked every spelling in the dictionary and had no music on in the background. Then, without another look at it, she sealed the envelope, closed her eyes, made a wish, and put it in her case. She actually made two wishes, because why waste an opportunity? So while her eyes were clammed shut and she asked her guardian angel to please please please make her Headmistress, she added a little postscript about Mark Samuels, which included specific requests about his good motives and his good thighs.

She opened her eyes and stood pondering in her living room. Was that the definition of a modern woman? Wishing for fulfilment in career, love and lust – in that order? Yes it was, she decided. She was the personification of today's woman because she wanted all of them equally. She felt all fired up until she got outside her home and reconsidered that she probably wouldn't get any of them. Which, probably, she thought, as she climbed into her boudoir, was the definition of an unhappy modern woman.

First thing Friday morning, she went straight to Miss James's office. She stood in the corridor outside it, staring at Janet's in-tray. There were a few A4-sized envelopes lying in it. Should she have a quick look and see if any of them were the same shape as hers? Did she want to know if anyone else had joined the competition? Or would it –

'Hi,' said Mark.

She spun round. 'Hi!'

He nodded at her envelope. 'Is that it?'

She nodded back. Then she put it in Janet's tray. Mark clapped, cheering quietly. She gave a little bow of her head and walked back to the staffroom, grinning like an idiot.

That morning in the meeting, after a Reception child had started sobbing hysterically at the puzzle and had to be taken back to her class by Janet (only marginally less horrifying, in Nicky's opinion), Miss James had another little surprise for her trusty Deputies.

'As you both know,' she grinned merrily, 'the summer trip is fast approaching. And of course, as my fiercely feuding Deputies, you won't want to miss a trick.'

'Of course,' enthused Rob.

'Absolutely!' said Nicky.

'And now that I know exactly where we all stand apropos my job,' Miss James gave them both an adoring smile, 'I will make sure that all the boring, silly interviews have taken place with the governors and with me, et cetera, et cetera, by the trip, so that I can spend that week with both of you – and any other applicants – before the final decision is made. Obviously, the ultimate decision goes to the governors, but they will definitely be asking me my opinion.' She slapped her papers. 'That is by far the fairest way, don't you both think?'

They nodded. After the meeting, even Rob seemed unable to find the right piece of the puzzle and only found a piece when Nicky did. They walked out of her office together, still in a daze.

'You realise what this is, don't you?' he whispered in the corridor.

'Yup.'

'It's a week-long fucking job interview.'

'Yup.'

'She's going to make us do absolutely everything,' he hissed. 'Every single job. Bitch. And for some reason, she is absolutely determined to make us feuding, bitter rivals.'

'Mm, yeah, I noticed that,' said Nicky. 'Why is that?'

Rob turned to her sharply before they went back into the staffroom and put his hand on the door handle, preventing her from entering.

'Maybe she's jealous,' he said. 'She knows we've got something special. Nicky, we can't let her do this to us,' he said.

Then, to her surprise, he grasped her by the elbow and steered her quickly towards the wall opposite, cornering her by a door. She shook his hand off and almost spat out her words.

'Rob, what makes you think you can keep turning our friendship on and off just when it suits you?'

'Eh?'

'That despicable "shag 'em" comment to Mar— the bursar at the fête. What on earth gives you the right –'

Rob hung his head down, his voice so low she barely heard it. 'I was jealous. I'm sorry. Unforgivable, I know.'

'*What?*' She was incredulous. 'Jealous of what?'

'Oh, come on, Nicky,' Rob was suddenly breathing hard, his eyes pleading. 'Aren't you sick of all this pretending?'

It would have taken a greater woman than Nicky Hobbs not to experience meltdown at these words. She looked up at him. His eyes looked haunted. Suddenly everything turned into sharp focus for her. This was it. Make or break. Closure. Or . . . (What was the opposite of closure? Grand opening?) Her knees buckled. Rob edged in closer.

She pushed him away fast with her knee.

'Rob,' she hissed. 'Not here. Not now.'

He moved back. 'When are we going to stop kidding each other?' he asked. 'And ourselves?'

She couldn't answer. She couldn't think. She was having enough trouble breathing.

'Seven years, Nix,' he said pleadingly. 'Seven years.'

She nodded.

'I know I joke about us,' he went on, 'but, Nick . . . you've got to know . . . there's not a day goes by when I don't wonder what would have happened, if only . . .'

She closed her eyes and shook her head. She'd stopped thinking about it for a while now. (Which meant she was winning. Hoorah!)

'I've changed,' he confessed in a whisper. 'I've matured. I want different things now. A home, a family, kids. Nicky, we're finally on the same page.'

She opened her eyes. What was he saying?

'Rob,' she managed, 'you can't just turn something this big on and off like this – it's all so sudden –'

'Sudden!' he laughed and then lowered his voice immediately. 'I've known you since you were practically still a child! Fancied you for two years before I did anything about it.'

'I thought it was one year –'

He let out a sad laugh. 'I lied. I was playing it cool,' he said. 'That's nearly a decade, Nicky. And I've never stopped fancying you. Every single day in that bloody staffroom –'

She thought of Amanda and cooled.

'Your timing's never been good,' she said. 'But this really is . . . you're just annoyed with Miss James trying to pit us against each other –'

'No!' he held up his hands. 'She's made me see sense. Trying to turn our future into her last petty power game.' They looked at each other, neither breathing, their faces inches apart. Nicky was so stunned – and constricted – that she didn't notice Mark appear silently from his office, almost beside them, spot them, and disappear as quickly and silently as he'd appeared.

'I'm sorry if it feels sudden,' said Rob. 'To be honest, I wasn't expecting this either. But now that it's out there, please . . . just promise me you'll think about it.'

'Think about what, exactly?'

'Us. The real thing. Seriously. I think about it all the time. If we just . . . decided to sod the consequences for once; went with our gut feelings instead of our minds. Just imagine the life we'd have together . . . the *family* we'd finally let ourselves have –'

The staffroom door opened and they sprang apart. Two minutes later, they were both inside with Pete and Ally, and apart from the odd earnest glance from Rob, he acted as if nothing had happened. Nicky's hands shook for an hour.

For the rest of the day, she felt her life had completely changed perspective. It was as if her pupils were a fantastic precursor to her life instead of a worthy alternative to it. It made such a difference, just believing that her dream of motherhood could actually one day be a reality.

At lunch-time, she was passing Mark's door when it opened and he appeared in the doorway. They stopped and looked at each other, and she felt strangely removed from him, as if she hadn't seen him for a long time.

'Hello,' he said.

Miss James appeared from her office.

'Hello, hello, hello,' she said. She joined them both. 'Did you know,' she told Nicky, 'that Rob, your worthy adversary, has been helping organise chess club all term?'

'No!' replied Nicky, eyes wide. 'Good! Good for him.'

'Isn't it?' Miss James smiled. There was a pause.

'Shall I tell Miss James what we were just talking about?' Mark asked Nicky.

'Er . . .' she answered.

'She's being modest,' he told Miss James. 'She just offered to help me organise the table quiz.'

Miss James gave a little squeal. 'Did you? Oh, wonderful girl! I'm so proud of my Deputies. I'm proud of all my staff. Oh, I do know how to pick the best, don't I? When do your meetings start?'

'The preliminary one's tonight, actually,' said Mark. 'At my place. Eight, on the dot. Miss Hobbs was just telling me she could make it.'

Miss James's eyes shone at her. 'You can tell me all about it tomorrow morning!' she said.

'Actually,' Mark said to his boss, 'I was going to ask you if I could have a quick word.'

'Mi office es su office!' Miss James beamed. 'You can tackle Eastern Europe while you're there.'

'Excellent.' He turned to Nicky. 'So eight tonight, then. I'll e you my address.'

She nodded and watched him follow Miss James into her office.

After Miss James's door shut in front of her, Nicky stood looking at it for a while. Her head was in a spin. She wondered how she'd be feeling about spending an evening with Mark if she hadn't recently worked out a possible secret motive for his support and if Rob hadn't suddenly started talking like something out of Mills and Boon this morning. Were her internal organs pulsating to the *Mambo* because of Rob's sudden declaration of a decade of secret lust this morning or because of Mark's spontaneous table quiz meeting? She had absolutely no idea. All she knew was that it was definitely the *Mambo*.

When school finished, she set up her laptop in the staffroom. If there was no email from Mark, she'd assume that he had been bluffing. She logged on. Under the title *Meeting* was his address and a message.

Mi casa es su casa . . . See you tonight. x

She stared at the kiss. How could a small letter, a typewritten, lower-case letter, feel so significant?

What should she do? Would Oscar be there? Would Oscar mind that his teacher was coming to his house? Did he even know about this? Or would Oscar be away tonight?

In which case, would they be alone? In Mark's house? All evening? Or would it be a completely above-board meeting, with a secretary and everything? If so, who would that be? Amanda? Martha? Janet? Rob? (As for Rob, what the crap was going on there?) What would Mark be like in his own home? What would the décor be like? Would he have a live-in partner there? An au pair? A *wife*? Would she be tall and blonde or tanned and wiry? Did the table quiz actually exist? Or was he just trying to get her on his own? If so, why?

Oh dear oh dear oh dear.

She'd thought that when she handed in her application all her worries would subside for a while.

Ally walked into the staffroom and she glanced at her.

'Blimey, what's the matter?' asked Ally. 'You look as if you've seen a ghost.'

'I've got to go to a spontaneous fundraising meeting at Mark's house tonight,' she said. Oh, and Rob offered to father my children, she thought.

Ally's eyes widened. 'A "spontaneous" fund-raising meeting? Wow.'

Nicky didn't reply.

Ally sat down next to her. 'It's just a meeting,' she said soothingly.

'A spontaneous meeting.'

'So act spontaneous. You'll be fine.'

Nicky nodded. 'I'm feeling very stressed.'

Ally nodded slowly. 'And wear perfume.'

Nicky nodded again. 'Thanks.'

At five minutes to eight, she parked her car two houses away from the address she'd been given and sat in silence. Her thoughts were as tangled as her intestines. She was dressed in clothes Oscar saw her in every day. She was here in a professional capacity. She was a teacher. Mark was the bursar. This was a meeting.

She looked in the rear-view mirror for the fifth time. Her freckles had multiplied from spending most of Saturday in the sun. She frowned at her reflection. Everything had changed since Saturday. She had hated Rob then and had had a crush on Mark. Now . . . she just didn't know what she felt.

She tutted and told herself it was just a fundraising meeting, heaved open the car door and made her way to the number house she'd been given. She stood outside it and checked the address again. It was not what she'd expected at all. She'd imagined something grand and masculine, possibly with columns, but this was a nondescript end-of-terrace semi with, if she wasn't very much mistaken, nets.

She rang the doorbell and turned to look at the road. The evenings were getting much lighter now. Summer was on its way. Still, she thought, she should have worn a hat.

She heard the door open behind her and turned round. To her delight, Oscar stood at the door, beaming at her.

'Hello!' she exclaimed. 'How's my favourite pupil called Oscar?'

Laughing, he stepped back into an elegant and spacious hall.

'Daddy's just changing,' he said, with an ear-to-ear grin. 'I'm meant to ask you if you want some wine.'

'Are you indeed?' She raised her eyebrows.

'Yes.'

Oscar led her into the kitchen where he opened a bottle of white with so much concentration he almost forgot she was there. She scanned the room for signs of a woman's touch, but the signs were too confusing: a borderline chintzy blind and sunshine-yellow kitchen cupboards, but minimalist furniture and completely bare walls. She looked for photos. Nothing. A timetable was stuck to the fridge with Oscar's weekly after-school activities inked in in red capitals. Ooh, and a photo of Oscar, Daisy, Mark and Lilith in a garden, looking suspiciously like a happy family.

When the bottle opened, Oscar cheered and started shouting upstairs. 'I did it! I did it!' As Nicky heard footsteps coming down the stairs, her mouth dried and she swallowed hard. She turned to greet Mark, who came into the kitchen towel-drying his hair. He was in jeans and a simple V-necked green T-shirt that emphasised both the greeny blue of his eyes and the width of his shoulders. She gave him a quick professional smile, wholly appropriate for a supper quiz meeting, then when he turned round, stared at the back of his neck and the breadth of his shoulders as he stretched up to get the glasses. Just a meeting, she told herself. Just a meeting.

'Did Oscar ask you if you wanted wine?' Mark asked her.

'Well —' she began.

'I told her I had to,' Oscar explained.

'That's not quite the same thing,' his father told him.

'Oh,' said Oscar, studying Mark pour out two full glasses and one small one.

'It's fine, really,' said Nicky. 'To be honest, I'm not sure how appropriate it would be anyway.'

Mark gave her a mildly quizzical expression. 'Appropriate?' he repeated, handing her a glass. 'What do you mean?'

'Well,' she said. 'Wine at a fundraising meeting. In front of a pupil.'

'Ah,' breathed Mark, nodding slowly. 'Yes. I see.'

Nicky raised her glass and downed most of her wine in one.

For half an hour they sat round the kitchen table drinking wine, the conversation punctuated by Mark's 'Don't rush it, sweetheart, savour it'. Nicky felt like she was glimpsing the secret backstage banter of her favourite band. Only once did she forget herself. 'You're going to get tipsy if you drink at that speed,' she warned, smiling at Oscar. Oscar looked across at his dad for approval. She followed his gaze, remembering herself too late. She apologised quickly. To her relief, Mark nodded at Oscar. 'She's not a teacher for nothing,' he added. 'She speaks with great wisdom.'

'And considerable experience,' she murmured into her glass.

They all laughed, Oscar the loudest, because although he didn't understand the joke, their laughter put him on a high. Thanks to his high the conversation was easy and fluid. Nicky felt so relaxed that after a while, she felt able to ask if anyone else was coming.

'Such as?' asked Mark.

'I don't know,' she said, pretending. 'Amanda – I mean Miss Taylor? Miss Matthews? Anyone?'

'Miss *Taylor*?' repeated Oscar, looking at his dad. 'Is she coming?'

Mark gave Oscar a quick look and then turned to Nicky.

'Well,' he explained slowly, 'seeing as there's no meeting and it was the first thing that came into my head,' he said, 'it would be a bit odd if they turned up. Unless you mentioned it to them, of course.'

Nicky tried to think of something to say, but it was hard to concentrate over the four-part chorus of the 'Hallelujah' going on in her head. She wished she'd worn perfume.

'I suppose I'd better go and do my homework,' said Oscar quietly. He turned to his dad. 'Can I come down when I've finished?'

'Of course, gorgeous boy.'

Oscar turned to Nicky, suddenly shy.

'Night, Miss Hobbs,' he said.

'Night-night, Oscar,' she replied. 'Good luck with your homework. I'll see you tomorrow.'

'Unless you're still here by the time I've finished,' he corrected before running upstairs.

Feeling wrong-footed, wrongly dressed and all giggly, Nicky followed Mark to the cosy corner of the kitchen, where she sat on the two-seater sofa by the French windows, tucking her skirt under her legs. He joined her there, sitting nearly in the middle, facing her and leaning forwards, one leg stretching out in front of her.

'So,' she began, 'it appears I am here under false pretences.'

'Well,' allowed Mark, arm resting on the top of the sofa, 'you could put it like that, I suppose. I just hated Miss James playing you off against Rob so obviously. But to be honest, it would be great if you could help me with the table quiz. I've never organised one myself and it would mean that, well, I won't get stuck organising it with Martha. Or worse still, Amanda.'

'Ooo-ooh,' giggled Nicky, exhilarated. 'Nasty.'

Mark smiled. 'Honest.'

She smiled back. 'Honest *and* nasty,' she said. 'Better and better.'

They discussed Amanda cautiously at first, and when it became obvious that they concurred wholeheartedly, their observations grew less and less cautious.

'It's her duplicity I can't bear,' he said. 'I don't trust a word she says.'

She nodded furiously. 'I know!' she cried. 'Every smile's like a little lie.'

'Yes!'

They laughed. 'Rob and Pete can't see it at all,' she went on. 'For obvious reasons. She's been following us – well, *them* – well, *Rob* – around for ages. Like a little . . . stray dog.'

He laughed. 'Oh yes?'

'Yes,' sighed Nicky. 'I mean, she obviously still really fancies him.'

'Mmm,' agreed Mark. 'In a bitter, twisted, vengeful way.'

She gave a smiling nod and pondered this for a while. This all felt like yesterday's news, after Rob's impassioned plea to her this morning. She felt disloyal discussing Rob with Mark, but for some bizarre reason, she felt just as disloyal, if not more so, not telling Mark the latest about herself and Rob. Were her loyalties shifting? She was just about to mention something – she didn't know what – when Mark spoke again. He eyed her above his wine glass.

'Do you think it's really over between Rob and Amanda?' he asked slowly.

She paused. Then she nodded firmly.

'At the Christmas party,' he went on, 'you seemed to be . . . involved. If I may be so bold.'

She gulped down some wine. 'Involved?'

'In the garden. I came out and you two were hugging.'

'Oh yeah. No, no,' she said. 'We hadn't . . . talked for quite a while.'

'Ah.' Mark nodded. 'I see.'

'You know . . . as part of the gang. He said he missed me. As a friend.'

Mark nodded. 'And now you're . . . all friends again.'

'Well . . .' She scrunched up her nose, remembered her freckles and unscrunched it quickly. 'It's probably a bit more complicated than that, actually,' she said softly.

Mark said lightly, 'Ah. I see.' He spoke slowly and carefully. 'Would I be right in saying that you and Rob once went out with each other?'

She gave the smallest of nods, her eyes on her drink. 'A long time ago,' she whispered.

'But sometimes,' he asked tentatively, 'there's still a little chemistry there?'

Now there was a tricky one. If Mark had asked her before fireworks night, she'd have said nothing serious. (But was that because she'd been in denial?) If Mark had asked her immediately after fireworks night, she'd have said No Way. (Because she kissed Rob thinking of Mark, and in a cynical ploy to get closure with him. And it had worked.) If he'd asked her when Rob was dating Amanda, she'd have maintained the no. (But was that because she'd been angry and jealous?) If he'd asked her after Rob had chucked Amanda and begged her to be friends again, she'd have probably admitted yes sometimes. (But was that really because she felt victory over Amanda?) If he'd asked her just after the 'shag 'em' comment, she'd have said she genuinely hated him. And after this morning's epic turnaround? She had no idea, but she did know she was beginning to feel seasick.

'Well, it's complicated,' she repeated.

'I see.'

There was a long pause.

'Well,' she said, for some reason desperate not to misinterpret herself to Mark, 'I did kiss him. Once. Fairly recently, I suppose. A while before you came to the school.'

He raised his eyebrows in a silent question.

'Well,' she blundered, 'technically several little times under the umbrella title of "Once".' She coughed.

Mark propped his head in his elbow which was on the back of the sofa, his face now inches away from hers. She wanted to stay there for ever.

'And . . . what happened?' he whispered.

'He kissed me back,' she whispered back.

Mark nodded slowly. 'That was decent of him,' he allowed.

'Well, he's a polite boy.'

Mark roared with laughter and she stopped herself from jumping on him there and then. Instead she used the opportunity to lean forward and whisper, 'Are you a spy?'

He roared again.

No,' he laughed, shaking his head. 'I'm not a spy. I'm just the new boy trying to understand the office politics.'

'Ah! I see.'

'So.' He smiled. 'After the kiss?'

She'd never realised before how highly charged the word 'kiss' was. It was very highly charged. It kept highly charging her.

She grimaced. 'It got complicated for a bit,' she replied. 'But it's much more simple now.'

'Is it?'

'I think so.'

He smiled and drank some of his wine. She decided, on reflection, never to tell him that she kissed Rob the night she'd first seen him at the fireworks display because her insides were all lit up with nowhere to go. Nor would she tell him that, if she were being completely honest, she had actually seen flashes of Mark under her eyelids during the kiss with Rob. No. She would stop short of telling him that, because it might make her sound just a little bit completely barking. Instead, she kept her eyes down.

'How so?' asked Mark.

'Well, basically because I didn't want to start anything with him.' She gave a little shrug. 'The End.'

She heard Mark suck in breath through his teeth and tut a few times.

'I see,' he said, a slight smile on his lips, and still leaning in towards her. 'And since then?'

For some reason, the relief Nicky felt at being able to answer this was enormous.

'It's funny you should ask,' she said. 'He's just started making serious noises again, all of a sudden. Just after this morning's meeting, in fact.' She tried to laugh, but looked away when she realised her eyes had moistened. 'But I think that's just because Miss James is trying to get us to gang up against each other and . . . it sort of spurred him to get back at her.'

Unable to look Mark in the eye, she didn't see his features relax into a beam.

'Excellent reason to get serious with someone,' he said.

'Yeah well, that's what I mean,' said Nicky. 'It's complicated. It's all over the place. But basically we're old news. Very old news. He's been out with Amanda since me and he'll probably go out with her again. And I don't envy either of them.'

'Mm.'

'Anyway,' she said, bravely looking up, 'I don't want to talk about him.'

Mark's eyes seemed to light up from inside, as if the tiny family living in his head were switching on their evening lamps. His eyes were so expressive that she went gooey just looking at them. Wow. This moment was delicious. She just wanted it to go on and on. She wanted to bottle it.

'Of course,' said Mark. 'Sorry. Change of subject.'

She realised she was just sitting there smiling at Mark. And he was smiling back at her with a smile so pensive and slight that she felt intrusive looking at it. Intrusive and soft-centred.

After a lengthy silence, she took a gulp of wine and, in doing so, lifted her eyes to meet Mark's. His skin was utterly perfect. She thought of her freckles and managed a tight little grin. She could feel his soft breath on her cheeks.

There was a long silence. She cleared her throat. 'So anyway,' she said, huskily, 'about this table quiz –'

'Fuck the table quiz,' murmured Mark, edging closer, and she almost had a coronary. It was the sexiest thing she'd ever heard. She'd never be able to hear the words 'table quiz' again without feeling faint. They locked eyes and hovered timelessly, before his gaze slid down to her lips. She swallowed. She heard him swallow. She looked down at his lips.

He leant ever so slightly towards her, his face tilting fractionally. Feeling dizzy, she leant towards him. He stopped suddenly. She stopped suddenly. He looked back up at her eyes. She looked back up at his. He gave a fraction of a smile. He looked back down to her lips. Her back was beginning to ache. Then he softly brushed her thigh with a warm hand and started leaning and tilting towards her again, his breathing thick. Her eyelids fluttered shut.

'Hello!' cried Oscar from the kitchen. They both leapt two feet in the air. Nicky spilt her wine and Mark knocked his shin on the sofa leg.

'Hello!' they both shouted.

Oscar froze. They froze. Oscar's cheeks reddened and his eyes filled. He raced out of the room. Mark raced after him, but when he heard Oscar's door slam, he stood on the stairs for a moment before coming back down.

He found Nicky in the hall.

'I'd better go,' she said, looking at the floor. She got her scarf a bit tangled and decided just to carry it.

'Right,' said Mark.

'Right. Bye.'

'Bye.'

It wasn't until Nicky had been in bed for a while that the liquid wooziness stopped completely. As she fell asleep, her phone bleeped. She stretched across to her bedside table.

Night-night, my lovely rival! Rx

She flung herself back on her pillow and groaned.

Meanwhile, after tidying up the kitchen, turning out the lights and locking up, Mark tapped on Oscar's door. When he heard a muffled 'Come in', he tiptoed into the dark room. Oscar was curled up in bed.

Mark sat on his bed and leant over him.

'Sorry,' squeaked Oscar.

He hugged him and Oscar sat up and cried in his father's chest.

24

During the next month, Nicky had no choice but to focus on the issues at hand. She had real, proper work to do for the table quiz, which did exist and was now only three weeks away. She had masses of organising to do for the summer trip to Bournemouth, which was to start nine days before the end of term. With only one and a half days of school after it, she had final-ever reports for thirty children to write before the end of term. And, she was informed during a morning meeting, she now had two headship interviews, one with Miss James, the other with six of the school's governors, to look forward to. Meanwhile, she had her Joint Deputy hinting at babies in every other text and a knee-trembling crush on her favourite pupil's father.

Focus, focus, focus.

But first things first. The morning after the 'meeting', her first priority was to sort things out with Oscar. Poor, poor Oscar. After she'd got home from Mark's, and spent a few heady hours replaying certain aspects of the evening, she moved on to replaying Oscar's cameo, though key, appearance. The more she remembered his expression the more wretched she felt.

Bright and early the next morning – five o'clock to be precise – she realised she must apologise to him personally. She emailed Mark as soon as she got to work.

She deleted several versions in her quest to find the right tone for such an email. It was a toughie.

Dear Mark, she began.

Too formal.

Mark.

Too cold.

Dear Mr Right?

Too needy.

How difficult could it be? All she wanted to do was ask how Oscar was. After half an hour, ten minutes before she knew the staffroom would be buzzing, she finally found the right tone.

How's Oscar? she wrote.

Nicky.

She clicked Send and then gasped. There was an email for her. From him. He was in already. Down the corridor. Probably in a black suit, white shirt, no tie and his Adam's apple.

How are you? it said.

Mark.

Her throat squeaked. Their emails had crossed each other. She leapt up to go to his office. As she reached the staffroom door, she almost knew what was going to happen next before it happened. She waited a second and then, lo and behold, the door opened and there stood Mark.

'Hi!' they both said.

'Our emails crossed over,' he said. 'I thought I might as well just come and talk to you.'

'Yes. Me too. How's Oscar?'

'Fine,' he said. 'He just felt terrible because he thought he'd interrupted something personal.'

Nicky's hand flew up to her mouth. 'Poor thing!' she cried. 'I've got to talk to him.'

'He's fine!' insisted Mark. 'How are you?'

'Is he in already?' she asked.

'Yep. In class. Reading his book.'

'I'll go up,' she stepped forward to pass him.

'How are you?'

She looked at him and shook her head. 'I can't . . . It's about Oscar. I feel terrible.' She lowered her voice to a whisper. 'I'm his teacher, for goodness' sake.'

'I know.' Mark stepped back. 'Absolutely. Talk to him.'

She ran up the stairs and found Oscar sitting in his seat, reading his book.

'Oscar, my love,' she started. He could barely look her in the eye. She went to him and knelt down beside him, careful not to make the physical contact too intimate. It almost hurt. She wanted to hug him till his teeth twanged.

'You are a wonderful boy,' she whispered.

He nodded one sharp nod.

'I had no right to make you feel uncomfortable in your own home.'

Another sharp nod and a sniff.

'You have nothing to be embarrassed about at all.'

Another nod, another sniff.

When she returned to the staffroom, Ally was there and the others weren't.

'So?' whispered Ally, as soon as she got near.

'It was a real meeting,' whispered Nicky.

'And?'

Nicky took a deep breath. She mustn't tell her. This was dangerous. It could lose her her job.

'*And?*' repeated Ally.

'We nearly kissed.'

Crap.

Ally blinked at her. 'That was some meeting,' she murmured.

'*Nearly.*'

'I've been thinking,' murmured Ally. 'Perhaps I should reconsider my principle of not getting involved in school activities.'

'Don't tell anyone,' begged Nicky. 'Promise.'

Ally looked hurt. 'Who would I tell?'

'I don't know. Pete. Rob.'

'Are you kidding?' said Ally. 'And risk them swapping your secrets for a fumble with Amanda?' She snorted. 'I'd rather pickle my own eyes.'

Pete arrived and joined them immediately.

'Hello, laydeez!' he said. 'Who wants a coffee?'

'Ooh lovely!' said Ally.

'You star!' said Nicky.

They watched him go to the kettle.

'Bless,' said Nicky fondly.

'I know,' sighed Ally. 'It's like watching a child in the body of a slightly bigger child.'

After that day, Nicky made a point of going to the canteen for lunch later than usual, and she completely stopped popping in to see Mark in his office. He kept his distance too. She made Ally promise never to mention the meeting again.

Suddenly, and purely coincidentally, her list of jobs had grown so long it had practically doubled and she only had time to think about Mark properly in the privacy of her own home. Purely due to lack of time she didn't even have the chance to chew the situation over slowly – usually twice, like a pensive cow – with Claire, which was her usual way of dealing with this kind of problem. There was just so much to do.

When she wasn't finalising table quiz arrangements, which involved marketing, enjoying convoluted phone calls with members of the PTA about *University Challenge* versus *The Weakest Link*, selling tickets during lunch-hours, collecting prizes for the raffle, organising the dinner ladies, emailing Mark with the latest updates about it (two PTA members were writing the quiz, Mark was collecting the money from all the teams and sorting final numbers), finalising numbers, allergies and dietary requirements for the summer trip to Bournemouth, which involved writing to parents, hassling parents and then collating replies (Rob was organising the trip's daily itinerary, and Miss James was finalising the hostel because the owner was an old friend), or writing thirty reports (with no music in the background), she was just teaching, really.

It came as no surprise to Nicky that her biggest worry soon became the table quiz.

Partly because it was the first hurdle to jump, but mostly because it would mean spending two and a half hours in Mark's company (which she now found so confusing that the only thing she believed in was his name) in front of Miss James, most of the other teachers and about a hundred parents. And it would mean dealing with the PTA, dinner ladies and her boss. Let alone Rob, her arch-rival who was now merrily talking procreation; Ally, who knew about her history with Rob and her recent history with Mark and had been known to get so drunk at school functions that she got confused over what was a secret and what was a public announcement; Pete, who may or may not know about what had happened with Rob; and Amanda, her new best friend and ally whom she despised and who despised her.

Now, what did one wear for such an evening?

Summer had been last week, so Nicky's choice of skirts was narrowed down to three. The previous weekend (midsummer) she'd been doing her weekly shop and happened to find herself in a posh chemist where, as a little treat to herself, she spent practically half her monthly salary on some new, sheer stockings and a Clarins cleanser. Perhaps when she was Head she'd be able to afford toner too.

Hours before the table quiz, she was feeling stressed, so she allowed herself a break from organising the Bournemouth trip and preparing for her interviews. She got home before six and in only three hours, she was nearly ready.

She kept to her simple work uniform of skirt, heels and fitted top, except that tonight, she took the plunge and decided to wear something slightly different. It was an evening do, after all. Tonight's skirt was smart and fitted but made of black leather. Tonight's shoes were that bit higher, and did things to her ankles and calves that, combined with the sheer new stockings, worked on testosterone as nectar to a bee. And tonight's tight-fitting top was low-cut, fitted and short, yet thanks to its overall casual design, looked as if it wasn't really trying.

She twirled round in the full-length hall mirror, and straightened the seam at the back of her new stockings. She could hardly apply her lipstick, her hand was shaking so much. When the doorbell suddenly buzzed, she had to start again because she felt the clown mouth ruined the overall look. She made her way carefully down the stairs in her heels and opened the door to Claire. She had begged Claire to come. Claire's car was bigger than hers which would give them room to take all the raffle prizes. She'd have asked Ally but she lived on the other side of the school, and anyway, Ally just turning up was a major step. With a lift from her sister, Nicky had the perfect excuse not to accept a lift from Rob. And Claire could provide much-needed, unconditional, sisterly moral support.

'Bloody hell!' cried Claire, when she saw her. 'You're wearing that?'

'Why?' Nicky froze.

'Um . . . nothing.'

Nicky glanced at her watch. She didn't have time to change.

'Well, thanks for your support,' she mumbled, going back up the stairs. 'I feel drunk on high self-esteem now.' She thrust a cuddly dog the size of a pony into her sister's arms. 'Come on. There's loads to do. We'll do it in two trips.'

A quarter of an hour later, they were ready to go.

'You do look lovely,' said Claire, as she started the car. 'I –'

'Just drive,' said Nicky.

'No, really,' said Claire. 'It was just –'

'I don't want to hear it.'

'Will you stop interrupting me! It was just that *I* felt

underdressed because I didn't realise it was a posh do.'

'It's not a posh do!' wailed Nicky. 'I'm ridiculously overdressed.'

'But it looks good.'

'Stop talking and drive.'

After Claire got lost, making them late, Nicky seriously considered going back home and telling everyone tomorrow that she'd completely forgotten to come because she'd been so traumatised by the latest plot twist in *Emmerdale*. It felt marginally less excruciating than turning up late to an evening she'd helped organise, wearing a dead cow.

As Claire parked, Nicky tried to open the door, but the child-lock was on. She watched helplessly as parents walked past the car, up the path.

'Oh good,' mumbled Claire, unlocking the doors, 'I won't be the only one in jeans.'

Nicky tried to get out of the car quickly (not easy in her outfit), making do with slamming the door very heavily.

Guests had only just started arriving, but all the staff were there. One dinner lady was placing the regulation green cups and saucers plus jumbo packs of custard creams on trolleys in the corner of the hall for the half-time refreshment break, the other was hefting vast bottles of lemonade, water, what looked like hundreds of bottles of cheap wine, plus paper cups into the middle of each table. The quizmasters – parents of a Year 3 child, who did charity quizzes for a hobby (and were nearing divorce, partly due to doing charity quizzes for a hobby) – were seated on the podium at the front of the hall, arguing volubly over the microphone system. Amanda and Mark were chatting in the far corner. Nicky squinted at them, questioning what he'd told her about his thoughts of

Amanda, before looking away fast. Ally and Pete were sitting on one of the tables with Martha and her boyfriend. Rob was walking slowly round the hall, next to Miss James, hands clasped behind his back like a visiting dignitary.

Hoping that Miss James wouldn't spot her arriving this late, Nicky hurried her collection of raffle prizes over to the podium, then made her way over to the dinner ladies to thank them for getting there so promptly. Then she caught Mark's eye over the top of Amanda's head, and he gave her a wide, open smile. Amanda turned round to see who he was smiling at. Mark gave the nod and, together, they approached Nicky and Claire. Miss James and Rob were approaching from the other side of the hall and they all met in the middle. Nicky tried to wear the expression of someone who had been there for the past hour.

'Nicky!' cried Amanda, running the last bit of the way towards her. 'You made it! Excellent! Now we're all here.' She took both her hands in hers and, arms outstretched, looked her up and down. 'Wow! Look at *you*. Boy oh boy. I can see why you were this late! Very, very sexy. I didn't know you wore leather. But if it makes you look that amazing, to hell with having a conscience!'

Nicky felt anything but amazing, with her arms stuck in the air, and tried fruitlessly to pull her hands out of Amanda's. She had to introduce Claire to them all with her arms still up. They remembered Claire from when she'd been in observing the teachers' assistants and conversation was easy. After Amanda finally dropped her hands, Nicky decided to go and sit down.

'Bloody hell,' whispered Claire, following behind.

'What?' muttered Nicky.

'She's a bitch, isn't she?' said Claire. 'Why does she hate you so much?'

Nicky stared at the centre of the table, seeing nothing, her head buzzing. Soon everyone else from their team had joined them. Nicky was seated between Miss James and Claire. Rob was on the other side of Miss James. Amanda was on his other side. Mark sat next to Claire. Then came Ned, his wife, Ally and Pete, and Martha and her boyfriend.

Ally and Pete were in their most scornful and sarcastic moods. Martha was in a foul mood. This put her boyfriend in an even fouler mood. Ned was nervous. This made his wife even more nervous. Rob was ebullient. Amanda was more ebullient. Mark was tense. Nicky was even more tense.

'Isn't this *fun*?' squealed Miss James, pouring wine into everyone's paper cups.

They nodded and, almost as one, downed their drinks. The microphone suddenly roared with feedback, announcing the quizmaster. 'Er, hello, everyone,' he began, and then laughed a nervous laugh. 'Can you hear me at the back?'

'NO!' shouted everyone at the back.

Nicky thought she might actually kill someone before the evening was out.

'Er, welcome to Heatheringdown's table quiz,' said the quizmaster, and then laughed a nervous laugh, which was already getting on Nicky's nerves. 'Er, first of all, I must tell you something that, over the years, my wife and I have learnt that one ignores at one's peril.' He laughed again.

The hall buzzed with anticipation.

'Er, you will notice,' he continued, 'that there is a big bottle of lemonade in the middle of your table.' He laughed once more.

There was a murmur of suppressed excitement.

'Er, you must, I repeat, *must*, open this slowly,' said the quizmaster gravely. No laugh. 'Otherwise, er, you will be drenched.' He laughed.

Everyone waited for the punchline.

'Now,' he began, with a laugh. 'Er, here are the rules for tonight's quiz . . .'

In exactly the same way that there is only really one winner on every team of four in *University Challenge* and three lucky members of his or her team, there proved to be only really one winner on Table number 10. And no one was more surprised than Martha to discover that it was her boyfriend. The others made valiant attempts and occasional lucky guesses, but he was an encyclopaedia of quiz knowledge. Meanwhile, Nicky was trying to ignore Rob's fixed gaze on her and hoping that Mark was able to as well.

During the half-time refreshment break, Mark stood up. 'Who wants to help me and Nicky sell the raffle tickets?' he asked.

There was silence. Miss James looked round the table.

BANG! went a bottle of lemonade behind them, followed by the rowdy hysterics of a drunk, and now soaked, table.

'*Perfect* way to show off that fantastic skirt.' Amanda smiled up at Nicky. 'No point wasting it sitting down.'

'You can say that again,' winked Rob. Nicky stood up, somewhat unsteadily, thanks to two paper cups of cheap wine, and saw Rob and Amanda lean forward to chat to Miss James. Of course. There was no way they were going to waste this opportunity to bend her ear. She looked at Ally and Pete, but they were busy badly refilling their cups and doing Bagpuss impressions. She caught up with Mark, which was quite a feat in her outfit. He gave her an enormous smile. He had had four cups of wine.

'How do you think it's all going?' he asked. 'And the quiz?' They both laughed, though in truth Nicky wasn't exactly sure why.

'Fabulous,' she said, sincerely. 'Well done.'

'Well done to you too,' he replied. 'How are you doing?'

'Well,' said Nicky, 'obviously I'm really glad I wore this skirt, otherwise I don't know what Amanda would have got her claws into all evening.'

Mark laughed. 'She's just jealous,' he said.

She gave him a look. He returned it.

'What of?' she asked bravely.

'Where shall I start?' he said softly. Nicky's knees turned to foam. 'Right,' he said. 'See you back at the table. I want every single one of those tickets sold. Or else . . .'

'Or else?' Nicky smiled.

He gave her a look up and down and her insides obediently followed it. 'Where shall I start?' he repeated, even softer this time, before walking away.

She turned, all wobbly, and went in the opposite direction, feeling attached to him by elastic. Or that might have been the drink.

To her surprise, she enjoyed selling the tickets. Or rather, she was happy while she was doing it. Until the end.

'What are the prizes?' asked one of the fathers, his jacket drenched with lemonade.

She gave him her best smile. 'They only cost one pound,' she said.

'I know,' he said. 'What are the prizes?'

'A meal for two at the fantastic local Chinese restaurant,

397

a colour television, a cuddly toy, an Xbox, a bottle of champagne and a very nice box of very nice chocolates.'

'What make?'

'Um. Godiva.'

'The colour television, what make?'

'I don't know.'

'Oh.'

'But the chocolates are Godiva.'

There was a pause. With a big sigh, he found a pound coin in his pocket.

'Go on, then,' he sighed. 'It's for a good cause.'

She smiled, thanked him from the bottom of her heart and hoped with all of it that his table wouldn't win.

When she sat down at her table again, it didn't take long to work out that everyone had been conscientiously finishing the wine. Rob had just gone round the table pouring the last of it into their cups. Conversation stopped abruptly at her return and a table of red faces smiled blurrily up at her. There was an awkward pause.

Nicky sat down heavily. 'If I don't win the cuddly dog,' she said, 'I want my money back.'

Amanda's laughter was louder than everyone else's and she finished with a sighed 'Oh dear, oh dear', as if she'd laughed so much her sides were aching.

BANG! went another bottle of lemonade and Table 4 was drenched. More raucous hysteria.

After the quiz ended, all the parents left, some drenched, most drunk, some carrying raffle prizes, and some all three. Nicky counted up the ticket money, Mark made his goodbyes to both of the quizmasters, who hadn't talked to each other since Round 6, and the dinner ladies tidied everything up. Meanwhile Rob and Amanda, who seemed suddenly distinctly sober, kept Miss James amused.

Ally came and sat down next to Nicky. She was carrying the cuddly dog, which was the size of a pony.

'I'm thinking of calling him Pete,' she said, punching him on the nose. 'Are you all right?'

Nicky grunted. 'I suppose it could be worse.'

'Yeah, you're right.'

'You think?' rushed Nicky. 'How?'

'Um. You could have got lemonade all over you?'

Nicky tried to smile.

'Or won this fluffy dog and have to go home on the night bus.'

'Oh dear.' Nicky looked at Ally. 'You're going to get killed.'

'I'm so glad you talked me into coming.'

'I'll ask Claire to give you a lift home,' said Nicky.

'No, it's all right,' said Ally. 'I'm kidding. Rob's just offered to give us all a lift home.'

'Has he? That was nice of him.'

'In front of Miss James.'

'Wanker.'

'I know,' agreed Ally. 'Utter creep.'

'Yeah.'

'I said yes, of course.'

'Of course. Make him go via Watford.'

They turned to Claire as she joined them. She was carrying the Godiva chocolates. Ally made Claire kiss Pete the dog before making her goodbyes. Claire sat down next to Nicky and opened the chocolates.

'God, look at Rob and Amanda,' hissed Nicky, taking a

chocolate. 'You'd think they were the President and First Lady, wouldn't you?'

'I know,' said Claire, chewing a toffee. 'You certainly get the feeling that he's the Headmaster-in-waiting.'

Nicky stared at her sister.

'Have you any idea what being supportive actually means?' she asked.

Claire tutted. 'I don't mean Miss James feels that he is, I mean he acts like he is.'

Nicky sighed. 'Tell me what the hell they'd been saying about me while I was doing the raffle tickets,' she ordered.

'I'll tell you in the car.'

'No. Tell me now, so I can do damage limitation before I leave, and actually sleep tonight.'

Claire sighed before taking another chocolate. 'Amanda said what a lovely couple you and Mark would make.'

Nicky's eyes doubled in size. She turned to look at Amanda just as Amanda burst into laughter at something Miss James had just said.

'Don't worry, it totally backfired,' said Clare, 'because then Ned started saying how lovely you were and his wife agreed and they said they couldn't understand why you weren't married.'

Nicky stared at Claire.

'So,' Claire went on, 'Martha said you were probably too much of a career woman and men were intimidated by that. And then Amanda said that she bet you'd give it all up in a trice, as soon as you had a family. You were one of those women and everyone knew you were desperate for kids. And it was all bound to happen soon because Mark and you were so keen on each other. She bet money on you being preg-

400

nant within the year and giving up the rat-race to become a full-time mum within two. Then Ally started saying that you could easily juggle both, and Pete agreed and said that you'd make a very good juggler, though it probably wouldn't be ideal to start with babies, especially your own.'

Claire took another chocolate and then looked at Nicky. 'God, Nick,' she said. 'You've gone white. Say something.'

Nicky shook her head. 'I can't think of anything nasty enough,' she whispered.

When they finished counting, Nicky asked Claire to take the amount to Mark while she went to wait for her in the silent, dark car. She couldn't face anyone. She didn't want to go home; she just wanted to be there now. She wanted to be knocked unconscious until she was in bed.

She sped up towards the hall door, hoping no one would call her name. She had gone beyond the point of no return and was seconds away from crying. It was probably the drink, but she didn't know it was possible to feel hate this powerfully. She hated Rob for not hating Amanda, or at least pretending to and not standing up for her about being a career woman. She hated Amanda for saying those things in front of Miss James. She hated Miss James for making her and Rob compete. And for always smiling and being in such a bloody good mood all the time – what pills was that woman on? She hated her for pretending that she didn't know how much work went into everything. She hated Pete for always making jokes the whole bloody time. She hated Claire for being so honest all bloody evening. And she hated Mark for looking keen on her in public and yet being so unreadable to her.

As she walked down the empty, darkened corridor,

heading towards the exit, her tears started coming. She sniffed loudly and let out a choked sob, its echo ringing out past the wall display of the solar system. Just as she opened the school's entrance to the playground, she heard the door from the hall behind her swing open into the corridor. Someone wasn't far behind. She sped up. She didn't want any of them to see her like this. By the time she was halfway across she was sober. She'd already got Claire's car key out of her bag. She ran a little of the way until she reached the path. The gentle curve of the lamp-posts at the side of the path and fairy lights in the conifers always made the path look like a fairy grotto at night, but as the sound of the footsteps behind Nicky stopped, indicating that whoever was behind her had now also reached the squidgy tarmac too, she didn't care. As soon as Claire's car hove into view, she pointed her key at the car and started clicking desperately, nearly sobbing with frustration when nothing happened, like a desperate radar-wielding *Star Trek* extra. Finally she heard the loud click of the car doors unlocking. She sped up and yanked at the passenger door. It didn't open and she almost pulled her back out. She'd forgotten the child-safety lock. The person behind her was catching up. Frantically, she pressed the car key again. The person behind her was now gaining. Suddenly, with a tiny little click, the passenger door unlocked. Now she could hear the footsteps again, which meant the person was in the car park. It sounded like a woman. If it was Amanda, there was every chance she'd hit her and then keep on hitting.

She pulled open the car door and just as she was about to jump in, she heard Miss James sing out her name. She moaned silently, wiped her face fast, smiled and turned to face her boss.

'Congratulations!' trilled Miss James. 'Well done, my dear.' Her voice was an octave higher than usual, her arms stretched towards her. 'What a wonderful, wonderful evening! You should be very, very, very, very, *very* proud of yourself.'

Nicky tried not to burst into tears. 'Thank you,' she squeaked. 'Glad you enjoyed it.'

'Enjoy it? *Enjoy* it! I loved it. *Loved* it! Adored every minute of it! So funny! The lemonade! Genius!' She burst into laughter, before suddenly going serious and pointing at Nicky. 'You clearly have superb organisational skills.'

'Yes. It was fun organising it. '

'And you can clearly work well as one of a team.'

'I'd like to think so. It was a good team as well,' breathed Nicky, her hand on the door handle.

'Of course!' agreed Miss James, nodding. 'Indubiter-bibbly.'

'Mm.'

Miss James just wasn't getting the hint. Instead, to Nicky's horror, she even leant in closer, swaying softly like a conifer in the breeze, her eyes so near that Nicky could see the reds of them. Then she whispered very, very loudly, 'That young Miss Taylor!' She widened her eyes. 'She's a little turn-up for the books, isn't she?'

'Oh?' mumbled Nicky, dreading the worst. 'H-how do you mean?'

Miss James gave her a big wink, which involved her entire body and made her look like she was trying to prevent middle-aged leakage. 'My dear,' she confided, 'the girl's a completely conniving cow.' She tapped her nose, missed, and almost poked herself in the eye. Then she squeezed Nicky's arm and finally left her in peace.

25

'Right,' began Claire, from across Nicky's dining-room table. 'Now then, Miss Hobbs –'

'She doesn't call me Miss Hobbs,' interrupted Nicky.

Claire shot her a look over her glasses. 'Excuse me,' she said shortly, 'this is meant to be a role-play.'

'Well, there's no point in doing a role-play if it's not convincing,' said Nicky. 'She doesn't call me Miss Hobbs.'

'What does she call you? Nicky?'

'"My dear". "Dear girl".' Nicky tried to think of some more.

Claire frowned. 'Doesn't sound very professional. What does she call Rob?' she asked drily. '"Boss"?'

Nicky shut her eyes. 'Just begin the interview.'

Claire coughed. 'Well, my dear,' she began again, 'what qualities do you think you can bring to this job?'

The practice interview went well. During it, Nicky was forced to reorganise a few key answers and devise a method for remembering everything, which entailed a combination of mnemonics and imaginary headlines. After three hours and much repetition, she thought her brain might dissolve.

'What time is the interview?' asked Claire.

'Eight.'

'What time is Rob's?'

'Seven.'

'Hmm.'

Nicky sighed. 'Don't ever tell me what that "hmm" means.'

'No, I just –'

'I don't want to hear it.'

'– think you've got longer to sleep in –'

'Hah!'

'– or prepare.'

Nicky rubbed her eyes. She knew she couldn't possibly prepare for another question. She'd even thought of a compelling answer for what she'd do if she got pregnant, apart from 'sell my story of immaculate conception to the press'.

She'd thought through and round every possible angle that Miss James might pursue in tomorrow's interview. In fact, she'd thought of every single aspect of this job. And the more she'd thought about it, the more she knew she wanted it. And the more she wanted it, the more nervous she got. Her stomach was so full of nerves there was no room for anything else in it, least of all food. She hadn't eaten any dinner. At 11 p.m., just after Claire had left, she forced some toast and tea down her throat but had to leave most of it.

She slept well, which is to say, she didn't wake up all night. But she dreamt terribly. She had her recurring exam nightmare, where she was doing A-levels and had just discovered she had to do Maths instead of English and Classics. Her best friend (Marianne Sunderland – two boys, one surgeon husband, own beachwear catalogue business) was trying to help her but could only speak Chinese.

When Nicky woke, her cheeks were damp. She looked at her clock just as its alarm went off. She listened to Radio 4 as she got ready for her interview, just in case Miss James surprised her and asked her something topical. When she got into her car and tuned in again, she realised that she hadn't heard a single word. She didn't even know who today's presenters were. She changed the channel to Classic FM, but it was adverts mostly for digital radios and she didn't want one. She couldn't even listen to this one properly. She turned it off and decided to role-play another interview. By the time she arrived at school, her lower inner lip was shredded and her stomach was concrete.

She sat in her car, steadying her breath. When her mobile phone bleeped with a text message, she smiled immediately. She took it out and read it.

Brk a leg. Preferably Rob's. Ally x

For a full minute, she envied Ally her late mornings and stress-free days. And then, after the minute was over, she got out of her car and smoothed down her smart interview skirt.

She walked up the path and studied the numbers and alphabet on the ground. If she got the job, she'd get them repainted. And possibly change the G-gnu for a G-goat.

Five minutes later, she stood in the silent staffroom blinking up at the clock. Half past seven. Rob had been in there for half an hour. She had half an hour to kill. Her body shivered, as if someone had just walked over her grave. Her hands were freezing. She decided, for want of anything else to do, to boil the kettle even though she didn't want tea or coffee. Then she decided to redo her make-up, and when the kettle boiled before she was halfway through, she just stopped and looked at it, mascara wand in hand.

Sitting there like that, she asked herself why she was quite this nervous. She had had job interviews before. She had passed a lifetime's worth of exams. She picked up her mirror again. She brought it closer to her face and stared at the delicate, precisely parallel lines beginning their journey down the soft skin from the outer corner of her eyes to the tip of her cheekbones.

'Hiya. How are you?' came Mark's voice from the door.

She almost dropped the mirror.

'OK, thanks,' she answered. Her lips were now quivering with cold.

He walked into the staffroom and she thought he might bend down to hug her, but he just stopped short of reaching that far. 'You'll be fine,' he said.

Nicky's eyes darted past him as the staffroom door opened. When Ned appeared, there was a stunned silence. Ned almost turned round and walked back out again, then seemingly thought better of it, stayed – that is, he tried to shrink into nothingness where he stood – and whispered hello.

When they said hello back, he nodded. He continued nodding all the way to his locker.

'You're in early,' said Nicky, for want of anything better to say.

He gave a little start and half turned to her, his face looking worryingly like the face of someone who'd just shat himself. Which was well within the realms of possibility.

When Amanda came in, he looked like he'd just done it again. Nicky sympathised.

'Ooooh!' laughed Amanda, looking from Ned to Nicky and back again. 'Of course! It's today, isn't it? I forgot! So! Are we all ready, then?'

There was a moment of sudden communal under-standing. Nicky looked at Ned. He nodded a bit more, eyes firmly on the floor. She wanted to be able to speak. Then Amanda turned to Ned, who was now even paler than Nicky.

'What time's yours?' she asked him.

Ned could barely bring himself to look at Nicky. He managed a turn of the head, but that was as far as he could do. His eyes skimmed the floor as his mouth did an impersonation of a smile. The skin round his lips was hospital-green.

'It was my wife's –' he began.

'No!' said Nicky. 'You don't need to explain. Good luck, Ned. Go for it!'

'So!' Mark turned to Amanda. 'What time's yours?'

Amanda laughed. 'I'm not going for it!' she said. 'God, I'm not remotely ambitious.'

Ned excused himself. Probably to change his trousers, thought Nicky. As he walked past her, she said, more to him than Amanda, 'There's nothing wrong with a bit of ambition.'

Ned shut the door behind him. Nicky could feel Mark looking at her. She wanted very much to look back at him, but knew that Amanda was looking and that she'd probably cry.

'Good luck,' she heard him say lightly.

'Thanks,' she replied.

He strode across the room, opened the door and stepped back as Rob appeared before them all. The two men nodded a greeting to each other, and as Mark left, Rob entered, grinning at Amanda and Nicky.

'Well?' asked Amanda. 'How was it? Don't keep us in suspense! Was it OK?'

He blew out air through tight lips and shrugged. Behind him, Miss James popped her head round the door and smiled.

'Hello, team!' she said and then looked at Nicky. 'Are you ready, my dear?'

Nicky picked up her case and followed Miss James to her office. As she walked past Mark's office, she heard his door quietly click shut. She carried on walking behind Miss James.

Behind the bursar's door, Mark was making a rather delicate phone call. As he waited for someone to answer, he paced the floor.

'Fortune Green Senior School?' came the receptionist's voice at the other end.

'Hello,' he said. 'It's Mark Samuels here, I'm returning Mr Davies's call from yesterday.'

'Ah yes, hello.' Her smile was audible over the phone. 'The Headmaster's free now,' said his receptionist. 'I'll put you through.'

Miss James stood back at the door to her office and let Nicky go in before her. Nicky gave a respectful smile to Miss James's shoes as she passed them. Miss James shut the door quietly behind them. The first thing Nicky saw was a governor sitting in an extra chair behind Miss James desk, to her right. He looked like a thin, kindly Father Christmas, except slightly older. He had a white beard and the most mesmerising white furry eyebrows that jumped up, like two terriers whose owners had just come home, every time he smiled.

'This is Mr Godfrey-Smythe,' introduced Miss James. 'Nicky Hobbs, our other Joint Deputy Head.'

Nicky put forward her hand, determined to give him a confident handshake that spoke of kindness, warmth and empathy, yet firmness and discipline. Smiling, with jumping eyebrows, he took her hand in his and vibrated it sideways for a moment.

'Right, well,' said Miss James as she sat down at her desk, 'I suppose we'd better get started, hadn't we?'

Nicky nodded and licked her lipstick. She crossed her legs and held her hands in her lap. She gave Miss James – and Mr Godfrey-Smythe – a broad, warm smile. She breathed deeply and slowly. She had a headache.

Miss James propped her glasses on her nose, picked up the top application form and glanced at it, holding it away from her face. No smile. Nicky looked at her face without its smile. There were such deep lines from the corners of her nose to her chin that they looked drawn on. Her lips were surprisingly thin. Miss James suddenly banged the form down on her desk and looked up at her.

'Oh, just talk to me,' she said, taking off her glasses. 'Why the job, my dear? Tell me Why The Job.'

Mr Godfrey-Smythe's eyebrows trampolined ecstatically.

'Well,' Nicky started, sitting forward. She began by headlining her qualities, explaining how each one matched what she thought were the qualities of a good head teacher. Then she went back to each in turn and elaborated. All the while, Miss James stared intently at her, nodding slowly. Nicky concluded by repeating her headlines and underlined them with a hopeful smile. Miss James continued to nod slowly. Then she stopped nodding and sat back in her chair. There was a moment of pure silence. The moment expanded.

And then, ever so slowly, into the silence, came the low, quiet whiffle of a hedgehog making its way across the office. When Miss James looked briefly down at her notes, Nicky took the opportunity to glance at Mr Godfrey-Smythe. He was out cold, head back, mouth open. He was now displaying nose hair that competed admirably with his eyebrows.

'Are you happy?' asked Miss James suddenly.

Now, there was a question Nicky had not prepared for. She felt as if she'd turned over a Maths exam paper and found a question on Henry IV. Her body went into shock. God knows where her blood was rushing to, but it wasn't her brain.

Focus, focus, focus.

If she answered yes, would she come across as too content and therefore not in need of promotion? If she answered no, would she come across as someone too unhappy to be a headmistress? She opened her mouth to speak, as intrigued to hear what she was going to say as Miss James appeared to be.

'It's such a strange time of life, isn't it?' asked Miss James. 'Your thirties. Isn't it? You're not young any more, but you're not old yet. You're not really anything. You've still got to prove yourself in the world, yet you should already be halfway there.'

At this point, Nicky still believed they were having a conversation and saw a tree-lined avenue of conversation that would lead them both to the perfect glade of Nicky Hobbs, Headmistress. She liked Miss James's style. She opened her mouth with every intention of talking.

'Of course,' went on Miss James, 'it was all very different

in my day. I was a rarity. Still am, mostly. At least you're among others like you, young feisty women, all climbing up that long, slippery pole – that sharpest of sharp learning curves – together.'

Nicky decided now was not the time to ask why feisty was an adjective only ever used to describe women or pets. Meanwhile, she tried hard not to stare at Mr Godfrey-Smythe. Had Miss James fixed his drink? Or had he woken up and started taking notes?

'And none of you,' said Miss James, sitting forward, 'not one of you poor dears can have any idea how far you'll get up that long, slippery pole. Or what life's cruel hand will throw at you on the way up.' She sighed. 'By my age, of course, you know a little bit more. Even if you haven't got very far up that pole, and you've made a complete mess of your life, at least you *know*. There's something very reassuring about that.'

Nicky had lost sight of her avenue. She nodded with great enthusiasm and tried to ignore the bubble of stress rising up into her chest.

'But then, of course,' sighed Miss James, 'all too soon, along comes retirement. And suddenly, you're right back at the beginning again. Right back at the bottom of another long, slippery pole. Will you get to the top? Will it all work out? Have you finally stopped learning or is there still loads more to learn? Will you be on another sharp learning curve? What will life throw at you while you're climbing up your retirement pole? Illness, dementia and death, or long sunny afternoons and boules tournaments? Will you be allowed to finish the journey of fulfilment? Or, in some cases, start it? Will you even recognise it?'

'Hmm,' said Nicky thoughtfully. 'Yes, I –'

'I suppose,' said Miss James, 'we never really know the answer to any of those questions until we are, literally, on our deathbed. And up until that moment, that very last moment of our lives, that very last breath we take, we are all just climbing up one slippery pole after another.'

Nicky didn't move. Mr Godfrey-Smythe spluttered slightly, stopped and resumed whiffling. Miss James didn't look, but merely waited for it to end.

'Look at your poor little pupils, for instance,' she went on. 'They're finally about to reach the top of the long, slippery pole of primary school. To plant their own Year 6 flag right at the very pinnacle of that pole! They've lived through a whole year of being the big fish in a little pond. They have reached the top. And what reward do they get for that? They get to go right to the bottom of the next slippery pole. The long, slippery pole of secondary school! To be the bottom of the dung-heap. The smallest fish in the biggest pond they've ever seen. The bottom of the sharpest learning curve of all. Poor little mites! And then they'll struggle up that pole – falling in and out of all the pitfalls of adolescence, exams, first heartbreak, parent problems – and for what? Another bloomin' pole. Sixth-form college! Then – if they're "lucky" – university. Then a career. Then their first job. Second job. Third job. It never ends, does it?'

Nicky shook her head. There was a long silence. Should she just start talking? Or would that wake Mr Godfrey-Smythe?

Miss James leant forward, her eyes sparkling. Nicky leant in.

'I want to learn how to scuba-dive,' whispered Miss James.

'Ooh!' breathed Nicky.

'Of course, they don't teach it at my local pool.' She leant back again. 'I'm ahead of my time. Like my mother before me. Maybe I'll just go on some advanced swimming course first. And of course I've got so many books to read. That's one thing a head never gets time to do.'

'Ah,' said Nicky.

'Ah, *reading*,' sighed Miss James luxuriously. 'Reading is wonderful. It's one of life's joys, isn't it? And yet how often do we do it? I mean, it's ironic, isn't it? We teach our children how to master this exquisite language of ours – the language of Chaucer, of Wordsworth, of Shakespeare – and then, as adults, we don't do it, do we? Do you? Do you read?'

'Um . . .' Christ, what on earth was the correct answer to that? She'd just been told that a head never has time to read. 'Um . . .' she repeated. 'Well –'

'Of course,' went on Miss James, 'you read books for work, but do you ever have time to read for *yourself*? Really read for your own pure pleasure? To exercise those little grey cells? To escape! To let your imagination run wild? To get inside someone else's head? Now, here's a little secret I can let you into. Ah, dear me. The last book I read was the first *Harry Potter*. Don't tell anyone else that. Shocking, isn't it? Shocking.' She tilted her head slightly and gave Nicky a small smile. 'Anyway, where were we?' she asked kindly. 'Gosh, I do rattle on, don't I?' She put on her glasses and looked up at the wall clock. 'Oh my goodness me!' she exclaimed. 'You should have stopped me. Now *that's* something a head *has* to be able to do. Absolutely imperative. Take control!' She hit the desk forcefully. 'Take control!' she repeated.

415

Mr Godfrey-Smythe woke with a jump. His eyes landed on Nicky. She tried to give him a reassuring smile, but it was hard when you weren't feeling very reassured yourself.

'Yes . . . well,' said Nicky, 'I –'

'Now, my dear. Have you got any questions?' asked Miss James.

Oh dear God, thought Nicky. She was stunned. How on earth had she and Claire not thought of that question? She hadn't rehearsed for the only real question she'd got. What questions do you ask a headmistress about being a head-mistress? Will I be able to afford Clarins?

'Um . . .' she murmured.

Miss James smiled at her. 'Take your time, poppet,' she said, kindly. 'This is your moment.' She turned and grinned at Mr Godfrey-Smythe who gave them both a kindly look, his eyebrows jumping for a bone.

Nicky's heart hammered against her chest.

'No need to be nervous, my dear,' said Miss James softly.

This isn't nerves, thought Nicky hotly. This is hate.

'Actually,' she said.

'Yes?'

'I don't think I have, really. I just think you learn the important things on the job.'

Miss James sat back in her chair and just looked at her as if she'd said the most amazing thing she'd ever heard.

'Interesting,' murmured Miss James, nodding slowly. 'Interesting.'

Afterwards, as Nicky's hand was vibrated sideways by a smiling Mr Godfrey-Smythe, she felt her body go light with relief and her head go heavy with tension. She watched Ned follow Miss James like a lamb to the slaughter and wanted to reassure him that all he'd have to do was listen and occasionally, if he felt like showing a streak of assertiveness, nod.

'Well? How was it?' Rob asked her, Amanda hovering close by.

'Fine,' said Nicky. 'How was yours?'

'Fine,' said Rob. They nodded at each other.

Teaching Year 6 that day was a blessed relief. Nicky performed one of her most enjoyable science lessons, that of mixing sodium bicarbonate with water first, then lemon juice, orange juice and, finally, vinegar. The results were increasingly exciting, finally resulting in bangs good enough for any kid, let alone a Year 6. The children were beside themselves with excitement at the reaction to vinegar. And Nicky was beside herself with teaching them something she knew was fun and that they'd never forget. It was such a lovely lesson, and compared with her interview, such a sane interlude, that it really did help her forget the madness of her morning interview and fear of her afternoon one with the governors, due at 5.30. She loved all her children today – their eager faces, their spontaneous laughter, their unbounded joy when they got the answers right, their team spirit and support for others – but most of all she loved Oscar. It was a small reminder that, even if she'd wanted to, she couldn't rush into Mark's office and collapse in a small heap all over him. All her kids were a tonic; Oscar, though, was something bordering on therapy.

At lunch, the gang reconvened, but there was a new awkwardness to it due to this morning's interviews. Neither Rob nor Nicky were spilling any beans, no matter how much the others asked, and Ally and Pete were not impressed at being left out. Pete tried to change the subject by asking how Ally's morning had gone.

'I'm sorry,' said Ally curtly, 'but I don't want to talk about it.'

'No, of course,' replied Pete. 'I shouldn't have asked.'

'What about your morning?' asked Ally.

'I couldn't possibly say,' said Pete. 'It might jeopardise my entire career. Although I did have a Lion bar at break.'

'Did you?' asked Ally in shock. 'Tidy your desk this instant.'

'I don't have a desk.'

'Well, tidy mine then.'

'You don't have one.'

'I don't? Right, that's it. I'm resigning.'

Conversation turned to something bland and none of them were interested in it at all.

By 4.30, Nicky had developed a headache so big she was convinced it was meant for someone else's head. She resisted taking any tablets until after school finished, when she finally had no choice. In desperation, she took three. By 5 p.m., she felt high, but barely awake. She made it to a café near the school where she ordered two double espressos. By the time she was on her way back to school her body didn't know which way was up.

As she walked back in, she passed Mark and Oscar coming out. She beamed at Oscar and gave Mark a fast, friendly smile. They smiled back. After she'd passed, they stopped and turned to watch her.

'Is she all right?' Oscar asked his father.

'I don't know,' murmured Mark.

At 5.30 Nicky was called into an interview with six governors. As soon as she walked in, she realised this was going to be a very different experience from her first interview. For a start, she got a chance to speak, and even to speak about the vacancy of Head Teacher at Heatheringdown. Secondly, it soon became clear that no one was going to fall asleep in this meeting. Mr Godfrey-Smythe had clearly done his part for the interview effort and was now doubtless at his gentlemen's club whiffling and displaying his nasal hairs over a whisky. The only problem was that the room was so full of underlying tension that she felt like the least important thing in it.

Before the second question had been posed to Nicky, it became clear that she was merely a pawn in a long-term battle of wills between Governor Smith and Governor Atkins. Governor Smith was Brutus to Governor Atkins's Caesar. Everyone else in the room was a key member of the senate. She was some guy in a toga. The political and personal conflicts were impossible for Nicky to predict or overcome. All she could gather was that they all seemed far more interesting and important than her answers. When Governor Atkins asked a question, Governor Smith's eyes rose skyward or he smirked secretly behind a bony finger or sat back elaborately in his chair. He would then, rather pointedly, ask the next question and Governor Atkins would sit, motionless, his face reddening with every second of Nicky's answer. By the end of the interview, she almost didn't want the job any more.

'Now then, Miss Hobbs,' said Governor Smith, 'we've heard a lot about your ideas for the future and all very sensible it sounds. I only have one more question for you and that is to ask you whether you have ever held any similar positions of responsibility in any other aspects of your life?

Your private life, for instance. I mean,' he pointed to her CV, 'it doesn't say here if, for example, you have children of your own. I think it goes without saying that motherhood is –' he bestowed a gracious smile on both female governors – 'the ultimate responsibility.'

Nicky looked at the female governors. One was busy writing, the other stared back at her. Was this a trick question? Legally, he couldn't ask her if she was planning to start a family within the next few years, but there was every chance he wanted to know. Despite the irregularity of his question, she had rarely found her single status a selling point and she wasn't going to let that one go.

'You're absolutely right,' she said with a smile. 'No, I'm not a mother. But I am very content and I'm sure we'd all agree that that's the best role model for children.'

There was a pause which did not convince her that they'd all agree on anything.

'However,' she continued, 'I do have three nieces who I look after a lot. *Whom* I look after a lot,' she said. 'Often for whole weekends. But . . . no, I don't have my own children. This gives me much more time to focus on my pupils, prepare their work, mark their work, help them work on their displays, et eteca, without feeling that I should be rushing elsewhere. I do not clock-watch at all. Far from it.'

Governor Smith looked at her, nodded slowly and then wrote something down. Nicky decided now was not the moment to question if he had asked Rob whether he was a father.

'I don't think we need to worry about Miss Hobbs's ability to look after children.' Governor Atkins smiled, leaning forward towards her. 'Year 6 teacher for the past three years

420

with excellent SATS results speaks for itself, does it not, Miss Hobbs?'

'I'd like to think so,' she replied, adding Governor Atkins to her Christmas card list. 'And of course, thirty sets of parents trust me enough to spend five hours a day in charge of their children. That's a big responsibility and one I'm proud to have.'

All the male governors nodded enthusiastically at her.

'Are you saying that teachers are more responsible for children than their own parents?' asked Governor Morris, mother of four.

'No!' replied Nicky. 'Of course not! Parents spend far more time with their children. But there are still many hours in the week when I am entirely responsible for their children's physical and emotional welfare, and it's not a responsibility I take lightly.'

'Yes,' Governor Morris smiled, 'but the question is not whether you are up to your present job, but whether you are up to a headship.'

'I think,' added Governor Atkins, 'that Miss Hobbs was merely using her experience as a teacher to answer the question.'

'And I think,' added Governor Smith, 'that Governor Morris's comment was, as usual, most pertinent and useful.'

'Thank you.' Governor Morris smiled at Governor Smith.

'My pleasure.' Governor Smith smiled back.

Nicky considered getting them all to kiss and make up. She was grateful when after only an hour, they let her go. Caesar won the battle by standing up and showing her out. She turned to say goodbye to the others and caught Brutus making eye contact with his comrades. She got out fast.

26

If Nicky had been hoping for some kind of hint from Miss James about the way the land lay during the next morning's meeting, she would have been in for a big let-down. Luckily she hadn't been. She was, however, hoping very much that she would be able to make it through the day. The stress of yesterday and the overdose of headache pills had put her eyelids on a different speed from the rest of her body. Why did her head always seem out of control? It was almost as bad as her hair. She wondered sometimes if the two were linked. If her hair were naturally sleek and 'manageable' (as they termed it in those infuriating adverts where women's hair was made of molten metal), would the pain in her head be as manageable? If she thought for one minute that the two were causally linked, she'd go straight out and buy a hair iron.

The others didn't seem to have had any bad effects from yesterday's interview. In fact, Miss James and Rob were on tip-top form and both enjoyed a great gossip together about Harry Potter. Even the Year 4 at the puzzle table was allowed to join in. Nicky conserved her energy and focussed on keeping her eyelids up.

After Harry Potter, Miss James then told them a joke she'd been told 'recently' which they both recognised as Ned's favourite, nay only, joke. They all laughed loudly.

As the meeting progressed, it dawned on Nicky that the clues were all there, should she wish to find them. Rob and Miss James were now old friends, and Ned had been able to deliver his joke properly, something he rarely managed to do in the staffroom.

Not that she was downhearted or anything, but facts were facts. She was doomed.

By the time Miss James asked her and Rob for updates on the Bournemouth trip and instructed them to start nagging their respective teachers to complete their reports in time for her to sign them all, Nicky felt that she was just bluffing by being there.

After the meeting, she stood at Miss James's puzzle with a despondent heart, while Miss James had a quick word outside with Janet.

Nicky frowned at the wretched puzzle helplessly. 'Isn't this thing finished yet?' she mumbled to Rob. 'They're usually done by now, aren't they? This one's gone on for ages.'

He shrugged. 'It's only a puzzle,' he said, sticking a piece somewhere in the former Yugoslavia. Nicky watched him wander out of the office and then looked back down to the puzzle. She stared at it some more. *It's only a puzzle*, she told herself. *It's only a puzzle*. She scanned it slowly, her eyes twizzling in and out of focus. *Only eight hours till bedtime*, she thought. *It's only a puzzle*.

She let her eyes focus on the southern coast of Spain, where she'd been on holiday a couple of years ago. She wondered idly if she'd be able to find the resort she'd visited.

She looked all along the coastline which, thanks to the entire population of Heatheringdown, was now satisfyingly complete. She looked again. The resort she remembered wasn't there. She frowned heavily. And, if she wasn't very much mistaken, the coastline itself seemed to be waving in the wrong direction. And then she spotted some lettering which she was sure was Czech and not Spanish. She kept her finger on the spot, blinked very hard and started examining the rest of the puzzle. Sure enough, there were pieces in it that had been forced to fit, their colours and lettering completely wrong.

Miss James came in, saw her and laughed.

'Gosh, my dear!' she said. 'Still here?' She walked to her desk and started hunting for today's assembly notices. 'That one's taking for ever, isn't it? I think it's the longest one yet.'

'Um,' said Nicky. 'Miss James.'

'Hmm?' She was delving through her papers.

'I think I've spotted something.'

'Hmm?'

Nicky looked at her and waited. Miss James looked up.

'I have a feeling I know why it's taking so long,' said Nicky.

'Oh yes?'

'People have been cheating.'

Miss James's features froze so instantly she looked like a photo. 'What do you mean?' Her voice was cold.

'Well,' Nicky looked back at the puzzle, 'some of the pieces are wrong. They've just been put anywhere.'

Miss James came to look. Nicky pointed at the pieces. They stood there for a while and then Miss James said, almost inaudibly, 'Thank you.'

That morning in assembly Miss James made no jokes and when she caught her glasses on her necklaces, she merely untangled them. She spoke gravely about the fact that somewhere in the school there was a cheat. Maybe several. And not just any cheat. A cheat in the biggest team game the school had ever undertaken. A cheat who had not just let down themselves, but let down the entire school.

There was silence.

Miss James explained that the puzzle on her desk in her office was not just a puzzle. It was a symbol. A symbol of a society working together towards a worthy purpose, that of creating a decent, hard-working, honest generation of men and women. She was ashamed and disheartened. And to have this happen just before the end of the school year, and days before her own retirement after twenty years as Head-mistress, was doubly disheartening. She expected to have the culprit – or culprits – in her office at lunch-time.

When no culprit appeared, she did the same the next day, with an ultimatum this time. If no one had come forward to admit their behaviour, the entire school would lose the half-day holiday from the last day of term. It would not be a half-day, it would now be a full day. By the end of the week, she was stony-faced throughout assembly. There were no jokes, there were no anecdotes.

The morning meetings changed too. They were now short and sorry affairs with Miss James going through the motions. The puzzle table lay empty and the new blank space it left in the room looked oddly naked.

After one such meeting, Nicky held back and asked Miss James if she was all right.

Miss James looked at her.

'I have been lied to,' she said simply.

To her surprise, Nicky began to long for the return of Miss James's infuriating smiles. Meanwhile, she got back to filling her own capacity for worry to breaking point. The deadline for numbers for the Bournemouth trip was tomorrow morning nine o'clock sharp. Her deadline for relaying dietary requirements to the hostel was the day after, which would mean checking all the forms and invariably calling the parents who had forgotten to fill that bit in. She also needed to finish organising five days' worth of activities for those pupils not going on the trip in good time to give to the teacher overseeing them while she was away, as well as finish all her end-of-year reports because there would be so little term-time after the trip. Reports were no longer the two-line judgements of yesteryear. Nicky had to find enough positive, encouraging and inspiring things to say about each child to fill a small booklet. In some cases, it was the most creative writing she did all year. Plus she still had a detailed, loving letter to write to her entire class for their end-of-year book which was being painstakingly assembled by one of the mothers.

Even without a full-time job, this amount of work could easily fill a week, possibly four days if she didn't sleep. But she liked her sleep. It was getting harder and harder to get up in the mornings and she had on occasion even been known to press her alarm snooze button.

The next day, her worry capacity zoomed up to the red zone. She was in the staffroom when Amanda almost ran up to her, eyes and smile wide with anticipation.

'You'll never guess who's coming on the trip!' she declared.

'Well, that'll save time,' replied Nicky dully, without pausing from what she was doing.

Ally and Pete laughed heartily at this and Rob offered a smile.

'Go on,' Amanda demanded. 'Guess. I'm *so* excited!' Amanda turned to Rob.

'Blimey.' Rob smiled. 'The Queen?'

Amanda shrieked with laughter. 'Wrong sex.'

'Prince Philip?'

'No!'

'Shergar,' suggested Pete.

'Rumpelstiltskin,' offered Ally.

Amanda was now only talking to Rob. 'I'll give you a clue. He works at this school, but he's not a teacher. Has a child in Year 6 called Oscar. Blond hair. And green eyes.' She looked at Nicky, incapable of controlling a smirk. Martha joined them.

'You are *kidding* me!' Martha told Amanda. They both shrieked.

'Nope!' laughed Amanda. 'Go and have a look for yourself. He's on the list. Next to his little boy. Just under me!' She shrieked with laughter again.

Now Nicky stared openly at Amanda, finally shocked into reacting.

'*You're* coming?' she said, trauma overriding her politeness chip.

'Of course!' laughed Amanda. 'I'm not going to miss a treat like that.'

Nicky grimaced. 'Are you actually aware of how much work this trip will involve?' she asked. 'It's not a holiday.'

Amanda's smile stiffened on her face. 'Thank you, Miss

Hobbs. I'm perfectly aware of what is involved in a school trip.'

'We're going to the British seaside, Amanda.'

'I know where we're going.'

'On the coast.'

'I know.'

'With colleagues, not friends.'

Amanda affected a smiling concern. 'Oh, you seem really shaken up about this.'

'On a glorified coach trip.'

'I had no idea you'd be this upset.'

'Sleeping in a hostel! Sharing showers! *Working!*'

The others weren't laughing any more and Amanda's smile vanished so completely it was hard to believe it had ever existed.

'I know,' said Amanda pointedly, 'and I'm going. Get over it.'

Nicky turned to Ally and Pete.

'You see?' she told them desperately. 'If Amanda can do it, you two can.'

'If Amanda can do it,' retorted Ally loyally, 'anyone can.' She turned to Amanda. 'No offence, Amanda.' She turned back to Nicky. 'But I'd rather teach, thanks. And I want to have a week without you all. Especially without Miss James and Janet. I'm going to steal all the envelopes. It'll be fun.'

'I want to see Gwen doing assembly,' said Pete.

They all turned to him. 'Why?' asked Nicky.

He lowered his voice to a whisper. 'Apparently, she's big in her local amateur dramatics society. She's been having special coaching. The theme's Reproduction.'

'Oh! Excellent!' laughed Ally. 'I can't wait.'

Nicky was officially depressed. The nightmare had grown to Hitchcockian dimensions. Every day and every night for a whole week being scrutinised by Miss James (who had now not smiled for days). Every day and every night for a whole week competing with Rob who was either playing it cool or hinting at their possible future. And at the same time she would need to maintain order, discipline, fun, variety and comfort for forty kids away from home, some for the first time. No Ally for much-needed moral support. And every day and every night for a whole week in close contact with Mark, who made her head shrivel and her body swell from too much thought. And all this while being observed by that wily witch Amanda.

'I've put my name down!' screeched Martha. 'I'm coming too!'

And Martha.

Nicky left the room to have a look at the list, followed close on her heels by Ally. Sure enough, there was Mark's name, next to Oscar's. (Just above Martha's and below Amanda's.) They stared up at the list.

'By the way,' murmured Ally, 'you might have gone at Amanda a bit strong in there.'

'Why the hell is he going?' Nicky asked. 'For a start, what's Oscar doing going on this trip in the first place? Everyone knows it's for the underprivileged kids.'

'Maybe Oscar wanted to join in with the other kids for a change.'

'Then why's he bringing Daddy?'

Ally looked at her. 'First you hated Mark Samuels for not being involved enough in his son's life, now you're angry because he's getting too involved. He can't win, can he?'

Nicky turned to Ally. 'You honestly think he's going on a crappy work trip to Bournemouth to be involved in his son's life?'

'What are you insinuating, Miss Hobbs?' asked Ally, her eyes wide. 'That Mark Samuels has an ulterior motive?'

Nicky spoke through gritted teeth. 'He's a man, isn't he?'

'So what do you think it is, then?'

'I don't know. But I don't like it.'

'Why? If he's after anyone, it's you. You're the one he's tried to kiss.'

'How do I know that?' Nicky turned to Ally suddenly. 'I'm just the one I *know* about. For all I know, he's tried it on with all of us. Amanda's in his office all the time. The first time I went in there he was so red I thought he was going through the male menopause.'

'Well, he hasn't tried it on with me,' argued Ally.

'I mean, think about it,' continued Nicky, 'this is a man who engineered a fake meeting at his house just so he could try and get off with his son's teacher. Which involved lying to our boss and, now I think about it, risking my career had Miss James found out the truth. For all we know he's doing things like that with all of us. I wonder how many others he's tried it on with?'

'So do I,' retorted Ally. 'This is meant to be an equal opportunities school.'

'Maybe all those bitchy things he said to me about Amanda were just to make me *think* he was on my side.' Her voice rose. 'Yes! He sounded me out first before laying into her. Like he was finding out my opinion before he gave his; you know . . . lulling me into a false sense of security, so I opened up and told him what the right thing to say was.' Ally

430

shook her head. 'Maybe,' continued Nicky, 'he did the same to her about me. He's ingratiating himself with all of us, one by one, like we're all . . . I don't know . . .'

'Gibbering morons?'

'I'll tell you one thing.'

'The aliens are coming?'

'I bet he got a darn sight further with Amanda than he did with me.' She gasped. 'And if Oscar hadn't interrupted us just before he and I . . . you know . . . God knows what would have happened. I bet I'd have stayed over. I could have lost my job over him. Jesus Christ. What the hell was I thinking?'

'"I'm happy"?' suggested Ally.

'I mean, how much do I really know about this man? All I *know* is that he was a crap father for the first decade of his son's life. I also *know* that he lied to his boss – and mine – just to get a quick snog. Those are the only things I actually *know* about him. Everything else is just flirting and wishful thinking. His idea of climbing the career ladder is probably sleeping with the next Headmistress! He's from the *City*, Ally. They do things like that there.'

They stared at each other. Finally, Ally let out a long, deep sigh.

'Nicky,' she said softly, 'I hate to stop you mid-breakdown, but you are forgetting one important thing.'

Nicky frowned and then gasped. 'Of course! His au pairs!'

Ally stared. 'No! Nicky, listen to me. He liked you before Miss James's job came up.'

'Did he?'

'Yes!' cried Ally. 'He gave you that glowing review in front of everyone, remember?'

'Ah yes, but I was still the Deputy Head, wasn't I? Still pretty high up.'

'Nicky!' shouted Ally. 'This is not *Carry On Up the Staffroom*. You are going to have to get a grip.'

'You know what?' said Nicky suddenly, turning to Ally. 'There's only way I could believe his intentions with me were genuine.'

'How?'

'If he left the school.'

'*What?*'

'Then I'd know it was about me and not his poxy job at Heatheringdown.'

'Look,' said Ally, 'I know you've been working really, really hard recently, but you've got to get a grip. Mark Samuels is going on a week-long school trip to be with his boy. End of story.'

Nicky stood motionless.

'Nicky?'

'Yeah,' she sighed wearily. 'Yeah. Sorry. I've just got so sick of all the politics.'

'It's OK. It's nearly the end of term.'

'Yeah. Maybe you're right.'

'Good. No ulterior motive,' said Ally.

'No ulterior motive,' repeated Nicky.

'OK?'

'OK.'

'Now. Do you think you're ready to come back into the staffroom?'

Nicky nodded and slowly, they went back in together.

Across the corridor, Mark sat in his office, staring at his list of emails. He'd done it. And it hadn't been nearly as unpleasant as he'd thought it would be. In fact, Miss James seemed so preoccupied she almost didn't notice. Yes, she admitted she was surprised and extremely disappointed – his appointment here had lifted morale no end – but when he'd honestly explained his rationale, she'd had the good grace to say that she completely understood. It was a real pity it had to happen so soon, as well. So little time for everyone to get their minds round it. She told him that he would be sorely missed and she would announce the news to the rest of the staff after the school trip. But until then, he was not to tell a soul. She did not want the school trip spoilt by news that she felt sure would bring everyone down.

And so Mark had found he had no choice. If he wasn't allowed to tell anyone that he was leaving – and however desperately he wanted to tell Nicky, there was no way he'd risk her career by landing her that kind of secret – and there were only two more days of term after the school trip, he'd had no choice. Of course he didn't want to go on the stupid trip – who in their right mind would? But he knew that if he didn't buy himself some extra time with Nicky, it would be too late. He wouldn't have any excuse to see her again. As long as he didn't tell her that he was leaving, he could maybe actually get somewhere with her. So he'd persuaded Oscar to go on the school trip and signed them both up.

27

Nicky's bedroom window was as wide open as it went, and a humid breeze rippled over her clothes, which lay prone and lifeless on her bed like sunbathing models. She and Ally stared at each item in turn, Nicky trying to envisage them as the clothes of a future headmistress, Ally trying to envisage them as the clothes of a hot chick on the pull.

Claire was also due in ten minutes to help Nicky decide what to pack. Which meant Nicky had ten minutes to give herself a manicure, face pack and home-wax.

As she ran to the bathroom, Ally followed her and sat on the edge of the bath, watching her spread depilatory cream on her legs, mud on her face and Lovechild! varnish on her nails.

'You do realise,' Ally said, 'that Rob is going to pop a toothbrush in his top pocket two minutes before leaving.'

'I know,' replied Nicky through her face pack. 'Everything's easier for men.'

'They don't even have to sit on cold toilet seats to wee,' agreed Ally. 'Bastards.'

By the time Claire arrived, Nicky had a mud-brown face, vibrant-red nails and scarlet-pimpled legs.

'Whe-hey!' said Claire, as Nicky tried to remove the cream and mud. 'Sexy.' She went ahead into the bedroom. 'Right,' she said, scanning the bed. 'How long you going for? A month?'

'A week,' said Nicky, following Ally into the room.

'A week?' repeated Claire.

'I told her it wasn't enough,' said Ally.

Claire stared at the clothes. 'You're taking this much crap for one week?'

Nicky breathed evenly, her fingers fanned on her hips. 'No,' she said. 'You're going to help me decide what to take for a week. Without crushing my self-esteem.' There was a pause. 'Do you think you can manage that?'

'I don't crush your self-esteem,' replied Claire. 'You take things far too seriously.'

Nicky counted to ten for her fingernails to dry. Then she counted to fifty for her anger to subside.

'Right,' said Claire, picking up Nicky's favourite skirt. 'Well, this is gorgeous.'

'Thank you.'

'If you want a holiday shag.'

'Exactly!' said Ally.

Nicky put it back in the wardrobe, without giving it another glance. 'That's exactly the help I need.' She stared at her wet thumbnail. 'Damn.'

'Wha—?' said Ally.

Claire was now holding up a pair of pedal pushers and frowning hard.

'What do you think?' asked Nicky tentatively.

'Difficult to say,' mused Claire. 'Tell me about them.' Ally stood behind Claire, shaking her head furiously at Nicky.

'Very comfortable,' listed Nicky, 'can sit on the grass without worrying about my knickers showing, make my bum look big but my ankles small, in the Gap sale two years ago, go with everything.'

'Perfect,' said Claire, holding them up towards Nicky, eyes already on the next item.

Within half an hour, the ideal future-headmistress wardrobe was selected and Nicky had smudged eight nails. Claire popped to the toilet, leaving Ally and Nicky alone.

'Has she always been this scary?' whispered Ally.

'Ye-es,' replied Nicky thoughtfully. 'I think motherhood did it to her.'

'Remind me never to become a mother.'

Nicky shook her head. 'No, I mean becoming a mother to me when she was so young. Right. I'm going to redo my nails. Back in a mo.'

Ally sat on the bed frowning. Then, when she heard Nicky shut herself in the bathroom, she leapt to action. She opened the case and added two of the sexier skirts Nicky had discarded. She thought about adding the fuchsia cardigan and strappy summer sandals, but changed her mind. She didn't want to overdo it. Then she made a hasty exit.

Nicky locked her luggage without looking inside, ruining her nails again, and left for town to spend half her salary on a haircut and the other half on a hat to hide it under. As she'd left her home, she'd looked up at the sky. The sun had phoned in its work today, leaving a hot, grey sky hanging over hot, grey people. This holiday was going to be unutterably terrible, she'd decided. Three hours later, on her journey back, she considered texting Rob to ask how smart his holiday wardrobe would be, but thought better of it. For a start, he'd only reply that her text would be one of their grandchildren's favourite anecdotes one day, and secondly, she didn't want to show how much she cared before she'd even got on the coach.

Meanwhile, as the morning dampened into early afternoon, Rob returned home an hour earlier than usual. He picked up his mail from the doormat and flicked through it while wandering into his bedroom to pack. He sat down heavily on his bed and stared at the envelope in his hand. He turned it over. He let the moment last. Here, in his hand, was his future. Here was the long-awaited reply from a private school in London, where he'd been interviewed six weeks ago. He was holding his future. He felt sure the interview had gone well.

He made a decision: if he got this job, he would bunk off Bournemouth. Dead relative – funeral, etc. He thought of Amanda and Nicky on the coach without him and smiled. *Too good to be true*, he repeated like a mantra as he tore open the envelope. He read the letter. He stopped smiling. Then he read it again, scrunched it up and threw it on the floor, swearing. He stood up, opened his wardrobe and started throwing clothes into the open suitcase behind him. This was now more than a trip. This was the job interview of his life. Everything else had been leading up to this. He was going to be the next Head of Heatheringdown. Whatever it took. Within five years he'd double its size and get the best SATS results in London and then move to a posh, fancy private school in the south. And then he'd drive a car like that cocky shit Mark Samuels.

He stopped, turned round, and looked at the untidy pile of clothes in the suitcase. Then he took them all out and folded them up neatly before putting them back in again. He decided he would phone Pete later and see if he could extract any interesting goss from the gang. Girls told each other everything and sometimes Ally had a blind spot when it came to Pete.

If he had phoned Pete then, he'd have only got his answerphone. Pete was sitting inelegantly in his local YMCA changing rooms, a small towel covering his modesty, leaning hard against his locker, his concave chest wheezing gently. When he got his breath back, he'd have a shower. Until then he'd just sit there trying not to look at anyone. He closed his eyes. Did women really prefer men with rolls of flesh? Men with hair smothering their shoulders? Men with stomachs that went all the way round their backs? Men whose sweat kamikaze-ed off them when they turned round?

Perhaps he should stop going to the gym. How could something that was meant to make you feel better about yourself involve stripping naked in front of other men? Men who, it just so happened, went regularly to the gym? Anyway, it was making absolutely no difference at all. She was no more interested in him than she'd been before he'd started to keep fit. What was it to her that he could now lift heavier weights than two months ago? And run for another fifteen minutes? She couldn't care less if he could carry a truck on his back.

Once, to his horror, she'd actually caught him eyeing her, and the look she'd thrown him was one of utter contempt. As if he'd just told her he liked doing it with sheep, or something. It had taken him a week to look her in the eye again. He sighed heavily and pulled himself to his feet. Then he wrapped his towel round him, before padding slowly to the showers.

Meanwhile, after she'd left Nicky's, Ally spent the day mooching round Muswell Hill before taking the bus home to Finsbury Park. She had considered walking into Crouch End and taking the bus from there, which would have been great exercise, but she'd had too much to carry, and anyway, what was the point? She could walk a mile every hour and eat nothing but vegetables for the rest of her life and still look more like Superman than Lois Lane. She wondered if people looked at her and marvelled at her size? Did the gang pity her? She'd once caught Pete's eye focus on her ample bosom and then, when he saw that she'd seen, he looked sharply away. It was the expression of shame on his face when he looked away that had hurt her more than anything. As if her breasts were just so big, and the expanse of her back so broad, that he was just embarrassed for her. Mind you, what did she expect from someone whose thighs were probably the size of her shins?

While some of her staff were preparing for the trip, Henrietta James stood looking out of the living-room window at the neat little garden beyond, her long hair and smooth skin belying her true age. A robin was pecking at the hanging bird-food. She'd give herself another five minutes before putting the vegetables on. She heard her mother shuffle in behind her.

'I see you're all packed, then.'

She nodded.

'I shan't call if anything happens,' her mother informed her, sitting down with a groan. 'No need to spoil your holiday.'

'It's not a holiday,' repeated Henrietta, turning to face her mother. 'It's work.'

Her mother tutted. 'You've retired, girl. Leave on a high.'

Henrietta thought of the puzzle cheat and then went into the kitchen to get the vegetables started.

At about the same time, Oscar was sitting on top of his Samsonite suitcase while Mark tried to shut it through his legs. It had been a fun day. They'd started packing straight after breakfast. Every now and then his dad had asked a packing question, and it had been his job to phone Daisy and repeat the question, so she could ask her mum. Lilith had then told Daisy the answer, Daisy told him and he told his dad. It had been the most fun packing ever. He went to bed early but couldn't fall asleep for ages.

In direct contrast, Mark went to bed late and fell asleep instantly. He had known that once he'd handed in his resignation at Heatheringdown, lots of things would fall into place. He enjoyed his job, but when he'd got the phone call from Fortune Green School – Heatheringdown's feeder senior school and the school Oscar would be going to in September – offering him the same post but for significantly more money, he knew he would be mad to refuse. Lilith had been right. He simply wasn't earning enough. Yes, they had plenty of savings, but it took courage to live off savings. This way, he would be able to live off his current earnings instead of his past earnings and still be able to walk into school with Osc (until Osc would be too cool to walk in with his dad, of course).

And then as soon as he'd handed in his resignation, everything made sense. He knew without a shadow of a doubt that he was hopelessly in love with Nicky Hobbs because the thought of not seeing her every day depressed him. He hadn't even left the school yet and already he was missing her. It hurt him every time they said hello in the corridor, because he knew it was only for a few more days. It hurt every time he saw her car in the car park and knew that he'd missed bumping into her. It hurt every time Oscar talked about her, because he wasn't with her and was jealous of whoever was.

And so, after much persuading, Oscar agreed to go on the school trip with him. At first he'd been so adamantly against going that, to get him to agree, Mark had been forced to tell him about his new job, after swearing him to secrecy. It had worked. Oscar was persuaded. Not only was he persuaded, he was thrilled. Not about the trip – that would be awful – but about starting senior school in September at the same time as his dad. He wasn't scared any more.

Mark had known that there was every chance Oscar would come round to the idea of the school trip before he himself had. But he hadn't realised quite how quickly that would happen. They hadn't even left home yet and already the boy was enjoying it more than he was. In fact, he could honestly say that he'd never hated packing for a holiday so much in his life. He had allowed what he'd thought was a generous half-day for it, but it had just gone on and on. By lunch-time he'd had a shopping list of necessities he'd never realised were necessities before, because five-star hotels supplied them as a matter of course. As the packing had expanded to fill the entire day, he'd begun to have serious doubts about his decision to go on this trip with Oscar. What sort of place expected you to bring your own soap?

How could anything be defined as a holiday, when you had to carry the most basic contents of your own bathroom cabinet there with you? After they'd labelled everything (what for? So a thief would know the name of the person whose item he'd stolen?) they went to the local chemist where he discovered the existence of holiday-sized containers.

Then later, while he'd been preparing an easy pasta dinner, it had suddenly occurred to him that during all his previous holidays he had had an au pair keeping house during his absence. He would have to remember to cancel the milk last thing tonight and the newspapers tomorrow morning and empty his fridge of anything that might go mouldy within the week. And empty the kitchen bin ready for the dustmen later in the week. He would have to ask Lilith to put out the bins the night before the dustmen were due. This holiday had better be good, he thought. And then he thought of Nicky.

By the time he'd finished clearing up from dinner, packed his own bag and clambered into bed, he needed a holiday. And not one where they didn't supply the bloody soap. He shut his eyes and imagined Nicky packing for the same trip. He wondered if she'd ever been on a holiday where she didn't need to pack her own soap. He saw her lying by a pool in a bikini. The next morning he woke with a start. He stared ahead of him, and saw Nicky lying by a pool in a bikini.

A mile away, Nicky opened her eyes and lay quite still for a while. She mentally ticked off all the items on her packing list. Then she got out of bed, opened her wardrobe, pulled out a pretty fuchsia cardigan and a pair of strappy sandals and tucked them on the top of her luggage. She stopped and stared at the two short skirts lying on the top, before a slow smile widened her lips. She stretched across to her phone and dialled Ally's number.

28

Claire drove Nicky to school so that Nicky's car wouldn't be left unattended in the car park for a week. It was a Saturday morning and they were the first ones there. As they sat in the car, facing the entrance, waiting for everyone else to arrive, Claire plonked a paper bag in Nicky's lap.

'What's this?' asked Nicky.

'It's a paper bag,' said Claire.

Nicky opened it. Inside was a pair of earrings, a necklace and bracelet.

'The girls chose them,' said Claire. 'They'll go with the skirts I told you not to pack.'

Nicky blinked. 'How did you know I'd packed them?'

Claire shrugged. 'When did you ever listen to me?'

Nicky gave a tight grin and Claire said, 'it's a pleasure.'

When the coach turned into the car park, they got out of the car and lugged Nicky's hold-all across the empty playground. The day wasn't going to be a stunner, but youth was on its side and the early-morning air was fresh, bordering on frisky.

'Don't do anything I wouldn't do,' quipped Claire, as they kissed goodbye, and Nicky stopped herself from saying, 'What, like leave it too late to have children?'

She stood at the coach door as it sighed and slid open. The smell of coach hit her in the back of her throat.

'Morning!' said the coach driver as he stepped down. 'Just you, is it?'

'Looks like it,' said Nicky.

He took her bag and placed it in the boot, then ambled back to stand next to her.

'I hate coaches,' Nicky said quietly. 'I always forget till I have to get in them.'

Two people carriers turned into the car park, packed with at least five children each.

'I hate kids,' sighed the coach driver. 'I never bloody forget that.'

Nicky grinned. She took out her copy of the list ready to tick off names. She smiled at the two mums as they approached.

'Will they serve cheese there?' greeted one before she'd reached her.

'I don't know,' Nicky said. 'Why?'

'Well, he hates it. Won't eat it.'

'Is it an allergy?'

'Might as well be, he hates it that much.'

'Did you fill that in on the form? Because if you did, it'll be fine.'

'What form?'

'The consent form you sent back. There was a section on allergies.'

'Well, it's not an allergy.'

'No. But he won't eat it.'

'Won't go near it. Won't be in the same room as it. Mr Pattison knows.'

'Ah well, that's all right.'

'Is Mr Pattison coming?'

'Yes.'

'Where is he, then?'

Nicky smiled. 'I don't know. Shall we phone him?'

'Go on, then.'

Nicky dialled his mobile. She was put on to voicemail.

'Hello, Mr Pattison, it's Miss Hobbs. I have –' she asked the mother's name – 'Mrs Jennings here who just wants to check that you are cognisant of the fact that Jamie will not, at any point on the holiday, be in the same room as cheese.'

She rang off.

By now the coach was surrounded by cars, like a mother pig with her suckling piglets. Parents milled round the car park trying to ignore their nerves while children raced round, slowly getting on them. Nicky placed her handbag on the very front window-seat of the coach, on the left, and then returned to the car park, where she roamed around chatting to parents and ticking names off lists. She spotted Martha-Plus-One approach. She checked that there was only one piece of luggage, but still had her doubts that the boyfriend wouldn't try stowing away in the boot.

When Miss James was dropped off by a male 'family friend', Nicky stared. The headmistress wore pink tracksuit bottoms and matching jacket over a spotless white T-shirt. Nicky stopped herself from greeting her boss with a kiss and made do instead with a hearty hello. As the family friend drove away, they stood side by side, observing the gathering.

'Nice weather for it,' said Miss James after a while. Nicky asked her if she wanted to meet the driver and then watched her as she obligingly wandered up to the coach door, her

446

clean white sneakers crunching on the gravel, and offered him her hand. It was as if she'd already retired, and in doing so had shed a decade in age. Which begged the question that, if Nicky were to take her place, would she look a decade older?

She looked down at her watch. Still half an hour to go before take-off. Where the hell was Rob? Just as she thought this, his car turned into the entrance. He roared right up to the coach and leapt out of his car.

'Morning, sunshine,' he greeted her, his usual private wink at the ready.

'Are you going to leave your car here all week?' asked Nicky.

'Yep,' he muttered. 'With any luck it'll get stolen.'

'Why are you late?'

'Bloody overslept, didn't I?' he muttered.

'It's OK,' she said. 'We weren't going to leave without you. I'd have got the coach to pick you up from your home if I'd had to.'

He allowed her a small smile. 'I'm sure you would have,' he said. He indicated Miss James with his head. 'Did she say anything?'

'Yes,' whispered Nicky loudly. 'She said, "I'll show that Pattison to be late on my shift."' She shrugged and opened her eyes in innocent wonder. 'I wonder what she meant by that?'

'Ha ha,' he said, his eyes still on Miss James and he went to greet her. Nicky watched him apologise repeatedly to her. Her observation was interrupted by a cheery hello. She steeled herself and then turned to Amanda. Her lower jaw slowly gaped open, like a Thunderbird puppet's lower jaw.

'All aboard!' sang out Amanda.

She was wearing a light summer dress, high-heeled wedge espadrilles, big floppy hat and sharp shades. She looked ready for a cruise. Or rather, she looked gorgeous, and ready for a luxury cruise. Glossy lipstick brought out the pink, healthy glow in her cheeks, exemplary use of expensive foundation gave her the silken complexion of a Hollywood starlet, and when she lifted her shades, Nicky found herself looking into immaculately eye-lined, enhancingly eye-shadowed, meticulously mascaraed eyes. Every single eyelash was standing to attention. She stared for a while, wondering what life must be like for a woman like Amanda. What did she do when everyone else was writing their New Year's Resolutions? Exfoliate?

'Wow, Amanda!' she managed. 'Dressed to kill, eh!'

'Oh, I wouldn't say that!' grinned Amanda. 'Dressed for a summer holiday, more like!' She took her time to look Nicky up and down. 'Are you coming with us?' she asked innocently. While Amanda then made a great display of greeting Rob, Nicky found herself unable to function. Her brain was clogging up with all the different answers she should have given.

She caught sight of Ned, at the other side of the car park. Even at that distance she could make out the stoop of his shoulders. He walked slowly from the passenger seat to the boot of the car, took out a small case, and walked slowly to the driver's seat, where his wife sat. He bent down while she opened the window, kissed her, turned and approached the gathering. When he saw Nicky, he gave a little nod before studying the ground in front of her feet. She put her hand on his arm.

'Ned.' He stopped. 'Good luck with the job interview.'

He looked at her. 'Thanks,' he said and stepped up on to the coach. He half turned towards her. 'You too.'

There was a sudden glut of arrivals twenty minutes before the coach was due to leave and both pupils and teachers started boarding. Nicky looked down her list. Daisy, Oscar, Mark Samuels still to come. She pressed her biro against Mark's name until it made a dent in the paper. She added a dent on one or two random names.

She looked up and grinned at the surprising sight of Ally and Pete approaching.

'We thought we'd come and see you off,' said Ally.

'And laugh,' added Pete.

'Oh, thanks, guys!' Nicky grinned.

Janet, Miss James's trusty PA, who had less choice about being on this trip than the two Deputies did, loomed towards them. She'd had to get a temp in to cover her while she was away, which everyone knew meant she'd be working overtime or after term time to catch up. But everyone also knew that Miss James couldn't possibly do without her, even on a school trip.

'Hello!' said Nicky.

'Oh, piss off,' muttered Janet, low enough for none of the kids to hear, and got on the coach.

Nicky looked at Ally and Pete.

'You lucky, lucky bastards,' she whispered.

'Luck's got nothing to do with it,' laughed Pete. 'It's sheer lack of ambition.'

Then they followed Janet into the coach to wish everyone a hearty bon voyage.

Lilith's car turned into the car park and drove right up to

the coach, parking next to Rob's. As soon as she parked, all the doors flew open and Daisy, Oscar, Mark and Lilith leapt out. Mark ran to the boot and started unpacking luggage straight into the coach's boot while Lilith hugged Daisy, and Oscar ran to Nicky. She ticked his name off the list and he climbed inside the coach without a look back. After she'd marked Daisy in, and waved hello to Lilith, she turned her attention to Mark.

'Hi.' He grinned down at her.

She held her pen to paper. 'Name?' she asked, with an attempt at a professional smile that was more like an arch grin.

He laughed. 'Samuels, Miss.'

She pretended to look for his name. 'You're late, Samuels.'

'How's it going?' he asked quietly.

She put the pen to her lips as if thinking. 'Oh, you know,' she sighed with a little shrug, 'purgatory.'

He smiled and she watched his lips part as he prepared to speak. Then she watched him jump almost two feet in the air as Rob bellowed from the coach, 'Get a move on, Samuels! We're all waiting for you!'

Ally and Pete jumped out of the coach and grinned goodbye to them both. Nicky followed Mark on to the coach and everyone cheered. When Rob cried out, 'Oscar! Have a word with your dad!' there was a cacophony of laughter.

Miss James had moved Nicky's bag from the left seat to the right seat across the aisle and placed herself in the optimum front-window seat that Nicky had chosen. Nicky eased herself into the aisle seat behind the driver. Miss James glanced a smile at her across the aisle before looking back

450

out of the window and Nicky reminded herself that technically there were ten more days before Miss James retired.

Rob stopped chatting to the driver and stood, feet wide apart, at the front of the coach facing everyone. He welcomed them all and began a roll-call. Nicky watched him perform some jokes and funny voices, wondering if he'd offered to do this for Miss James or had been asked to by her. She stole a glance at Miss James, who was watching Rob, an enigmatic smile on her lips. Nicky tried to look at him from outside herself, as if she was Miss James. Tall, slim, olive-skinned, dark-haired, handsome (if you like your men with big features) and unarguably good with kids. A future headmaster? A future father? A future sperm donor, maybe?

When he finished, he looked down at her as if she was the only person in the coach. She blinked the look away. He squeezed in front of her, sitting down by her side in the window seat, as the coach set off. She looked out across him to the car park below. Martha's boyfriend stood motionless. Ned's neat little wife had got out of her car and was watching, her arms crossed against her tiny frame. Ally and Pete were playing tag. Lilith got smaller and smaller, her smile fading with each wave.

After they'd finished tag, Ally and Pete watched the coach disappear and then wandered slowly across the playground.

'What shall we do now?' asked Pete.

'Brunch?' said Ally.

'Thought you'd never ask.'

They played tag again to his car.

In the coach, the children began a rowdy rendition of 'A Hundred Green Bottles' and Miss James suddenly sat up and moved across to the seat next to her, so as to be nearer to Nicky and Rob. Nicky thought she might be about to ask one of them to complain about the noise, but instead she smiled across the aisle at them.

'I forgot to tell you both,' she started and then stopped dramatically. Rob leant towards her, across Nicky, his hand on the furry headrest behind her head. He was so close she could smell the cool freshness of his underarm deodorant and the citrus tang of his aftershave. She turned her head to Miss James.

'The governors were very impressed with both of you,' mouthed Miss James. 'And they've asked me to give my verdict after I return from this trip.'

She looked from one to the other. Nicky could feel Rob nod furiously next to her face. If he'd been any closer she'd have got stubble rash. She blinked in amazement at Miss James. Had the woman finally lost the plot? This was totally inappropriate, let alone tantamount to suggesting they just shoot it out in a duel when they got to Bournemouth. Why was Miss James so intent on them being rivals? However, she was delighted she was still in with a chance.

'And, of course,' she smiled at them both in turn, 'you both know how I feel about you.'

'What about Ned?' whispered Rob, his hand, hidden from Miss James, touching Nicky's shoulder, as if they were conspirators, not rivals.

Miss James shook her head sadly, closing her eyes. Then she opened them, started nodding and said that he may well become one of the next Deputies. Or even *the* Deputy. She'd be telling him on the journey. Best for him to know as soon as possible. This was left hanging in the air. Rob's hand didn't move from Nicky's shoulder.

'What about external applicants?' he asked.

'All highly impressive,' admitted Miss James. She let that linger, before concluding, 'But not quite impressive enough.'

The coach took a sharp right corner and Rob leant in towards Nicky. She was forced to gently move him away and was rewarded with a sly glance. Miss James sat back into her seat and immediately fell fast asleep. Her head lolled against the window until it finally lodged there. After a good ten minutes, Rob moved back into the furthest corner of his seat, squashed up against the window and then motioned for Nicky to join him there. She sidled nearer.

'Howdee, sexy thing,' he whispered. 'Future Yummy Mummy. Foxy ladee —'

She raised an eyebrow.

'Well,' he sighed. 'It's better than playing the game she wants us to play.'

He had a point. It was beginning to feel like they were pawns in some sad little chess game going on in Miss James's brain. Nicky glanced back at Miss James to see if she was listening. She was snoring gently. She turned back to Rob and almost knocked noses with him. He had moved his head towards her. He whispered into her ear, close enough for her to feel his breath down her neck.

'She wants us to compete with each other,' he informed her.

Nicky edged her head back and whispered just as deliberately back in his ear, 'We *are* competing with each other.'

He shrugged. 'Not if we decide to be on the same side,' he whispered even closer, his mouth now touching her hair.

She shivered. Then nodded fractionally.

'You and me. Finally,' he whispered, leaning towards her as he spoke. 'Instead of you against me.'

Nicky moved her head away slightly.

'I'll let you into a secret,' he whispered.

Her eyes swivelled to him.

'I've been applying for other jobs at the same time.'

She nodded once.

'No bites . . . as yet.'

Another nod.

There was a long pause while Miss James snorted and resettled. Nicky started forming a polite but firm sentence in her head about having decided, after lengthy consideration, etc., etc., etc., that she'd rather have babies with someone she loved and who loved her. All in all, probably best for the baby, blah, blah, blah.

'You know what I think?' asked Rob before she'd got further than the third blah.

'Um,' she said slowly, 'Man U will win?'

'No. I'm going to be really honest,' he prefaced. 'You may not like it.'

She turned to face him. 'I've got BO?' she whispered.

He ignored her. 'Believe it or not,' he whispered slowly and clearly, 'this is all . . . much harder . . . for *me* . . . than *you*,' he said.

She blinked. 'What is?' she asked. 'Sitting in a coach?'

'I've never really admitted this before,' he said, looking down, 'but you're not the only one with a clock ticking, you know.'

She frowned, envisaging him as Captain Hook in *Peter Pan*, with a haunting tick-tock echoing inside his abdomen.

'What are you talking about, Rob?' she asked squarely.

He now moved his head back towards the window and spoke so quietly she had to inch her neck forward like a tortoise not to miss anything.

'If I don't get a headship before I'm thirty-five,' he whispered ever so slowly, 'I'll never get one. I'll have left it too late. Like you and babies. Except, of course, you could adopt.'

She balked. 'Women have babies in their mid-forties,' she told him, forgetting to whisper. 'Men become headmasters into their bloody sixties.'

'SSSSSSHHHHHH!' Rob shrank in his seat. Nicky shrank with him. 'Keep your voice down,' he whispered. 'Don't want to wake her.'

Nicky repeated herself in a whisper.

'What?' he replied. 'And have a five-year-old when you're fifty? No thanks.'

Nicky looked ahead. 'Rob. It's awfully sweet of you to worry about me and my non-existent babies, but you really don't have to. You just worry about your –'

He gripped her hand in his and spoke with a new urgency. 'Nicky, don't you get it? I care about you. I don't want you crying every time you get a promotion.'

'I cried once.'

'But facts are facts,' he admitted. 'Unfair, anachronistic and sexist though it may be, if you become Head, you won't be able to have children for years and –'

'*WHY?*' she exclaimed.

'SSSSHHHH!' He laughed and she found herself giggling with him. They shrank in their seats. Then she repeated her question in a whisper and he looked at her as if she'd just asked him what two plus two equalled.

'Because you'll be in an incredibly pressurised new job,' he explained. 'Try telling the governors you want six months' maternity leave after they've just given you the headship.' He laughed. 'You'd get two weeks off if you were lucky.'

Nicky was silent.

'On the other hand,' he continued, 'because we live in an unfair world, if I got the job, it wouldn't make any difference at all. Except it would speed things up for you – for us.'

'Hmm.'

'Let's just say, for argument's sake,' he began, curling his body in towards her, 'that you and I *were* an item – as if we'd taken things one step further on Bonfire Night, or never even broken up – and say we were planning to start a family now, we could start immediately. We could start right now!' He laughed again and whispered in her ear, 'We could go up to the back of the coach now. That would put a stop to those fucking green bottles!' They were both smiling now. 'You'd get your maternity leave and could even go part-time if you wanted – or not, if you didn't want – and I could bring home enough bacon for all of us.'

She stayed silent.

'On the other hand,' he continued, moving away slightly, suddenly thoughtful, 'if *you* got the job, and *I* didn't . . . I'd be struggling on a deputy's salary and you'd be lucky to get a fortnight off. And you would end up missing the best years of his life.'

Nicky looked at Rob. 'His?' she smiled. 'Has he got a name, too?'

Rob smiled back. 'Hypothetically speaking.'

'Exactly,' she said. 'It's hypothetical. So it's not really an issue, is it?'

He looked at her. 'You keep forgetting us, Nicky.' He opened his eyes wide to give her a deeply serious look. 'It could be, Nick,' he whispered. 'It could *already* be, if we'd taken things further on Bonfire Night. It's all much easier than you think. You're the one making it complicated.'

She did wish he'd stop bringing up the night in the kitchen. It confused her. Maybe, just maybe, Rob was right. Maybe they had always been meant to be together. And Mark was the distraction, keeping her from getting on with her life. She hadn't even kissed Mark; for all she knew he could be a lousy kisser. (Perhaps she should do it just for research.) At least she knew that Rob was a good kisser. And more. Well, when he was in the mood to take his time. Otherwise it was just your everyday TV sex – or what Nicky now called man-sex – lots of mild violence, which men thought was passion, very little build-up. But basically they'd been happy together. OK, in the seven years since then, she'd changed in many ways, but then, Rob probably had too. She hoped. In fact, now she came to think about it, he'd always been a bit selfish sexually. She hadn't realised it until she'd gone on to have other relationships after him. She wondered if he had changed in that way. Not only that but after those first few heady months theirs had been a very volatile relationship. Again, at the time she'd thought that was what made it so passionate. Now, her idea of the perfect relationship was almost the opposite of that. But then they'd both grown up, hadn't they? If they started again it would be different, wouldn't it? She replayed the kitchen kiss and found it slightly disconcerting that her main memory of it was that she'd been thinking of Mark all the way through it. But wasn't that, she asked herself, normal? Wasn't that real life? Didn't lots of happily married people do that? Was she waiting for something that didn't exist? Was Claire right? Was it all about settling for something? Maybe that was why the phrase was 'settling down'; because you did it when you'd settled for someone. Otherwise the phrase would be something like 'soaring up', wouldn't it?

Two motorway junctions went past.

'Just think about it,' Rob said and then got up, giving her a soft touch on her shoulder as he did so, and walked down the coach.

Nicky looked out of the window and watched the blur of people in their cars and wondered how they'd all achieved their own little comfort zone of a family. Thousands of them out there, whizzing past in tidy foursomes. How come so many ordinary people managed to do something so monumental? Had all of them found their one true love and then had the children of their dreams? Or had they all settled with what they could get? Or had they just not thought about it and let it happen? Had any of them, she wondered, gone back to their first love?

'Excuse me, Miss Hobbs, is this seat taken?' came a deep voice behind her.

She turned and looked up to see Mark standing next to her seat. The sun was smudged behind his head, creating a halo effect. She tried to ignore this, and nodded. He stepped over her to sit in Rob's seat.

'Hello,' he said. 'I've come for some adult conversation.'

'What a good idea.' She smiled. 'Let's find an adult.'

He laughed. Then he sat back and turned to look at her. She gave him an easy, non-committal smile. He gave her a delicious one back. He leant his head back. She leant hers back too. They smiled. Then they smiled a bit more. They kept on smiling. And then, when they'd finished smiling, they started again. Then Mark gave a little laugh. She gave one back.

Behind them, the eightieth bottle accidentally fell, led by a raucous Rob. They smiled.

'You know what?' he whispered.

'What?' she whispered back. He was leaving the school and wanted her children?

'I hate children.'

She stopped smiling. 'Except Oscar,' she breathed.

'Of course except Oscar.'

'I love them,' she said quietly.

He grimaced 'Bleagh. You haven't just lived through twenty green bottles in your ear.'

'No.'

'I'm looking forward to Oscar growing up,' he said. 'I think he'll be a great adult. A good mate.'

She nodded. 'I bet he was a lovely baby.'

Mark nodded vaguely. 'I missed most of it. Hard work though. Wouldn't go through that again. No, I much prefer him now.'

He turned to smile at her again. She tried to return it, but it was hard when you felt like your stomach had just been pummelled.

'Hello,' said Miss James suddenly, with a yawn. 'Are we nearly there yet?'

'I don't think so,' said Nicky. She stepped forward and asked the driver. He told them not long now.

Nicky relayed the message and then leant over to Mark.

'So,' he said, looking up at her, 'about this adult conversation.'

'I really ought to check on the children,' she managed to say. 'No peace for the wicked.'

She went and joined Rob.

Mark sat still at the front of the coach. He only got up when Rob returned twenty minutes later. They swapped places without a word.

29

The hostel was located, the luggage unpacked, the coach dismissed and the children settled before the teachers realised the full implications of Miss James's booking mistake. Nicky was the last to hear about it, because she'd been busy dealing with two bunk-bed disputes and one severe case of homesickness leading to vomiting. And that was just the children.

She had popped her head round the door of what she'd thought was the female teachers' room, only to find everyone in there, except Miss James, whose voice could be heard arguing with the hostel manager from the other end of the corridor.

'Apparently,' Rob grinned gleefully, 'there seems to have been a "miscommunication" and we're all in the same room. So it looks like you girls are bunking in with us.'

Nicky was concentrating so hard on not looking at Mark that it took a while for this information to sink in. She ended up staring at Rob for ages. He continued to smile at her as he lay slowly back on the bottom bunk nearest the door, putting his arms behind his head.

'So,' she said slowly, 'we're all in here together? Men and women? Together?'

Amanda, Martha, Mark, Ned and Janet all nodded slowly.

'Er, Robert, did you just call us "girls"?' Amanda asked. She was lying on the bottom bunk opposite Rob, on her stomach, her legs swinging in the air and her chin on her hands. She looked like something out of a Busby Berkeley number.

'Anyway, who says this isn't *our* room?' Martha added, leaning against Amanda's bed. 'And *you're* bunking in with *us*? There's a lot more women than men.'

'Good point, sister!' exclaimed Amanda. 'After all, Miss James would hardly have forgotten to book *herself* a room, would she?'

This was met with an awkward pause. It was the first mention of the fact that this was all Miss James's fault. Nearly the entire room tried to ignore this comment. Martha, however, was not going to let that go. She was just entering the bitching phase of her job. She'd been at the school for a whole academic year now, so no longer thought of herself as new. She felt secure, and she had got over the honeymoon period long enough ago to have started picking fault with everything. At the same time, she was still fresh, and disillusionment had yet to set in, so there was a youthful, almost positive energy to her bitching. 'That's right!' she responded happily to Amanda. 'It's *our* room and the *boys* are bunking in with us! Ah dear!' she laughed. 'This is all *so* typical! Good thing the old bat's retiring, eh?'

The room went quiet again. Miss James's retirement was not something Rob, Nicky or Ned wished to dwell on, let alone within this context. Ned had been informed by Miss James on the coach that he hadn't got the headship, but

462

would be considered for the post of Deputy, should a vacancy occur. He had gone back to his seat without looking at Rob or Nicky.

'Whoops!' giggled Amanda. 'Don't mention the war!' She did a stage wink at Martha.

Martha giggled. Amanda then asked Martha if she wanted to share a bunk with her. Nicky turned her back on them to stop the premonitions of them sharing secret diaries next. She was feeling too low to be able to tolerate them.

For want of anything else to do, she studied the room. It was long and narrow, filled to bursting point with four wide, tall bunk beds; two in each corner, facing the centre of the room. The space dividing them all was so narrow that you could easily reach across and pull the hair of your sleeping neighbour, should you so desire. The door at one end led on to the noisy corridor, the other to the communal bathroom. On the other side of the corridor lay the children's dorms, far too near for comfort, but then this 'holiday' was not about comfort.

Already the space between the beds was full of rucksacks and clothes. Amanda and Martha were now sharing the left corner bunk, at the bathroom end, and next to it Ned had done an impressive job of hiding himself on the bottom bunk, leaving just his well-darned socks visible. He was below the top bunk where Miss James's bag lay. That left two bunks, both at the corridor end. Rob lay proprietorially on the bottom bunk to Nicky's left. Opposite him, on the bottom bunk to her right, sat Mark, very still, eyes down. In the middle of the room stood an imposing Janet, looking cross. No change there then.

Nicky looked down at Mark. He didn't move. She turned

to Rob. He grinned and winked. She looked over at Amanda. Amanda was overtly observing her, a knowing smile on her lips.

She just didn't know what to do. If she shared with Mark, it would mean climbing above him every night and, more terrifyingly, climbing down every morning after a full night's tormented sleep, her hair looking like a crocheted two-piece. What if she talked in her sleep? What if she talked in her sleep about him? Or worse, what if *he* talked in his sleep? Worse still, what if he talked in his sleep about Amanda? Even worse than all that, what if he looked keen on her in front of Miss James and Miss James assumed Nicky would become a full-time mum in two years and give her job to Rob? The less she had to do with Mark the better. But if she took the bed opposite him, he'd have an even better view of her and, more relevantly, she'd have a spectacular bird's-eye view of him and she'd expend so much energy trying not to watch him, she'd have none left for the kids. On the other hand, if she slept above Rob, she wouldn't put it past him to try and join her on the top bunk as soon as lights were out and start their family right here, right now. She was still standing, trying to decide, and she knew Amanda was still scrutinising her. Maybe she should sleep in the showers.

She looked at Janet.

'Well,' she shrugged at her. 'Where do you want to sleep?'

'At home,' replied Janet shortly, before climbing the ladder above Mark's bed.

Nicky turned to Rob.

'Right,' she said. 'Looks like we're sharing.'

'I thought you'd never ask!' he grinned. 'Do you prefer going on top?'

The room wolf-whistled. Oh dear God, thought Nicky as she climbed up the ladder above Rob. It was going to be a long, long week.

At first, Pete thought that all they'd talk about was Rob, Nicky and Amanda and what might happen on the trip. But they didn't. They'd spent all day together now – an unprecedented amount of time together, alone – and they hadn't mentioned the others once. Not only that, but it hadn't even been his idea to see the matinée. They'd sat with their legs over the backs of the chairs in front, gripping firmly on to their sweets, popcorn and fizzy drinks and laughed hoarsely at each other's jokes, which were all funnier than the ones in the film. When they came out, they blinked in the afternoon light. The weather was turning.

'I'm starving,' said Pete.

'Me too,' said Ally. 'What shall we eat?'

'Pizza?' he suggested.

She nodded for a while. 'Mm,' she decided eventually. 'Perfect.'

Meanwhile, Rob had arranged for a brisk beach walk along the East Cliff towards Boscombe. It only took one hour to get the children ready and just half an hour to find Miss James's glasses. They were under Ned's bed and by the end of the walk he had almost finished apologising.

By the time they had all made it to the beach, Nicky was ready to throw herself into the sea. She was dwelling on Mark's comments on the coach. If the man of your dreams didn't want children and you did, it was a no-brainer. Walk away. She'd heard stories where women assumed they'd changed their blokes' minds only to discover ten years on that he'd gone and had the snip one lunch hour. She wanted Mark, but not as viscerally, as desperately, as her primeval need to have babies. And she wasn't in the business of changing a man's mind purely for her selfish needs. She was, however, heartbroken. She was bringing up the rear of the crocodile, holding hands with the spasmodically weeping homesick child and envying her. If only going back home would sort out all her problems. From the back, she had an all-too perfect view of everything. She could see the black bruises of clouds as they hurtled across the white sky, she could see the foam roar off the grey sea, she could see the piercings on every teenager who passed and she could see Janet's back. It was getting closer and closer to Mark's back as they trudged onward and ever onward. They would make a good match, she thought. Was he going after every single staff member in turn? She felt a pang every time Janet looked in profile towards him and smiled. Nicky had no idea Janet's lips could go up. And then, if Nicky wasn't very much mistaken, through the sea spray, she actually saw Janet laugh. Nicky knew it was a laugh because her shoulders shook. Good God, the woman was almost as tall as he was. She was so tall they could even kiss just by accident.

Feeling sick of the sights Bournemouth had offered so far, Nicky forced herself to look elsewhere. She scanned the crocodile and, halfway down it, spotted Amanda and Martha deep in delicious conversation. Watching them did actually take her mind off things, because it soon became apparent that she was witnessing the beginning of something deeply significant. For here were two women sharing their first bonding bitch session, a vital, primary stage in a certain kind of intense, female friendship; a moment where the dynamics and hierarchies are seared into the friendship's unique, impenetrable psyche. They were embarking on a voyage of discovery of shared hates. And from the look of things, these two were going to be bosom buddies for a very long time.

She looked at the front of the crocodile and there could just make out Rob walking next to Miss James, a humble half a step behind, his hands held behind his back. She felt a tinge of admiration, almost pride, instead of jealousy, so she forced herself to take this one step further and imagine herself becoming his lifelong partner. At least her children would have long legs and fierce ambition. This intriguing thought gave her no stirrings of ecstasy, but on the plus side, it gave her no heartache either.

Tired from too much thinking, she decided to turn her attention to the children. Perhaps she should just spend time with them this week. Yes, that would do her good. If there was one thing to stop you dwelling on worries you couldn't control, it was being with children when they needed you most. Nothing focuses your mind quite like a child being sick. She squeezed the child's hand she was holding and they exchanged pallid smiles. Then she tried to find the back of Oscar's head. She couldn't find it. At first she panicked, but stopped herself and scanned the crocodile again. Second time round she realised why. Oscar was looking at her, his face an indistinct blur through the cold rain. She was just about to wave when he turned away. He didn't look back once during the entire walk.

Two hours later, they returned to the hostel as bedraggled, bone-weary and bored as they were drenched, all in need of a hot chocolate and warm blanket. One child was heard complaining of frostbite. Nicky made a decision. She would forget all about the adults on this trip, forget about the job, about Rob's surreal suggestions, and all her conflicting feelings for Mark. She would pretend she was looking at the children through a microscope.

She spent the rest of the day solely in their dorms, talking to them, listening to them, and helping them get ready for bed. She stayed with them until the very last one had fallen asleep (until the middle of the night, of course, when at least one would wake up hysterical with homesickness or fear of the dark, or both). The evening dissipated faster than the sea spray, which she could almost taste on her skin and in her hair. Oscar was already asleep when she went to say goodnight to his dorm.

Later that evening, they had their first teachers' meeting and Nicky was pleased to discover that she was almost too exhausted to care about all the tensions and undercurrents in their small, stuffy dorm. By now all she really cared about was her sticky, salty hair. It was going to take hours to dry unless she slept on it wet, which never created a good look the morning after. If she'd been given a choice now of whether to become Headmistress or wash her hair, she'd have chosen the latter.

Rob's itinerary was the major topic on everyone's mind.

'I suppose,' said Miss James, flashing him a big smile, 'that we find ourselves in a position where making a compromise is the only choice.'

Nicky's eyes turned involuntarily to Mark, and then, as a pathetic subterfuge, she gave everyone else an identical look. They were all sitting, two per bed, on the top bunks in their room. Miss James had hoped – as they all had, in fact – that the lounge would be free every evening, and they could conduct their meetings in it just like last year. But the hostel was doing very well this year and apparently three families wanted to use it. Miss James was planning to demand a refund at the end of the holiday. Janet's first job of the holiday was to keep notes of absolutely everything that went wrong, no matter how small. No one was in any doubt that Janet was the woman for the job. Clearly, Miss James's friendship with the manager had been overstated.

'I completely agree,' Rob reassured Miss James. 'You're absolutely right.'

'Good, good, good.' Miss James grinned, hitching her legs under her bottom. Ned, who was sharing her bunk, moved away to give her more room.

'However,' said Rob, 'it did take me months to get this itinerary *exactly* right. It may not look like it to the casual onlooker, but there is actually a complex, structured symbiosis at work here.'

Nicky tried very hard not to look at Mark. She ended up looking at Amanda, who was staring at her, her expression a dare.

'What's that, my dear?' asked Miss James. Nicky wasn't sure if Miss James had misheard or misunderstood.

'Well,' began Rob, 'there's a theme to the itinerary.'

'Ooh, *lovely*,' replied Miss James.

'And more than just a theme,' continued Rob, 'there's a slow but steady build-up to the theme, so that by the end of the week, the kids will, hopefully, have learnt something as well as had a good time.'

'If you don't mind me asking,' started Janet, in a tone that told him she couldn't care less if he did, 'what did the kids learn from an afternoon in the rain?'

Nicky gave a small laugh of agreement. Amanda stared at her. Martha studied her toes intently, classic loyal behaviour to the alpha female bitch. Nicky realised that she must have come up in their bonding bitch earlier.

'Good question,' laughed Rob. 'Well, they enjoyed their hot chocolates afterwards and they all learnt that your body can do things it might not want to, if you put your mind to it.'

'If you don't mind me saying,' started Janet, in a tone that told him she'd get a great deal of pleasure if he did, 'this is meant to be a holiday. The pupils' parents have paid good money for them to come away on it. If they go home and tell them they hated it, we'll be inundated with complaints. Last year we just had fun.'

'And *that*,' Miss James grinned, reaching her arms out towards Janet, 'is why this fine plain-talking lady has been my PA for ten years.' She turned to Rob. 'I do not doubt, for one second, that the theme, structure, symbiosis and slow-building lesson of this holiday are splendid, my good man. But what we must never forget is that we are not in control. We are merely servants. Public servants for the country's parents. And these parents have paid us their hard-earned money to send their children on a holiday, not a week-long lesson. We do not want any complaints.'

There was silence.

'Apart from mine, of course,' she finished, looking at Janet. 'Of which there shall be plenty.' Janet nodded.

'Absolutely,' agreed Rob. 'So, what do you suggest, Miss James?'

Miss James blinked at him. Then she turned, smiling, to Nicky.

'What do you suggest, my dear? We haven't heard much from you yet this evening.'

'Um,' Nicky sat up. She felt like she was climbing up on to a tightrope. 'Well, I suppose we could keep to Rob's suggested itinerary, and then if there happens to be a weather situation, we just move on to the next one on the list. And then as soon as the weather is good again, we go straight back to the one we missed off. That way the order isn't too messed up.'

Miss James turned to Rob.

'Robert?'

'I think that's excellent,' he said, almost happily.

'Good, good, good.'

'But,' he said, suddenly struck by a thought, 'who decides what a "weather situation" is?'

'Ooh, good point,' exclaimed Miss James. Amanda and Martha nodded thoughtfully.

'Well,' said Amanda softly, 'I don't know if it's relevant . . .'

There was a pause.

'Oh, I'm sure it is,' encouraged Miss James.

'Well, just for the record, I *love* walking in the rain!' Amanda smiled. 'Very rejuvenating. And it's excellent for the skin.'

'Is it?' asked Miss James. 'I didn't know that.'

'Oh yes,' confided Amanda. 'Keeps the skin young.'

'I shouldn't imagine nine- to eleven-year-olds care much about that,' responded Janet drily, doodling in her minutes pad. Amanda stared across at Janet, her big blue, blinking eyes making a show of amazed anger, like a parent might

471

look at a child just before giving them a telling-off, or a Mafia boss might look at a new member just before ordering cement. Janet finished her doodle.

Nicky looked away. She didn't want Amanda to know she'd witnessed her powers fail.

It was increasingly obvious to Nicky that Janet was indestructible. And it wouldn't take Amanda long to work that out too. There were some people in life who were simply too thick to notice when they were being bullied, and there were those, like Janet, who had some emotional bits of their brain missing and genuinely didn't care. In exactly the same way that Amanda knew instinctively that Martha and Nicky noticed and cared, she'd work out that Janet didn't. But Janet would never be a danger, because anyone strong enough not to care about the alpha female bitch, also didn't bother taking sides. Janet was a loose cannon.

Nicky thought of the homesick child.

'Right,' said Miss James clapping her hands, after the meeting was over. 'Mark, dear, you're the nearest to the door, could you just pop out and ask for a round of cognac for us?' She turned to them. 'I think we could all do with a little nightcap, don't you?'

It was quickly decided that the women would now carry out their ablutions, while the men swiftly agreed to have their nightcap in the bar. After much bartering over who would stay sober enough to keep an eye on the children's dorms tonight and who would be able to get in the drinks, Ned, Rob and Mark shared the first round of the holiday and Miss James, Amanda, Janet and Martha enjoyed night-caps in the dorm, lying on their beds reading, while Nicky bagsied the first wash. She didn't know whether to be

472

touched or horrified that they'd all been so understanding about how long her hair would need to dry. When she came back, her hair up in a towel, she found a wholly silent dorm.

As she went to her bed, Miss James silently picked up her washbag and, with a quick smile her way, went into the corridor. Almost as soon as she was out of the room, Amanda sat up. 'Bloody hell,' she whispered hoarsely. 'It's like going on holiday with your fucking grandparents.'

Martha laughed uproariously, shushed furiously by Amanda. Nicky and Janet smiled.

'I tell you what, though,' continued Amanda, 'that Mark Samuels, eh? What is he doing single?'

Janet laughed. It was a surprising noise.

'He can fiddle with my figures any day,' whispered Amanda.

Janet snorted and they all laughed.

Nicky shut her eyes, which was the nearest she could get to shutting her ears, and turned to lie on her side, facing the wall.

'Don't you agree, Nicky?' Amanda asked.

Nicky opened her eyes and looked at the wall. She knew Amanda couldn't see her from where she was. She was safe.

'I've never really thought about it,' she said, and yawned.

God, she missed Ally. She wondered what she was doing now.

Ally was getting in another couple of drinks at her local pub. She stood at the bar and wondered if it was just her imagination or were they both not talking about the elephant in the room? She turned back to Pete suddenly. He gave her a small, nervy smile. She turned back fast. Bloody hell. She wasn't imagining it. Her hands went clammy.

Behind her, Pete's small frame went cold. He stared at the back of Ally's head. He knew that look of hers. That look was contempt. That look was 'no'. That look was 'just good friends'. What the hell had just happened? Everything had been going so well. What had he done wrong? He tried to smile at her as she walked back to him, but it took a massive effort. They started their drinks in silence. Then Ally said, 'I wonder how they're doing?'

At the same time, in the hostel lounge in Bournemouth, Mark was getting in the second round and when he returned, Rob was talking and Ned smiling a simple smile. Rob looked up at Mark and beamed.

'All right, Markie Mark? We were just saying that that Janet's a bit of a surprise, isn't she?'

Mark smiled as he sat down. 'Is she?'

Rob gave a whistle. 'Those jeans.' He shook his head. 'They do things to her arse that I wouldn't mind doing myself.'

Mark smiled into his pint.

'I prefer her in a skirt myself,' said Ned, with sudden force. 'In the light you can see everything. And I mean *everything*.'

Rob and Mark stared at him. He finished his pint and then went to the bar for the next round.

'Well!' murmured Rob.

'Well, *well*,' agreed Mark.

'Well, well, *well*,' concurred Rob.

Mark nodded.

'I think the pressure's getting to him,' shared Rob.

474

Mark nodded. They both looked across the room at Ned. He was sitting at the bar, slowly munching peanuts from the bowl.

'Thank God I don't have to worry about the promotion business,' sighed Rob.

'Oh yes?'

Rob sat forward. 'Don't tell anyone this, but . . .' He tapped his nose and then nodded.

Mark frowned. Rob glanced at Ned still at the bar. Then he sat further forward.

'Me and Nicky,' he whispered. Then he winked.

'What?' asked Mark.

'It's win-win, mate.' Another wink, another tap on the nose.

'What is?'

'It's a secret,' whispered Rob. 'Her and me.'

'What? You and Nicky? Hobbs? An item?'

Rob forced a laugh. 'More than an item, mate. If I get the job, we're starting a family.'

'I honestly think,' Pete told Ally, 'that he has grown up and finally wants to have babies with her.'

'Oh *bollocks*!' cried Ally. 'If people made babies by filling out a form and sending it to the partner of their choice, do you think Rob would still want to do that with Nicky? Or anyone come to think of it. Why do you think procreation involves sex? It's so that men actually do it. Rob does not want babies. He's trying it on.'

'Now –' tried Pete.

'I'm telling you, Rob does not want babies,' interrupted Ally. 'Never has. But for some reason he's now using it as a line to get into her pants.'

'Bloody hell,' said Pete, shaking his head. 'You really hate men, don't you?'

'No,' said Ally firmly, shaking her head. 'It's just that I've gone seriously off Rob. I will never forgive him for going out with Amanda. He's a shit.'

'No he isn't,' said Pete. 'And he's my mate. So please don't talk about him like that.'

'Calling Nicky a prick-tease just because she didn't want to shag him? After all they've been through together —'

'I told you that on strict condition you never brought it up again,' shot Pete. His face went ashen. 'You didn't tell Nicky he said that, did you? He'd kill me.'

Ally was hurt and angry. 'Of course I didn't! You made me swear not to. On my *Corrie* videos.'

'Good.' Pete drank some of his pint. 'Look. He was just pissed off. Stupid macho pride.'

'Macho pride, my arse!' shouted Ally. 'She was his close friend. And he goes around —'

'He didn't "go around",' reminded Pete. 'He just told me. I'm his mate. I bet you know loads about Rob from Nicky that you don't tell anyone. Let alone me.'

Ally looked at him and gave a minute shake of the head. 'She'd never call him anything as bad as a prick-tease, whatever he did to her.'

'Well,' sighed Pete. He spoke slowly. 'I'm not saying Nicky isn't nicer than him.'

Ally nodded. 'Exactly. He's a shit.'

'Why are you so hard on him?' asked Pete suddenly.

Ally gave him a pained look. 'Because I actually thought he was different from all the others.'

Pete stared for a moment, then knocked back his drink in one.

'Different?' he repeated, looking at his glass. He cleared his throat. 'How?'

She shrugged. 'I thought he had a brain,' she said simply. 'And wouldn't want a girlfriend he'd have to explain his jokes to.'

Pete nodded.

'You men are all the same,' said Ally. 'Predictable as fuck.'

It was something she'd said many times before, but this was the first time she'd said it while Pete was drunk.

'That's a bit unfair,' he said.

She looked at him squarely. 'Is it?' she asked. 'You don't see someone like Rob going for someone like me, do you?'

He looked back at her. 'Do you want him to?'

'No,' said Ally. 'But that's not the point.'

'You don't see the likes of Nicky going for the likes of me,' he retorted.

Ally stared at him. 'I . . . I didn't . . .' she mumbled, her face going red.

He raised his eyebrows at her. In response she said contemptuously, 'I think you've just proved my point.'

'Eh? How?'

'Because . . .'

'Yes?'

'Because you fancy Nicky but . . .' She came to an eloquently sudden stop.

'But?' he forced.

She shook her head. 'Nothing,' she whispered.

'But,' he finished for her, 'she's out of my league. It works both ways, you know.'

Ally shrugged at her pint.

'Except,' said Pete crossly, 'that I don't fancy Nicky and you do fancy Rob. And Mark. And anyone in a pair of trousers, it seems.'

'No I don't.'

'Then why do you go on about them all the bloody time?' She shot him a look. 'Revenge.'

'What against? All the men in the world?'

'No, because you go on about Amanda all the bloody time.' She came to an abrupt halt.

She couldn't look up again, so she finished her pint in silence.

When Ned came back from the bar, Rob greeted him like a long-lost friend. Mark took his drink and drank up quickly, not listening to the conversation around him. He should have guessed, he told himself. 'Complicated', she'd said in the car when they first discussed her promotion. And then she'd continued to use that word at the faux meeting at his house, even just before they almost kissed. Well, complicated was definitely one word for it, he thought bitterly. The biggest mistake of her life. That was another. So. She was secretly engaged to Rob, her rival for the promotion. No wonder it had been such an enormous decision for her to go for it. And there he'd been, pushing her and supporting her, and all this time calling Rob names, like a right clueless idiot. That explained them snogging together outside at the Christmas party! Amanda must be a subterfuge. Everything fitted together now. Except, he pondered, all those things she'd told him about Rob that night when they'd nearly kissed. She admitted they'd had a snog, and had gone out in the past, and had even admitted it was still complicated, but nothing more. Had she, in fact, been trying to tell him, without actually telling him? Hoping he'd put two and two together to make five?

God, he'd made a complete fool of himself. The first time he'd let go since Helen, and he'd gone and fallen for a taken woman. A woman who'd lied to him, let him make a fool of himself and, to top it all, chosen a prize wanker instead of him. Galling. That was another word for it.

An hour later, Ned, Rob and Mark were putting the world to rights. They agreed that teachers should earn more, women couldn't drive and had a natural aptitude for ironing (and if you asked them, most of them admitted to actually enjoying it), and the torment of trying to fight women for their jobs at the same time as trying to bring home the bacon was lowering men's sperm count. In a hundred years they'd all be extinct. Working women were literally destroying mankind. Mark almost felt sorry for Rob – you had to hand it to him, being in love with his rival put him in a really tough emotional position. He slapped him on the back and announced that the world was in a mess.

They sat in silence for a while.

'I hate fucking women,' said Ned suddenly.

They frowned hard at him, which had the bonus of getting him temporarily back into focus.

'No, hold on . . .' he said. 'I don't mean that . . .'

'Yeah, we know what you mean, mate,' said Rob.

'I mean,' insisted Ned, 'I fucking hate women.'

'But you're a happily married man –' said Rob.

Ned let out an explosive laugh that was so venomous the

others were stunned into silence. 'I'm not allowed to buy my own fucking lunch,' Ned told them, 'in case I flirt with someone in the canteen.'

Rob and Mark stared. White spittle was gathering in the corner of Ned's mouth.

'I have to phone halfway through every day,' he said, his voice rising, 'so she knows I haven't left her.'

Rob and Mark were motionless. Ned's eyes were watery and red.

'I don't *want* to leave her,' he told the table forcefully. 'But,' he pointed his finger somewhere towards the Gents, 'I wouldn't mind giving Janet a good seeing-to. He punctuated this with a belch. 'Right. Who wants another one before bed?' he asked.

Mark and Rob landed their pint glasses in front of him.

When the pub bell rang, Pete swore.

'Why the swearing?' asked Ally, dully. 'It was inevitable, you know.'

'I can't drive,' he said. 'I'm drunk.'

She shrugged and looked at his shoulders as she spoke. 'You'll have to kip at my place, then.'

'Oh, OK. Cheers.'

''Sall right,' she said.

They walked out of the pub separately, Pete ahead by a few feet. When he got outside he kept walking for a bit, then turned round and waited for Ally, his hands in his pockets. When she opened the pub door into the night, he took a step towards her. She walked towards him and they met in the middle.

30

When Ned, Rob and Mark returned to the dorm at 11.30, it was already pitch black and silent. They collided into everything at least twice and made shushing noises to wake the dead. The only thing that was missing from a Ray Cooney farce was the laughter. If they'd known that none of the women were asleep it would have saved a lot of trouble.

Janet had just returned from the children's dorms where she'd been looking after a vomiting child for the past two hours. Nicky had been back for an hour after talking and cuddling a homesick child. She now lay with her face to the wall, blinking in the dark, unable to sleep. What on earth had the men been talking about all evening? Ned, Mark and Rob? Surely the only thing they had in common was the fact that they ate food. She was trying to work out whether she felt more relaxed now she knew where Mark was, or less relaxed because he was in the same room as her, when a terrifying roar of thunder filled in the dorm. Or rather, Ned farted. It was the most awful noise Nicky had ever heard, as if terrorists had exploded a stink bomb inside her head. But at least it stopped anyone being able to pretend they were asleep. Miss James sat up in her top bunk and ordered Ned

481

to open the window and then drink two pints of water before going to sleep. Janet was to get the water and stay with him until he'd finished. Rob turned on the light and Mark went to shower. Meanwhile, Amanda and Martha laughed till they wept. Even Nicky smiled. When all their eyes had grown accustomed to the light and the after-effects of the explosion, they watched Ned stumbling up his bunk ladder to open the window, and all shared a rare moment of finding something in common to laugh at. It took him six attempts.

'For goodness' sake, Ned,' shot Miss James eventually. 'I'm surprised at you. Really.'

'Sorry,' he said. 'Sorry, sorry, sorry, sorry, sorry. Sorry. Sorry.'

'There's no need to keep repeating yourself,' said Miss James. 'We heard you perfectly well the first time.'

Amanda and Martha squawked with uncontrollable laughter.

Rob turned to Nicky on the top of their bunk, his face level with hers.

'That's not the only surprise,' he murmured. 'Our Ned's a bit of a dark horse.'

When Mark returned to the dorm, wearing just his pyjama bottoms, and drying his hair on a towel, he found Rob leaning on Nicky's bunk, murmuring softly to her. They were laughing together and her face was hidden behind his. God, thought Mark. It was so obvious once you knew. It was a miracle no one else had spotted it. When Rob walked past him to the shower, they smiled at each other and Rob slapped him on the arm. Mark made sure not to look at Nicky, even though he felt her eyes were on him.

'Right!' ordered Miss James hotly. 'Let's all get some sleep now. We've got a busy day tomorrow.'

Unfortunately, it was she who woke everyone up, half an hour later, when she got out of bed to go to the toilet and forgot she was on a top bunk. Fortunately, she landed on Ned's duvet, which he'd pushed off him in his sleep, and his rucksack, which he'd forgotten to store under his bed. Unfortunately, she needed the toilet three times a night. Rob suggested she sleep on the bottom bunk but she said she was far too claustrophobic for that. After the third time she'd fallen off the top, Rob found a spare mattress and placed it next to her bunk. Ned woke on it the next morning, after one of the best night's sleep he'd ever had.

The next morning it was decided that, as there was no 'weather condition', Rob's itinerary could be kept to, and all was well with the world. This meant a fun-packed morning at the aquarium, followed by a fun-packed afternoon at the fair. Then back to the hostel for tea, reading, showers, gradual winding down of the children and inevitable winding up of the adults, followed by lights out in the children's dorm. Then bartering for nightcaps and night duties, and then Nicky washing her hair as early as possible so as to get in some vital sleep before Miss James started falling off her bunk to go to the toilet.

Breakfast was finished within the hour and by nine o'clock a crocodile made up of pairs of nine- to eleven-year-olds accompanied by eight rapidly ageing adults reached the main section of Bournemouth's pier.

It was a typical British scene, with acres of white sky above and acres of white flesh below. On the main concourse stood candyfloss stalls, burger stalls and a merry-go-round.

Further back from the sea was an expanse of freshly cut grass, complete with a pretty slip of a river, crazy golf and a real live bandstand. On it an amateur brass band played old favourites, some in tune, softened by the seashore sounds of the melancholy wail of seagulls and toddlers. Beautiful young foreign students wandered through it all with bemused looks on their windswept faces.

The crocodile shivered at the aquarium door, waiting for it to open. Miss James stood at the front with Rob, while Nicky walked down the side of it, doing a headcount, just in case anyone had escaped on the ten-minute walk, which frankly, she'd considered doing herself.

Oscar stood next to his dad. He put his hand in his and squeezed. His dad looked down and smiled, which Oscar thought made him look sadder. When Miss Hobbs walked past, ticking off everyone's names, Oscar felt his dad sort of shrink. He stood closer.

When they went in, Oscar used the opportunity to watch him more than the fish. He watched his dad like a hawk. Through vast water-filled tanks of sharks and piranhas he watched him gaze at the glass. At one point he even thought he was going to rest his head against it. And what about Miss Hobbs? She kept shooting his dad these sharp little glances of disappointment. What had happened?

If only he could ask his dad. But he couldn't. It wasn't their way. Just like he would never ask his dad if he loved Miss Hobbs. He just knew his dad did, and he knew his dad knew he knew. But he had to find out what had happened. He asked Daisy and, as they went round the aquarium, she taught him the ways of cunning.

'Rule number one: never ever say what you mean,' she began.

'What do you mean?' he asked.

'Well, for example, if you want to go to swimming on Saturday, you don't say, "I want to go swimming on Saturday," because then your dad will say no. You say, "Did you know that eight out of ten children don't exercise enough? And the most common cause of childhood obesity is lack of exercise?" Then you say, as if it's just occurred to you, "Daddy, can I watch television all weekend?"' She looked at Oscar with a self-satisfied grin. 'See?'

He looked at her in amazement.

'That's fantastic,' he said in awe.

'I know,' she said. 'And the beauty is, not only do you get your own way, but they think it was their idea.'

As they came out of the aquarium and took their ice creams on to the pier, Oscar and his dad went to sit on the beach together. Oscar felt uncomfortable, as if he was lying. But he knew it was the only way to find out.

'Dad,' he started. He gave a little cough and hoped he wasn't going red. 'I like Miss Hobbs.'

Mark smiled and looked at him. He stroked his head. 'Good. She's a good woman to like.'

'Do you?' Oscar mumbled, eyes down.

Mark sighed. 'Yes,' he said eventually. 'Yes I do. Very much.'

There was a long pause. Oscar was embarrassed for his father at how easy this was. Somehow he'd expected more from him.

'Like . . . you liked Mummy?' he croaked.

Mark gave him a look and Oscar looked away.

'When did you grow up to be so clever?' asked Mark gently.

'Does she like you back?'

Mark shook his head. 'It appears she's already taken.'

'What? She's got a boyfriend?' Oscar blurted that bit out, but he couldn't keep up the Daisy way. He felt a shocking sense of betrayal at this news. Just then, Rob walked past and, as if he knew what they were talking about, gave Mark a secretive sort of smile. Mark watched him go. Oscar quizzed him with his face and Mark said softly, 'He told me. Man to man.' Then he gave Oscar a kiss and handed him the rest of his ice cream to finish.

Oscar finished it. He was upset, but ice cream was ice cream.

Half an hour later, Daisy and Oscar were strapped into their climbing equipment and climbing a painted plastic wall in the middle of the pier. Daisy was ahead of Oscar.

'Mr Pattison and Miss Hobbs?' repeated Daisy, looking down at Oscar. 'You are *kidding* me.'

'I'm not,' said Oscar hotly, fixing his foot on a step and pulling himself up to her level. 'I hate her. How can she want him instead of my dad?'

'She doesn't. And anyway, Mr Pattison's with Miss *Taylor*. Anyone can see that.'

'No he's not!' shouted Oscar.

'Yes he is!' shouted Daisy back.

'How do you know?'

'I know.'

'Oh, you know everything,' muttered Oscar darkly.

Daisy almost fell off her bit of plastic wall, she answered him so aggressively. 'I do know, so there. If you want to ignore me, more fool you, Oscar Samuels.'

They both looked down and saw the rest of the children queueing for their turn. In front of the children, Mr Pattison stood near Miss James, Miss Taylor standing at the back of the queue.

Oscar looked back up.

'Daisy.'

'What?'

'Do you want to be a detective?'

Daisy's eyes lit up.

That afternoon, they sat apart from everyone else at teatime. They were busy constructing a secret language and code. During reading time, they did surveillance. And by bed-time the plan was ready.

The next day was the first day of the treasure hunt, to be done every morning until the end of the holiday. The questions to be answered each day came from the area of Bournemouth they had seen that day. During the treasure hunt, the children were under strict instructions to find an adult on the hour, every hour, to let them know they hadn't been killed or abducted, or merely escaped to do something more fun instead. They were forbidden to go near roads or shops.

On the top of the four-page quiz, next to Rob's name as quiz deviser, was the address of the police station; the name of the friendly local policeman to ask for; the name and address of the hostel they were staying at; a list of questions, that, if posed by strangers, should be considered inappropriate, and a signal to run away and contact the police; plus all the teachers' mobile phone numbers. Underneath was the instruction to HAVE FUN!

Daisy and Oscar stared at the first question.

Up, up, up and stay. Winking from above . . .

'It doesn't make any sense,' she said finally, scrunching up her nose.

'I know,' said Oscar. 'Why would anyone pick Mr Pattison over my dad?'

Daisy looked up at Oscar. 'I meant the treasure hunt.'

Oscar was looking through her. 'Look! Over there!'

She shot round. Mr Pattison was standing on the grass section, near the bandstand. In one hand he held the sheet of papers on which to mark down the children's hourly register, in the other his mobile, on which to tell the other teachers which children were still alive. He kept looking at his watch.

'Right,' said Daisy, standing. 'Let's go.'

'Wait!' hissed Oscar. 'He mustn't see us.'

They watched him a bit more.

'You keep an eye on him,' said Oscar, 'I'll be back in a minute.'

Before she had a chance to argue, he'd gone. She held up her printed treasure hunt and watched Mr Pattison from behind it. He kept checking his watch every thirty seconds or so. He was definitely waiting for someone. Or he was very, very bored. She scanned the area. Her heart jumped when she saw Miss Hobbs ambling towards the bandstand, just approaching the crazy golf and the tethered hot-air balloon. A secret assignation! Maybe Oscar's dad was right! Miss Hobbs was walking very slowly, her papers and mobile in a pretty bag over her shoulder, her head down. Just before she reached a bench, she looked round, as if she was looking for someone. She was definitely acting suspiciously. Daisy looked across the grass to see if Mr Pattison had seen her. Yes. He had. He had gone all still and was staring at her. Daisy couldn't breathe. Was Mr Pattison going to approach Miss Hobbs? And if so, why? And if not, why not?

Daisy stared.

No. He didn't approach her. Instead, he turned and walked away along the pathway, then up some steps towards the shops, nowhere near Miss Hobbs's bench. Then he wandered round the other side of the bandstand, making himself no longer visible. Daisy followed him to the bridge crossing the little river beside the bandstand, then she stepped slowly towards the path leading behind the bandstand. Strictly speaking, she wasn't allowed here. She looked back to Miss Hobbs. Miss Hobbs was now sitting on the bench, her bag next to her lap, her head up, eyes shut. She was sunbathing, her long hair fanned out behind her, falling down the back of the bench. Daisy stared at her hair. It looked different here. The curls had become even tighter, like ringlets, and the colour had gone light and glossy. It was beautiful. Daisy glanced further back, towards the pier. She couldn't see Mr Samuels anywhere. Or Miss Taylor. When she looked back at Mr Pattison, he was now glancing left and right, left and right.

Where the hell was Oscar? She looked back again and there he was; she could just make him out, running back to her, his socks falling down. When he reached her, she spoke quickly.

'Postman Prat is definitely waiting for someone.'

She pointed at Mr Pattison.

'Good,' said Oscar. He held up a disposable camera. They did a high-five. Then they looked back at Mr Pattison.

He'd gone. Vanished. They stared left, then right. Then they looked up, towards the shops, behind the bandstand, and both gasped at what they saw. There was Miss Taylor. Coming down from the shops. In a rush. They raced back, and stood on the other side of the river, where they were allowed to be, pretending they were looking into it. They didn't know Miss Taylor very well because she had never taught them. They didn't know the limits of her temper, or the strength of her humour. They didn't know her at all. She was swinging a carrier bag against her legs and a handbag over one shoulder. They moved behind a tree, and Oscar got his camera ready. But she was walking too quickly. When she reached the path, she turned right along it, away from the restricted area. They looked at each other. Why was she doing that? Where did it lead? It was a strictly forbidden area for the children, and all the teachers were meant to be contactable throughout the treasure hunt.

They followed.

The river went on for ages, leading them across the city centre where they both looked at the pebble mosaic of a mermaid, into the upper gardens and past the war memorial. She was now walking very fast. She checked her watch and sped up until she was almost running. And then, all too soon, she slowed down again. She was now approaching some tennis courts. And there, standing in front of them, looking cross, was Mr Pattison. Miss Taylor gave a small wave.

He called out, 'Where the bloody hell have you been?' to which she replied, 'Oh, gimme a break.'

Daisy and Oscar stopped and slipped behind a tree. Oscar

490

held his camera to his eye. He had to lean it against his face to stop it shaking.

Miss Taylor and Mr Pattison met with a fierce kiss, their mouths like magnets. It actually made a noise and Daisy and Oscar stifled a snort. Then Daisy whispered, 'Told you,' and Oscar gave her a swift elbow to the ribs. Then he realised he had to wind on the camera. Luckily, Miss Taylor and Mr Pattison were still kissing. Daisy was staring with undisguised disgust on her face. 'They look like they're eating each other,' she whispered. 'I'm gonna vom.'

Oscar held the camera in place and, concentrating hard, pressed his finger firmly down. The camera clicked so loudly that he and Daisy leapt up and fled, almost falling over in their haste.

When they reached the bandstand, in a fraction of the time it had taken to go the other way, they collapsed on the grass in hysterics and caught their breath.

'Do you think you got it?' asked Daisy eventually.

Oscar shrugged. 'Who cares? I'll just tell my dad.'

At teatime, they sat apart from everyone else again, at the far end of the dining hall, observing the teachers. Miss Taylor and Mr Pattison acted like nothing had happened, and Mr Pattison was wandering down the aisles, teasing the kids, passing them anything they needed and occasionally chatting to Miss Hobbs.

Oscar asked Daisy how she had known they were an item. She told him that she hadn't known, she'd guessed, just from the way she looked at him during assembly.

'What? All lovey-dovey?' asked Oscar.

Daisy shook her head. 'No. Angry. Like my nan looks at her boyfriends when they annoy her.'

Daisy then asked Oscar why his father thought that Mr Pattison and Miss Hobbs were an item in the first place. He told her that Mr Pattison had told him.

Daisy took this information in slowly.

'Well then,' she said. 'He's a big fat liar.'

'Or he's two-timing Miss Hobbs,' said Oscar. 'That's horrid!'

'Well, most men are shits,' Daisy explained. 'My mum told me.'

'My dad isn't!' retorted Oscar.

'No.' Daisy nodded. 'You're right. Not any more.'

They turned to watch the reformed Mr Samuels, who was sitting with all the other adults, including Miss Hobbs, but not talking to anyone.

'But on the plus side,' Daisy continued, 'it does mean that Mr Pattison thinks he needs to put your dad off. Which means he thinks – or is scared – that your dad and Miss Hobbs might actually get together.'

Oscar frowned. Daisy sensed he needed more information.

'Maybe Miss Hobbs has told him she likes your dad, or something. Why else would he need to make up that lie?'

Oscar shook his head. 'I don't know. I don't understand any of it.'

'Well, don't you worry,' said Daisy contentedly. 'I do. And I've decided. I'm going to be a private detective when I grow up.'

Oscar looked at her with something approaching awe and fear.

The next day, Oscar and Daisy accidentally left the camera in their dorm, so couldn't get the film developed. They wouldn't have had much time anyway, as the class went on a day-trip to an adventure playground and there wasn't a chemist in sight. They had decided that they had to give Oscar's dad proof when they told him of their discovery, so it would have to wait another day. On the coach trip to the playground, though, they were able to finish the treasure hunt.

She lies not in water, but in stones
Bordered by commerce, instead of sailors' bones

was the mermaid they'd seen in the city centre.

Thank you is a simple word, and words cannot express
How deep our gratitude goes on, for what you gave to us

was the war memorial.

It was easy once you got into the swing of it. You just had to remember that Mr Pattison was a self-righteous, pompous twit. It also helped having gone beyond the restricted area before all the other kids.

The next day was meant to be a full day doing the treasure hunt. Because Oscar and Daisy had finished theirs, they were going to do some more spying and Oscar could get his film developed. He was so excited he could barely sleep all night. As it happened, they didn't have any luck with the spying, but after lunch they sat behind the bandstand, where they knew – thanks to following Mr Pattison – that they would be invisible to everyone else. They fought over the photos.

'I took it!' shouted Oscar.

'If it wasn't for me you wouldn't have known anything!' shouted back Daisy.

They opened them together.

The photo was blurred, and mostly of Mr Pattison. But if you looked really carefully, you could make out a bit of Miss Taylor's hair. And, through his legs, some of her skirt. It was proof enough. It reminded them both of the kiss and they made loud, slurpy noises on their arms and laughingly pushed each other away a lot, to compensate.

Then they practised how Oscar would tell his dad in the most dramatic and important way possible. He needed quite a lot of tutoring on this from Daisy, so it was decided that if his dad bought him a thank-you present, Daisy was to get half of it.

It wasn't until after tea that Oscar got his father alone. There was one hour before bedtime, during which he was meant to be reading and then getting ready for bed. He knocked on the adults' dorm door. His dad opened it. He was alone. The others were all either chatting to some children, preparing things for tomorrow or having their turn to get rat-arsed.

'I've got something to tell you,' announced Oscar. 'Something very dramatic and important.'

'Oh yes?'

'Daisy and me saw Mr Pattison kissing Miss Taylor yesterday,' he blurted. 'I mean, *really* kissing her. Like he was angry.'

He waited for his father to start crying and hug him. Mark stared at his son.

'How on earth do you know this?'

'We spied on them! Look! I took a photo.' He thrust the photo in front of his dad's face.

Mark jerked his head back and blinked at it.

'Bloody hell,' he whispered. 'What the hell am I looking at, Oscar?'

Oscar could barely get the words out.

'You're looking at them kissing. Look, that's her hair, behind his head. And that's her skirt through his trousers. You have to squint a bit –'

His dad pushed the photo down. 'I meant "What the hell have you done?"'

'I took it!' cried Oscar excitedly. 'To show you! We spied on them! Daisy knew it all along!'

'What on earth has got into you, Osc?' his dad whispered.

Oscar backtracked. 'I told Daisy what you said about Miss Hobbs and Mr Pattison. And she said Mr Pattison was Miss *Taylor's* boyfriend, not Miss *Hobbs's* boyfriend. And she was right. She thinks men are shits. Is that true, Dad?'

His dad just stared at him.

'Well, aren't you going to do anything?' asked Oscar. 'Tell Miss Hobbs? Tell Miss Taylor? Tell Mr Pattison?' He paused. 'Buy me a bike?'

'Tell Miss Hobbs?' repeated his dad. 'And be the one to break her heart about the man she wants to spend the rest of her life with? And then hope she falls into my arms out of gratitude?'

'*Yes!*' cried Oscar. Gosh, his dad was such an idiot some-times. 'Daisy would like a bike too, but I said I couldn't promise. But she was ever so good, though. She's going to be a private detective when she grows up. She really helped –'

'Is that what you do with our secrets?' shouted Mark. 'Run and tell Daisy? Are you going to tell her about my job, too?'

'No!'

'And as for you wanting a reward for spying on someone, I'm absolutely speechless.'

'But —'

'I'm . . . I'm so disappointed in you, Oscar, I don't know what to say.'

Oscar went hot. He wanted to hide from his father, but he wanted a hug at the same time.

'Well, I'm going to tell Miss Hobbs if you're not,' he said, his breath coming fast.

'Don't be an idiot,' shot his father.

'I'm not an idiot!' shouted Oscar. 'You are!'

'Oscar!'

Oscar raced out of the room. He went straight to bed and lay curled up, face to the wall. Daisy tried to get him to talk but he just pushed her away.

That night, Mark decided not to join Rob in the lounge. It was Ned's turn to stay sober. Janet joined Rob, though, and drank him under the table. Unfortunately, Nicky had decided to as well, unable to spend another evening in the company of Amanda and Martha and finding it impossible to stay still when she knew Mark was with the others. By the time she realised he wasn't joining them, she knew it would have looked too forced to walk out. She was stuck with the wrong crowd again.

After the first night, Miss James had forbidden any of them to drink too late, so after an hour, Rob, Janet and Nicky returned to the dorm. They found Miss James fast asleep, her raucous snoring punctuating the whispers of Amanda, Martha and Mark, who were all sitting on Amanda's bottom bunk. Nicky felt so envious she could almost taste it. Rob held the door open for Nicky, and when she caught Mark's eye briefly, he looked away.

After the events of the first night, a nocturnal routine had evolved in the adults' dorm. Ned was strictly forbidden to sleep on the mattress next to his bed until Miss James had used it three times. She had always done this by midnight, and after then, Ned lay in the middle of the dorm, letting out thunderclaps that shattered everyone's dreams. The novelty of these violent outbursts had worn off and no one found them funny any more. Revenge was taken by stepping on his sleeping face en route to the bathroom. By the end of the trip, Miss James had a bruised coccyx, hip and knee, and Ned had a swollen jaw.

Oscar woke early the next morning, remembered the argument with his dad, and didn't speak to Daisy once, all the way through breakfast. Afterwards they sat on the grass and tried to forget everything and pretend they were doing the stupid treasure hunt. Daisy told Oscar that if they couldn't work on his dad, they were going to have to work on Mr Pattison or Miss Taylor.

'I don't want to help him,' said Oscar. 'I hate him.'

'No, you don't,' said Daisy impatiently. 'You're angry with him. Because you love him so much. But because you're emotionally stunted you can't handle the emotion. All men are emotionally stunted. My mum said.'

'But Miss Hobbs loves Mr Pattison.'

'No, she doesn't,' said Daisy evenly.

'How do you know?'

'I know.'

'Oh just leave me alone!'

'Don't you want Miss Hobbs and your dad to be together?'

Oscar gave a shrug. Then he thought of how he'd ruined everything the night Miss Hobbs had come to their house. He had to make it up to his dad, even if his dad hated him for it.

'Don't think of doing it for your dad,' said Daisy, reading his mind. 'Do it for you.'

Oscar nodded. He thought of Miss Hobbs spending time with them at the weekend, going swimming with him, and introducing him properly to her eldest niece.

But what should they do next? They tried thinking of something conclusive, something brilliant, but all they could come up with was leaving the photo on Miss Hobbs's pillow.

No. That was immature and cowardly, they decided. It was also not a good enough photo.

So, they decided to do what any good detective does when he or she doesn't know what to do next. They were going to do some more spying. And this time they needed to be able to hear what was being said. And there was only one way to do that.

31

There were now only two more days of the holiday left. Daisy and Oscar knew they had to do their spying tomorrow evening because there was a day-trip to Brownsea Island on the last day, and they would all be getting back to the dorms too late. Evenings were the only time when teachers had any free time alone.

They spent the whole night making their plan, except between the hours of three and five, when things went a bit hazy before Oscar woke to dribble on his arm and Daisy snuffling into her elbow. By 6 a.m. their entire plan was settled and given a name, complete with codes. By 7 a.m., when the morning bell was rung to get up, they were ready for a good night's sleep.

Oscar was so excited that he couldn't eat a thing for breakfast. Luckily he was too tired to, anyway. Even more luckily, breakfast was kippers. The day was boring, merely a stretch of time to be crossed before spying could commence and Plan O-D (Oscar-Daisy) could be put into action.

When evening came, they exchanged the secret sign (a scratch on the left earlobe with the right index finger) during tea, and snuck away to their empty dorm. They sat behind the half-open door. From here they had a perfect view of who was coming in and out of the adults' dorm opposite. They went over their plan.

'If you go in and someone's in there?' asked Daisy.

'Plan A,' Oscar said.

'Which is?'

'Pretend I want to talk to them.'

'And if someone's in the bathroom?'

'Plan B.'

'Which is?'

'Hide.'

'And?'

'Spy.'

Daisy nodded. 'Right. Now. I'll be out here. If you hear "tu-whit, tu-whoo", what does it mean?'

Oscar looked at her. 'Someone's doing a crap impersonation of an owl.'

'Oscar! This is serious.'

'Someone's coming.'

'If you hear it twice?'

'All clear.'

'Right.'

They heard something. Daisy looked out into the corridor, Oscar peeked through the crack in the door.

'Hobbit approaching,' she whispered urgently. 'Hobbit in hole.'

'I know,' hissed Oscar. 'I'm next to you.'

'Well, go on, then!'

Oscar tutted. 'She'll still be in there.'

'She might be in the bathroom.'

'Give her two more minutes.'

500

Daisy looked at her watch. Exactly two minutes later, she said, 'Right. Go on.'

Oscar jumped up and skidded in his socks across the empty corridor and into the adults' dorm. He heard Daisy giggling behind him. The dorm was empty, the door leading to the bathroom showing an engaged red strip under the handle. Plan B it was. Hide. And Spy. Heart hammering, he glanced back at the dorm door. If he left now, no one would be any the wiser. He looked again at the bathroom door. He crouched down and lay flat on his back next to the nearest bed, preparing to slide under. He came face to face with the bottom of it. There wasn't enough room for him. He heard the toilet flush, and leapt up. What should he do now? It hadn't occurred to him that there wouldn't be room to hide under a bed. Where else was a self-respecting child to hide in a teachers' dorm? He climbed to the top bunk, whipped up the duvet and lay under it, as flat as could be. Quickly, he sat up again and piled some of the clothes scattered at the foot of the bunk on top of the duvet. He was a natural! Then he lay back down again, completely flat, piling a jumper round his head, but leaving his ear nearest the wall uncovered, so he could hear everything clearly. This was perfect. He could hear everything and was totally invisible. He heard the bathroom door open – Miss Hobbs! – and shut again behind her. He could hear her humming. It couldn't have gone better.

Then he fell asleep.

Across the corridor, sitting cross-legged on the floor, Daisy picked up her magazine and opened her emergency supply of biscuits stolen from the kitchen earlier in the day. Then her eyes shut and she leant back heavily, the door closing behind her.

Nicky sat on the bottom bunk – Rob's bed – too knackered to climb into hers. Why was Mark ignoring her? Had he picked up on her innermost thoughts and found them repulsive? Had he told her that he hated children expressly to stop her from imagining anything ever going on between them? Oh, the humiliation. Still, she told herself immediately, if he persisted in calling kids awful and kept ignoring her, it would definitely make it much easier to go with Rob's white-picket-fence vision of life together. A girl could be offered much less and live quite happily on that, she told herself, thinking of Claire.

She lay back on Rob's bed and let out a low, heavy sigh. The door opened.

'Hey!' said Rob. 'Starting without me? I knew you were competitive, but that's ridiculous.'

She shot up into sitting position. 'I'm too knackered to climb into my bed. Honestly, it's an obstacle course just to get to sleep.'

Rob laughed and sat down next to her.

'Don't worry, Nicky,' he said softly. 'Not long now.'

She managed a small smile. 'Yeah, then the longest job interview known to man will be over.'

'Yeah,' said Rob, sidling closer to her, 'and then we can ignore the old bat and just get on with our lives, eh?'

Nicky leant her back against the wall and looked at him.

'Mr Pattison, if I didn't know you better, I'd think you were trying to put me off the race before it was over,' she said archly.

To her surprise Rob answered seriously.

'Hardly!' he cried. 'Fucking hell! I'm only the guy offering you everything you've ever wanted instead of winning a stupid old bat's idea of a race.'

Nicky frowned.

'Everything I've ever wanted,' she repeated, nodding dully.

'Yeah!' He sounded piqued. 'Kids, husband, financial security, the whole kit and caboodle. But if you want to go ahead and win some fuck-off stupid race instead –'

'Ah!' she said, suddenly getting it. 'I see, you mean everything I ever wanted when I was twenty-three!'

He looked at her and his eyes went suddenly soft. 'I know you, Nicky,' he said with a gentle urgency. 'Better than anyone else in the world. And I know you haven't changed that much.' He put a large hand on her thigh.

'You don't know me more than *I* know me, Rob,' she said, moving his hand off her thigh.

'Sometimes you're your own worst enemy,' he whispered, putting his hand back, more gently this time.

She tried to concentrate.

'And sometimes our worst enemies are our friends in disguise,' she said, putting it back.

That seemed to really annoy him. 'What the hell does that mean?'

She hadn't meant to annoy him, she was just talking hypothetically, while trying to keep his hand off her thigh. But now she'd started, she'd better keep going.

'You know,' she said, sweetly, 'if you really felt strongly for me, as you claim to do, you'd be happy for me trying to be Head. I'm happy for you. I don't keep trying to talk you out of it, do I?'

'It's exactly because I do feel strongly for you that I'm

trying to help,' pleaded Rob. 'I know you, Nicky, and I know that you're not thinking this through! If you settled down with me, you'd have the family you always wanted within a year and you wouldn't give a shit about this stupid promotion.'

'Will you stop going on about me and kids!' cried Nicky. 'You're bloody obsessed!'

'Nicky, you can try and pretend to yourself, but I know the truth. I'm the one you finished with because I didn't want to give you children before you were twenty-five! I'm the one whose shoulder you cried on because you thought promotion meant no kids, remember?'

'I was twenty-three, Rob! What the hell did I know about myself? I thank God I never rushed into having kids that young. And I only cried once! It was just the shock of it. You seem to forget that I didn't cry when the headship came up.'

'Look, *you* may be in denial, but *I* can see it like it is,' said Rob. 'You're not getting any younger. If you want more than one child – and I know you do – you'll have to pop them out quickly. And believe me, you won't have the time or energy to be a head teacher of a school as well. And you'll be such a good mother that you won't care anyway!'

'What the hell gives you the right to tell me what I want and don't want?'

There was a pause.

'Love?' he said softly. There was that hand again.

There was another pause.

'And anyway,' she said, trying to lighten the tone while moving his hand again, 'maybe I'll find a man who's already got a family. Maybe I'll be a fantastic stepmum and a brilliant headmistress at the same time.'

'Oh for fuck's sake, Nicky!' To her amazement, Rob started shouting. 'You're so fucking naïve. You live in cloud-cuckoo-land. Which planet are you from? It's like watching you try to do Miss James's pathetic puzzle every morning. You must have wasted hours doing it.'

'Oh sod off!' cried Nicky. 'Just because you're Puzzle-King doesn't mean I can't be a good headmistress.'

'I'm not Puzzle-King!' Rob was almost hysterical. 'That's exactly what I mean – you're so naïve! Nicola, I cheat!'

Nicky gasped. 'What? Every time? Every morning?'

'Of course every morning! I've got better things to do than find the last bit of Yugoslavia because she's too lazy to do her own fucking hobby! The whole school would be an academic year ahead if it wasn't for her fucking puzzles.'

'You're kidding me!' gasped Nicky. 'You're the puzzle cheat? You're why I've had to cancel a back massage because I'm now in school on the last afternoon of term?'

'Don't blame me, blame Miss James! The woman is mental! And because of our morning meetings, we're ending up finishing her puzzle for her! Or rather *you* are! Every single morning you waste half an hour doing it for her! If you counted up how much time you've spent doing her puzzle this year, you'd probably have been able to learn a new language by now. Did you never stop to think why Janet never actually steps into her office?'

There was a long silence.

As it happened, Nicky had stopped to think why Janet never actually stepped into Miss James's office and she had decided it was because Janet was an unfriendly old sow.

'You see?' continued Rob, calmer now. 'You haven't got the cynicism needed to be a decent head teacher. You'd be too busy helping everyone do their puzzles.' He laughed, then spoke softly. 'Anyway, I know that you don't want someone else's family.' He brushed her hair with his hand. 'You want your own.'

'Well, that shows how little you know me.' She shook his hand off.

Rob sat silently for a moment before speaking again, this time his voice full of disbelief and coming out through gritted teeth.

'You're not seriously talking about that arrogant prick and his little prat of a son, are you?'

'Don't talk about them like that!'

They were now staring at each other, their breathing heavy. Then to Nicky's amazement, Rob suddenly threw himself on to his knees in front of her. For some reason it reminded her of a bad comedy sketch and she had to hide a laugh when she realised he wasn't joking.

'Marry me, Nicky,' he said desperately, as if his life depended on it.

'P-pardon?' she managed.

'You heard. Marry me. Live dangerously. Sod the consequences. Let's just do it.'

He jumped up and sat next to her again. His hand gripped her hand.

'You're mad,' she said. 'Leave me alone. You're scaring me.'

'Why not?'

'That's not a good reason to get married, Rob.'

'I've heard of worse. Why the hell not?'

'Touched as I am by this romantic proposal,' said Nicky, 'I shall have to force myself to say no.'

Rob stood up again and started pacing. 'So you're going to chuck in your one last chance at real happiness for a cocky shit who's already got one of his own?'

'You don't know what you're talking about.'

'I know that someone else's shitty little ten-year-old son is not your idea of the perfect family.'

'Oscar is not shitty. Stop talking about him like that.'

'I taught him for a year too, remember. Hardly got a word out of him all year. And he's been giving me the evil eye all holiday. Gives me the creeps.'

'You know what?' flashed Nicky. 'If he's giving you the evil eye, Rob, chances are you're evil.'

Rob opened his eyes wide. 'Oh, that's really rational talk, that is.'

'He's a wonderful kid,' she said breathlessly, 'and I adore him.'

'Jesus Christ, Nicky! Listen to yourself! You sound like an over-emotional schoolgirl. Do you honestly think that you're headmistress material? Oscar's just a normal little shit of a kid. And his dad's a smug git who thinks he can ponce in here and charm all the pussy into his bed with his posh suits, his flash car and superdad act. And what I can't believe is that you – you, Nicky, one of the brightest women I know – are falling for it all! And you're going to turn your back on your only chance of happiness for that!'

There was a long pause.

'Just leave me alone, Rob.'

'Nicky . . . I'm trying to *help* –'

'Get out.'

'I don't want you to get hurt –'

'Get out.'

'I'm telling you because I care.'

'GET OUT!'

There was a pause.

'OK,' said Rob. 'Just promise me one thing. Don't let him ruin your dreams, Nicky.'

He slammed the dormitory door behind him. Nicky wasn't quite sure why she started sobbing, she just knew that a lot of tears needed to come out and sobbing seemed as good a way as any to make that happen. She fell back on to Rob's bed and let it all come out.

She didn't even hear the door open. It was only when she heard Mark's voice near her ear asking her what was wrong that she jumped up.

'Oh! Sorry!' she said. 'Please. Now's not a good time,' she said, sitting up and sniffing hard. 'Please. Just leave me alone.'

'What's wrong?' The pain in Mark's voice made the tears come again. He sat down next to her and she suddenly felt so safe she needed to cry some more. She tried not to look at his long thigh stretching out on the bed next to her. Or notice the charge through her body that came just from the feel of his frame so near hers. She remembered the table quiz meeting at his house and almost went from sobbing straight to coronary. She had to get back into control. Remember, she told herself, this was a man who had gone to great pains to let her know he didn't want children and had then ignored her all week. He was also a man who had a persuasively strong motive for making friends with her.

He was also a man with really long thighs.

'Please,' she said quietly. 'Please. Just leave me alone.'

'Nicky, please,' he echoed, his voice like a velvet pulse that went straight to where it counted. 'Who's upset you?'

'No one. Me.'

'Is it Rob? Nicky, tell me. What's he done?'

Nicky let out a noise – either a laugh or a cry, she herself couldn't tell. There was a long, increasingly uncomfortable pause and she decided that Mark was now wondering whether to hold her in his strong, manly arms or have her sectioned. She wondered if he was the kind of versatile chap who could do both.

Damn, what did she have to lose?

'He proposed, actually,' she said, her voice suddenly hard. There was silence.

'Proposed? . . .' Mark trailed off. 'To you? I thought . . .'

'What?' She looked at him. 'That "every cell in my body" was made for something other than marriage?' asked Nicky pointedly. 'Is it so hard to imagine that someone may actually want to marry me? And have a future with me?'

It felt like the most dangerous thing she'd ever said in her life. She envisaged her guardian angel smacking its forehead and going for a tea break.

'Since you ask,' she heard Mark finally say, 'it's what I imagine all the time.'

Well, that was what she thought he said, but of course he could have said anything, the throbbing in her ears was so loud. Wait, he was speaking again.

'In fact,' she heard him say, 'I can't think of anything else.'

She heard that. She looked at him. He looked at her. She looked at him a bit more. He looked at her a bit more, with great big thumping knobs on.

'Really?' she whispered, her voice all wispy.

'Yes!' Mark's voice was tremulously intense. 'Nicky!' he said. 'You must know how I feel about you. Don't you?'

She gasped. Was that angels she could hear overhead?

'I know it's doomed,' he went on. 'I know you're in love with Rob, but . . . I can't help it. I utterly adore you.'

She stared at him. Now, somewhere in that romantic declaration he'd taken a wrong turn. She repeated it, conscious that her reply was important with a capital IMPORTANT.

'I'm not in love with Rob,' she said quietly, fairly sure that this was the salient point to hold on to.

It was his turn to stare at her. She gave as good as she got. Within moments they were staring at each other again.

'Really?' he said and started to laugh, even though Nicky was fairly sure no one had told a joke. At least, she thought, not her.

'Really!' she repeated, laughing too. 'He's driving me nuts. Keeps trying to talk me into having his babies every time I see him. He's convinced we've got this thing going on, like he and I are starting up again. I don't want to annoy him because, well, he's my rival and I know how competitive he can be when he's angry, but, to be honest, it's beginning to get spooky. And a bit unnerving.'

Mark was really laughing now and so was she. It felt so good to talk honestly about Rob for a change.

'Oh my God!' cried Mark. 'Thank God! Nicky, I'm mad about you. I don't know what I'd do without you.'

She was just considering fainting when he enveloped her in his arms and ever so gently touched her lips with his. Her entire body went zing. She saw fireworks under her eyelids as they began a soft, tender kiss. Then suddenly they were both laughing. Then just as suddenly they weren't. She didn't know how it happened but they were now lying next to each other and her arms were round his neck and his were round her waist. His touch was so gentle it was slightly shaky.

On the bed above them, Oscar scrunched up his eyes. What the hell was happening now? There was complete silence.

Had they gone? He waited for an eternity. Nothing.

They must have gone. He couldn't hear a thing. He should leave. As soon as possible. He pulled the duvet off him and sat up.

He stood up on the bed and then heard a giant, echoing human owl hoot four times and then a door slam shut. He jumped down the ladder and came face to face with Mr Pattison. Mr Pattison's face was puce. Oscar almost jumped back up the ladder. Then he followed Mr Pattison's gaze and stared in amazement. There was his dad and Miss Hobbs, lying on the same bed together! Miss Hobbs was all flushed and his dad had lipstick on. It was like trying to work out one of those maths puzzles that started with 'If it takes a snail forty-eight hours to go two metres . . .' He'd never been good at those.

For a moment everyone stared at everyone else. It was so quiet Oscar thought he'd gone deaf.

'Oh my giddy aunt,' whispered Mr Pattison eventually. Oscar thought he saw Mr Pattison start to smile, but then he went all serious instead. 'This is all deeply disturbing.' He turned to Oscar. 'All in front of the boy. Very unprofessional.'

To Oscar's astonishment, Miss Hobbs looked angrily at him.

'Oscar Samuels!' she said faintly. 'What on earth are you doing in here?' She jumped up and straightened her top.

Oscar stared at his dad, who jumped up too, but his dad was even angrier than she was.

'Oscar! Explain yourself!'

'Actually,' said Mr Pattison, 'I think I'm more interested to hear Miss Hobbs's explanation. Let's see . . . the Deputy Head snogging the school bursar in front of her own pupil – a pupil who happens to be the bursar's son.' He shook his head. 'I'm not sure I'd be able to live with myself if I don't mention this to Miss James.'

'But! You . . .' started Oscar. He wanted to say that he'd seen him snogging Miss Taylor, but the words just didn't come out.

Mr Pattison looked at him with studied surprise. 'Yes, Oscar?' he said slowly. 'I . . .'

And then to Oscar's utter amazement, instead of thanking him, Miss Hobbs started shouting at him. She gave him a detention for tomorrow, an essay to write on Why You Shouldn't Hide in People's Rooms. He wanted to shout back at her, but he couldn't speak. He hated her. And his dad. And Mr Pattison. He ran out of the room and launched himself on to his bed before the tears came.

32

Rob, Mark and Nicky stared at each other in the bedroom.

'You wouldn't dare tell Miss James,' Mark said to Rob, his voice low and trembling.

'Don't tell me what I would or wouldn't do,' shot Rob. 'You arrogant prick.'

'*I'm* the arrogant prick?' yelled Mark. 'I'm not the one proposing to one woman while shagging another!'

'*What?*' said Nicky.

'Don't listen to him, Nicky,' said Rob. 'He's just trying to shit you up.'

'I'm not!' shouted Mark. 'You're shagging Amanda, you hypocrite.'

'Oh *I'm* the hypocrite?' said Rob. 'I've never lied about my feelings. You're the one pretending to be a right-on new man to get into her pants while telling the lads in the bar that it's women like her who are bringing down civilisation as we know it.'

'*What?*' said Nicky.

'What?' said Mark.

'You say one thing but you do another,' said Rob.

'Well, so do you,' said Mark.

'Well, so do you,' mimicked Rob.

'Both of you, shut up,' snapped Nicky. 'I've heard enough from both of you.'

'Nick—' they started.

'SHUT UP!'

They shut up.

'Mark,' said Nicky, in a low voice, 'what do you mean, he's shagging Amanda?'

'Nicky!' cried Rob. 'This is *me*. Rob. Don't listen to him, he'd say anything to get into your pants! Which reminds me, what the hell did I just see?' He turned to Mark. 'D'you like to make your son watch, Samuels? You sick bastard –'

'Rob,' cut in Nicky, 'what you saw there was . . .'

'Nicky!' pleaded Mark. 'You don't have to explain anything to him.'

Nicky looked at him. 'Mark, don't you get it? I've lost it. I just got off with the bursar in front of my pupil, who happens to be his son.' She shrugged. 'It's hardly *Dead Poets Society*, is it?'

'Oh no, Nicky,' Mark grimaced, 'that was a *crap* film.'

'Nicky,' said Rob solemnly, 'I think you have to seriously consider what just happened.'

'Oh shut up,' said Mark. 'You –'

'Mark.' Nicky turned to him. Her voice was low. 'He's right.'

'Nicky,' said Mark, his voice soft and urging, 'we didn't do anything wrong.'

Rob let out a harsh laugh.

'Yes we did,' said Nicky sadly. 'Listen to me. I'm very confused at the moment, but I do know that this is my career and I like my career. Spending time with you at the moment is probably the most reckless thing I could do in my career to date.'

'Why?'

'I have to focus,' Nicky went on. 'Stay sharp.'

'Nicky,' insisted Mark, 'listen to me.'

'Why the hell should she?' asked Rob quietly. 'What does she know about you, eh? Does she know that you think women with careers are destroying mankind? Does she know that you think women should do the ironing while their men go out to work?'

'WHAT?' cried Nicky.

'I don't know what you're talking about,' said Mark.

'Oh yeah?' said Rob. 'It's amazing what pearls comes out of a charmer's mouth when he's had a drink or two.'

Mark turned to Nicky, his voice almost frantic. 'I was drunk out of my skull because he'd just told me you and he were about to start a family together.'

Nicky stared at Rob.

'Bollocks!' laughed Rob in amazement, his eyes wide. 'Blimey, mate, your porkies just get bigger and bigger. Nicky, I don't know what he's talking about.'

'I tell you, Nicky,' insisted Mark, 'I was drowning my sorrows at the thought of you starting a family with someone else.'

'But I thought you didn't want to start another family,' said Nicky.

Mark looked genuinely astonished. 'I never said that!'

'You did,' said Nicky, 'to me, on the coach on the way up here. You said you wouldn't go through having a baby again.'

'I wouldn't go through having Oscar!' said Mark. 'It was

hell. He lost his mother when he was four. It was a nightmare. I'd bloody love more children. Oscar's been begging for a baby brother or sister for –'

'Hah!' interrupted Rob. 'That's not the kind of talk you talked with the lads at the bar.'

They both turned on him. 'Shut up!'

Nicky shook her head. 'I'm so confused,' she said quietly. 'All I know is that I don't really know who either of you are. What your motives are. And I'm also very confused about myself at the moment.'

There was silence. Eventually Nicky sighed and shook her head. 'But the one thing I do know is that Oscar is my pupil.'

'Oh, just give it up, mate,' Rob told Mark. 'Don't you know when you're beaten?'

'Piss off, Prattison,' hissed Mark.

Rob balked. 'Don't you *dare* call me Prattison, you fuck. That was her nickname for me years before you came on the scene in your stupid designer suits. You think because you've got a penis for a car that you can get whatever you want –'

'Do you *want* my car, or something?' asked Mark. ''Cos you go on about it an awful lot.'

'No thanks,' said Rob. 'I've got my own penis, thanks.'

'Oh yeah, we all know that,' shot back Mark. 'And you're keeping it busy too –'

Nicky let out a heart-stopping scream. They both stopped and looked at her. She stared at them.

'Don't you think someone should go and see how Oscar is?' she asked. 'Preferably his father?'

Mark turned from Rob to her, his expression dark. 'Please don't pretend to teach me how to be a father any more,' he said, his voice hollow. 'I know perfectly well that Oscar's

516

gone. I had thought it would be more appropriate for his teacher to go to him in this instance. He knows that however angry I may get with him sometimes, I love him unconditionally and will never leave him, but he's never had a teacher shout at him like that. A teacher he cares so much about. Especially as this is a disciplinary issue, not a parental one.'

'Sorry,' she whispered. 'I'll go to him.' And she left the room without another look at either of them.

The last happy day of the holiday was to be spent taking a day-trip via the ferry to Brownsea Island, a beautiful pine-tree-clad island in Poole Harbour. Nicky had been there years ago as a child, during the one holiday she remembered going on with her parents, and all she could remember about it was the harrowing lovesick wail of the peacocks, their tails erect as a display of desperation. She offered to stay behind with the detention children.

As well as Oscar, there were a few other children staying behind, three with detentions and one with tummy upset. The four on detention wrote their essays in the dining room and Nicky spent her morning wandering to and from them and the one lying listlessly on her bed.

The last evening of the trip was spent, thanks to Rob's itinerary, putting on a show of sketches for each other. The hostel owner had finally allowed them the lounge, seeing as no one else had used it the entire time they'd been there. There would be the usual reunion party the following evening, back at school; a disco, bad lighting, sausages on a stick and the children getting more action than the adults. Nicky couldn't wait.

The sketch show was as hellish as anyone could imagine

and the children couldn't get enough of it. Nicky sat at the back. Rob was in most of the skits, and was compère and chief clapper in the audience. He also announced the winner of the treasure hunt and gave out prizes. Oscar and Daisy didn't even come third. As Nicky sat watching him, she felt she was observing a winner racing to the finishing line. The more she watched him, the more she wanted to believe that he was on her side. She watched Amanda to see if there were any signs that what Mark had said was true about Rob and her. They barely made eye contact all night, and when they did, it was hardly the stuff of passion. In fact, Amanda spent most of the night chatting to Martha and, if anything, Rob flirted more with Martha than Amanda.

No. Mark must have lied about Rob shagging Amanda.

So she started asking herself how much she actually knew about Mark, but her answers kept getting interrupted by very distracting memories of the kiss they'd shared, which knocked any kiss she'd ever had with Rob into an old tin hat. That really wasn't helping at all.

After Oscar starred in a sketch he'd written himself about doing the daily treasure hunt, which poked merciless fun at the laborious questions, he went back to his dorm to change. The sketch had gone well and he was in high spirits. Nicky was staring so intently at Rob, who was pretending to find the sketch hilarious, that she missed Mark follow his son out of the lounge. But Amanda didn't.

Mark reached Oscar's dorm and stood in the doorway.

'Hi there,' he said quietly. Oscar jumped. He stood up straight. Then he turned his back and continued to change his clothes in silence. Mark couldn't believe how tall and straight his boy's back was. It was beautiful.

'That was fantastic,' he said. 'Well done.'

'Thanks,' said Oscar.

Mark stepped into the room.

'C'mon, Osc,' he said. 'Let's be friends.'

Oscar's tears came fast and furious, as usual. He wiped them away with the heel of his hand. Mark went and hugged him.

'I was only trying to help,' squealed Oscar into his chest.

'Shhh, I know, sweetheart.'

'Sorry,' mumbled Oscar. 'Sorry.'

Why did it always break Mark's heart to hear Oscar apologise? 'It's all right,' he soothed. 'I was touched that you'd go to that much trouble to try and help me, even if it was misguided.'

Oscar put his arms round his father's waist and wiped his eyes on his jumper. Mark kissed the top of his head, something he wouldn't be able to do for long without a step-ladder. Then they both stepped away. Mark walked slowly back towards the door.

'Dad!' called Oscar across the room.

'Mmhm?'

'I'm so glad you're leaving here.'

'Yeah,' said Mark. 'So am I. It's all got a bit complicated, hasn't it?'

'*Leaving?*' came Amanda's shocked voice from the doorway. Mark and Oscar jumped.

'Why on earth are you leaving, Mark?' she asked.

After the show, the children had pillow fights in their dorms, and the adults went to the bar to drink themselves silly. Nicky had volunteered to stay sober tonight in case any of the children were sick from overeating or just plain delirium at being so near to going home, so she was the first to leave the bar. She wasn't followed for another two hours. There was no way Martha was leaving before Amanda. Amanda wasn't going till Rob did. Rob was staying close to Mark, but not too close. And Mark was going nowhere near Nicky and staying very near alcohol. Miss James was enjoying one of the last nights of her career. And Ned and Janet, to no one's surprise by now, were going to out-drink them all.

Amanda went to get a round in, and Rob joined her at the bar, purportedly to help with the drinks. They smiled at each other and then glanced back at the others.

'I found out something very interesting this evening,' she said.

He raised his eyebrows. 'Oh yeah? A penny for your thoughts.'

'Oh, my thoughts are worth much more than that.'

'A pound, then.'

She smiled again. 'Nowhere near enough.'

'How about . . .' he took a deep breath, 'a big fat diamond ring?'

Amanda's eyes lit up. 'Now you're talking,' she whispered.

He smiled.

'How about bringing the deadline of our . . . little "deal" forward?' she asked.

He gave her a sideways look. 'Keep talking.'

'We come clean about us as soon as Miss James announces that you're the next Head. We don't wait the full year since we made the deal,' she sighed as if conjuring up the scene, 'dear me now, all that time ago, in Gwen's little garden, on New Year's Eve.'

520

They shared a conspiratorial laugh.

'I'll never believe,' murmured Rob, 'that she actually walked into the garden while we were discussing it.'

'I know!' laughed Amanda. 'I had to smudge my lipstick to make it look like we'd been snogging. Hilarious.'

'And I had to pretend I was pissed. Completely overdid it.' He looked at her and smiled. 'It's been fun, hasn't it, though, Mand?'

'I've never been so turned on before,' she confided, flashing her eyes at him. 'There's something so . . . sexy about keeping it secret from everyone.' She leant in to him and touched his ankle with the heel of her shoe. She heard his breathing deepen. 'Especially when she thinks you're making eyes at her in the staffroom. I don't know what I'll do for amusement once all this is over.'

'In which case, why do you want to bring the deadline forward?' he asked.

'Ah, that's easy,' she sighed elaborately. 'Eventually every girl needs to feel secure. Even a girl like me.'

Rob thought about it. 'Could be awkward.'

'Well,' she sighed. 'OK. If you don't want this piece of information, Miss Jean Brodie'll get it on with Mark and then you'll have no leverage with which to put off your worthy opponent.'

He shook his head. 'I'm not sure I've got that much leverage any more,' he said. 'I was so sure I had her in the palm of my hand, like putty . . . I swear she was buying the baby clothes. But . . . I don't know . . .'

'You need this piece of information,' said Amanda urgently. 'I'm telling you it'll swing it.'

His breathing quickened. 'God, you're an amazing woman.'

'I know.' She didn't so much smile as smoulder. 'Well, it took a strong woman to talk you back into my bed that night.'

He gave her a laddish leer. 'There wasn't much talking, as I recall.'

'Well,' she murmured, 'there had to be some compensation for letting Mark give Miss Jean a lift home from the pub.'

He looked at her properly. 'Compensation. That's one word for it. Tell you what – I'll know you're playing away from home if you ever organise another fundraising meeting.'

She giggled. 'Me?' she said innocently. 'Play away from home? Never. Not once I've got the man I want. Unless, just maybe . . . if the deadline isn't brought forward.'

He smiled. How could he have ever thought that little Nicky was his type? Amanda was a far more worthy partner than he could ever have hoped for. They say that behind every successful man is a woman, and she was no exception. Her ambition was pure and simple: to help him achieve his potential, and be there on his arm when he did it. It was beautiful in its simplicity.

'OK,' he said. 'It's a deal. As soon as Miss James announces me as the new Head, I'll tell everyone we've been secretly engaged since New Year.'

She smiled and leant in.

'You won't miss chasing Miss Hobbs?'

He smiled at her. 'Miss Who?'

She leant in closer before she spoke again.

'Are you ready for your . . . information?'

'Yes.'

She brushed his forearm with her breast.

'Mark Samuels is leaving,' she said slowly and clearly.

He was stunned. 'When?'

'At the end of this term.'

'This term?' Rob's eyes were large.

She nodded slowly. 'Yup. In two days' time.'

Rob stole a glance at the crowd in the mirror behind the bar before looking back at Amanda.

'Brilliant.'

'The question is,' murmured Amanda, 'what to do with this nugget.'

Rob smiled. 'That's easy.' He leant forward and whispered something in her ear. She gasped, leant back and smiled widely at him.

'Are we a dynamite team or what?' she whispered, in awe.

'I'll keep Martha busy,' he said with a wink.

'I bet you will,' she said.

'Well, duty calls.'

'And that impressive speed of thought,' she murmured, stroking his ankle with her own, 'is why you are going to be such a good Head at Heatheringdown Primary School.'

Nicky lay on Rob's bottom bunk, her hair in a towelled turban, blinking up at the ceiling.

She'd just tried phoning Ally, but her answerphone was on again. She didn't want to keep leaving messages, so she'd just hung up.

She was going to have to work this one out on her own. Which was a shame, because she'd never been any good at multiple-choice. To summarise:

Whom Do I Trust, Rob or Mark?

1 Is Rob . . .
a) shagging Amanda (who he knows has no sense of humour)?
b) a worthy suitor who wants to marry me and have a family with me?
c) a genuine friend who really does know me better than I know myself and just wants what is best for me?

2 Is Mark . . .
a) a morally reprehensible chameleon, who cunningly changes his story to get on with whoever he is with? After all, he had claimed to hate both Amanda and Rob, yet Amanda's often in his office, and on this holiday alone, he must have spent hours drinking with Rob.
b) A misogynist pig in disguise, who will only reveal his true colours when he's got you under his spell?
c) Cynically trying to lure me into his bed and confidence so that he can control Heatheringdown once I'm Headmistress?
d) The One? Hopelessly in love with me and future sire of my progeny?

When the dorm door opened, she looked up, glad of any interruption. Even when she saw Amanda, she didn't mind. Amanda yawned a hello and started drivelling on about how much everyone was drinking.

'Ned's a big surprise, isn't he?' she asked finally.

'What do you mean?' asked Nicky, pulling herself up on to her elbows. 'The drinking or the wind?'

'Well.' Amanda smiled, 'it's a tough call. I mean, he's so good at both.'

They laughed.

'Honestly, though,' said Amanda, perching her tiny bottom by Nicky's feet on the bed. 'They're all going for it out there tonight.'

'Are they?' mumbled Nicky, sitting up. She took her hair out of her towel and started to gently dry it.

'Mm. I'm just too knackered,' said Amanda, folding her long legs under her and leaning against the wall. 'I don't know where Rob gets all his energy from.'

'Mm.'

'It's funny,' said Amanda mildly, 'I can't believe we went out with each other now.'

Nicky gave her a cautious smile. 'You were mad about him,' she said quietly.

'I know,' Amanda smiled. 'For ages. Made a real fool of myself.'

'Why do you say that?'

Amanda shrugged half-heartedly. 'Well, you do, don't you? When you're blinded by a crush.'

Nicky looked down, but she was surprised to hear that Amanda's voice was thick with emotion. 'It was never really me he wanted,' she said. 'But I don't think I'm telling you anything you don't already know.'

Nicky shook her head slowly.

'You look tired,' said Amanda softly.

Nicky nodded, closing her eyes. 'I am.'

'You were right. It's been much harder work than I imagined.'

Nicky blushed.

'I'm just glad it's over.' Amanda stretched.

Another nod.

'It's a shame about Mark, though,' continued Amanda.

'Hmm?'

'Mark. It's a shame he's leaving,' said Amanda. 'I mean,' she went on, 'I suppose if you think about it, it's not all that surprising. Oscar's leaving, so what's left here for him? But it was nice having a decorative man around the place for a change.'

Nicky felt as if Amanda had just leant over and scooped out her insides. She knew Amanda was still talking because her lips were still moving. 'I don't think he's told anyone else. Apart from us. And Miss James, of course.'

She turned to Nicky properly, for the first time since she'd come in, and her body made an abrupt halt. They stared at each other, Amanda taking in Nicky's shocked expression.

'Oh my God,' she whispered. 'What's the – you did know, didn't you? You knew he was leaving?'

Nicky could barely shake her head.

'Oh no,' whispered Amanda, her eyes filling. 'He's going to kill me.'

'Don't worry,' croaked Nicky. 'I won't tell him.'

'I just assumed he'd told you,' whispered Amanda. 'I thought you were . . . friends.'

Nicky shook her head. 'He hasn't told me anything.'

'God, sorry.' Amanda actually started crying. 'It's amazing how wrong you can get it sometimes . . . I keep getting it wrong.'

'So, when's he going?'

'I'm not sure I should –'

'Oh come on, you might as well now.' Nicky tried to sound light-hearted.

Amanda kept her head down. 'End of term. Two days after we get back. He only told me because . . .' Her voice drained away.

'Go on,' allowed Nicky.

Amanda shook her head, then spoke quietly. 'He said he wanted us to stay in touch after he'd gone. I assumed, of course, that he'd say the same to you.'

There was silence. Nicky was motionless.

'He made me promise not to tell anyone,' confided Amanda, 'but I assumed that didn't include you.'

'It's OK.'

'Nicky!' urged Amanda suddenly, turning her moist eyes to her. 'You've got to promise me you won't tell him I told you.'

Nicky nodded.

'I mean it,' said Amanda. 'He'll be so upset with me. He hasn't even signed contracts yet. And Miss James made him promise not to tell anyone.'

'Don't worry,' said Nicky. 'I've already forgotten it. I couldn't give a damn what he does.'

'I'm sorry,' said Amanda significantly and Nicky nodded her appreciation. Then Amanda squeezed her hand and they sat in miserable silence for a few moments. Then Amanda gave a massive yawn, and wandered forlornly into the shower room.

So, thought Nicky, turning to the wall. He's leaving. That meant that her stupid ulterior motive fear was groundless. There had been no hidden agenda for that life-changing kiss. Which was lucky, seeing as that kiss was so life-changing it was going to lose her her promotion and possibly even her whole career. But he had confided in Amanda about his new job and told her that he wanted to stay in touch after he'd gone. And he hadn't so much as mentioned he was bored with his job to her. What the hell was going on? Was he after Amanda too? Had they even kissed already?

But remember, she reminded herself, there had been no hidden agenda for that amazing, life-affirming kiss. And on that thought, she found a final burst of energy to finish off drying her hair and climb up to her bunk where she fell into a deep sleep that not even Ned's nocturnal blasts could pierce.

When she woke up, she felt strangely at peace with the world. Mark kissed her because she was her, and not because she might become the next Head. But he had told Amanda his secrets before her. There was no doubt she was confused about him, but it didn't matter any more. Because the most liberating thing that had come out of this was that she had suddenly realised she didn't give a flying fart whether Rob was or wasn't shagging Amanda, except in trying to work out his motives. Closure didn't come more complete than that.

And so the fun-packed holiday was over. After breakfast, there were two hours to finish packing up and board the coach. Nicky bagged herself the front seat again keeping her eyes down as everyone boarded. But when Rob climbed the steps, she looked up, moved her bag and gestured for him to join her. He did so, albeit reluctantly.

She found she could barely look at him.

'I think we need to talk,' she started. 'We've both been through loads and this year's been a really hard time. I want you to know that I'm sorry if I ever confused you about us or gave you mixed signals. To be honest, I was very confused about you.'

Rob was nodding slowly. 'Was?' he said eventually.

'Yes. I know now that . . . we're not meant to be.'

Rob nodded slowly.

'Rob,' she said, 'I have to know something. Did you mean it when you said you'd have to tell Miss James about that silly snog with Mark?'

He leant closer to her. 'Of course not,' he whispered. 'I was just so . . . angry and amazed, Nicky. That you could do that in front of the kid.'

'But we didn't really do anything . . .' Her voice trailed off.

'Well, how do you explain what I saw, then?'

'I don't know. I don't know anything any more. He was just suddenly there!'

'I always thought you were so in control,' said Rob sadly. 'But recently, I don't know what's happened to you. That was . . . an unbelievable thing for you to let happen.'

'I know, I know. But I can tell you it won't happen again. It was a mistake. It turns out he was playing me along. I can't tell you how I know, I just do.'

Rob looked at her. 'Sorry, Nicky. I always said he was a –'

'Yeah, all right. You were right. Well done you.'

They watched the road for a bit.

'But,' continued Nicky, 'at least you know it means it won't happen again. I'm back in control.'

'That's hardly the point, is it?' asked Rob. 'I mean, can you imagine the consequences of that if you were Head?'

'Oh, don't.'

'I mean if you did get the job, Nicky – and we both know

there's every chance of that – we'd both have to live with knowing that you'd done that.'

Nicky shook her head.

'A deputy head doing something like that is very different from a head doing that,' said Rob. 'Do you really think you could honestly say, hand on heart, that you know you wouldn't make that sort of mistake again?'

The tears were a surprise to her, and she didn't even wipe them away. After everything, it had come to this. She spoke quietly. 'I'll withdraw my application,' she said with a small sniff.

There was a pause.

'It's probably for the best,' agreed Rob, handing her a tissue and holding her hand. 'And you know I'd never tell anyone what you did in front of Oscar.'

'Thanks.'

'When will you do it?' he asked suddenly.

She shrugged. 'Don't know,' she said. 'At tonight's party?'

Rob let out a low sigh. 'You're very brave, Nicky Hobbs. I'm proud of you. And you know I'll be there for you.'

'Thanks. I know you will.'

'It's your decision,' he murmured. 'I guess you had to come to it yourself.'

Nicky nodded slowly, as if her head was too heavy for her neck. 'Yes,' she said quietly. 'It's my decision.'

33

Nicky stood with the other teachers in the car park, bidding a fond farewell to the children as they were collected by smiling parents, most of whom looked ten years younger than the previous week.

In truth, she found it hard to bid any of the fond farewells with any real fondness. And sometimes she even forgot the farewell bit too. She was depressed about Mark, but she was devastated about the headship.

She watched Mark chatting happily to other parents. She watched Amanda flick her hair over her shoulder. Did he really want her? And what about the revelatory Amanda! She'd actually cried with empathy when she thought she'd put her foot in it. How could you get someone so wrong? Amanda must get that all the time, she thought, looking at her long legs. Maybe you could be lonely being so beautiful. Nicky turned and watched Rob do the rounds, chatting to all the parents and playfully teasing the kids, and wondered what changes he'd bring to the school next year. If she didn't lose her job, she'd be there as a friend for him, his trusty, loyal Deputy. She watched Miss James hugging every child to her bosom, even the ones she was collecting detention essays from, and wondered whether the woman would miss her life as Head or turn away and never look back. She watched Ned greet his wife with a perfunctory peck and wondered whether the woman had a weak sense of smell or a strong nerve.

Then she set to wondering how tonight's inevitably excruciating disco could possibly top such a trip. What evils awaited her amidst the paper bowls of Cheesy Wotsits? Perhaps Ned would ask her to dance and, after holding her breath throughout 'Three Times a Lady', his wife would then murder her in a jealous rage. It felt strangely calming to be prepared for the worst.

She turned away from the throng and saw a couple ambling towards her. She almost didn't recognise them. She knew the silhouettes well, but had never seen them like this before, and so did not register who they were. It was only when they were within a few feet and unmistakably Ally and Pete that a penny the size of a planet dropped, as if from the skies. There were no obvious clues – they weren't holding hands, they weren't even touching, they weren't even smiling very much, it was just that something was different. A slow smile warmed her face as she realised it was the space between them that had changed. Pete stood a vital inch closer to Ally than usual, his left shoulder consciously posed behind her right shoulder, instead of next to it, achieving a subtly protective air. And her body seemed conscious, to the tips of her hair, of where his ended. Every tilt of her frame was an interaction with his.

Nicky stared at them both, her understanding growing with her smile. She bid a silent goodbye to her best friend, and then ran up to greet them.

'So how was it?' Ally grinned.

'Hell on earth,' Nicky grinned back. 'What about you two?'

She looked at them and grinned expectantly. They looked at each other and grinned expectantly. Then they looked back at her and grinned expectantly.

'Great!' said Ally.

'Yeah,' said Pete, nodding significantly. 'Great.'

'Great!' said Nicky. 'That's . . . *great*!'

Oscar was suddenly at her side.

'Miss Hobbs, I need to tell you something.'

Nicky watched Pete join Rob before turning absent-mindedly to Oscar.

'Not right now, sweetheart,' she said. She looked back at her friend. Ally was beaming.

'You look *great*!' said Nicky, with a warm smile.

'It's about Miss Taylor,' said Oscar. 'And my dad.' Nicky froze. She turned to Oscar.

'Please, Oscar, not now.' She waited for him to leave. As he walked slowly away, Ally turned the beam on her and Nicky basked in it for a moment. Then Ally gave her a most significant raise of her eyebrows and slowly leant in, as if to share a confidence.

'I tell you,' she grinned, 'I *feel* great!' She nodded repeatedly.

Nicky stopped herself from telling her that that was great.

'Oh,' she said instead, deciding that she might as well join in all the sharing. 'I'm withdrawing my application for Head. Mark's an un-bee-leev-able kisser. But I think he's actually after Amanda. Amanda's nicer than we thought. And if Rob wants to, he could lose me my job.'

'What?' Ally looked stricken.

'So!' exclaimed Nicky quickly. 'What have you been up to?'

It might have been an awkward moment if Oscar and Mark hadn't suddenly appeared by Nicky's side.

'Hello there,' Nicky said to Oscar, unable to meet Mark's eye. 'What did you want to tell me?'

'Miss Taylor –' he started.

She didn't know what she'd have done if Rob hadn't suddenly joined them and loitered, almost protectively. It worked. Oscar and Mark left almost as quickly as they'd appeared. She called after Oscar, ran to him and hugged him goodbye.

'See you tonight at the party,' she said to him.

He nodded miserably.

'You have to come!' she said. 'I'll want a dance with you!'

He suddenly became alert. 'OK,' he said. 'The first dance. Promise. You have to promise.'

She laughed. 'I promise!'

As she watched him get in the car she felt as wretched as she'd ever felt in her life. As they drove away, she turned her back, but that didn't stop the desire to be in the car with them both swamping her. She turned to Ally.

'What are you doing now?' she asked, in a small voice.

'I'm meeting Pete's mum for the first time.'

Nicky forced an excited response. 'Good luck!' she said.

'I don't need luck,' said Ally grimly. 'I need a miracle.'

Nicky watched them leave together. Then she watched the car park slowly empty, leaving her standing alone. Twenty minutes later, Claire arrived.

By now Nicky could barely raise a smile. As her sister drove

534

her home, attacking her with questions about the holiday, she answered in monosyllables. Eventually Claire gave up.

'I didn't have to pick you up, you know,' she told her. 'I'm not your personal chauffeur.'

Nicky tried to answer, but the lump in her throat kept getting in the way. She sniffed. Claire looked at her hard, then suddenly leant across her, took an emergency box of tissues and bar of chocolate out of the glove compartment and put them both in her sister's lap. By the time they'd reached Nicky's flat, Claire knew everything.

As soon as they got in, Claire put the kettle on and poured Nicky a big glass of wine. While Nicky drank the wine and the kettle boiled, she phoned Derek to tell him she'd be home a little later than planned.

'Well, you'll just have to make the dinner then,' Nicky heard Claire say into the phone. 'There's chicken and fresh salad in the fridge.' When she then heard her ring off with 'I'm not going to tell you which shelf, Derek, I'm going to watch you grow by learning', she even managed the first genuine smile of the day. It felt strangely good.

Claire joined her at the kitchen table, plonking a mug of sweet tea in front of her. She pulled a chair close, and took Nicky's hand in a firm squeeze.

'All that's happened,' she summarised, 'is that you haven't got a promotion, which you might not have got anyway. The rest is unpleasant, but it's over. And you don't know that he's after Amanda. You only know her side of it.'

Nicky nodded, but it didn't stop the tears coming.

'Believe me,' insisted Claire, 'if he's after Amanda, you don't want him,' she added, her squeeze almost hurting Nicky's hand.

535

Nicky sniffed. 'He's got lovely forearms,' she murmured.

Claire sighed.

'And hair. I loved his hair.'

Claire nodded.

'Did I tell you how good a kisser he was?'

Claire gave a pained nod.

'That was it,' squeaked Nicky. 'My life has peaked. It's downhill from now on.'

'Nicky, believe me,' said Claire. 'You will get over him. And, don't forget, there is always Rob. He's been constant all the way through.'

'I don't want Rob,' she said so softly Claire didn't even try and argue.

When the phone went, they looked at each other. They heard Rob on the answerphone saying that he'd pick Nicky up in an hour, just in case she was too tired to drive to the party. No need to call back. They drank their tea in silence.

An hour later, thanks to an endless stream of positive support from Claire and another generous glass of alcohol, Nicky was feeling much better. She wasn't dressed to kill tonight but she could certainly have got manslaughter. She wore a tight, slinky pair of pedal pushers, which accentuated her waist and gently rounded hips, before coming to a tailored end just below the knee, emphasising the fleshy curve of her calves and delicate lines of her ankles. They had, of course, been rejected from the packing pile. These she topped with a simple cotton tank top, which effortlessly showed off the curves of her upper arms and cleavage, while camouflaging the tiny curve of her belly. She finished it off with her favourite pair of pumps, which were easy, graceful and subtle. She wore no make-up. Just the act of applying it would have made her feel needy. She didn't look at her reflection in the mirror before answering the door to Rob.

Before Rob started the car, he turned to Nicky.

'How you doing?'

She was able to flash him one of her finer smiles. It was amazing what the body could do when it had to.

'I'm good,' she said. 'You?'

'Fine.'

There was a pause.

'Are you,' he said slowly, 'sure you're up to talking to Miss James tonight?'

She nodded. 'Yep. It's a bit of a relief, actually.'

There are only two major flaws with holding a disco in a school hall for teachers and pupils; namely the venue and guests. Apart from that, it's the perfect party. Nicky and Rob arrived early, to find a Year 3 parent behind the mixing desk performing a comedy cameo worthy of a BAFTA. If ever a baseball cap should have been worn the right way round, it was on him. On the front of his mixing desk was a handwritten poster announcing *Skool Disco!!! Only Rebels Apply!!!*

Beside him stood three trestle tables in a row, covered in *Harry Potter* paper tablecloths and matching plates, each offering sausages on sticks, a ton of chocolate in assorted packaging, almost as many crisps and some Cheesy Wotsits. At the far end stood a smaller trestle table with thirty bottles of Diet Coke and two cartons of orange juice.

'Bloody hell,' murmured Rob.

'I know,' replied Nicky. 'They've really pushed the boat out this time. Must be because she's leaving.'

As the words were out of her mouth, the unmistakable voice of Miss James came from behind them.

'Helloooo! Hello! Hello, hello, hello, hello, hello!'

They turned to greet her. She was on such a high that it was hard not to be infected by some of it, and amazingly, Nicky found herself already adapting to the knowledge that Rob was the next Head, she was his next Deputy, Mark was most probably a cad and life would still go on. After all the greetings were over, Rob leapt up on to the stage to shut the curtains, 'for added ambience', and Nicky started greeting the eager disco-goers, some of whom had brought their own iPods just in case the music was 'wank'.

But gradually her positive mood disappeared as an increasingly familiar tension started to take its hold again. She wasn't quite sure what she was most tense about: Finding a convincing excuse with which to withdraw her application; telling Mark how hurt she was that he'd confided in Amanda and not her – thus betraying Amanda and revealing the depth of her own feelings for him; or being asked to dance by Ned and being murdered by his wife in a jealous rage.

The trestle tables were filling up nicely now as nearly all the children had arrived and taken their positions by the chocolate. There would be chocolate-rage fights within the hour. There was little variety in the choice of disco-wear; the girls all looked like street prostitutes, the boys like rappers.

Nicky spotted Daisy and looked for Oscar while desperately hoping she wouldn't find Mark before he found her. She found Lilith instead, standing in the doorway, staring at the DJ in undisguised disbelief. Nicky approached her and they greeted each other warmly.

'Tell me,' said Lilith, crossing her arms. 'Is he being ironic?'

Nicky focussed. 'It's difficult to tell,' she mused.

'Mm.' They watched him for a bit longer. As the 'Birdie Song' started and a secret smile played on his face, Lilith's eyes lit up.

'Yes! He's being ironic!' she cried. 'I have to get me some of that.' And she was gone. Nicky watched his eyes warm as he leant over the mixing desk to hear Lilith's request.

The volume increased, The Boomtown Rats came on and some of the kids even started dancing. Two had already started energetic snogging. When Miss James approached Nicky, dancing to 'I Don't Like Mondays' and popping Maltesers, Nicky decided now was her moment.

'Could we have a word?' she shouted in Miss James's ear.

'I know!' laughed Miss James. 'Isn't it?' She executed a slow twirl. Then she gave Nicky a wink and pulled her to the edge of the hall where they could actually hear each other.

'No need to tell the others,' she confided, pulling out a hip flask from her bra and offering it to her. Gratefully Nicky accepted. It was neat vodka. Miss James gave her a wink. 'A bit like a Fisherman's Friend, only for headmistresses,' she said.

'Um, yes,' said Nicky, when her voice returned. 'About that. I need to have a word.'

'Aha!' cried Miss James, looking past her. Nicky followed her gaze and found herself looking at Mark. He was as pleasing on the eye as he was a shock to her system. In fact, the two were probably linked. She greeted him as coolly as she could, which meant her body heat shot up through the ceiling. He greeted her just as coolly. She saw Oscar hanging back behind him, watching her. Mark started to move away and she beckoned to Oscar. But Miss James reached forward and took Mark firmly by the arm.

'Mark!' she cried. 'Ah, Mark! Mark, Mark, Mark.' She shook her head and sighed. 'Ah! Mark.' Then she turned to Nicky. 'He's leaving us, you know.' She turned back to Mark. 'I know, I know! I told you not to tell anyone, and now here I am, blabbing away like a schoolchild. But . . . ah, dear me. *Mark.*'

Mark turned to Nicky and they looked at each other. Nicky didn't know what expression to pull, so she didn't pull one at all.

'I was going to tell you,' he said. 'But I wasn't allowed to.'

She nodded evenly. 'It's all right,' she said. 'I knew already.'

He frowned. 'How?'

'Ah, dear me!' cried Miss James. 'Marcus, Marcus, Marcus!' She turned to Nicky and sighed. 'Don't you think?' she said.

Nicky nodded. 'Yes,' she said. 'I do a bit.'

'How did you know?' repeated Mark.

She looked at him. 'Things get round. Girls talk.' Before he could respond, she turned and walked away, grateful she wasn't wearing high heels because each step was hard to take.

Suddenly she felt herself being bodily swept to the side of the hall.

'Who told you?' Mark whispered in her ear. 'It wasn't that bitch, Amanda, was it?'

She tried to move away, but he wasn't letting her. His grip on her arm was firm.

'How can you call her a bitch?' she said crossly, moving her arm away. 'Do you mind? People will see.'

'So what?' he said urgently. 'Miss James is leaving. She doesn't care. I'm leaving, so I'm no longer the bursar. And in two days' time, Oscar's not one of your pupils. So what are you running away from?'

They stared at each other.

'You,' she said simply.

It seemed to do the job. He stepped back.

'Right,' his voice was all quiet. 'I see. Well, don't worry. I'm not going to beg. I won't come in again this term. I've only got to pack up my things and I'll do that in the holidays. We only came to see you, so we'll be going.'

Nicky kept her eyes down.

'Good luck with everything,' he said.

'Hello there,' cut in Rob, suddenly next to Nicky. 'Hope I'm not interrupting anything too important –'

'No, not really,' said Mark. 'I was just going.'

'No! Don't go,' said Nicky desperately. Mark stopped. 'I – I want to dance with Oscar.'

'Well, I very much doubt he'll want to dance with you,' said Mark.

'Well, you haven't got time anyway, Nicky,' said Rob urgently. 'I think you'd better do it before she's too far gone.' He nodded in the direction of Miss James who was now shimmying down a wall.

'Do what?' started Mark. He stared at Nicky.

'I'm withdrawing,' she said simply. 'Turns out I wasn't the best man for the job after all.'

The look he gave her hurt her more than she could have imagined. It told her that she was not the woman he'd thought she was. Worse, it told her that even though he was leaving the school, he still desperately wanted her to be the next Head because he believed in her. He'd been genuine all along. And yet he wanted to stay in touch with Amanda.

Thankfully, Rob guided her gently away, towards Miss James, while Mark went to get his and Oscar's coats.

Rob and Nicky found Miss James standing on the edge of the dance hall, watching Amanda dancing in the middle of it.

'Isn't she a clever mover?' she said, as they approached. 'Irresistible, I'd say.'

'Miss James,' said Nicky. 'I – I need to talk to you.'

'Yes, my dear,' she said. She turned to Rob. 'Oh hello, Rob. Do stay, charming boy.'

'Thank you, Miss James.'

'Not at all.' She turned back to Nicky. 'What can I do for you, my dear?'

'I want to talk about my application for the headship.'

Miss James's smile vanished.

'I – I . . .' Nicky went on before coming to a halting stop. Rob pinched her arm. 'I – I . . . don't think . . . I should . . . I need to withdraw . . .'

Miss James stared at her. Then she looked at Rob. 'Gosh! This is all rather . . . puzzling, isn't it?' she said. Then she smiled at him sweetly. 'But you seem to be so good at puzzles, perhaps you'll be able to make it out.' He was momentarily unable to answer. Suddenly Miss James clapped her hands.

'Ooh! That reminds me!' she cried. 'I've got a speech to make.' She squeezed both their arms. 'Don't go away.'

They watched her as she ran up the stairs on to the stage.

'What happened there?' asked Rob, his hand squeezing her arm tightly.

She leant against the wall and watched Mark and Oscar leave, feeling as if her soul was wandering indifferently away. They didn't even cast a glance back as they opened the hall door and started the long walk down the path. The door stayed open and a gentle summer breeze wafted in.

Meanwhile, Miss James popped behind the curtains and returned to the front of the stage with her trusty satchel under one arm and a microphone in her hand. As if on cue, the lights went up and the disco stopped. The room burst into hysterical, E-number-fuelled applause. Nicky stared out of the open hall door, watching the last shadows of Mark and Oscar walk down the path outside, further and further away from her life. Oscar kept looking back, but Mark put his arm round the boy's shoulder and he fell in step with his dad. How could something so slight hurt so much? She made to follow, but two things happened. Amanda walked across the hall and leant laconically in the open doorway, a hair-flicking, smiling sentry. And Rob forcibly stopped Nicky from moving by tightening his grip on her arm.

'You'll see him at school,' he whispered. 'This is important.'

'One two three,' echoed Miss James's voice round the hall, tapping the microphone with her finger. 'One two three. One two three, one two three, one two three. HELLO, EVERYBODY!'

The room cheered.

'I thought tonight was an appropriate time to announce my successor.'

The room fell silent. You could have cut the tension with a plastic palette knife.

'But first,' said Miss James, 'I have a rather special essay to read.'

To the murmur of the crowd, she put the microphone on the floor and bent down to fish inside her bag. She pulled out an essay, picked up the microphone and, standing up, put her glasses on the tip of her nose.

'*Why I Shouldn't Hide In Someone Else's Room,*' she read out, '*by Oscar Samuels.*'

There was a gentle murmur as everyone tried to find Oscar. Nicky's thoughts were fast and simple. She was going to die. Her body went into flight-or-shite mode. She searched frantically for Lilith, hoping that Lilith might run out and catch Oscar before he'd left. But Lilith was too busy looking into the eyes of the DJ, who now had time to look properly back into hers. Where was Daisy? Daisy was gorging on chocolate. She tried to run after Oscar, but Rob pushed her back against the wall, hitting her head against it, and hissed, 'Don't even think it,' into her face. She'd have fainted, but Rob probably wouldn't have let her.

Outside, in the soft summer dusk, Oscar started to cry. Mark squeezed his shoulder but felt too depressed to be able to help him. Every step felt like another mile away from her. Why didn't she want him? Was her career so much more important to her than he was? He was about to blame her for this before he realised that only recently his own career had stood in the way of everything. How could he blame her for doing what he had done for so long? And yet, the pain.

'Do you know anything about this?' Rob hissed at Nicky as Miss James began to read Oscar's essay.

544

'No,' hissed Nicky back. 'You might be in luck. He might withdraw my application for me. He may even ruin my entire career.'

Rob's face showed something between impatience and anger. 'Well then,' he said. 'Let's just wait and see.'

'*I am in detention,*' (read out Miss James), '*as punishment for spying on my teachers. But I do not need punishment. I've already had my punishment. I have learnt things about adults, about injustice and about love that they don't teach you in school. Things I never wanted to know: There aren't always happy endings. Adults are not all good. The baddies do sometimes win. Lying does get you what you want. And true love doesn't make everything all right.*

To be more specific, this is what I learnt on my school trip at Heatheringdown Primary.'

Nicky was dumbstruck. Was she about to watch her life swirl down the plughole? What would Oscar have written about the kiss?

'*One:*' (Miss James continued), '*Mr Pattison is having a secret affair with Miss Taylor.*'

Nicky's entire body did a swooping jump in the air without physically moving. The room gasped. While Miss James paused dramatically, Nicky felt Rob's body stiffen beside her. His fingers burrowed deeper into her arm. She blinked a few times.

'*Two: Mr Pattison proposed to Miss Hobbs and then when my father accused him of lying about his affair with Miss Taylor, lied again, saying that he wasn't and then calling my father a liar.*'

Nicky tilted her head. Eh? How many liars were there again? Rob started swearing under his breath.

'*Three: Miss Hobbs likes Mr Pattison, even though we have called him "Slimy Sir" since Year 3. Daisy says Miss Hobbs likes him because although he is slimy with her she doesn't notice because he is very good-looking, if you like that sort of thing. Daisy's mum says that Mr Pattison is harmless to look at but poisonous to touch. A bit like a jellyfish.'*

The room found this hilarious. Daisy started jumping up and down with excitement. She ran across the hall to her mum and they hugged as they continued to listen, with matching smiles on their faces.

'Four: Mr Pattison admitted to Miss Hobbs that he is the puzzle cheat.'

The entire room gasped as one. Even the DJ gasped. Then there was uproar. Miss James had to pause before she could continue.

'He told her that because she didn't cheat at the puzzle every morning, she'd never be a good headmistress. This means because of him we are all having an extra half-day at the end of our school year.'

Angry shouts started to fill the hall and they didn't notice Miss James swallow hard before continuing.

'Five: Mr Pattison thinks Miss James is –' (she paused) *'– "mental".'*

More uproar. Shouts of 'Shame!' Miss James smiled at her crowd and fought back the tears.

'Six: Mr Pattison uses the F-word even more than Year 5.'

'Seven: Miss Taylor, who is having a secret affair with Mr Pattison (See Point One), eavesdropped on a private conversation between me and my dad about him leaving his job. Then she forced my dad to tell her about it, even though he had not even told Miss Hobbs yet (and he's in love with her) because he had been told not to by Miss James.'

Nicky gasped and pulled her arm away from Rob. As if he'd come out of a trance, he ran to the steps beside the stage. By the time he'd reached them, the first sausage flew through the air, hitting him squarely on the head. He never made it up to the stage. It was amazing what children could sacrifice when sacrifice was needed. Chocolates, crisps, Cheesy Wotsits, lemonade bottles and even two full cartons of orange juice.

Mark and Oscar reached G for Gnu.

'Would you like some chocolate when we get home?' asked Mark.

Oscar shook his head and sniffed.

'We could watch *Johnny English* again,' suggested Mark.

Another shake and sniff and they lapsed into silence as they approached the end of the learning-curve path. On the squidgy tarmac, Mark suddenly stopped and knelt down, holding Oscar's arms with his hands.

'Osc, don't cry, sweetheart,' he said. 'She didn't mean to upset you. She still wanted to dance with you. She loves you. It's me she doesn't love.' But Oscar kept crying and shaking his head. Eventually he leant on his father and mumbled into his father's neck, 'Is it because I spied on her that she doesn't want us?'

'Oh, no!' Mark took his boy in a hug as Oscar started sobbing.

Nicky didn't see what happened to Rob after the chocolates hit him, because she sprinted out of the hall across the playground, down the learning-curve path and towards the car park. She missed Miss James announce 'the wonderful Miss Hobbs' as her successor, missed Amanda leave smartly by the side exit without a backward glance, and thankfully missed the sight of Ned and Martha getting it on in the canteen on top of the custard creams.

She yelled Mark's name until she was hoarse.

Silence.

She started to run again, and by the time she reached the G for Gnu (which she'd change to Goat if she ever got to be Head), she had to pause for breath. She heard a car engine start and began to run again, sobbing as she went. When she reached the car park, she saw a car drive out. It wasn't Mark's. She scanned the car park desperately. There at the bottom was Mark's car and there were Mark and Oscar, about to get in. She yelled their names, her voice now tinny and high. They stopped and looked over to her. She waved pathetically at them. They stared. She walked slowly towards them, her legs unstable, her breath too loud for her to hear herself practise what to say. When she reached them, Oscar came and stood next to his father. She looked at them both.

'I'm so sorry,' she offered, in a cracked voice. 'Oscar, I'm sorry!'

Oscar ran forward and they met in a fierce, somewhat squeaky hug, Nicky kneeling on the ground, their heads almost level. They leant their foreheads together. Eventually, she moved away.

'I think you owe me a dance,' she said, tearfully.

'Miss Taylor!' he rushed. 'She overheard –'

'I know,' said Nicky, stroking his hair. 'I know everything, my love.' Mark had wandered nearer, and was now standing about a foot away, his frame shadowed by a gentle summer sunset. She looked at him as she said, 'Miss James has just read out your son's detention essay to the entire school.' She held Oscar's hand.

Oscar took in a gallon of air and Mark whooped. They all started laughing.

Then Mark stopped laughing and stepped towards her.

'So you know I was telling the truth,' he said quickly. 'About Rob. About me. And how I feel about you. How we both feel about you. You know I love you – we love you – we both love you –'

'Da-ad!' cried Oscar, blushing fiercely. 'Da-ad!'

'Actually,' Nicky stood up, a sob of laughter escaping, 'Oscar said it even more eloquently than you. If you can imagine that.' She was still holding Oscar's hand, partly to stop her own from shaking. 'I'm so sorry, Mark,' she said and she felt Oscar's hand squeeze hers. She squeezed it back as she asked his father quietly, 'Can you forgive me?'

'Yes! Yes, oh yes,' he said and they all met in a hug in the playground, Mark making a slight hiccupy noise from his throat. And then the three of them started laughing, swaying and hugging more. And Nicky learnt another lesson, that it was possible to love two people this much at the same time.

The Nanny
Melissa Nathan

When Jo Green takes a nannying job in London to escape her small-town routine and ineffectual boyfriend Shaun, culture shock doesn't even begin to describe it. Because walking into the Fitzgerald family's designer lifestyle is like entering a parallel universe . . .

Dick and Vanessa are the most incompatible pair since Tom and Jerry, and their children are downright mystifying. Suddenly village life seems terribly appealing.

Then, just as Jo's starting to get the hang of Tumble Tots, karate practice and cleaning out the guinea pigs, the Fitzgeralds acquire a new lodger, and suddenly Jo's sharing her nanny flat with the distractingly good-looking but insufferably grumpy Josh. So when Shaun arrives on the scene, things can only get trickier.

The Waitress
Melissa Nathan

Katie Simmonds wants to be a film director. Last week she wanted to be a writer, the week before that an educational psychologist, and the week before that a florist. One thing Katie isn't short of is ambition, but she knows for certain that none of her ambitions are to be a waitress. Unfortunately, Katie Simmonds is a waitress.

Hassled by customers, badly paid and stuck with the boss from hell, Katie's life hasn't turned out quite as she'd planned. As for relationships, she's starting to discover that a career choice isn't the only commitment she has problems with. But just when she thinks that things can't get any worse, the café where she works is taken over by the last man in the world she wants to see again.

arrow books